WIELAND

CHARLES BROCKDEN BROWN

WIELAND

OR, THE TRANSFORMATION:
AN AMERICAN TALE
AND OTHER STORIES

*Introduction and Notes
by Caleb Crain*

THE MODERN LIBRARY
NEW YORK

Charles Brockden Brown

Charles Brockden Brown—novelist, essayist, short-story writer, magazine editor, and political pamphleteer—has been called America's first professional writer. He was born in Philadelphia on January 17, 1771, to Quaker parents, Elijah and Mary Armitt Brown. Although a precocious student, Brown was hampered by physical frailty and bouts of melancholy, which would shadow him throughout his life. He studied at the Friends' Latin School from age eleven to sixteen, before becoming apprenticed to a local lawyer; Brown's parents had decided that law was the best career for him, while his brothers became successful merchants.

Brown, however, had more interest in literature, and during his apprenticeship he composed poetry and essays and cofounded the Belles Lettres Club in 1787. Dedicated to philosophical and political discussion, the club encouraged Brown's literary endeavors. In 1789, he published a series of essays in the *Columbian Magazine* under the pseudonym "The Rhapsodist," in which he questioned the politics and moral standing of the new American republic. Having resigned from his fledgling law career in 1792, Brown cofounded the Friendly Club in 1793 with friends Dr. Elihu H. Smith and William Dunlap. During visits to New York, Brown sought advice and support from them as he tried to start a professional writing career.

Brown completed his first novel, *Sky-Walk,* in 1797. Although the complete manuscript was never published, one chapter appeared in March 1798 in *The Weekly Magazine of Original Essays, Fugitive Pieces, and Interesting Intelligence.* Brown also finished *Alcuin; A Dialogue,* a fiction in the form of a dialogue between a male schoolteacher and a female advocate of women's rights. Parts of *Alcuin* were printed in the *Weekly Magazine* as "The Rights of Women." Other essays and short stories published during 1798 demonstrate Brown's didacticism, such as "The Man at Home" and "A Series of Original Letters." At the end of 1798, Brown had entered a period of increased creative production and had had his first major success.

In September 1798, Brown's novel *Wieland; or, The Transformation* was published. Based on the true story of a religious fanatic who killed his family, *Wieland* is a macabre tale of psychological terror narrated by a young woman. The novel garnered favorable critical attention and has become Brown's best-known work. His American Gothic style, which combined psychological and supernatural elements, would later influence other American writers such as Poe and Hawthorne. As *Wieland* went to press, Brown was already at work on his second major novel, *Ormond; or, The Secret Witness,* which appeared in February 1799. Also narrated by a woman, the well-received *Ormond* is a melodramatic novel that explores innocence, seduction, and murder in the world of a sixteen-year-old orphan. Themes that recur in Brown's writing—the rights of women, excessive religion, social problems, moral integrity, and the supernatural—surface in *Ormond.*

The reception of *Wieland* and *Ormond* brought Brown fame, and he provided two more manuscripts to his publisher in quick succession. *Arthur Mervyn; or, Memoirs of the Year 1793* was published in two parts in 1799 and 1800, and some chapters were serialized in the *Weekly Magazine. Arthur Mervyn* chronicles the adventures of a young man in Philadelphia during the yellow-fever epidemic as he encounters murder, theft, and dishonesty. Brown's next novel, *Edgar Huntly; or, Memoirs of a*

Sleep-Walker, was excerpted in the first issue of his new magazine, *The Monthly Magazine and American Review,* in April 1799. Like *Wieland, Edgar Huntly* was written in Gothic style, although Brown had added the rugged American wilderness as the setting for this psychological murder mystery. The book appeared later that year, with great success; volume three included an historical short story, "Death of Cicero: A Fragment."

After the publication of these four novels, Brown turned his attention to journalism and the *Monthly Magazine,* where he served as editor. During 1799 and 1800, he wrote numerous reviews, essays, and stories, including "Thessalonica: A Roman Story," "Portrait of an Emigrant," "Friendship," "The Trials of Arden," "A Lesson on Concealment: or, Memoirs of Mary Selwyn," and most notably, "Memoirs of Stephen Calvert." The *Monthly* ceased publication in December 1800, and in 1801 Brown started a quarterly, *The American Review and Literary Journal.*

In the same year, Brown published two novels that differed considerably from his previous fiction. *Clara Howard* and *Jane Talbot* are epistolary romances written in a sentimental style on the subject of marriage and morality at the turn of the century. Brown continued working on the *American Review* until it went out of business in 1802, and his serial essays on "Female Accomplishment" ran in *Port Folio* that year. In 1803, Brown founded another journal, *The Literary Magazine and American Register* in which he published several essays and stories, including "Memoirs of Carwin, the Biloquist," an unfinished novel written in 1798 as a prelude to *Wieland.* At this time, Brown began writing and distributing pro-expansionist political pamphlets that criticized the Jefferson administration, and he published a translation of C.F.C. Volney's *A View of the Soil and Climate of the United States.*

After a four-year courtship, Brown married Elizabeth Linn in 1804, and they had four children. To support his new family, Brown worked in his brothers' import business until it closed in 1806 and provided editorial material to the *Literary Magazine* before and after it was renamed *The American Register; or, General Repository of History, Politics, and Science* in the same year. He spent the remaining years of his life composing political tracts on trade and commerce issues and a series of

"Scribbler" essays for *Port Folio* magazine. A massive two-volume geography manuscript on which he had been working was lost.

On February 22, 1810, Brown died at the age of thirty-nine from tuberculosis. His prolific oeuvre includes nonfiction that reveals much about early American culture and fiction that broke ground and paved the way for a national literature.

Contents

Biographical Note   v

Introduction *by Caleb Crain*   xi

A Note on the Text   xxv

Wieland; or The Transformation:
    An American Tale   1

Memoirs of Carwin the Biloquist   235

Thessalonica: A Roman Story   297

Walstein's School of History.
    From the German of Krants of Gotha   327

Death of Cicero, a Fragment   341

Appendix: An Account of a Murder Committed
    by Mr. J[ames] Y[ates], upon His Family, in
    December, a.d. 1781   361

Notes   367

INTRODUCTION

Caleb Crain

1.

Until the starchily phrased, quirkily researched, zigzag-plotted fiction in this book, there was little reason to think that Gothic writing would come to America. The genre appeared to be distinctly European. It depended on the conflict of utopian ideals with ancient fears, and Americans were too practical for either—or so the national myth would have it. There might be specters haunting Europe, but the United States was too busy making money to lose sleep over them.

Shortly before the eighteenth century's end, however, a young lapsed Quaker from Philadelphia named Charles Brockden Brown discovered how to unnerve the bold new nation. To bring the Gothic style across the Atlantic, Brown began by "discarding the hacknied machinery of castles, banditti & ghosts," as the playwright William Dunlap, his friend and later his biographer, explained. Brown realized that the United States had new fears, which required new expression. For his first published novel, therefore, he turned to something domestic and plain: the human voice, the vessel of a person's identity and authority.

In a representative democracy, the citizen's voice is the source of power. But how secure is a voice? How do you know you are listening to the right one? Two decades after the Revolution, the American republic was anxious that it might be harboring one utopian ideal after all: itself. And citizens could not rid themselves of the fear that their nation, like other utopias, might crack up and cease to exist.

2.

The fear was not groundless. In the 1790s, the United States faced threats from within and without, and it was not always clear which was which. Consider the danger posed by Edmond Genet, whom revolutionary France had sent as its minister to the United States in 1793. America still owed France a debt of gratitude for its aid in the Revolutionary War, and Genet was welcomed with a tour of fetes that stretched from Charleston to Philadelphia. The sentiment was imprudent; France had just declared war on Great Britain, and the United States could not afford to take sides. Genet, however, took advantage of the surge of affection by enlisting Americans as sailors on French privateers. He made plans to recruit soldiers in Kentucky for attacks on Louisiana, then the property of Great Britain's ally Spain, and he also had hopes of taking Florida and Canada. When President Washington reminded Genet that America was and intended to remain neutral, Genet angrily declared that he would appeal to the people directly by petitioning Congress for Washington's removal.

Genet had misjudged. In America, Congress did not depose presidents as wantonly as the National Convention decapitated executives in France. More or less harmlessly, Genet's outrageous mission collapsed. But the episode was alarming, not least because it would have been hard to say whether Genet posed an external or an internal threat. Did the danger consist in Genet as foreign agent or in the domestic response to him? The Federalists in Washington's administration viewed with suspicion the Democratic Societies that had sprung up across the country, like toadstools after rain, to welcome the French minister.

Republican politicians like Thomas Jefferson and James Madison, on the other hand, viewed with a symmetrical suspicion those Americans who sympathized with France's enemy, the commercial juggernaut Great Britain. In 1795, the Federalist diplomat John Jay brought home a treaty with Great Britain that proposed to sacrifice a small portion of American honor for two large boons: better terms for maritime trade and the withdrawal of British forces from the American West. In their role as America's first opposition party, Republicans encouraged voters to regard the treaty with high-minded paranoia: Had Americans fought the Redcoats so bitterly in order to sell the nation's dignity later at a good price? Could the merchants of New York and New England be trusted to distinguish their financial interests from their patriotic duty? It took some time for the people's pride to give way to the people's greed.

Each party was anxious that the other would compromise the nation's integrity—that it would confuse inside and outside by mistaking another country's interest for America's. The challenge in the 1790s was to steer a course between France and Great Britain, and between the French ideology of radical liberation and the British one of fiscal prudence.

Under the presidencies of George Washington and John Adams, the federal government inclined slightly toward Britain and fiscal prudence. The leading thinker during both administrations was Alexander Hamilton, who as Washington's secretary of the treasury almost single-handedly built the infrastructure for American capitalism. Hamilton defined his political philosophy, and thus the rationale of Federalism, as "1st the necessity of *Union* to the respectability and happiness of this Country and 2 the necessity of an *efficient* general government to maintain that Union." The definition sounds so reasonable and matter-of-fact as to be indisputable, and therein lay the problem: the Federalists never learned to differentiate between opposition to their policies and opposition to government per se.

They saw themselves as the party of virtue. And as long as virtue governed, any limits to the government's power—in the form of, say, explicit guarantees of the freedom of the press or the right to bear arms—seemed to be unnecessary obstructions. Hamilton had even argued in *The Federalist* that since America had no king to restrain, there would be no point to a bill of rights. (In an early indication of his differences with Hamilton, James Madison had seen to it that one was ratified anyway.) In 1794, the Federalist reign of virtue and prudence met a serious challenge in the western counties of Pennsylvania, where the people rebelled against an excise tax that Hamilton had set on whiskey. The rebels dispersed as soon as Washington summoned troops, but a certain innocence was lost and a certain governmental blindness set in. Hamilton was probably correct in believing that his whiskey tax was efficient and not overly burdensome, but he was incapable of seeing that the protest against it was genuine. In frontier Pennsylvania, whiskey was traded as money and valued as a symbol of social unity. The tax upset people. But Hamilton insisted that resentment of it was a mere pretext that had been exploited by subversive elements.

Once Washington retired from politics in 1796, Federalist virtue became precipitously less popular. In June and July 1798—as Brown's novel *Wieland* was being typeset—the Federalists unwisely attempted to write their distrust of political opposition into law. The Naturalization Act of 1798 extended the residency period required for citizenship from five to fourteen years. It backfired; Irish immigrants were panicked into registering to vote in great numbers, and nearly all of them would vote Republican. The Alien Enemies Act enabled the president to apprehend during wartime anyone deemed an enemy of the nation, and the Alien Act allowed the president during peace or war to expel any aliens he considered dangerous. Adams thought these acts excessive, and both would expire unenforced. Finally, and most notoriously, the Sedition Act made it a crime to libel the U.S. government. This, too, backfired. In *The Age of Federalism,* the historians Stanley Elkins and Eric McKitrick note "the almost comic clumsiness, the sheer political ineptitude" with which the Federalists prosecuted their enemies on charges of libel—turning their slanderers into heroes, antagonizing their own supporters, and ensuring the victory of Thomas Jefferson in the presidential election of 1800.

3.

Jefferson's peaceful triumph, however, was far from certain in early 1798, when Charles Brockden Brown was at work on *Wieland; or, the Transformation: An American Tale*. It was not then clear how, or whether, the United States would survive its crisis. It was natural for a writer like Brown to worry about the nation's end, and his education prompted him to turn to the classics as he imagined how it might come about. After all, Athens may have been the birthplace of democracy, but Rome had been the death of it.

In Republican Rome, as in early national America, the relationship in politics between voice, virtue, authority, and violence had been an open question for a time. Americans felt the historical analogy keenly. During the Revolution, John Adams had addressed his wife—and Alexander Hamilton had addressed his fiancée—as Portia. George Washington had ordered a performance of Addison's tragedy *Cato* for his troops at Valley Forge. In the 1790s, when the American republic was felt to be precarious, politicians began to see one another as Roman villains. To cast aspersions on the Republican Jefferson, for example, the Federalist Hamilton recalled a well-known twist in Roman history: "It has aptly been observed that *Cato* was the Tory—*Caesar* the whig of his day. The former frequently resisted—the latter always flattered the follies of the people. Yet the former perished with the Republic [and] the latter destroyed it." Hamilton, like Cato, was associated with the interests of the upper class. His counterintuitive insinuation was that Jefferson, by pandering to the people and prattling about their rights, was more likely to attempt a coup like Caesar's.

Cato was one of the two great Roman heroes Americans looked up to. The other was Cicero, Rome's master of oratory. Together, Cato and Cicero had foiled the conspiracy of Catiline, a demagogue who had hoped to murder the senators in 63 B.C. After Caesar crossed the Rubicon in 49 B.C. and entered Italy, Cato fought him in the civil war, committing suicide in 46 B.C. when he saw that Caesar would prevail. Cicero, on the other hand, made peace with Caesar and retreated to the study of philosophy during his dictatorship. It would be impossible to say which hero Americans loved more. George Washington, as a man of action, modeled himself on Cato. John Adams, as a man of letters, followed Cicero.

Cicero was the natural choice for a politician with a literary sensibility. According to Plutarch, Cicero was "the one man, above all others who made the Romans feel how great a charm eloquence lends to what is good, and how invincible justice is, if it be well spoken." To American politicians, he represented the power that words could lend virtue in a republic—the power that rhetoric could oppose to rule by force. He represented, in other words, rule by voice. Cicero was the only kind of aristocrat that Adams believed in: a man who could "command *two votes; one besides his own*." It would have been hard to find an ambitious young lawyer in late-eighteenth-century America who did not aspire to emulate him.

4.

At least one law student of the era had doubts, however. As the reader will discover, the great orator of the Roman Republic haunts the fiction by Charles Brockden Brown collected in this volume, and he is not always a welcome ghost.

Born in 1771, Charles Brockden Brown was the fifth son of Elijah and Mary Brown, who were practicing Quakers. According to the historian Peter Kafer, Brown's father had attempted a career as a merchant and failed. Despite financial assistance from his brother-in-law, Elijah was censured by his fellow Quakers in 1768 for failure to pay his debts. After a brief detour into smuggling, he lapsed into mere copying; he became a scrivener, like Melville's Bartleby. In 1784, he was imprisoned for debt. As Charles later recalled in a letter to a friend, he kept his father company: "When eleven or twelve years of age I spent twelve hours in each day, that is, . . . I passed the night, for 8 months together in a *Jail*. In an apartment in which my slumbers were [continual]ly woken by the clanking of chains and bolts & iron doors. Where my ears were continually assailed by blasphemies or obscenities."

The Brown family was not alone in its troubles. As a group, Pennsylvania Quakers suffered a tremendous loss of prestige and power in the late eighteenth century. For decades they had controlled the state legislature and sat at the top of Philadelphia high society. The Revolution abruptly demoted them. As pacifists, they were sidelined by military events. And observant Quakers could not in good conscience swear allegiance to the commonwealth of Pennsylvania or the new republic, and so their loyalty was widely suspected and they were subjected to legal and financial penalties. Tom Paine's famous attack on the Quakers at the end of *Common Sense* was only one among many. On September 5, 1777, Revolutionary authorities arrested nearly a score of Quakers, including Elijah Brown, and deported them to Virginia for eight months. As Kafer observes, the Enlightenment rhetoric of the American Revolution—the talk of inalienable rights and universal freedoms—no doubt clashed with the Brown family's personal experience of the Revolutionaries' actions, which must have looked on the ground very much like harassment of a minority on account of its religious faith.

The Browns pinned what hopes they had of recuperating their status and wealth on young Charles, whose genius showed itself early in such eccentric passions as geography and shorthand. He began to study law in 1787. Perhaps it was then that he began his careful reading of Cicero, the profession's patron saint. (In Melville's tale, Bartleby's employer owns a plaster bust of the orator, probably a standard fixture in law offices.) Brown would have found extravagant praise of Cicero in such books as Hugh Blair's *Lectures on Rhetoric and Belles Lettres*, which functioned for Federalist-era Americans as both a handbook for public speakers and a treatise on aesthetics. Blair wrote that Cicero's "name alone suggests every thing that is splendid in oratory." Blair had a telling criticism, however: "In most of his orations, . . . there is too much art; even carried [to] the length of ostentation. There is too visible a parade of Eloquence."

Too much art would be Brown's problem with oratory as well. He became fascinated with its power, and in his letters he began to play with the feelings of his friends unscrupulously. He feigned a wish for suicide, for example, and he concocted a story of a secret marriage and sudden widowerhood. Eloquence, Brown discovered, was amoral. To arouse and shape another person's emotions with words involved a kind of trickery, and yet the instrumental use of this trickery in law hardly seemed worthy of its potential. "No one was ever less calculated for the drudgery of business than myself," Brown complained to a friend. "Science and Literature are the Idols of my soul: Love and friendship constitute my existence." As late as 1795, Brown would still be pretending to his family that he hoped to pass the bar someday. But it was a ruse. As the merchant Thomas P. Cope recalled years later, Brown

> was poor, nor had his parents the means of conferring on him anything beyond a bare subsistence in their family. They pressed him continually to the practice of the law & his friends, who believed him to possess the necessary qualifications for becoming a shining character in that leading profession, urged their suit, but they urged in vain. He had too much good nature to deny them flatly; he gave expectations of compliance but, without sufficiently explaining his objections, he secretly fostered a determination adverse to their wishes & was fully resolved never to appear at the bar. In this very embarrassing situation he became unhappy . . .

For the better part of a decade, Brown's lies and poverty rendered him miserable. "I am sometimes apt to think," he wrote to his friend William Dunlap, "that few human beings have drunk so deeply of the cup of self-abhorrence as I have." But he was determined, as Dunlap later wrote in his biography, "to become exclusively an author, [which] was at that time a novelty in the United States."

He nearly succeeded. Between 1798 and 1801, Brown wrote half a dozen novels. In a portrait that James Sharples painted in these years, Brown looks both clammy and excitable. He has a pixie's face, with the vulnerable, delicate expression of someone who ought to be wearing glasses. It is without question the image of an author—an identity that Brown owed to a small circle of friends his age who cooperated by seeing him as one.

Chief among these friends was the doctor and poet Elihu Hubbard Smith. In the decade that saw Congress move from New York to Philadelphia, Brown traveled in the opposite direction. He followed Smith to New York, where Smith had assembled something he called the Friendly Club, a group of doctors, lawyers, writers, artists, and businessmen, most of them in their twenties, who met weekly during winters to discuss literature and current events. Brown found the milieu intoxicating. In New York, one Philadelphia friend observed, "C[harles] seems to be in his element & I am glad to see him enjoy himself. He flutters & hops about like a bird & I don't know whether I shall be able to catch him again without salt."

From Smith, Brown received encouragement of his writing and an education in radical philosophy. Smith taught Brown deism and vegetarianism. Most important, he introduced him to anarchy, as propounded by William Godwin, husband to Mary Wollstonecraft and father to Mary Shelley, in his *Enquiry Concerning Political Justice* (1793). Every form of government, Godwin believed, would prove to be an unnecessary evil once people learned to tell the truth, no matter how embarrassing, and to form their own opinions about justice. The theory liberated Brown, because it discomfited in equal measure the political authority launched by the American Revolution, which had oppressed his parents, and the religious authority of Quaker doctrine, which had hobbled them. Cicero's voice would not save the republic, and God's voice would not save the soul. Salvation was not, perhaps, to be had at all. But justice might be reached through sincerity and a salutary distrust of any voice but one's own. *"Godwin came, & all was light,"* quipped Smith, amused by the alacrity of Brown's conversion.

5.

A clever artist disguises his hand, and Brown chose to put Godwin's doctrine in the mouth of his archvillain. It appears as the credo of Ludloe, the mastermind who misleads Carwin long before the action of *Wieland* begins. In the fragment titled "Memoirs of Carwin the Biloquist," Ludloe's Godwinian anarchy is set forth explicitly, but in the finished novel *Wieland*, it figures, more quietly, as a disruption of the social fabric—an unraveling in the carpet, rather than a pattern there.

The ostensible philosopher is Cicero, whose bust is set up by Theodore Wieland in the hillside temple, where Father Wieland had formerly worshiped, every noon and midnight. The marble head is meant to signal an advance. From barbarism and religion, the Wielands in America have risen to enlightenment, and the temple has become a place where sociability and scholarship mix. Whereas Father Wieland was superstitious and barely literate, Theodore is so at home with Latin that he debates questions of textual purity with his friends. As Clara Wieland, Theodore's sister, boasts, "Here a thousand conversations, pregnant with delight and improvement, took place." In the enlightened world, it is safe to question authority; in fact, it is one of the great pleasures. And so Theodore's dearest friend is Henry Pleyel, who also loves the Latin orator but does not take him quite as seriously. Clara reports that in conversations with Pleyel, "even the divinity of Cicero [was] contested."

Of course no one would have claimed that Cicero was replacing God literally. No one would have intended to claim that, at any rate. But as Brown's half jest—and the novel's ensuing catastrophes—indicate, one cannot replace God figuratively without also replacing him literally.

Half a dozen years later, while editing *The Literary Magazine and American Register,* Brown would repeat the joke in an essay titled "Ciceronians." Between the fourteenth and sixteenth centuries, Brown wrote,

> the votaries of Cicero . . . formed a sort of fraternity, in which, strictly speaking, Cicero was a divinity, an object of worship. They did not put up prayers to Cicero as to a saint or martyr.—They did not believe in his powers of protection or intercession. In this sense they were not his worshippers; but they deserved this name, inasmuch as they devoted all their studious and contemplative hours to his works; as they conceived all his opinions, moral, political, and critical, to be infallibly true, and his language to be the only medium through which a reasonable being ought to convey his thoughts.

When, at last, academic study so etiolated the bodies of the Ciceronians that they neared death, they "appeared in their last agony to be less pleased with the hope of the presence of God, than of meeting with this demon of eloquence."

Like most jokes, this one depends on an incongruity. God is an absolute. Cicero, on the other hand, was what an eighteenth-century political observer would have called a trimmer: in striving to save the ship of state, he often adjusted his sails according to the prevailing political winds. There is something ridiculous about taking as a supreme authority a person known for the elegant use of words. When right depends merely on the well-said, and the well-spoken are observed to say whatever is convenient, nervous minds begin to long for a more rigorous deity.

Furthermore, Cicero was "a poor *philosopher*," as Brown observed in an 1805 essay titled "On the Merits of Cicero." Brown pretended in that essay that a recent attempt at reading the *Discussions at Tusculum* fell victim to bad timing: "It was, indeed, somewhat unlucky that I just now lighted on this dialogue, which attempts to prove, *that pain is no evil*, for I had, at that moment, just escaped from the twinges of a tooth-ache." To a modern eye, the *Discussions at Tusculum* does look like two-parts wishful thinking and one-part throwing in the towel. "Supplement [courage] with self-control—the power to keep every emotion in check—and then every ingredient you could need for the happy life is yours," Cicero advises. Should pain and suffering threaten to overwhelm self-control, he recommends suicide: "If you are unable to face [the assaults of fate], there is nothing to prevent you from running away." It adds no luster to Cicero's glory to note that he did not even come up with this advice himself, but cribbed it from the Stoics.

Cicero makes, in other words, a very unsatisfactory god, and *Wieland* aims to disabuse the reader of any faith in him. When the novel's hero and narrator, Clara, narrowly avoids rape, the innocence she sheds echoes the *Discussions at Tusculum:* "I used to suppose that certain evils could never befall a being in possession of a sound mind; . . . that it was always in our power to obstruct, by his own death, the designs of an enemy who aimed at less than our life." Clara draws few morals from her tale, but one of them is that emotional reticence and suicidal resignation rarely lead to happiness.

Only one aspect of Cicero would have struck Brown as divine: his eloquence. In the dark glass of Brown's fiction, that eloquence is detached from Cicero's person—or, indeed, from anyone's person. It appears as ventriloquism, or biloquism, by which an adept may learn how "to speak where he is not," to borrow Clara's horrified turn of phrase. When Brown first began to explore the power of fiction in the early 1790s, he wrote to a friend of the pleasure it gave him: "In assuming the persons or placing ourselves in the situations of others, we enjoy a new kind of existence, and think and act in a manner wonderfully befitting our assumed characters." Ventriloquism was a demonic emblem of this art and may have reflected Brown's personal anxiety about his creative power. But it was an anxiety that resonated in Federalist America. Like a ventriloquist, the alien Edmond Genet had thrown his voice into America's domestic conversation, causing a disruption he could not have fully understood. And as it did in the Wieland family, this vulnerability to foreign voices could trigger in the Founding Fathers a punitive, near-delusional reaction.

In his novel, Brown asked dark questions about the nature of political authority in a republic: Does virtue give a leader license to use violence? If violence is necessary, is it because eloquence has failed? Or is it unwise to rely upon eloquence in the first place? Is eloquence no more likely than force to support virtue? Can ordinary people tolerate the anxiety caused by having to decide what is right for themselves? Or will they always prefer, even if they have to hallucinate the instructions, to be told what to do?

These questions would not have distracted someone like Alexander Hamilton, who was so confident of his virtue and authority that when Adams failed to hang any of western Pennsylvania's whiskey rebels, he upbraided the president for failing to exert "a salutary rigor." But it would be simpleminded to suggest that *Wieland* gives the lie only to the Federalist idea of America. When Clara sees Carwin in rustic disguise and begins to daydream about "how the plough and the hoe might . . . become the trade of every human being," Brown is sending up the romantic notion that farmers are somehow the salt of the earth. The ideal was precious to Thomas Jefferson, who unambiguously believed that "cultivators of the earth are the most virtuous and independent citizens." A few months after *Wieland* was printed, Brown mailed an inscribed copy to Jefferson, leader of the Republican party. Given his misty faith in agrarian goodness, the vice president might not have been sure how to take the compliment. After all, in the novel Brown comes very close to saying that on a farm, no one can hear you scream.

6.

Wieland was published on September 14, 1798. Five days later, Elihu Hubbard Smith died in New York's yellow-fever epidemic. Brown's career as a writer of serious fiction would survive his friend by less than two years. He would be forced to reinvent himself. By April 1800 he would find reasons "for dropping the doleful tone and assuming a cheerful one" and would thereafter abandon the Gothic style that marked his best writing. In the end, not only would Brown change into a critic and magazine editor, but he would disavow radical politics and keep mum about his lack of faith in Christianity. In October 1803 he would write in an editor's note that "I should enjoy a larger share of my own respect, at the present moment, if nothing had ever flowed from my pen, the production of which could be traced to me."

Brown wrote most of "Carwin the Biloquist" immediately after finishing *Wieland,* and he was probably propelled into it by an excess of what Nicholson Baker refers to as "the misleading momentum that . . . makes the completion of novels possible." It is included in this anthology for the light it sheds on *Wieland*'s villain. More suggestive and more artful are the final three stories here, written after Brown had lost his friend and moral anchor, Smith, but before he had forsworn fiction.

In "Walstein's School of History," Brown argues that the novel may provide as much moral guidance as history does. At the time, novels desperately needed such a defense. In his *Brief Retrospect of the Eighteenth Century* (1803), Samuel Miller gave a typical condemnation of the genre: "There is no species of reading which, promiscuously pursued, has a more direct tendency to discourage the acquisition of solid learning, to fill the mind with vain, unnatural, and delusive ideas, and to deprave the moral taste." It was perhaps in recognition of the arguments in "Walstein's School of History" that Miller made an exception for his friend Brown, whom he praised for "being the first American who presented his countrymen with a respectable specimen of fictitious history."

In "Thessalonica" and "Death of Cicero," Brown strove to live up to the standards and goals of the fictional Walstein. As Walstein recommends, in Brown's two Roman stories "the facts are either collected from the best antiquarians, or artfully deduced from what is known, or invented with a boldness more easy to admire than to imitate." And Brown, like Walstein, aims for his stories to provide "a model of right conduct." There is a catch, however. The heroes of both tales are highly skilled politicians with good intentions; we know Cicero's talent as an orator, and we sense that Julius Malchus is an able diplomat and administrator. But they have survived into eras when virtue has no place in government, and religion has only a cynical one. Voices that hope to convince by their reason and beauty alone will fail. In the world these stories describe, right conduct may be possible, but a happy ending is not. As the nation's first Gothic novelist, Brown felt obliged to remind America that the head of Cicero had been displayed as the symbol of a new political order once before—in the flesh, by the man who had arranged for his murder.

———

CALEB CRAIN is the author of *American Sympathy: Men, Friendship, and Literature in the New Nation.* He lives in Brooklyn.

A NOTE ON THE TEXT

Wieland, or the Transformation was first published in 1798 by T. & J. Swords, and its fragmentary sequel, "Memoirs of Carwin the Biloquist," was first published serially between 1803 and 1805 (though Brown had written a large part of it in 1798) in *The Literary Magazine and American Register* (a journal Brown started in 1803). "Thessalonica" first appeared in the May 1799 volume and "Walstein's School of History" in the August 1799 of *The Monthly Magazine and American Review*, another journal Brown had founded in 1799. "Death of Cicero" was first published as an appendage to the second printing to volume 3 of *Edgar Huntly, or Memoirs of a Sleep-Walker* (Philadelphia: H. Maxwell, 1799–1800). *Wieland, or the Transformation, and Other Stories* has been set from these first published editions, as they were the only ones to appear in Brown's lifetime, and according to the editors of the Bicentennial Edition of *Wieland* and *Carwin* published by Kent State University Press, there is no reason to believe that the variants in the first and second English editions (the first published in 1811 and the second in 1822) of *Wieland* or in the second American and first English edition of *Carwin* (the former published in 1815 and the latter in 1822) were made on the basis of revisions by Brown that his family might have discovered after his death and given the publishers.

In addition to substituting a short *s* for the long *s* (*f*) typically found in English-language books of the eighteenth century, and to regularizing the use of quotation marks and silently correcting printer's errors, the following substantive emendations have been made based on a consultation with the Bicentennial Edition:

p. 14, line 15: "designed" has been replaced with "deigned."

p. 19, line 32: "rend" has been replaced with "rendered."

p. 20, line 15: a comma has been inserted after "selects."

p. 63, line 26: "panic struck" has been replaced with "panic-struck."

p. 73, line 15: a semi-colon after "others" has been replaced with a colon.

p. 80, line 4: "can" has been replaced with "cannot."

p. 81, line 12: "those" has been replaced with "these."

p. 92, line 30: "real" has been replaced with "realized."

p. 134, lines 16–17: commas have been inserted after "now" and "thought."

p. 145, line 5: "comest" has been replaced with "camest."

p. 148, line 11: "effected" has been replaced with "affected."

p. 157, line 7: "a" has been inserted before "criminal."

p. 159, line 14: "these" has been replaced with "those."

p. 172, line 22: "affected" has been replaced with "effected."

p. 212, line 18: "those" has been replaced with "these."

p. 220, line 19: "not" has been inserted after "was."

p. 229, line 1: "him" has been inserted after "predisposed."

p. 238, line 2: "affect" has been replaced with "effect."

p. 247, line 30: "I" has been inserted after "could."

p. 250, line 22: "not" has been inserted after "was."

p. 252, line 7: "I" has been inserted after "and."

p. 256, line 28: "This" has been replaced with "His."

p. 257, line 10: a comma has been inserted after "guidance."

p. 257, line 12: a comma has been inserted after "topic."

p. 257, line 22: "destruction" has been replaced with "destructive."

p. 258, line 7: commas have been inserted after "novelty" and "however," and the comma after "disappearing" has been deleted.

p. 261, line 20: a comma has been inserted after "transgressions."

p. 265, line 23: a comma has been inserted after the first "thousands" and deleted after the second.

In addition, there were numerous places where "Ludlow" instead of "Ludloe" was used in the *The Literary Magazine*'s publication of *Carwin*. The editors of the Bicentennial Edition note that this inconsistency seems to be the result of Brown having failed to follow through on a decision he had made to spell the character's name with an *e* rather than a *w*, and hence they adopt "Ludloe" throughout. On the other hand, they retain another variation in the spelling of a name, that of "Benington" / "Bennington," on the grounds that it appears that Brown had simply failed to decide which spelling to use. This Modern Library edition follows the Bicentennial Edition on both these matters.

WIELAND

From Virtue's blissful paths away
The double-tongued are sure to stray;
Good is a forth-right journey still,
And mazy paths but lead to ill.

ADVERTISEMENT

The following Work is delivered to the world as the first of a series of performances, which the favorable reception of this will induce the Writer to publish. His purpose is neither selfish nor temporary, but aims at the illustration of some important branches of the moral constitution of man. Whether this tale will be classed with the ordinary or frivolous sources of amusement, or be ranked with the few productions whose usefulness secures to them a lasting reputation, the reader must be permitted to decide.

The incidents related are extraordinary and rare. Some of them, perhaps, approach as nearly to the nature of miracles as can be done by that which is not truly miraculous. It is hoped that intelligent readers will not disapprove of the manner in which appearances are solved, but that the solution will be found to correspond with the known principles of human nature. The power which the principal person is said to possess can scarcely be denied to be real. It must be acknowledged to be extremely rare; but no fact, equally uncommon, is supported by the same strength of historical evidence.

Some readers may think the conduct of the younger Wieland impossible. In support of this possibility the Writer must appeal to Physicians and to men conversant with the latent springs and occasional perversions of the human mind. It will not be objected that the instances of similar delusion are rare, because it is the business of moral painters to exhibit their subject in its most instructive and memorable forms. If history furnishes one parallel fact, it is a sufficient vindication of the Writer; but most readers will probably recollect an authentic case, remarkably similar to that of Wieland.[1]

It will be necessary to add, that this narrative is addressed, in an epistolary form, by the Lady whose story it contains, to a small number of friends, whose curiosity, with regard to it, had been greatly awakened. It may likewise be mentioned that these events took place between the conclusion of the French and the beginning of the revolutionary war. The memoirs of Carwin, alluded to at the conclusion of the work, will be published or suppressed according to the reception which is given to the present attempt.

C. B. B.
September 3, 1798.

Chapter I.

I feel little reluctance in complying with your request. You know not fully the cause of my sorrows. You are a stranger to the depth of my distresses. Hence your efforts at consolation must necessarily fail. Yet the tale that I am going to tell is not intended as a claim upon your sympathy. In the midst of my despair, I do not disdain to contribute what little I can to the benefit of mankind. I acknowledge your right to be informed of the events that have lately happened in my family. Make what use of the tale you shall think proper. If it be communicated to the world, it will inculcate the duty of avoiding deceit. It will exemplify the force of early impressions, and show the immeasurable evils that flow from an erroneous or imperfect discipline.

My state is not destitute of tranquillity. The sentiment that dictates my feelings is not hope. Futurity has no power over my thoughts. To all that is to come I am perfectly indifferent. With regard to myself, I have nothing more to fear. Fate has done its worst. Henceforth, I am callous to misfortune.

I address no supplication to the Deity. The power that governs the course of human affairs has chosen his path. The decree that ascertained the condition of my life, admits of no recal. No doubt it squares with the maxims of eternal equity. That is neither to be questioned nor denied by me. It suffices that the past is exempt from mutation. The storm that tore up our happiness, and changed into dreariness and desert the blooming scene of our existence, is lulled into grim repose; but not until the victim was transfixed and mangled; till every obstacle was dissipated by its rage; till every remnant of good was wrested from our grasp and exterminated.

How will your wonder, and that of your companions, be excited by my story! Every sentiment will yield to your amazement. If my testimony were without corroborations, you would reject it as incredible. The experience of no human being can furnish a parallel: That I, beyond the rest of mankind, should be reserved for a destiny without alleviation, and without example! Listen to my narrative, and then say what it is that has made me deserve to be placed on this dreadful eminence, if, indeed, every faculty be not suspended in wonder that I am still alive, and am able to relate it.

My father's ancestry was noble on the paternal side; but his mother was the daughter of a merchant. My grand-father was a younger brother, and a native of Saxony. He was placed, when he had reached the suitable age, at a German college. During the vacations, he employed himself in traversing the neighbouring territory. On one occasion it was his fortune to visit Hamburg. He formed an acquaintance with Leonard Weise, a merchant of that city, and was a frequent guest at his house. The merchant had an only daughter, for whom his guest speedily contracted an affection; and, in spite of parental menaces and prohibitions, he, in due season, became her husband.

By this act he mortally offended his relations. Thenceforward he was entirely disowned and rejected by them. They refused to contribute any thing to his support. All intercourse ceased, and he received from them merely that treatment to which an absolute stranger, or detested enemy, would be entitled.

He found an asylum in the house of his new father, whose temper was kind, and whose pride was flattered by this alliance. The nobility of his birth was put in the balance against his poverty. Weise conceived himself, on the whole, to have acted with the highest discretion, in thus disposing of his child. My grand-father found it incumbent on him to search out some mode of independent subsistence. His youth had been eagerly devoted to literature and music. These had hitherto been cultivated merely as sources of amusement. They were now converted into the means of gain. At this period there were few works of taste in the Saxon dialect. My ancestor may be considered as the founder of the German Theatre. The modern poet of the same name[2] is sprung from the same family, and, perhaps, surpasses but little, in the fruitfulness of his invention, or the founders of his taste, the elder Wieland. His life was spent in the composition of sonatas and dramatic pieces. They were not unpopular, but merely afforded him a scanty subsistence. He died in the bloom of his life, and was quickly followed to the grave by his wife. Their only child was taken under the protection of the merchant. At an early age he was apprenticed to a London trader, and passed seven years of mercantile servitude.

My father was not fortunate in the character of him under whose care he was now placed. He was treated with rigor, and full employment was provided for every hour of his time. His duties were laborious and mechanical. He had been educated with a view to this profession, and, therefore, was not tormented with unsatisfied desires. He did not hold his present occupations in abhorrence, because they withheld him from paths more flowery and more smooth, but he found in unintermitted labour, and in the sternness of his master, sufficient occasions for discontent. No opportunities of recreation were allowed him. He spent all his time pent up in a gloomy apartment, or traversing narrow and crowded streets. His food was coarse, and his lodging humble.

His heart gradually contracted a habit of morose and gloomy reflection. He could not accurately define what was wanting to his happiness. He was not tortured by comparisons drawn between his own situation and that of others. His state was such as suited his age and his views as to fortune. He did not imagine himself treated with extraordinary or unjustifiable rigor. In this respect he supposed the condition of others, bound like himself to mercantile service, to resemble his own; yet every engagement was irksome, and every hour tedious in its lapse.

In this state of mind he chanced to light upon a book written by one of the teachers of the Albigenses, or French Protestants.[3] He entertained no relish for books, and was wholly unconscious of any power they possessed to delight or instruct. This volume had lain for years in a corner of his garret, half buried in dust and rubbish. He had marked it as it lay; had thrown it, as his occasions required, from one spot to another; but had felt no inclination to examine its contents, or even to inquire what was the subject of which it treated.

One Sunday afternoon, being induced to retire for a few minutes to his garret, his eye was attracted by a page of this book, which, by some accident, had been opened and placed full in his view. He was seated on the edge of his bed, and was employed in repairing a rent in some part of his clothes. His eyes were not confined to his work, but occasionally wandering, lighted at length upon the page. The words "Seek and ye shall find,"[4] were those that first offered themselves to his notice. His curiosity was roused by these so far as to prompt him to proceed. As soon as he finished his work, he took up the book and turned to the first page. The further he read, the more inducement he found to continue, and he regretted the decline of the light which obliged him for the present to close it.

The book contained an exposition of the doctrine of the sect of Camissards,[5] and an historical account of its origin. His mind was in a state peculiarly fitted for the reception of devotional sentiments. The craving which had haunted him was now supplied with an object. His mind was at no loss for a theme of meditation. On days of business, he rose at the dawn, and retired to his chamber not till late at night. He now supplied himself with candles, and employed his nocturnal and Sunday hours in studying this book. It, of course, abounded with allusions to the Bible. All its conclusions were deduced from the sacred text. This was the fountain, beyond which it was unnecessary to trace the stream of religious truth; but it was his duty to trace it thus far.

A Bible was easily procured, and he ardently entered on the study of it. His understanding had received a particular direction. All his reveries were fashioned in the same mould. His progress towards the formation of his creed was rapid. Every fact and sentiment in this book were viewed through a medium which the writings of the Camissard apostle had suggested. His constructions of the text were hasty, and formed on a narrow scale. Every thing was viewed in a disconnected position. One action and one precept were not employed to illustrate and restrict the meaning of another. Hence arose a thousand scruples to which he had hitherto been a stranger. He was alternately agitated by fear and by ecstacy. He imagined himself beset by the snares of a spiritual foe, and that his security lay in ceaseless watchfulness and prayer.

His morals, which had never been loose, were now modelled by a stricter standard. The empire of religious duty extended itself to his looks, gestures, and phrases. All levities of speech, and negligences of behaviour, were proscribed. His air was mournful and contemplative. He laboured to keep alive a sentiment of fear, and a belief of the awe-creating presence of the Deity. Ideas foreign to this were sedulously excluded. To suffer their intrusion was a crime against the Divine Majesty inexpiable but by days and weeks of the keenest agonies.

No material variation had occurred in the lapse of two years. Every day confirmed him in his present modes of thinking and acting. It was to be expected that the tide of his emotions would sometimes recede, that intervals of despondency and doubt would occur; but these gradually were more rare, and of shorter duration; and he, at last, arrived at a state considerably uniform in this respect.

His apprenticeship was now almost expired. On his arrival of age he became entitled, by the will of my grand-father, to a small sum. This sum would hardly suffice to set him afloat as a trader in his present situation, and he had nothing to expect from the generosity of his master. Residence in England had, besides, become almost impossible, on account of his religious tenets. In addition to these motives for seeking a new habitation, there was another of the most imperious and irre-sistable necessity. He had imbibed an opinion that it was his duty to disseminate the truths of the gospel among the unbelieving nations. He was terrified at first by the perils and hardships to which the life of a missionary is exposed. This cowardice made him diligent in the in-vention of objections and excuses; but he found it impossible wholly to shake off the belief that such was the injunction of his duty. The belief, after every new conflict with his passions, acquired new strength; and, at length, he formed a resolution of complying with what he deemed the will of heaven.

The North-American Indians naturally presented themselves as the first objects for this species of benevolence. As soon as his servitude expired, he converted his little fortune into money, and embarked for Philadelphia. Here his fears were revived, and a nearer survey of savage manners once more shook his resolution. For a while he relinquished his purpose, and purchasing a farm on Schuylkill, within a few miles of the city, set himself down to the cultivation of it. The cheapness of land, and the service of African slaves, which were then in general use, gave him who was poor in Europe all the advantages of wealth. He passed fourteen years in a thrifty and laborious manner. In this time new objects, new employments, and new associates appeared to have nearly obliterated the devout impressions of his youth. He now became acquainted with a woman of a meek and quiet disposition, and of slender acquirements like himself. He proffered his hand and was accepted.

His previous industry had now enabled him to dispense with personal labour, and direct attention to his own concerns. He enjoyed leisure, and was visited afresh by devotional contemplation. The reading of the scriptures, and other religious books, became once more his favorite employment. His ancient belief relative to the conversion of the savage tribes, was revived with uncommon energy. To the former obstacles were now added the pleadings of parental and conjugal love. The struggle was long and vehement; but his sense of duty would not be stifled or enfeebled, and finally triumphed over every impediment.

His efforts were attended with no permanent success. His exhortations had sometimes a temporary power, but more frequently were repelled with insult and derision. In pursuit of this object he encountered the most imminent perils, and underwent incredible fatigues, hunger, sickness, and solitude. The licence of savage passion, and the artifices of his depraved countrymen, all opposed themselves to his progress. His courage did not forsake him till there appeared no reasonable ground to hope for success. He desisted not till his heart was relieved from the supposed obligation to persevere. With his constitution somewhat decayed, he at length returned to his family. An interval of tranquillity succeeded. He was frugal, regular, and strict in the performance of domestic duties. He allied himself with no sect, because he perfectly agreed with none. Social worship is that by which they are all distinguished; but this article found no place in his creed. He rigidly interpreted that precept which enjoins us, when we worship, to retire into solitude,[6] and shut out every species of society. According to him devotion was not only a silent office, but must be performed alone. An hour at noon, and an hour at midnight were thus appropriated.

At the distance of three hundred yards from his house, on the top of a rock whose sides were steep, rugged, and encumbered with dwarf cedars and stony asperities, he built what to a common eye would have seemed a summer-house. The eastern verge of this precipice was sixty feet above the river which flowed at its foot. The view before it consisted of a transparent current, fluctuating and rippling in a rocky channel, and bounded by a rising scene of corn-fields and orchards. The edifice was slight and airy. It was no more than a circular area, twelve feet in diameter, whose flooring was the rock, cleared of moss and shrubs, and exactly levelled, edged by twelve Tuscan columns, and covered by an undulating dome. My father furnished the dimensions and outlines, but allowed the artist whom he employed to complete the structure on his own plan. It was without seat, table, or ornament of any kind.

This was the temple of his Deity. Twice in twenty-four hours he repaired hither, un-accompanied by any human being. Nothing but physical inability to move was allowed to obstruct or postpone this visit. He did not exact from his family compliance with his example. Few men, equally sincere in their faith, were as sparing in their censures and restrictions, with respect to the conduct of others, as my father. The character of my mother was no less devout; but her education had habituated her to a different mode of worship. The loneliness of their dwelling prevented her from joining any established congregation; but she was punctual in the offices of prayer, and in the performance of hymns to her Saviour, after the manner of the disciples of Zinzendorf.[7] My father refused to interfere in her arrangements. His own system was embraced not, accurately speaking, because it was the best, but because it had been expresily prescribed to him. Other modes, if practised by other persons, might be equally acceptable.

His deportment to others was full of charity and mildness. A sadness perpetually overspread his features, but was unmingled with sternness or discontent. The tones of his voice, his gestures, his steps were all in tranquil unison. His conduct was characterised by a certain forbearance and humility, which secured the esteem of those to whom his tenets were most obnoxious. They might call him a fanatic and a dreamer, but they could not deny their veneration to his invincible candour and invariable integrity. His own belief of rectitude was the foundation of his happiness. This, however, was destined to find an end.

Suddenly the sadness that constantly attended him was deepened. Sighs, and even tears, sometimes escaped him. To the expostulations of his wife he seldom answered any thing. When he deigned to be communicative, he hinted that his peace of mind was flown, in consequence of deviation from his duty. A command had been laid upon him, which he had delayed to perform. He felt as if a certain period of hesitation and reluctance had been allowed him, but that this period was passed. He was no longer permitted to obey. The duty assigned to him was transferred, in consequence of his disobedience, to another, and all that remained was to endure the penalty.

He did not describe this penalty. It appeared to be nothing more for some time than a sense of wrong. This was sufficiently acute, and was aggravated by the belief that his offence was incapable of expiation. No one could contemplate the agonies which he seemed to suffer without the deepest compassion. Time, instead of lightening the burthen, appeared to add to it. At length he hinted to his wife, that his end was near. His imagination did not prefigure the mode or the time of his decease, but was fraught with an incurable persuasion that his death was at hand. He was likewise haunted by the belief that the kind of death that awaited him was strange and terrible. His anticipations were thus far vague and indefinite; but they sufficed to poison every moment of his being, and devote him to ceaseless anguish.

Chapter II.

Early in the morning of a sultry day in August, he left Mettingen, to go to the city. He had seldom passed a day from home since his return from the shores of the Ohio. Some urgent engagements at this time existed, which would not admit of further delay. He returned in the evening, but appeared to be greatly oppressed with fatigue. His silence and dejection were likewise in a more than ordinary degree conspicuous. My mother's brother, whose profession was that of a surgeon, chanced to spend this night at our house. It was from him that I have frequently received an exact account of the mournful catastrophe that followed.

As the evening advanced, my father's inquietudes increased. He sat with his family as usual, but took no part in their conversation. He appeared fully engrossed by his own reflections. Occasionally his countenance exhibited tokens of alarm; he gazed stedfastly and wildly at the ceiling; and the exertions of his companions were scarcely sufficient to interrupt his reverie. On recovering from these fits, he expressed no surprize; but pressing his hand to his head, complained, in a tremulous and terrified tone, that his brain was scorched to cinders. He would then betray marks of insupportable anxiety.

My uncle perceived, by his pulse, that he was indisposed, but in no alarming degree, and ascribed appearances chiefly to the workings of his mind. He exhorted him to recollection and composure, but in vain. At the hour of repose he readily retired to his chamber. At the persuasion of my mother he even undressed and went to bed. Nothing could abate his restlessness. He checked her tender expostulations with some sternness. "Be silent," said he, "for that which I feel there is but one cure, and that will shortly come. You can help me nothing. Look to your own condition, and pray to God to strengthen you under the calamities that await you." "What am I to fear?" she answered. "What terrible disaster is it that you think of?" "Peace—as yet I know it not myself, but come it will, and shortly." She repeated her inquiries and doubts; but he suddenly put an end to the discourse, by a stern command to be silent.

She had never before known him in this mood. Hitherto all was benign in his deportment. Her heart was pierced with sorrow at the contemplation of this change. She was utterly unable to account for it, or to figure to herself the species of disaster that was menaced.

Contrary to custom, the lamp, instead of being placed on the hearth, was left upon the table. Over it against the wall there hung a small clock, so contrived as to strike a very hard stroke at the end of every sixth hour. That which was now approaching was the signal for retiring to the sane at which he addressed his devotions. Long habit had occasioned him to be always awake at this hour, and the toll was instantly obeyed.

Now frequent and anxious glances were cast at the clock. Not a single movement of the index appeared to escape his notice. As the hour verged towards twelve his anxiety visibly augmented. The trepidations of my mother kept pace with those of her husband; but she was intimidated into silence. All that was left to her was to watch every change of his features, and give vent to her sympathy in tears.

At length the hour was spent, and the clock tolled. The sound appeared to communicate a shock to every part of my father's frame. He rose immediately, and threw over himself a loose gown. Even this office was performed with difficulty, for his joints trembled, and his teeth chattered with dismay. At this hour his duty called him to the rock, and my mother naturally concluded that it was thither he intended to repair. Yet these incidents were so uncommon, as to fill her with astonishment and foreboding. She saw him leave the room, and heard his steps as they hastily descended the stairs. She half resolved to rise and pursue him, but the wildness of the scheme quickly suggested itself. He was going to a place whither no power on earth could induce him to suffer an attendant.

The window of her chamber looked toward the rock. The atmosphere was clear and calm, but the edifice could not be discovered at that distance through the dusk. My mother's anxiety would not allow her to remain where she was. She rose, and seated herself at the window. She strained her sight to get a view of the dome, and of the path that led to it. The first painted itself with sufficient distinctness on her fancy, but was undistinguishable by the eye from the rocky mass on which it was erected. The second could be imperfectly seen; but her husband had already passed, or had taken a different direction.

What was it that she feared? Some disaster impended over her husband or herself. He had predicted evils, but professed himself ignorant of what nature they were. When were they to come? Was this night, or this hour to witness the accomplishment? She was tortured with impatience, and uncertainty. All her fears were at present linked to his person, and she gazed at the clock, with nearly as much eagerness as my father had done, in expectation of the next hour.

An half hour passed away in this state of suspence. Her eyes were fixed upon the rock; suddenly it was illuminated. A light proceeding from the edifice, made every part of the scene visible. A gleam diffused itself over the intermediate space, and instantly a loud report, like the explosion of a mine, followed. She uttered an involuntary shriek, but the new sounds that greeted her ear, quickly conquered her surprise. They were piercing shrieks, and uttered without intermission. The gleams which had diffused themselves far and wide were in a moment withdrawn, but the interior of the edifice was filled with rays.

The first suggestion was that a pistol was discharged, and that the structure was on fire. She did not allow herself time to meditate a second thought, but rushed into the entry and knocked loudly at the door of her brother's chamber. My uncle had been previously roused by the noise, and instantly flew to the window. He also imagined what he saw to be fire. The loud and vehement shrieks which succeeded the first explosion, seemed to be an invocation of succour. The incident was inexplicable; but he could not fail to perceive the propriety of hastening to the spot. He was unbolting the door, when his sister's voice was heard on the outside conjuring him to come forth.

He obeyed the summons with all the speed in his power. He stopped not to question her, but hurried down stairs and across the meadow which lay between the house and the rock. The shrieks were no longer to be heard; but a blazing light was clearly discernible between the columns of the temple. Irregular steps, hewn in the stone, led him to the summit. On three sides, this edifice touched the very verge of the cliff. On the fourth side, which might be regarded as the front, there was an area of small extent, to which the rude staircase conducted you. My uncle speedily gained this spot. His strength was for a moment exhausted by his haste. He paused to rest himself. Meanwhile he bent the most vigilant attention towards the object before him.

Within the columns he beheld what he could no better describe, than by saying that it resembled a cloud impregnated with light. It had the brightness of flame, but was without its upward motion. It did not occupy the whole area, and rose but a few feet above the floor. No part of the building was on fire. This appearance was astonishing. He approached the temple. As he went forward the light retired, and, when he put his feet within the apartment, utterly vanished. The suddenness of this transition increased the darkness that succeeded in a tenfold degree. Fear and wonder rendered him powerless. An occurrence like this, in a place assigned to devotion, was adapted to intimidate the stoutest heart.

His wandering thoughts were recalled by the groans of one near him. His sight gradually recovered its power, and he was able to discern my father stretched on the floor. At that moment, my mother and servants arrived with a lanthorn, and enabled my uncle to examine more closely this scene. My father, when he left the house, besides a loose upper vest and slippers, wore a shirt and drawers. Now he was naked, his skin throughout the greater part of his body was scorched and bruised. His right arm exhibited marks as of having been struck by some heavy body. His clothes had been removed, and it was not immediately perceived that they were reduced to ashes. His slippers and his hair were untouched.

He was removed to his chamber, and the requisite attention paid to his wounds, which gradually became more painful. A mortification speedily shewed itself in the arm, which had been most hurt. Soon after, the other wounded parts exhibited the like appearance.

Immediately subsequent to this disaster, my father seemed nearly in a state of insensibility. He was passive under every operation. He scarcely opened his eyes, and was with difficulty prevailed upon to answer the questions that were put to him. By his imperfect account, it appeared, that while engaged in silent orisons, with thoughts full of confusion and anxiety, a faint gleam suddenly shot athwart the apartment. His fancy immediately pictured to itself, a person bearing a lamp. It seemed to come from behind. He was in the act of turning to examine the visitant, when his right arm received a blow from a heavy club. At the same instant, a very bright spark was seen to light upon his clothes. In a moment, the whole was reduced to ashes. This was the sum of the information which he chose to give. There was somewhat in his manner that indicated an imperfect tale. My uncle was inclined to believe that half the truth had been suppressed.

Meanwhile, the disease thus wonderfully generated, betrayed more terrible symptoms. Fever and delirium terminated in lethargic slumber, which, in the course of two hours, gave place to death. Yet not till insupportable exhalations and crawling putrefaction had driven from his chamber and the house every one whom their duty did not detain.

Such was the end of my father. None surely was ever more mysterious. When we recollect his gloomy anticipations and unconquerable anxiety; the security from human malice which his character, the place, and the condition of the times, might be supposed to confer; the purity and cloudlessness of the atmosphere, which rendered it impossible that lightning was the cause; what are the conclusions that we must form?

The prelusive gleam, the blow upon his arm, the fatal spark, the explosion heard so far, the fiery cloud that environed him, without detriment to the structure, though composed of combustible materials, the sudden vanishing of this cloud at my uncle's approach—what is the inference to be drawn from these facts? Their truth cannot be doubted. My uncle's testimony is peculiarly worthy of credit, because no man's temper is more sceptical, and his belief is unalterably attached to natural causes.

I was at this time a child of six years of age. The impressions that were then made upon me, can never be effaced. I was ill qualified to judge respecting what was then passing; but as I advanced in age, and became more fully acquainted with these facts, they oftener became the subject of my thoughts. Their resemblance to recent events revived them with new force in my memory, and made me more anxious to explain them. Was this the penalty of disobedience? this the stroke of a vindictive and invisible hand? Is it a fresh proof that the Divine Ruler interferes in human affairs, meditates an end, selects, and commissions his agents, and enforces, by unequivocal sanctions, submission to his will? Or, was it merely the irregular expansion of the fluid that imparts warmth to our heart and our blood, caused by the fatigue of the preceding day, or flowing, by established laws, from the condition of his thoughts?*

---

*A case, in its symptoms exactly parallel to this, is published in one of the Journals of Florence.[8] See, likewise, similar cases reported by Messrs. Merille and Muraire, in the "Journal de Medicine," for February and May, 1783. The researches of Massei and Fontana have thrown some light upon this subject.

Chapter III.

The shock which this disastrous occurrence occasioned to my mother, was the foundation of a disease which carried her, in a few months, to the grave. My brother and myself were children at this time, and were now reduced to the condition of orphans. The property which our parents left was by no means inconsiderable. It was entrusted to faithful hands, till we should arrive at a suitable age. Meanwhile, our education was assigned to a maiden aunt who resided in the city, and whose tenderness made us in a short time cease to regret that we had lost a mother.

The years that succeeded were tranquil and happy. Our lives were molested by few of those cares that are incident to childhood. By accident more than design, the indulgence and yielding temper of our aunt was mingled with resolution and stedfastness. She seldom deviated into either extreme of rigour or lenity. Our social pleasures were subject to no unreasonable restraints. We were instructed in most branches of useful knowledge, and were saved from the corruption and tyranny of colleges and boarding-schools.

Our companions were chiefly selected from the children of our neighbours. Between one of these and my brother, there quickly grew the most affectionate intimacy. Her name was Catharine Pleyel. She was rich, beautiful, and contrived to blend the most bewitching softness with the most exuberant vivacity. The tie by which my brother and she were united, seemed to add force to the love which I bore her, and which was amply returned. Between her and myself there was every circumstance tending to produce and foster friendship. Our sex and age were the same. We lived within sight of each other's abode. Our tempers were remarkably congenial, and the superintendants of our education not only prescribed to us the same pursuits, but allowed us to cultivate them together.

Every day added strength to the triple bonds that united us. We gradually withdrew ourselves from the society of others, and found every moment irksome that was not devoted to each other. My brother's advance in age made no change in our situation. It was determined that his profession should be agriculture. His fortune exempted him from the necessity of personal labour. The task to be performed by him was nothing more than superintendance. The skill that was demanded by this was merely theoretical, and was furnished by casual inspection, or by closet study. The attention that was paid to this subject did not seclude him for any long time from us, on whom time had no other effect than to augment our impatience in the absence of each other and of him. Our tasks, our walks, our music, were seldom performed but in each other's company.

It was easy to see that Catharine and my brother were born for each other. The passion which they mutually entertained quickly broke those bounds which extreme youth had set to it; confessions were made or extorted, and their union was postponed only till my brother had passed his minority. The previous lapse of two years was constantly and usefully employed.

O my brother! But the task I have set myself let me perform with steadiness. The felicity of that period was marred by no gloomy anticipations. The future, like the present, was serene. Time was supposed to have only new delights in store. I mean not to dwell on previous incidents longer than is necessary to illustrate or explain the great events that have since happened. The nuptial day at length arrived. My brother took possession of the house in which he was born, and here the long protracted marriage was solemnized.

My father's property was equally divided between us. A neat dwelling, situated on the bank of the river, three quarters of a mile from my brother's, was now occupied by me. These domains were called, from the name of the first possessor, Mettingen. I can scarcely account for my refusing to take up my abode with him, unless it were from a disposition to be an economist of pleasure. Self-denial, seasonably exercised, is one means of enhancing our gratifications. I was, beside, desirous of administering a fund, and regulating an household, of my own. The short distance allowed us to exchange visits as often as we pleased. The walk from one mansion to the other was no undelightful prelude to our interviews. I was sometimes their visitant, and they, as frequently, were my guests.

Our education had been modelled by no religious standard. We were left to the guidance of our own understanding, and the casual impressions which society might make upon us. My friend's temper, as well as my own, exempted us from much anxiety on this account. It must not be supposed that we were without religion, but with us it was the product of lively feelings, excited by reflection on our own happiness, and by the grandeur of external nature. We sought not a basis for our faith, in the weighing of proofs, and the dissection of creeds. Our devotion was a mixed and casual sentiment, seldom verbally expressed, or solicitously sought, or carefully retained. In the midst of present enjoyment, no thought was bestowed on the future. As a consolation in calamity religion is dear. But calamity was yet at a distance, and its only tendency was to heighten enjoyments which needed not this addition to satisfy every craving.

My brother's situation was somewhat different. His deportment was grave, considerate, and thoughtful. I will not say whether he was indebted to sublimer views for this disposition. Human life, in his opinion, was made up of changeable elements, and the principles of duty were not easily unfolded. The future, either as anterior, or subsequent to death, was a scene that required some preparation and provision to be made for it. These positions we could not deny, but what distinguished him was a propensity to ruminate on these truths. The images that visited us were blithsome and gay, but those with which he was most familiar were of an opposite hue. They did not generate affliction and fear, but they diffused over his behaviour a certain air of fore-thought and sobriety. The principal effect of this temper was visible in his features and tones. These, in general, bespoke a sort of thrilling melancholy. I scarcely ever knew him to laugh. He never accompanied the lawless mirth of his companions with more than a smile, but his conduct was the same as ours.

He partook of our occupations and amusements with a zeal not less than ours, but of a different kind. The diversity in our temper was never the parent of discord, and was scarcely a topic of regret. The scene was variegated, but not tarnished or disordered by it. It hindered the element in which we moved from stagnating. Some agitation and concussion is requisite to the due exercise of human understanding. In his studies, he pursued an austerer and more arduous path. He was much conversant with the history of religious opinions, and took pains to ascertain their validity. He deemed it indispensable to examine the ground of his belief, to settle the relation between motives and actions, the criterion of merit, and the kinds and properties of evidence.

There was an obvious resemblance between him and my father, in their conceptions of the importance of certain topics, and in the light in which the vicissitudes of human life were accustomed to be viewed. Their characters were similar, but the mind of the son was enriched by science, and embellished with literature.

The temple was no longer assigned to its ancient use. From an Italian adventurer, who erroneously imagined that he could find employment for his skill, and sale for his sculptures in America, my brother had purchased a bust of Cicero. He professed to have copied this piece from an antique dug up with his own hands in the environs of Modena. Of the truth of his assertions we were not qualified to judge; but the marble was pure and polished, and we were contented to admire the performance, without waiting for the sanction of connoisseurs. We hired the same artist to hew a suitable pedestal from a neighbouring quarry. This was placed in the temple, and the bust rested upon it. Opposite to this was a harpsichord, sheltered by a temporary roof from the weather. This was the place of resort in the evenings of summer. Here we sung, and talked, and read, and occasionally banqueted. Every joyous and tender scene most dear to my memory, is connected with this edifice. Here the performances of our musical and poetical ancestor were rehearsed. Here my brother's children received the rudiments of their education; here a thousand conversations, pregnant with delight and improvement, took place; and here the social affections were accustomed to expand, and the tear of delicious sympathy to be shed.

My brother was an indefatigable student. The authors whom he read were numerous, but the chief object of his veneration was Cicero. He was never tired of conning and rehearsing his productions. To understand them was not sufficient. He was anxious to discover the gestures and cadences with which they ought to be delivered. He was very scrupulous in selecting a true scheme of pronunciation for the Latin tongue, and in adapting it to the words of his darling writer. His favorite occupation consisted in embellishing his rhetoric with all the proprieties of gesticulation and utterance.

Not contented with this, he was diligent in settling and restoring the purity of the text. For this end, he collected all the editions and commentaries that could be procured, and employed months of severe study in exploring and comparing them. He never betrayed more satisfaction than when he made a discovery of this kind.

It was not till the addition of Henry Pleyel, my friend's only brother, to our society, that his passion for Roman eloquence was countenanced and fostered by a sympathy of tastes. This young man had been some years in Europe. We had separated at a very early age, and he was now returned to spend the remainder of his days among us.

Our circle was greatly enlivened by the accession of a new member. His conversation abounded with novelty. His gaiety was almost boisterous, but was capable of yielding to a grave deportment, when the occasion required it. His discernment was acute, but he was prone to view every object merely as supplying materials for mirth. His conceptions were ardent but ludicrous, and his memory, aided, as he honestly acknowledged, by his invention, was an inexhaustible fund of entertainment.

His residence was at the same distance below the city as ours was above, but there seldom passed a day without our being favoured with a visit. My brother and he were endowed with the same attachment to the Latin writers; and Pleyel was not behind his friend in his knowledge of the history and metaphysics of religion. Their creeds, however, were in many respects opposite. Where one discovered only confirmations of his faith, the other could find nothing but reasons for doubt. Moral necessity, and calvinistic inspiration, were the props on which my brother thought proper to repose. Pleyel was the champion of intellectual liberty, and rejected all guidance but that of his reason. Their discussions were frequent, but, being managed with candour as well as with skill, they were always listened to by us with avidity and benefit.

Pleyel, like his new friends, was fond of music and poetry. Henceforth our concerts consisted of two violins, an harpsichord, and three voices. We were frequently reminded how much happiness depends upon society. This new friend, though, before his arrival, we were sensible of no vacuity, could not now be spared. His departure would occasion a void which nothing could fill, and which would produce insupportable regret. Even my brother, though his opinions were hourly assailed, and even the divinity of Cicero contested, was captivated with his friend, and laid aside some part of his ancient gravity at Pleyel's approach.

Chapter IV.

Six years of uninterrupted happiness had rolled away, since my brother's marriage. The sound of war had been heard, but it was at such a distance as to enhance our enjoyment by affording objects of comparison. The Indians were repulsed on the one side, and Canada was conquered on the other. Revolutions and battles, however calamitous to those who occupied the scene, contributed in some sort to our happiness, by agitating our minds with curiosity, and furnishing causes of patriotic exultation. Four children, three of whom were of an age to compensate, by their personal and mental progress, the cares of which they had been, at a more helpless age, the objects, exercised my brother's tenderness. The fourth was a charming babe that promised to display the image of her mother, and enjoyed perfect health. To these were added a sweet girl fourteen years old, who was loved by all of us, with an affection more than parental.

Her mother's story was a mournful one. She had come hither from England when this child was an infant, alone, without friends, and without money. She appeared to have embarked in a hasty and clandestine manner. She passed three years of solitude and anguish under my aunt's protection, and died a martyr to woe; the source of which she could, by no importunities, be prevailed upon to unfold. Her education and manners bespoke her to be of no mean birth. Her last moments were rendered serene, by the assurances she received from my aunt, that her daughter would experience the same protection that had been extended to herself.

On my brother's marriage, it was agreed that she should make a part of his family. I cannot do justice to the attractions of this girl. Perhaps the tenderness she excited might partly originate in her personal resemblance to her mother, whose character and misfortunes were still fresh in our remembrance. She was habitually pensive, and this circumstance tended to remind the spectator of her friendless condition; and yet that epithet was surely misapplied in this case. This being was cherished by those with whom she now resided, with unspeakable fondness. Every exertion was made to enlarge and improve her mind. Her safety was the object of a solicitude that almost exceeded the bounds of discretion. Our affection indeed could scarcely transcend her merits. She never met my eye, or occurred to my reflections, without exciting a kind of enthusiasm. Her softness, her intelligence, her equanimity, never shall I see surpassed. I have often shed tears of pleasure at her approach, and pressed her to my bosom in an agony of fondness.

While every day was adding to the charms of her person, and the stores of her mind, there occurred an event which threatened to deprive us of her. An officer of some rank, who had been disabled by a wound at Quebec, had employed himself, since the ratification of peace, in travelling through the colonies. He remained a considerable period at Philadelphia, but was at last preparing for his departure. No one had been more frequently honoured with his visits than Mrs. Baynton, a worthy lady with whom our family were intimate. He went to her house with a view to perform a farewell visit, and was on the point of taking his leave, when I and my young friend entered the apartment. It is impossible to describe the emotions of the stranger, when he fixed his eyes upon my companion. He was motionless with surprise. He was unable to conceal his feelings, but sat silently gazing at the spectacle before him. At length he turned to Mrs. Baynton, and more by his looks and gestures than by words, besought her for an explanation of the scene. He seized the hand of the girl, who, in her turn, was surprised by his behaviour, and drawing her forward, said in an eager and faultering tone, Who is she? whence does she come? what is her name?

The answers that were given only increased the confusion of his thoughts. He was successively told, that she was the daughter of one whose name was Louisa Conway, who arrived among us at such a time, who sedulously concealed her parentage, and the motives of her flight, whose incurable griefs had finally destroyed her, and who had left this child under the protection of her friends. Having heard the tale, he melted into tears, eagerly clasped the young lady in his arms, and called himself her father. When the tumults excited in his breast by this unlooked-for meeting were somewhat subsided, he gratified our curiosity by relating the following incidents:

"Miss Conway was the only daughter of a banker in London, who discharged towards her every duty of affectionate father. He had chanced to fall into her company, had been subdued by her attractions, had tendered her his hand, and had been joyfully accepted by both parent and child. His wife had given him every proof of the fondest attachment. Her father, who possessed immense wealth, treated him with distinguished respect, liberally supplied his wants, and had made one condition of his consent to their union, a resolution to take up their abode with him.

"They had passed three years of conjugal felicity, which had been augmented by the birth of this child, when his professional duty called him into Germany. It was not without an arduous struggle, that she was persuaded to relinquish the design of accompanying him through all the toils and perils of war. No parting was ever more distressful. They strove to alleviate, by frequent letters, the evils of their lot. Those of his wife, breathed nothing but anxiety for his safety, and impatience of his absence. At length, a new arrangement was made, and he was obliged to repair from Westphalia to Canada. One advantage attended this change. It afforded him an opportunity of meeting his family. His wife anticipated this interview, with no less rapture than himself. He hurried to London, and the moment he alighted from the stage-coach, ran with all speed to Mr. Conway's house.

"It was an house of mourning. His father was overwhelmed with grief, and incapable of answering his inquiries. The servants, sorrowful and mute, were equally refractory. He explored the house, and called on the names of his wife and daughter, but his summons was fruitless. At length, this new disaster was explained. Two days before his arrival, his wife's chamber was found empty. No search, however diligent and anxious, could trace her steps. No cause could be assigned for her disappearance. The mother and child had fled away together.

"New exertions were made, her chamber and cabinets were ransacked, but no vestige was found serving to inform them as to the motives of her flight, whether it had been voluntary or otherwise, and in what corner of the kingdom or of the world she was concealed. Who shall describe the sorrow and amazement of the husband? His restlessness, his vicissitudes of hope and fear, and his ultimate despair? His duty called him to America. He had been in this city, and had frequently passed the door of the house in which his wife, at that moment, resided. Her father had not remitted his exertions to elucidate this painful mystery, but they had failed. This disappointment hastened his death; in consequence of which, Louisa's father became possessor of his immense property."

This tale was a copious theme of speculation. A thousand questions were started and discussed in our domestic circle, respecting the motives that influenced Mrs. Stuart to abandon her country. It did not appear that her proceeding was involuntary. We recalled and reviewed every particular that had fallen under our own observation. By none of these were we furnished with a clue. Her conduct, after the most rigorous scrutiny, still remained an impenetrable secret. On a nearer view, Major Stuart proved himself a man of most amiable character. His attachment to Louisa appeared hourly to increase. She was no stranger to the sentiments suitable to her new character. She could not but readily embrace the scheme which was proposed to her, to return with her father to England. This scheme his regard for her induced him, however, to postpone. Some time was necessary to prepare her for so great a change and enable her to think without agony of her separation from us.

I was not without hopes of prevailing on her father entirely to relinquish this unwelcome design. Meanwhile, he pursued his travels through the southern colonies, and his daughter continued with us. Louisa and my brother frequently received letters from him, which indicated a mind of no common order. They were filled with amusing details, and profound reflections. While here, he often partook of our evening conversations at the temple; and since his departure, his correspondence had frequently supplied us with topics of discourse.

One afternoon in May, the blandness of the air, and brightness of the verdure, induced us to assemble, earlier than usual, in the temple. We females were busy at the needle, while my brother and Pleyel were bandying quotations and syllogisms. The point discussed was the merit of the oration for Cluentius,[9] as descriptive, first, of the genius of the speaker; and, secondly, of the manners of the times. Pleyel laboured to extenuate both these species of merit, and tasked his ingenuity, to shew that the orator had embraced a bad cause; or, at least, a doubtful one. He urged, that to rely on the exaggerations of an advocate, or to make the picture of a single family a model from which to sketch the condition of a nation, was absurd. The controversy was suddenly diverted into a new channel, by a misquotation. Pleyel accused his companion of saying *"polliceatur"* when he should have said *"polliceretur."*[10] Nothing would decide the contest, but an appeal to the volume. My brother was returning to the house for this purpose, when a servant met him with a letter from Major Stuart. He immediately returned to read it in our company.

Besides affectionate compliments to us, and paternal benedictions on Louisa, his letter contained a description of a waterfall on the Monongahela. A sudden gust of rain falling, we were compelled to remove to the house. The storm passed away, and a radiant moon-light succeeded. There was no motion to resume our seats in the temple. We therefore remained where we were, and engaged in sprightly conversation. The letter lately received naturally suggested the topic. A parallel was drawn between the cataract there described, and one which Pleyel had discovered among the Alps of Glarus. In the state of the former, some particular was mentioned, the truth of which was questionable. To settle the dispute which thence arose, it was proposed to have recourse to the letter. My brother searched for it in his pocket. It was no where to be found. At length, he remembered to have left it in the temple, and he determined to go in search of it. His wife, Pleyel, Louisa, and myself, remained where we were.

In a few minutes he returned. I was somewhat interested in the dispute, and was therefore impatient for his return; yet, as I heard him ascending the stairs, I could not but remark, that he had executed his intention with remarkable dispatch. My eyes were fixed upon him on his entrance. Methought he brought with him looks considerably different from those with which he departed. Wonder, and a slight portion of anxiety were mingled in them. His eyes seemed to be in search of some object. They passed quickly from one person to another, till they rested on his wife. She was seated in a careless attitude on the sofa, in the same spot as before. She had the same muslin in her hand, by which her attention was chiefly engrossed.

The moment he saw her, his perplexity visibly increased. He quietly seated himself, and fixing his eyes on the floor, appeared to be absorbed in meditation. These singularities suspended the inquiry which I was preparing to make respecting the letter. In a short time, the company relinquished the subject which engaged them, and directed their attention to Wieland. They thought that he only waited for a pause in the discourse, to produce the letter. The pause was uninterrupted by him. At length Pleyel said, "Well, I suppose you have found the letter."

"No," said he, without any abatement of his gravity, and looking stedfastly at his wife, "I did not mount the hill."—"Why not?"— "Catharine, have you not moved from that spot since I left the room?"—She was affected with the solemnity of his manner, and laying down her work, answered in a tone of surprise, "No; Why do you ask that question?"—His eyes were again fixed upon the floor, and he did not immediately answer. At length, he said, looking round upon us, "Is it true that Catharine did not follow me to the hill? That she did not just now enter the room?"—We assured him, with one voice, that she had not been absent for a moment, and inquired into the motive of his questions.

"Your assurances," said he, "are solemn and unanimous; and yet I must deny credit to your assertions, or disbelieve the testimony of my senses, which informed me, when I was half way up the hill, that Catharine was at the bottom."

We were confounded at this declaration. Pleyel rallied him with great levity on his behaviour. He listened to his friend with calmness, but without any relaxation of features.

"One thing," said he with emphasis, "is true; either I heard my wife's voice at the bottom of the hill, or I do not hear your voice at present."

"Truly," returned Pleyel, "it is a sad dilemma to which you have reduced yourself. Certain it is, if our eyes can give us certainty, that your wife has been sitting in that spot during every moment of your absence. You have heard her voice, you say, upon the hill. In general, her voice, like her temper, is all softness. To be heard across the room, she is obliged to exert herself. While you were gone, if I mistake not, she did not utter a word. Clara and I had all the talk to ourselves. Still it may be that she held a whispering conference with you on the hill; but tell us the particulars."

"The conference," said he, "was short; and far from being carried on in a whisper. You know with what intention I left the house. Half way to the rock, the moon was for a moment hidden from us by a cloud. I never knew the air to be more bland and more calm. In this interval I glanced at the temple, and thought I saw a glimmering between the columns. It was so faint, that it would not perhaps have been visible, if the moon had not been shrowded. I looked again, but saw nothing. I never visit this building alone, or at night, without being reminded of the fate of my father. There was nothing wonderful in this appearance; yet it suggested something more than mere solitude and darkness in the same place would have done.

"I kept on my way. The images that haunted me were solemn; and I entertained an imperfect curiosity, but no fear, as to the nature of this object. I had ascended the hill little more than half way, when a voice called me from behind. The accents were clear, distinct, powerful, and were uttered, as I fully believed, by my wife. Her voice is not commonly so loud. She has seldom occasion to exert it, but, nevertheless, I have sometimes heard her call with force and eagerness. If my ear was not deceived, it was her voice which I heard.

" 'Stop, go no further. There is danger in your path.' The suddenness and unexpectedness of this warning, the tone of alarm with which it was given, and, above all, the persuasion that it was my wife who spoke, were enough to disconcert and make me pause. I turned and listened to assure myself that I was not mistaken. The deepest silence succeeded. At length, I spoke in my turn. Who calls? is it you, Catharine? I stopped and presently received an answer. 'Yes, it is I; go not up; return instantly; you are wanted at the house.' Still the voice was Catharine's, and still it proceeded from the foot of the stairs.

"What could I do? The warning was mysterious. To be uttered by Catharine at a place, and on an occasion like these, enhanced the mystery. I could do nothing but obey. Accordingly, I trod back my steps, expecting that she waited for me at the bottom of the hill. When I reached the bottom, no one was visible. The moon-light was once more universal and brilliant, and yet, as far as I could see no human or moving figure was discernable. If she had returned to the house, she must have used wonderous expedition to have passed already beyond the reach of my eye. I exerted my voice, but in vain. To my repeated exclamations, no answer was returned.

"Ruminating on these incidents, I returned hither. There was no room to doubt that I had heard my wife's voice; attending incidents were not easily explained; but you now assure me that nothing extraordinary has happened to urge my return, and that my wife has not moved from her seat."

Such was my brother's narrative. It was heard by us with different emotions. Pleyel did not scruple to regard the whole as a deception of the senses. Perhaps a voice had been heard; but Wieland's imagination had misled him in supposing a resemblance to that of his wife, and giving such a signification to the sounds. According to his custom he spoke what he thought. Sometimes, he made it the theme of grave discussion, but more frequently treated it with ridicule. He did not believe that sober reasoning would convince his friend, and gaiety, he thought, was useful to take away the solemnities which, in a mind like Wieland's, an accident of this kind was calculated to produce.

Pleyel proposed to go in search of the letter. He went and speedily returned, bearing it in his hand. He had found it open on the pedestal; and neither voice nor visage had risen to impede his design.

Catharine was endowed with an uncommon portion of good sense; but her mind was accessible, on this quarter, to wonder and panic. That her voice should be thus inexplicably and unwarrantably assumed, was a source of no small disquietude. She admitted the plausibility of the arguments by which Pleyel endeavoured to prove, that this was no more than an auricular deception; but this conviction was sure to be shaken, when she turned her eyes upon her husband, and perceived that Pleyel's logic was far from having produced the same effect upon him.

As to myself, my attention was engaged by this occurrence. I could not fail to perceive a shadowy resemblance between it and my father's death. On the latter event, I had frequently reflected; my reflections never conducted me to certainty, but the doubts that existed were not of a tormenting kind. I could not deny that the event was miraculous, and yet I was invincibly averse to that method of solution. My wonder was excited by the inscrutableness of the cause, but my wonder was unmixed with sorrow or fear. It begat in me a thrilling, and not unpleasing solemnity. Similar to these were the sensations produced by the recent adventure.

But its effect upon my brother's imagination was of chief moment. All that was desirable was, that it should be regarded by him with indifference. The worst effect that could flow, was not indeed very formidable. Yet I could not bear to think that his senses should be the victims of such delusion. It argued a diseased condition of his frame, which might show itself hereafter in more dangerous symptoms. The will is the tool of the understanding, which must fashion its conclusions on the notices of sense. If the senses be depraved, it is impossible to calculate the evils that may flow from the consequent deductions of the understanding.

I said, this man is of an ardent and melancholy character. Those ideas which, in others, are casual or obscure, which are entertained in moments of abstraction and solitude, and easily escape when the scene is changed, have obtained an immoveable hold upon his mind. The conclusions which long habit has rendered familiar, and, in some sort, palpable to his intellect, are drawn from the deepest sources. All his actions and practical sentiments are linked with long and abstruse deductions from the system of divine government and the laws of our intellectual constitution. He is, in some respects, an enthusiast, but is fortified in his belief by innumerable arguments and subtilties.

His father's death was always regarded by him as flowing from a direct and supernatural decree. It visited his meditations oftener than it did mine. The traces which it left were more gloomy and permanent. This new incident had a visible effect in augmenting his gravity. He was less disposed than formerly to converse and reading. When we sifted his thoughts, they were generally found to have a relation, more or less direct, with this incident. It was difficult to ascertain the exact species of impression which it made upon him. He never introduced the subject into conversation, and listened with a silent and half-serious smile to the satirical effusions of Pleyel.

One evening we chanced to be alone together in the temple. I seized that opportunity of investigating the state of his thoughts. After a pause, which he seemed in no wise inclined to interrupt, I spoke to him—"How almost palpable is this dark; yet a ray from above would dispel it." "Ay," said Wieland, with fervor, "not only the physical, but moral night would be dispelled." "But why," said I, "must the Divine Will address its precepts to the eye?" He smiled significantly. "True," said he, "the understanding has other avenues." "You have never," said I, approaching nearer to the point—"you have never told me in what way you considered the late extraordinary incident." "There is no determinate way in which the subject can be viewed. Here is an effect, but the cause is utterly inscrutable. To suppose a deception will not do. Such is possible, but there are twenty other suppositions more probable. They must all be set aside before we reach that point." "What are these twenty suppositions?" "It is needless to mention them. They are only less improbable than Pleyel's. Time may convert one of them into certainty. Till then it is useless to expatiate on them."

Chapter V.

Some time had elapsed when there happened another occurrence, still more remarkable. Pleyel, on his return from Europe, brought information of considerable importance to my brother. My ancestors were noble Saxons, and possessed large domains in Lusatia. The Prussian wars had destroyed those persons whose right to these estates precluded my brother's. Pleyel had been exact in his inquiries, and had discovered that, by the law of male-primogeniture, my brother's claims were superior to those of any other person now living. Nothing was wanting but his presence in that country, and a legal application to establish this claim.

Pleyel strenuously recommended this measure. The advantages he thought attending it were numerous, and it would argue the utmost folly to neglect them. Contrary to his expectation he found my brother averse to the scheme. Slight efforts, he, at first, thought would subdue his reluctance; but he found this aversion by no means slight. The interest that he took in the happiness of his friend and his sister, and his own partiality to the Saxon soil, from which he had likewise sprung, and where he had spent several years of his youth, made him redouble his exertions to win Wieland's consent. For this end he employed every argument that his invention could suggest. He painted, in attractive colours, the state of manners and government in that country, the security of civil rights, and the freedom of religious sentiments. He dwelt on the privileges of wealth and rank, and drew from the servile condition of one class, an argument in favor of his scheme, since the revenue and power annexed to a German principality afford so large a field for benevolence. The evil flowing from this power, in malignant hands, was proportioned to the good that would arise from the virtuous use of it. Hence, Wieland, in forbearing to claim his own, withheld all the positive felicity that would accrue to his vassals from his success, and hazarded all the misery that would redound from a less enlightened proprietor.

It was easy for my brother to repel these arguments, and to shew that no spot on the globe enjoyed equal security and liberty to that which he at present inhabited. That if the Saxons had nothing to fear from mis-government, the external causes of havoc and alarm were numerous and manifest. The recent devastations committed by the Prussians furnished a specimen of these. The horrors of war would always impend over them, till Germany were seized and divided by Austrian and Prussian tyrants; an event which he strongly suspected was at no great distance. But setting these considerations aside, was it laudable to grasp at wealth and power even when they were within our reach? Were not these the two great sources of depravity? What security had he, that in this change of place and condition, he should not degenerate into a tyrant and voluptuary? Power and riches were chiefly to be dreaded on account of their tendency to deprave the possessor. He held them in abhorrence, not only as instruments of misery to others, but to him on whom they were conferred. Besides, riches were comparative, and was he not rich already? He lived at present in the bosom of security and luxury. All the instruments of pleasure, on which his reason or imagination set any value, were within his reach. But these he must forego, for the sake of advantages which, whatever were their value, were as yet uncertain. In pursuit of an imaginary addition to his wealth, he must reduce himself to poverty, he must exchange present certainties for what was distant and contingent; for who knows not that the law is a system of expence, delay and uncertainty? If he should embrace this scheme, it would lay him under the necessity of making a voyage to Europe, and remaining for a certain period, separate from his family. He must undergo the perils and discomforts of the ocean; he must divest himself of all domestic pleasures; he must deprive his wife of her companion, and his children of a father and instructor, and all for what? For the ambiguous advantages which overgrown wealth and flagitious tyranny have to bestow? For a precarious possession in a land of turbulence and war? Advantages, which will not certainly be gained, and of which the acquisition, if it were sure, is necessarily distant.

Pleyel was enamoured of his scheme on account of its intrinsic benefits, but, likewise, for other reasons. His abode at Leipsig made that country appear to him like home. He was connected with this place by many social ties. While there he had not escaped the amorous contagion. But the lady, though her heart was impressed in his favor, was compelled to bestow her hand upon another. Death had removed this impediment, and he was now invited by the lady herself to return. This he was of course determined to do, but was anxious to obtain the company of Wieland; he could not bear to think of an eternal separation from his present associates. Their interest, he thought, would be no less promoted by the change than his own. Hence he was importunate and indefatigable in his arguments and solicitations.

He knew that he could not hope for mine or his sister's ready concurrence in this scheme. Should the subject be mentioned to us, we should league our efforts against him, and strengthen that reluctance in Wieland which already was sufficiently difficult to conquer. He, therefore, anxiously concealed from us his purpose. If Wieland were previously enlisted in his cause, he would find it a less difficult task to overcome our aversion. My brother was silent on this subject, because he believed himself in no danger of changing his opinion, and he was willing to save us from any uneasiness. The mere mention of such a scheme, and the possibility of his embracing it, he knew, would considerably impair our tranquillity.

One day, about three weeks subsequent to the mysterious call, it was agreed that the family should be my guests. Seldom had a day been passed by us, of more serene enjoyment. Pleyel had promised us his company, but we did not see him till the sun had nearly declined.

He brought with him a countenance that betokened disappointment and vexation. He did not wait for our inquiries, but immediately explained the cause. Two days before a packet had arrived from Hamburgh, by which he had flattered himself with the expectation of receiving letters, but no letters had arrived. I never saw him so much subdued by an untoward event. His thoughts were employed in accounting for the silence of his friends. He was seized with the torments of jealousy and suspected nothing less than the infidelity of her to whom he had devoted his heart. The silence must have been concerted. Her sickness, or absence, or death, would have increased the certainty of some one's having written. No supposition could be formed but that his mistress had grown indifferent, or that she had transferred her affections to another. The miscarriage of a letter was hardly within the reach of possibility. From Leipsig to Hamburgh, and from Hamburgh hither, the conveyance was exposed to no hazard.

He had been so long detained in America chiefly in consequence of Wieland's aversion to the scheme which he proposed. He now became more impatient than ever to return to Europe. When he reflected that, by his delays, he had probably forfeited the affections of his mistress, his sensations amounted to agony. It only remained, by his speedy departure, to repair, if possible, or prevent so intolerable an evil. Already he had half resolved to embark in this very ship which, he was informed, would set out in a few weeks on her return.

Meanwhile he determined to make a new attempt to shake the resolution of Wieland. The evening was somewhat advanced when he invited the latter to walk abroad with him. The invitation was accepted, and they left Catharine, Louisa and me, to amuse ourselves by the best means in our power. During this walk, Pleyel renewed the subject that was nearest his heart. He re-urged all his former arguments, and placed them in more forcible lights.

They promised to return shortly, but hour after hour passed, and they made not their appearance. Engaged in sprightly conversation, it was not till the clock struck twelve that we were reminded of the lapse of time. The absence of our friends excited some uneasy apprehensions. We were expressing our fears, and comparing our conjectures as to what might be the cause, when they entered together. There were indications in their countenances that struck me mute. These were

unnoticed by Catharine, who was eager to express her surprize and curiosity at the length of their walk. As they listened to her, I remarked
that their surprize was not less than ours. They gazed in silence on
each other, and on her. I watched their looks, but could not understand
the emotions that were written in them.

These appearances diverted Catharine's inquiries into a new channel. What did they mean, she asked, by their silence, and by their thus
gazing wildly at each other, and at her? Pleyel profited by this hint, and
assuming an air of indifference, framed some trifling excuse, at the
same time darting significant glances at Wieland, as if to caution him
against disclosing the truth. My brother said nothing, but delivered
himself up to meditation. I likewise was silent, but burned with impatience to fathom this mystery. Presently my brother and his wife, and
Louisa, returned home. Pleyel proposed, of his own accord, to be my
guest for the night. This circumstance, in addition to those which preceded, gave new edge to my wonder.

As soon as we were left alone, Pleyel's countenance assumed an air
of seriousness, and even consternation, which I had never before beheld in him. The steps with which he measured the floor betokened
the trouble of his thoughts. My inquiries were suspended by the hope
that he would give me the information that I wanted without the importunity of questions. I waited some time, but the confusion of his
thoughts appeared in no degree to abate. At length I mentioned the
apprehensions which their unusual absence had occasioned, and
which were increased by their behaviour since their return, and solicited an explanation. He stopped when I began to speak, and looked
stedfastly at me. When I had done, he said, to me, in a tone which
faultered through the vehemence of his emotions, "How were you employed during our absence?" "In turning over the Della Crusca dictionary,[11] and talking on different subjects; but just before your entrance,
we were tormenting ourselves with omens and prognosticks relative to
your absence." "Catharine was with you the whole time?" "Yes." "But
are you sure?" "Most sure. She was not absent a moment." He stood,
for a time, as if to assure himself of my sincerity. Then, clenching his
hands, and wildly lifting them above his head, "Lo," cried he, "I have
news to tell you. The Baroness de Stolberg is dead!"

This was her whom he loved. I was not surprised at the agitations which he betrayed. "But how was the information procured? How was the truth of this news connected with the circumstance of Catharine's remaining in our company?" He was for some time inattentive to my questions. When he spoke, it seemed merely a continuation of the reverie into which he had been plunged.

"And yet it might be a mere deception. But could both of us in that case have been deceived? A rare and prodigious coincidence! Barely not impossible. And yet, if the accent be oracular—Theresa is dead. No, no," continued he, covering his face with his hands, and in a tone half broken into sobs, "I cannot believe it. She has not written, but if she were dead, the faithful Bertrand would have given me the earliest information. And yet if he knew his master, he must have easily guessed at the effect of such tidings. In pity to me he was silent.

"Clara, forgive me; to you, this behaviour is mysterious. I will explain as well as I am able. But say not a word to Catharine. Her strength of mind is inferior to your's. She will, besides, have more reason to be startled. She is Wieland's angel."

Pleyel proceeded to inform me, for the first time, of the scheme which he had pressed, with so much earnestness, on my brother. He enumerated the objections which had been made, and the industry with which he had endeavoured to confute them. He mentioned the effect upon his resolutions produced by the failure of a letter. "During our late walk," continued he, "I introduced the subject that was nearest my heart. I re-urged all my former arguments, and placed them in more forcible lights. Wieland was still refractory. He expatiated on the perils of wealth and power, on the sacredness of conjugal and parental duties, and the happiness of mediocrity.

"No wonder that the time passed, unperceived, away. Our whole souls were engaged in this cause. Several times we came to the foot of the rock; as soon as we perceived it, we changed our course, but never failed to terminate our circuitous and devious ramble at this spot. At length your brother observed, 'We seem to be led hither by a kind of fatality. Since we are so near, let us ascend and rest ourselves a while. If you are not weary of this argument we will resume it there.'

"I tacitly consented. We mounted the stairs, and drawing the sofa in front of the river, we seated ourselves upon it. I took up the thread of our discourse where we had dropped it. I ridiculed his dread of the sea, and his attachment to home. I kept on in this strain, so congenial with my disposition, for some time, uninterrupted by him. At length, he said to me, 'Suppose now that I, whom argument has not convinced, should yield to ridicule, and should agree that your scheme is eligible; what will you have gained? Nothing. You have other enemies beside myself to encounter. When you have vanquished me, your toil has scarcely begun. There are my sister and wife, with whom it will remain for you to maintain the contest. And trust me, they are adversaries whom all your force and stratagem will never subdue.' I insinuated that they would model themselves by his will: that Catharine would think obedience her duty. He answered, with some quickness, 'You mistake. Their concurrence is indispensable. It is not my custom to exact sacrifices of this kind. I live to be their protector and friend, and not their tyrant and foe. If my wife shall deem her happiness, and that of her children, most consulted by remaining where she is, here she shall remain.' 'But,' said I, 'when she knows your pleasure, will she not conform to it?' Before my friend had time to answer this question, a negative was clearly and distinctly uttered from another quarter. It did not come from one side or the other, from before us or behind. Whence then did it come? By whose organs was it fashioned?

"If any uncertainty had existed with regard to these particulars, it would have been removed by a deliberate and equally distinct repetition of the same monosyllable, 'No.' The voice was my sister's. It appeared to come from the roof. I started from my seat. 'Catharine,' exclaimed I, 'where are you?' No answer was returned. I searched the room, and the area before it, but in vain. Your brother was motionless in his seat. I returned to him, and placed myself again by his side. My astonishment was not less than his.

" 'Well,' said he, at length, 'What think you of this? This is the self-same voice which I formerly heard; you are now convinced that my ears were well informed.'

" 'Yes,' said I, 'this, it is plain, is no fiction of the fancy.' We again sunk into mutual and thoughtful silence. A recollection of the hour, and of the length of our absence, made me at last propose to return.

We rose up for this purpose. In doing this, my mind reverted to the contemplation of my own condition. 'Yes,' said I aloud, but without particularly addressing myself to Wieland, 'my resolution is taken. I cannot hope to prevail with my friends to accompany me. They may doze away their days on the banks of Schuylkill, but as to me, I go in the next vessel; I will fly to her presence, and demand the reason of this extraordinary silence.'

"I had scarcely finished the sentence, when the same mysterious voice exclaimed, 'You shall not go. The seal of death is on her lips. Her silence is the silence of the tomb.' Think of the effects which accents like these must have had upon me. I shuddered as I listened. As soon as I recovered from my first amazement, 'Who is it that speaks?' said I, 'whence did you procure these dismal tidings?' I did not wait long for an answer. 'From a source that cannot fail. Be satisfied. She is dead.' You may justly be surprised, that, in the circumstances in which I heard the tidings, and notwithstanding the mystery which environed him by whom they were imparted, I could give an undivided attention to the facts, which were the subject of our dialogue. I eagerly inquired, when and where did she die? What was the cause of her death? Was her death absolutely certain? An answer was returned only to the last of these questions. 'Yes,' was pronounced by the same voice; but it now sounded from a greater distance, and the deepest silence was all the return made to my subsequent interrogatories.

"It was my sister's voice; but it could not be uttered by her; and yet, if not by her, by whom was it uttered? When we returned hither, and discovered you together, the doubt that had previously existed was removed. It was manifest that the intimation came not from her. Yet if not from her, from whom could it come? Are the circumstances attending the imparting of this news proof that the tidings are true? God forbid that they should be true."

Here Pleyel sunk into anxious silence, and gave me leisure to ruminate on this inexplicable event. I am at a loss to describe the sensations that affected me. I am not fearful of shadows. The tales of apparitions and enchantments did not possess that power over my belief which could even render them interesting. I saw nothing in them but ignorance and folly, and was a stranger even to that terror which is pleasing. But this incident was different from any that I had ever before known. Here were proofs of a sensible and intelligent existence, which could not be denied. Here was information obtained and imparted by means unquestionably super-human.

That there are conscious beings, beside ourselves, in existence, whose modes of activity and information surpass our own, can scarcely be denied. Is there a glimpse afforded us into a world of these superior beings? My heart was scarcely large enough to give admittance to so swelling a thought. An awe, the sweetest and most solemn that imagination can conceive, pervaded my whole frame. It forsook me not when I parted from Pleyel and retired to my chamber. An impulse was given to my spirits utterly incompatible with sleep. I passed the night wakeful and full of meditation. I was impressed with the belief of mysterious, but not of malignant agency. Hitherto nothing had occurred to persuade me that this airy minister was busy to evil rather than to good purposes. On the contrary, the idea of superior virtue had always been associated in my mind with that of superior power. The warnings that had thus been heard appeared to have been prompted by beneficent intentions. My brother had been hindered by this voice from ascending the hill. He was told that danger lurked in his path, and his obedience to the intimation had perhaps saved him from a destiny similar to that of my father.

Pleyel had been rescued from tormenting uncertainty, and from the hazards and fatigues of a fruitless voyage, by the same interposition. It had assured him of the death of his Theresa.

This woman was then dead. A confirmation of the tidings, if true, would speedily arrive. Was this confirmation to be deprecated or desired? By her death, the tie that attached him to Europe, was taken away. Henceforward every motive would combine to retain him to his native country, and we were rescued from the deep regrets that would accompany his hopeless absence from us. Propitious was the spirit that imparted these tidings. Propitious he would perhaps have been, if he had been instrumental in producing, as well as in communicating the tidings of her death. Propitious to us, the friends of Pleyel, to whom has thereby been secured the enjoyment of his society; and not unpropitious to himself; for though this object of his love be snatched away, is there not another who is able and willing to console him for her loss?

Twenty days after this, another vessel arrived from the same port. In this interval, Pleyel, for the most part, estranged himself from his old companions. He was become the prey of a gloomy and unsociable grief. His walks were limited to the bank of the Delaware. This bank is an artificial one. Reeds and the river are on one side, and a watery marsh on the other, in that part which bounded his lands, and which extended from the mouth of Hollander's creek to that of Schuylkill. No scene can be imagined less enticing to a lover of the picturesque than this. The shore is deformed with mud, and incumbered with a forest of reeds. The fields, in most seasons, are mire; but when they afford a firm footing, the ditches by which they are bounded and intersected, are mantled with stagnating green, and emit the most noxious exhalations. Health is no less a stranger to those seats than pleasure. Spring and autumn are sure to be accompanied with agues and bilious remittents.

The scenes which environed our dwellings at Mettingen constituted the reverse of this. Schuylkill was here a pure and translucid current, broken into wild and ceaseless music by rocky points, murmuring on a sandy margin, and reflecting on its surface, banks of all varieties of height and degrees of declivity. These banks were chequered by patches of dark verdure and shapeless masses of white marble, and crowned by copses of cedar, or by the regular magnificence of orchards, which, at this season, were in blossom, and were prodigal of odours. The ground which receded from the river was scooped into valleys and dales. Its beauties were enhanced by the horticultural skill of my brother, who bedecked this exquisite assemblage of slopes and risings with every species of vegetable ornament, from the giant arms of the oak to the clustering tendrils of the honey-suckle.

To screen him from the unwholesome airs of his own residence, it had been proposed to Pleyel to spend the months of spring with us. He had apparently acquiesced in this proposal; but the late event induced him to change his purpose. He was only to be seen by visiting him in his retirements. His gaiety had flown, and every passion was absorbed in eagerness to procure tidings from Saxony. I have mentioned the arrival of another vessel from the Elbe. He descried her early one morning as he was passing along the skirt of the river. She was easily recognized, being the ship in which he had performed his first voyage to Germany. He immediately went on board, but found no letters directed to him. This omission was, in some degree, compensated by meeting with an old acquaintance among the passengers, who had till lately been a resident in Leipsig. This person put an end to all suspense respecting the fate of Theresa, by relating the particulars of her death and funeral.

Thus was the truth of the former intimation attested. No longer devoured by suspense, the grief of Pleyel was not long in yielding to the influence of society. He gave himself up once more to our company. His vivacity had indeed been damped, but even in this respect he was a more acceptable companion than formerly, since his seriousness was neither incommunicative nor sullen.

These incidents, for a time, occupied all our thoughts. In me they produced a sentiment not unallied to pleasure, and more speedily than in the case of my friends were intermixed with other topics. My brother was particularly affected by them. It was easy to perceive that most of his meditations were tinctured from this source. To this was to be ascribed a design in which his pen was, at this period, engaged, of collecting and investigating the facts which relate to that mysterious personage, the Dæmon of Socrates.[12]

My brother's skill in Greek and Roman learning was exceeded by that of few, and no doubt the world would have accepted a treatise upon this subject from his hand with avidity; but alas! this and every other scheme of felicity and honor, were doomed to sudden blast and hopeless extermination.

Chapter VI.

I now come to the mention of a person with whose name the most turbulent sensations are connected. It is with a shuddering reluctance that I enter on the province of describing him. Now it is that I begin to perceive the difficulty of the task which I have undertaken; but it would be weakness to shrink from it. My blood is congealed: and my fingers are palsied when I call up his image. Shame upon my cowardly and infirm heart! Hitherto I have proceeded with some degree of composure, but now I must pause. I mean not that dire remembrance shall subdue my courage or baffle my design, but this weakness cannot be immediately conquered. I must desist for a little while.

I have taken a few turns in my chamber, and have gathered strength enough to proceed. Yet have I not projected a task beyond my power to execute? If thus, on the very threshold of the scene, my knees faulter and I sink, how shall I support myself, when I rush into the midst of horrors such as no heart has hitherto conceived, nor tongue related? I sicken and recoil at the prospect, and yet my irresolution is momentary. I have not formed this design upon slight grounds, and though I may at times pause and hesitate, I will not be finally diverted from it.

And thou, O most fatal and potent of mankind, in what terms shall I describe thee? What words are adequate to the just delineation of thy character? How shall I detail the means which rendered the secrecy of thy purposes unfathomable? But I will not anticipate. Let me recover if possible, a sober strain. Let me keep down the flood of passion that would render me precipitate or powerless. Let me stifle the agonies that are awakened by thy name. Let me, for a time, regard thee as a being of no terrible attributes. Let me tear myself from contemplation of the evils of which it is but too certain that thou wast the author, and limit my view to those harmless appearances which attended thy entrance on the stage.

One sunny afternoon, I was standing in the door of my house, when I marked a person passing close to the edge of the bank that was in front. His pace was a careless and lingering one, and had none of that gracefulness and ease which distinguish a person with certain advantages of education from a clown.[13] His gait was rustic and aukward. His form was ungainly and disproportioned. Shoulders broad and square, breast sunken, his head drooping, his body of uniform breadth, supported by long and lank legs, were the ingredients of his frame. His garb was not ill adapted to such a figure. A slouched hat, tarnished by the weather, a coat of thick grey cloth, cut and wrought, as it seemed, by a country tailor, blue worsted stockings, and shoes fastened by thongs, and deeply discoloured by dust, which brush had never disturbed, constituted his dress.

There was nothing remarkable in these appearances; they were frequently to be met with on the road, and in the harvest field. I cannot tell why I gazed upon them, on this occasion, with more than ordinary attention, unless it were that such figures were seldom seen by me, except on the road or field. This lawn was only traversed by men whose views were directed to the pleasures of the walk, or the grandeur of the scenery.

He passed slowly along, frequently pausing, as if to examine the prospect more deliberately, but never turning his eye towards the house, so as to allow me a view of his countenance. Presently, he entered a copse at a small distance, and disappeared. My eye followed him while he remained in sight. If his image remained for any duration

in my fancy after his departure, it was because no other object occurred sufficient to expel it.

I continued in the same spot for half an hour, vaguely, and by fits,
contemplating the image of this wanderer, and drawing, from outward
appearances, those inferences with respect to the intellectual history
of this person, which experience affords us. I reflected on the alliance
which commonly subsists between ignorance and the practice of agriculture, and indulged myself in airy speculations as to the influence of
progressive knowledge in dissolving this alliance, and embodying the
dreams of the poets. I asked why the plough and the hoe might not become the trade of every human being, and how this trade might be
made conducive to, or, at least, consistent with the acquisition of wisdom and eloquence.

Weary with these reflections, I returned to the kitchen to perform
some household office. I had usually but one servant, and she was a girl
about my own age. I was busy near the chimney, and she was employed
near the door of the apartment, when some one knocked. The door
was opened by her, and she was immediately addressed with "Pry'thee,
good girl, canst thou supply a thirsty man with a glass of buttermilk?"
She answered that there was none in the house. "Aye, but there is some
in the dairy yonder. Thou knowest as well as I, though Hermes never
taught thee, that though every dairy be an house, every house is not a
dairy." To this speech, though she understood only a part of it, she
replied by repeating her assurances, that she had none to give. "Well
then," rejoined the stranger, "for charity's sweet sake, hand me forth a
cup of cold water." The girl said she would go to the spring and fetch
it. "Nay, give me the cup, and suffer me to help myself. Neither manacled nor lame, I should merit burial in the maw of carrion crows, if I
laid this task upon thee." She gave him the cup, and he turned to go to
the spring.

I listened to this dialogue in silence. The words uttered by the person without, affected me as somewhat singular, but what chiefly rendered them remarkable, was the tone that accompanied them. It was
wholly new. My brother's voice and Pleyel's were musical and energetic. I had fondly imagined, that, in this respect, they were surpassed
by none. Now my mistake was detected. I cannot pretend to communicate the impression that was made upon me by these accents, or to

depict the degree in which force and sweetness were blended in them. They were articulated with a distinctness that was unexampled in my experience. But this was not all. The voice was not only mellifluent and clear, but the emphasis was so just, and the modulation so impassioned, that it seemed as if an heart of stone could not fail of being moved by it. It imparted to me an emotion altogether involuntary and incontroulable. When he uttered the words "for charity's sweet sake," I dropped the cloth that I held in my hand, my heart overflowed with sympathy, and my eyes with unbidden tears.

This description will appear to you trifling or incredible. The importance of these circumstances will be manifested in the sequel. The manner in which I was affected on this occasion, was, to my own apprehension, a subject of astonishment. The tones were indeed such as I never heard before; but that they should, in an instant, as it were, dissolve me in tears, will not easily be believed by others, and can scarcely be comprehended by myself.

It will be readily supposed that I was somewhat inquisitive as to the person and demeanour of our visitant. After a moment's pause, I stepped to the door and looked after him. Judge my surprize, when I beheld the self-same figure that had appeared an half hour before upon the bank. My fancy had conjured up a very different image. A form, and attitude, and garb, were instantly created worthy to accompany such elocution; but this person was, in all visible respects, the reverse of this phantom. Strange as it may seem, I could not speedily reconcile myself to this disappointment. Instead of returning to my employment, I threw myself in a chair that was placed opposite the door, and sunk into a fit of musing.

My attention was, in a few minutes, recalled by the stranger, who returned with the empty cup in his hand. I had not thought of the circumstance, or should certainly have chosen a different seat. He no sooner shewed himself, than a confused sense of impropriety, added to the suddenness of the interview, for which, not having foreseen it, I had made no preparation, threw me into a state of the most painful embarrassment. He brought with him a placid brow; but no sooner had he cast his eyes upon me, than his face was as glowingly suffused as my own. He placed the cup upon the bench, stammered out thanks, and retired.

It was some time before I could recover my wonted composure. I had snatched a view of the stranger's countenance. The impression that it made was vivid and indelible. His cheeks were pallid and lank, his eyes sunken, his forehead overshadowed by coarse straggling hairs, his teeth large and irregular, though sound and brilliantly white, and his chin discoloured by a tetter. His skin was of coarse grain, and sallow hue. Every feature was wide of beauty, and the outline of his face reminded you of an inverted cone.

And yet his forehead, so far as shaggy locks would allow it to be seen, his eyes lustrously black, and possessing, in the midst of haggardness, a radiance inexpressibly serene and potent, and something in the rest of his features, which it would be in vain to describe, but which served to betoken a mind of the highest order, were essential ingredients in the portrait. This, in the effects which immediately flowed from it, I count among the most extraordinary incidents of my life. This face, seen for a moment, continued for hours to occupy my fancy, to the exclusion of almost every other image. I had purposed to spend the evening with my brother, but I could not resist the inclination of forming a sketch upon paper of this memorable visage. Whether my hand was aided by any peculiar inspiration, or I was deceived by my own fond conceptions, this portrait, though hastily executed, appeared unexceptionable to my own taste.

I placed it at all distances, and in all lights; my eyes were rivetted upon it. Half the night passed away in wakefulness and in contemplation of this picture. So flexible, and yet so stubborn, is the human mind. So obedient to impulses the most transient and brief, and yet so unalterably observant of the direction which is given to it! How little did I then foresee the termination of that chain, of which this may be regarded as the first link?

Next day arose in darkness and storm. Torrents of rain fell during the whole day, attended with incessant thunder, which reverberated in stunning echoes from the opposite declivity. The inclemency of the air would not allow me to walk out. I had, indeed, no inclination to leave my apartment. I betook myself to the contemplation of this portrait, whose attractions time had rather enhanced than diminished. I laid aside my usual occupations, and seating myself at a window, consumed the day in alternately looking out upon the storm, and gazing at the picture which lay upon a table before me. You will, perhaps, deem this conduct somewhat singular, and ascribe it to certain peculiarities of temper. I am not aware of any such peculiarities. I can account for my devotion to this image no otherwise, than by supposing that its properties were rare and prodigious. Perhaps you will suspect that such were the first inroads of a passion incident to every female heart, and which frequently gains a footing by means even more slight, and more improbable than these. I shall not controvert the reasonableness of the suspicion, but leave you at liberty to draw, from my narrative, what conclusions you please.

Night at length returned, and the storm ceased. The air was once more clear and calm, and bore an affecting contrast to that uproar of the elements by which it had been preceded. I spent the darksome hours, as I spent the day, contemplative and seated at the window. Why was my mind absorbed in thoughts ominous and dreary? Why did my bosom heave with sighs, and my eyes overflow with tears? Was the tempest that had just past a signal of the ruin which impended over me? My soul fondly dwelt upon the images of my brother and his children, yet they only increased the mournfulness of my contemplations. The smiles of the charming babes were as bland as formerly. The same dignity sat on the brow of their father, and yet I thought of them with anguish. Something whispered that the happiness we at present enjoyed was set on mutable foundations. Death must happen to all. Whether our felicity was to be subverted by it to-morrow, or whether it was ordained that we should lay down our heads full of years and of honor, was a question that no human being could solve. At other times, these ideas seldom intruded. I either forbore to reflect upon the destiny that is reserved for all men, or the reflection was mixed up with images that disrobed it of terror; but now the uncertainty of life occurred to me without any of its usual and alleviating accompaniments. I said to myself, we must die. Sooner or later, we must disappear for ever from the face of the earth. Whatever be the links that hold us to life, they must be broken. This scene of existence is, in all its parts, calamitous. The greater number is oppressed with immediate evils, and those, the tide of whose fortunes is full, how small is their portion of enjoyment, since they know that it will terminate.

For some time I indulged myself, without reluctance, in these gloomy thoughts; but at length, the dejection which they produced became insupportably painful. I endeavoured to dissipate it with music. I had all my grand-father's melody as well as poetry by rote. I now lighted by chance on a ballad, which commemorated the fate of a German Cavalier, who fell at the siege of Nice under Godfrey of Bouillon.[14] My choice was unfortunate, for the scenes of violence and carnage which were here wildly but forcibly pourtrayed, only suggested to my thoughts a new topic in the horrors of war.

I sought refuge, but ineffectually, in sleep. My mind was thronged by vivid, but confused images, and no effort that I made was sufficient to drive them away. In this situation I heard the clock, which hung in the room, give the signal for twelve. It was the same instrument which formerly hung in my father's chamber, and which, on account of its being his workmanship, was regarded, by every one of our family, with veneration. It had fallen to me, in the division of his property, and was placed in this asylum. The sound awakened a series of reflections, respecting his death. I was not allowed to pursue them; for scarcely had the vibrations ceased, when my attention was attracted by a whisper, which, at first, appeared to proceed from lips that were laid close to my ear.

No wonder that a circumstance like this startled me. In the first impulse of my terror, I uttered a slight scream, and shrunk to the opposite side of the bed. In a moment, however, I recovered from my trepidation. I was habitually indifferent to all the causes of fear, by which the majority are afflicted. I entertained no apprehension of either ghosts or robbers. Our security had never been molested by either, and I made use of no means to prevent or counterwork their machinations. My tranquillity, on this occasion, was quickly retrieved. The whisper evidently proceeded from one who was posted at my bed-side. The first idea that suggested itself was, that it was uttered by the girl who lived with me as a servant. Perhaps, somewhat had alarmed her, or she was sick, and had come to request my assistance. By whispering in my ear, she intended to rouse without alarming me.

Full of this persuasion, I called; "Judith," said I, "is it you? What do you want? Is there any thing the matter with you?" No answer was returned. I repeated my inquiry, but equally in vain. Cloudy as was the atmosphere, and curtained as my bed was, nothing was visible. I withdrew the curtain, and leaning my head on my elbow, I listened with the deepest attention to catch some new sound. Meanwhile, I ran over in my thoughts, every circumstance that could assist my conjectures.

My habitation was a wooden edifice, consisting of two stories. In each story were two rooms, separated by an entry, or middle passage, with which they communicated by opposite doors. The passage, on the lower story, had doors at the two ends, and a stair-case. Windows answered to the doors on the upper story. Annexed to this, on the eastern side, were wings, divided, in like manner, into an upper and lower room; one of them comprized a kitchen, and chamber above it for the servant, and communicated, on both stories, with the parlour adjoining it below, and the chamber adjoining it above. The opposite wing is of smaller dimensions, the rooms not being above eight feet square. The lower of these was used as a depository of household implements, the upper was a closet in which I deposited my books and papers. They had but one inlet, which was from the room adjoining. There was no window in the lower one, and in the upper, a small aperture which communicated light and air, but would scarcely admit the body. The door which led into this, was close to my bed-head, and was always locked, but when I myself was within. The avenues below were accustomed to be closed and bolted at nights.

The maid was my only companion, and she could not reach my chamber without previously passing through the opposite chamber, and the middle passage, of which, however, the doors were usually unfastened. If she had occasioned this noise, she would have answered my repeated calls. No other conclusion, therefore, was left me, but that I had mistaken the sounds, and that my imagination had transformed some casual noise into the voice of a human creature. Satisfied with this solution, I was preparing to relinquish my listening attitude, when my ear was again saluted with a new and yet louder whispering. It appeared, as before, to issue from lips that touched my pillow. A second effort of attention, however, clearly shewed me, that the sounds issued from within the closet, the door of which was not more than eight inches from my pillow.

This second interruption occasioned a shock less vehement than the former. I started, but gave no audible token of alarm. I was so much mistress of my feelings, as to continue listening to what should be said. The whisper was distinct, hoarse, and uttered so as to shew that the speaker was desirous of being heard by some one near, but, at the same time, studious to avoid being overheard by any other.

"Stop, stop, I say; madman as you are! there are better means than that. Curse upon your rashness! There is no need to shoot."

Such were the words uttered in a tone of eagerness and anger, within so small a distance of my pillow. What construction could I put upon them? My heart began to palpitate with dread of some unknown danger. Presently, another voice, but equally near me, was heard whispering in answer. "Why not? I will draw a trigger in this business, but perdition be my lot if I do more." To this, the first voice returned, in a tone which rage had heightened in a small degree above a whisper, "Coward! stand aside, and see me do it. I will grasp her throat; I will do her business in an instant; she shall not have time so much as to groan." What wonder that I was petrified by sounds so dreadful! Murderers lurked in my closet. They were planning the means of my destruction. One resolved to shoot, and the other menaced suffocation. Their means being chosen, they would forthwith break the door. Flight instantly suggested itself as most eligible in circumstances so perilous. I deliberated not a moment; but, fear adding wings to my speed, I leaped out of bed, and scantily robed as I was, rushed out of the chamber, down stairs, and into the open air. I can hardly recollect the process of turning keys, and withdrawing bolts. My terrors urged me forward with almost a mechanical impulse. I stopped not till I reached my brother's door. I had not gained the threshold, when, exhausted by the violence of my emotions, and by my speed, I sunk down in a fit.

How long I remained in this situation I know not. When I recovered, I found myself stretched on a bed, surrounded by my sister and her female servants. I was astonished at the scene before me, but gradually recovered the recollection of what had happened. I answered their importunate inquiries as well as I was able. My brother and Pleyel, whom the storm of the preceding day chanced to detain here, informing themselves of every particular, proceeded with lights and weapons to my deserted habitation. They entered my chamber and my closet, and found every thing in its proper place and customary order. The door of the closet was locked, and appeared not to have been opened in my absence. They went to Judith's apartment. They found her asleep and in safety. Pleyel's caution induced him to forbear alarming the girl; and finding her wholly ignorant of what had passed, they directed her to return to her chamber. They then fastened the doors, and returned.

My friends were disposed to regard this transaction as a dream. That persons should be actually immured in this closet, to which, in the circumstances of the time, access from without or within was apparently impossible, they could not seriously believe. That any human beings had intended murder, unless it were to cover a scheme of pillage, was incredible; but that no such design had been formed, was evident from the security in which the furniture of the house and the closet remained.

I revolved every incident and expression that had occurred. My senses assured me of the truth of them, and yet their abruptness and improbability made me, in my turn, somewhat incredulous. The adventure had made a deep impression on my fancy, and it was not till after a week's abode at my brother's, that I resolved to resume the possession of my own dwelling.

There was another circumstance that enhanced the mysteriousness of this event. After my recovery it was obvious to inquire by what means the attention of the family had been drawn to my situation. I had fallen before I had reached the threshold, or was able to give any signal. My brother related, that while this was transacting in my chamber, he himself was awake, in consequence of some slight indisposition, and lay, according to his custom, musing on some favorite topic. Suddenly the silence, which was remarkably profound, was broken by a voice of most piercing shrillness, that seemed to be uttered by one in the hall below his chamber. "Awake! arise!" it exclaimed: "hasten to succour one that is dying at your door."

This summons was effectual. There was no one in the house who was not roused by it. Pleyel was the first to obey, and my brother overtook him before he reached the hall. What was the general astonishment when your friend was discovered stretched upon the grass before the door, pale, ghastly, and with every mark of death!

This was the third instance of a voice, exerted for the benefit of this little community. The agent was no less inscrutable in this, than in the former case. When I ruminated upon these events, my soul was suspended in wonder and awe. Was I really deceived in imagining that I heard the closet conversation? I was no longer at liberty to question the reality of those accents which had formerly recalled my brother from the hill; which had imparted tidings of the death of the German lady to Pleyel; and which had lately summoned them to my assistance.

But how was I to regard this midnight conversation? Hoarse and manlike voices conferring on the means of death, so near my bed, and at such an hour! How had my ancient security vanished! That dwelling, which had hitherto been an inviolate asylum, was now beset with danger to my life. That solitude, formerly so dear to me, could no longer be endured. Pleyel, who had consented to reside with us during the months of spring, lodged in the vacant chamber, in order to quiet my alarms. He treated my fears with ridicule, and in a short time very slight traces of them remained: but as it was wholly indifferent to him whether his nights were passed at my house or at my brother's, this arrangement gave general satisfaction.

Chapter VII.

I will not enumerate the various inquiries and conjectures which these incidents occasioned. After all our efforts, we came no nearer to dispelling the mist in which they were involved; and time, instead of facilitating a solution, only accumulated our doubts.

In the midst of thoughts excited by these events, I was not unmindful of my interview with the stranger. I related the particulars, and shewed the portrait to my friends. Pleyel recollected to have met with a figure resembling my description in the city; but neither his face or garb made the same impression upon him that it made upon me. It was a hint to rally me upon my prepossessions, and to amuse us with a thousand ludicrous anecdotes which he had collected in his travels. He made no scruple to charge me with being in love; and threatened to inform the swain, when he met him, of his good fortune.

Pleyel's temper made him susceptible of no durable impressions. His conversation was occasionally visited by gleams of his ancient vivacity; but, though his impetuosity was sometimes inconvenient, there was nothing to dread from his malice. I had no fear that my character or dignity would suffer in his hands, and was not heartily displeased when he declared his intention of profiting by his first meeting with the stranger to introduce him to our acquaintance.

Some weeks after this I had spent a toilsome day, and, as the sun declined, found myself disposed to seek relief in a walk. The river bank is, at this part of it, and for some considerable space upward, so rugged and steep as not to be easily descended. In a recess of this declivity, near the southern verge of my little demesne, was placed a slight building, with seats and lattices. From a crevice of the rock, to which this edifice was attached, there burst forth a stream of the purest water, which, leaping from ledge to ledge, for the space of sixty feet, produced a freshness in the air, and a murmur, the most delicious and soothing imaginable. These, added to the odours of the cedars which embowered it, and of the honey-suckle which clustered among the lattices, rendered this my favorite retreat in summer.

On this occasion I repaired hither. My spirits drooped through the fatigue of long attention, and I threw myself upon a bench, in a state, both mentally and personally, of the utmost supineness. The lulling sounds of the waterfall, the fragrance and the dusk combined to becalm my spirits, and, in a short time, to sink me into sleep. Either the uneasiness of my posture, or some slight indisposition molested my repose with dreams of no cheerful hue. After various incoherences had taken their turn to occupy my fancy, I at length imagined myself walking, in the evening twilight, to my brother's habitation. A pit, methought, had been dug in the path I had taken, of which I was not aware. As I carelessly pursued my walk, I thought I saw my brother, standing at some distance before me, beckoning and calling me to make haste. He stood on the opposite edge of the gulph. I mended my pace, and one step more would have plunged me into this abyss, had not some one from behind caught suddenly my arm, and exclaimed, in a voice of eagerness and terror, "Hold! hold!"

The sound broke my sleep, and I found myself, at the next moment, standing on my feet, and surrounded by the deepest darkness. Images so terrific and forcible disabled me, for a time, from distinguishing between sleep and wakefulness, and withheld from me the knowledge of my actual condition. My first panics were succeeded by the perturbations of surprise, to find myself alone in the open air, and immersed in so deep a gloom. I slowly recollected the incidents of the afternoon, and how I came hither. I could not estimate the time, but saw the propriety of returning with speed to the house. My faculties were still too confused, and the darkness too intense, to allow me immediately to find my way up the steep. I sat down, therefore, to recover myself, and to reflect upon my situation.

This was no sooner done, than a low voice was heard from behind the lattice, on the side where I sat. Between the rock and the lattice was a chasm not wide enough to admit a human body; yet, in this chasm he that spoke appeared to be stationed. "Attend! attend! but be not terrified."

I started and exclaimed, "Good heavens! what is that? Who are you?"

"A friend; one come, not to injure, but to save you; fear nothing."

This voice was immediately recognized to be the same with one of those which I had heard in the closet; it was the voice of him who had proposed to shoot, rather than to strangle, his victim. My terror made me, at once, mute and motionless. He continued, "I leagued to murder you. I repent. Mark my bidding; and be safe. Avoid this spot. The snares of death encompass it. Elsewhere danger will be distant, but this spot, shun it as you value your life. Mark me further; profit by this warning, but divulge it not. If a syllable of what has passed escape you, your doom is sealed. Remember your father, and be faithful."

Here the accents ceased, and left me overwhelmed with dismay. I was fraught with the persuasion, that during every moment I remained here, my life was endangered; but I could not take a step without hazard of falling to the bottom of the precipice. The path, leading to the summit, was short, but rugged and intricate. Even star-light was excluded by the umbrage, and not the faintest gleam was afforded to guide my steps. What should I do? To depart or remain was equally and eminently perilous.

In this state of uncertainty, I perceived a ray flit across the gloom and disappear. Another succeeded, which was stronger, and remained for a passing moment. It glittered on the shrubs that were scattered at the entrance, and gleam continued to succeed gleam for a few seconds, till they, finally, gave place to unintermitted darkness.

The first visitings of this light called up a train of horrors in my mind; destruction impended over this spot; the voice which I had lately heard had warned me to retire, and had menaced me with the fate of my father if I refused. I was desirous, but unable, to obey; these gleams were such as preluded the stroke by which he fell; the hour, perhaps, was the same—I shuddered as if I had beheld, suspended over me, the exterminating sword.

Presently a new and stronger illumination burst through the lattice on the right hand, and a voice, from the edge of the precipice above, called out my name. It was Pleyel. Joyfully did I recognize his accents; but such was the tumult of my thoughts that I had not power to answer him till he had frequently repeated his summons. I hurried, at length, from the fatal spot, and, directed by the lanthorn which he bore, ascended the hill.

Pale and breathless, it was with difficulty I could support myself. He anxiously inquired into the cause of my affright, and the motive of my unusual absence. He had returned from my brother's at a late hour, and was informed by Judith, that I had walked out before sun-set, and had not yet returned. This intelligence was somewhat alarming. He waited some time; but, my absence continuing, he had set out in search of me. He had explored the neighbourhood with the utmost care, but, receiving no tidings of me, he was preparing to acquaint my brother with this circumstance, when he recollected the summer-house on the bank, and conceived it possible that some accident had detained me there. He again inquired into the cause of this detention, and of that confusion and dismay which my looks testified.

I told him that I had strolled hither in the afternoon, that sleep had overtaken me as I sat, and that I had awakened a few minutes before his arrival. I could tell him no more. In the present impetuosity of my thoughts, I was almost dubious, whether the pit, into which my brother had endeavoured to entice me, and the voice that talked through the lattice, were not parts of the same dream. I remembered, likewise, the charge of secrecy, and the penalty denounced, if I should rashly divulge what I had heard. For these reasons, I was silent on that subject, and shutting myself in my chamber, delivered myself up to contemplation.

What I have related will, no doubt, appear to you a fable. You will believe that calamity has subverted my reason, and that I am amusing you with the chimeras of my brain, instead of facts that have really happened. I shall not be surprized or offended, if these be your suspicions. I know not, indeed, how you can deny them admission. For, if to me, the immediate witness, they were fertile of perplexity and doubt, how must they affect another to whom they are recommended only by my testimony? It was only by subsequent events, that I was fully and incontestibly assured of the veracity of my senses.

Meanwhile what was I to think? I had been assured that a design had been formed against my life. The ruffians had leagued to murder me. Whom had I offended? Who was there with whom I had ever maintained intercourse, who was capable of harbouring such atrocious purposes?

My temper was the reverse of cruel and imperious. My heart was touched with sympathy for the children of misfortune. But this sympathy was not a barren sentiment. My purse, scanty as it was, was ever open, and my hands ever active, to relieve distress. Many were the wretches whom my personal exertions had extricated from want and disease, and who rewarded me with their gratitude. There was no face which lowered at my approach, and no lips which uttered imprecations in my hearing. On the contrary, there was none, over whose fate I had exerted any influence, or to whom I was known by reputation, who did not greet me with smiles, and dismiss me with proofs of veneration; yet did not my senses assure me that a plot was laid against my life?

I am not destitute of courage, I have shewn myself deliberative and calm in the midst of peril. I have hazarded my own life, for the preservation of another, but now was I confused and panic-struck. I have not lived so as to fear death, yet to perish by an unseen and secret stroke, to be mangled by the knife of an assassin, was a thought at which I shuddered; what had I done to deserve to be made the victim of malignant passions?

But soft! was I not assured, that my life was safe in all places but one? And why was the treason limited to take effect in this spot? I was every where equally defenceless. My house and chamber were, at all times, accessible. Danger still impended over me; the bloody purpose was still entertained, but the hand that was to execute it, was powerless in all places but one!

Here I had remained for the last four or five hours, without the means of resistance or defence, yet I had not been attacked. A human being was at hand, who was conscious of my presence, and warned me hereafter to avoid this retreat. His voice was not absolutely new, but had I never heard it but once before? But why did he prohibit me from relating this incident to others, and what species of death will be awarded if I disobey?

He talked of my father. He intimated, that disclosure would pull upon my head, the same destruction. Was then the death of my father, portentous and inexplicable as it was, the consequence of human machinations? It should seem, that this being is apprised of the true nature of this event, and is conscious of the means that led to it. Whether it shall likewise fall upon me, depends upon the observance of silence. Was it the infraction of a similar command, that brought so horrible a penalty upon my father?

Such were the reflections that haunted me during the night, and which effectually deprived me of sleep. Next morning, at breakfast, Pleyel related an event which my disappearance had hindered him from mentioning the night before. Early the preceding morning, his occasions called him to the city; he had stepped into a coffee-house to while away an hour; here he had met a person whose appearance instantly bespoke him to be the same whose hasty visit I have mentioned, and whose extraordinary visage and tones had so powerfully affected me. On an attentive survey, however, he proved, likewise, to be one with whom my friend had had some intercourse in Europe. This authorised the liberty of accosting him, and after some conversation, mindful, as Pleyel said, of the footing which this stranger had gained in my heart, he had ventured to invite him to Mettingen. The invitation had been cheerfully accepted, and a visit promised on the afternoon of the next day.

This information excited no sober emotions in my breast. I was, of course, eager to be informed as to the circumstances of their ancient intercourse. When, and where had they met? What knew he of the life and character of this man?

In answer to my inquiries, he informed me that, three years before, he was a traveller in Spain. He had made an excursion from Valencia to Murviedro,[15] with a view to inspect the remains of Roman magnifi-

cence, scattered in the environs of that town. While
scite of the theatre of old Saguntum, he lighted upon
on a stone, and deeply engaged in perusing the work of the
Marti.[16] A short conversation ensued, which proved the stranger to be
English. They returned to Valencia together.

His garb, aspect, and deportment, were wholly Spanish. A residence
of three years in the country, indefatigable attention to the language,
and a studious conformity with the customs of the people, had made
him indistinguishable from a native, when he chose to assume that
character. Pleyel found him to be connected, on the footing of friendship and respect, with many eminent merchants in that city. He had
embraced the catholic religion, and adopted a Spanish name instead of
his own, which was CARWIN, and devoted himself to the literature and
religion of his new country. He pursued no profession, but subsisted
on remittances from England.

While Pleyel remained in Valencia, Carwin betrayed no aversion to
intercourse, and the former found no small attractions in the society of
this new acquaintance. On general topics he was highly intelligent and
communicative. He had visited every corner of Spain, and could furnish the most accurate details respecting its ancient and present state.
On topics of religion and of his own history, previous to his *transformation* into a Spaniard, he was invariably silent. You could merely
gather from his discourse that he was English, and that he was well acquainted with the neighbouring countries.

His character excited considerable curiosity in this observer. It was
not easy to reconcile his conversion to the Romish faith, with those
proofs of knowledge and capacity that were exhibited by him on
different occasions. A suspicion was, sometimes, admitted, that his
belief was counterfeited for some political purpose. The most careful
observation, however, produced no discovery. His manners were, at
all times, harmless and inartificial, and his habits those of a lover of
contemplation and seclusion. He appeared to have contracted an affection for Pleyel, who was not slow to return it.

My friend, after a month's residence in this city, returned into
France, and, since that period, had heard nothing concerning Carwin
till his appearance at Mettingen.

On this occasion Carwin had received Pleyel's greeting with a certain distance and solemnity to which the latter had not been accustomed. He had waved noticing the inquiries of Pleyel respecting his desertion of Spain, in which he had formerly declared that it was his purpose to spend his life. He had assiduously diverted the attention of the latter to indifferent topics, but was still, on every theme, as eloquent and judicious as formerly. Why he had assumed the garb of a rustic, Pleyel was unable to conjecture. Perhaps it might be poverty, perhaps he was swayed by motives which it was his interest to conceal, but which were connected with consequences of the utmost moment.

Such was the sum of my friend's information. I was not sorry to be left alone during the greater part of this day. Every employment was irksome which did not leave me at liberty to meditate. I had now a new subject on which to exercise my thoughts. Before evening I should be ushered into his presence, and listen to those tones whose magical and thrilling power I had already experienced. But with what new images would he then be accompanied?

Carwin was an adherent to the Romish faith, yet was an Englishman by birth, and, perhaps, a protestant by education. He had adopted Spain for his country, and had intimated a design to spend his days there, yet now was an inhabitant of this district, and disguised by the habiliments of a clown! What could have obliterated the impressions of his youth, and made him abjure his religion and his country? What subsequent events had introduced so total a change in his plans? In withdrawing from Spain, had he reverted to the religion of his ancestors; or was it true, that his former conversion was deceitful, and that his conduct had been swayed by motives which it was prudent to conceal?

Hours were consumed in revolving these ideas. My meditations were intense; and, when the series was broken, I began to reflect with astonishment on my situation. From the death of my parents, till the commencement of this year, my life had been serene and blissful, beyond the ordinary portion of humanity; but, now, my bosom was corroded by anxiety. I was visited by dread of unknown dangers, and the future was a scene over which clouds rolled, and thunders muttered. I compared the cause with the effect, and they seemed disproportioned to each other. All unaware, and in a manner which I had no power to explain, I was pushed from my immoveable and lofty station, and cast upon a sea of troubles.

I determined to be my brother's visitant on this evening, yet my resolves were not unattended with wavering and reluctance. Pleyel's insinuations that I was in love, affected, in no degree, my belief, yet the consciousness that this was the opinion of one who would, probably, be present at our introduction to each other, would excite all that confusion which the passion itself is apt to produce. This would confirm him in his error, and call forth new railleries. His mirth, when exerted upon this topic, was the source of the bitterest vexation. Had he been aware of its influence upon my happiness, his temper would not have allowed him to persist; but this influence, it was my chief endeavour to conceal. That the belief of my having bestowed my heart upon another, produced in my friend none but ludicrous sensations, was the true cause of my distress; but if this had been discovered by him, my distress would have been unspeakably aggravated.

Chapter VIII.

As soon as evening arrived, I performed my visit. Carwin made one of the company, into which I was ushered. Appearances were the same as when I before beheld him. His garb was equally negligent and rustic. I gazed upon his countenance with new curiosity. My situation was such as to enable me to bestow upon it a deliberate examination. Viewed at more leisure, it lost none of its wonderful properties. I could not deny my homage to the intelligence expressed in it, but was wholly uncertain, whether he were an object to be dreaded or adored, and whether his powers had been exerted to evil or to good.

He was sparing in discourse; but whatever he said was pregnant with meaning, and uttered with rectitude of articulation, and force of emphasis, of which I had entertained no conception previously to my knowledge of him. Notwithstanding the uncouthness of his garb, his manners were not unpolished. All topics were handled by him with skill, and without pedantry or affectation. He uttered no sentiment calculated to produce a disadvantageous impression: on the contrary, his observations denoted a mind alive to every generous and heroic feeling. They were introduced without parade, and accompanied with that degree of earnestness which indicates sincerity.

He parted from us not till late, refusing an invitation to spend the night here, but readily consented to repeat his visit. His visits were frequently repeated. Each day introduced us to a more intimate acquaintance with his sentiments, but left us wholly in the dark, concerning that about which we were most inquisitive. He studiously avoided all mention of his past or present situation. Even the place of his abode in the city he concealed from us.

Our sphere, in this respect, being somewhat limited, and the intellectual endowments of this man being indisputably great, his deportment was more diligently marked, and copiously commented on by us, than you, perhaps, will think the circumstances warranted. Not a gesture, or glance, or accent, that was not, in our private assemblies, discussed, and inferences deduced from it. It may well be thought that he modelled his behaviour by an uncommon standard, when, with all our opportunities and accuracy of observation, we were able, for a long time, to gather no satisfactory information. He afforded us no ground on which to build even a plausible conjecture.

There is a degree of familiarity which takes place between constant associates, that justifies the negligence of many rules of which, in an earlier period of their intercourse, politeness requires the exact observance. Inquiries into our condition are allowable when they are prompted by a disinterested concern for our welfare; and this solicitude is not only pardonable, but may justly be demanded from those who chuse us for their companions. This state of things was more slow to arrive on this occasion than on most others, on account of the gravity and loftiness of this man's behaviour.

Pleyel, however, began, at length, to employ regular means for this end. He occasionally alluded to the circumstances in which they had formerly met, and remarked the incongruousness between the religion and habits of a Spaniard, with those of a native of Britain. He expressed his astonishment at meeting our guest in this corner of the globe, especially as, when they parted in Spain, he was taught to believe that Carwin should never leave that country. He insinuated, that a change so great must have been prompted by motives of a singular and momentous kind.

No answer, or an answer wide of the purpose, was generally made to these insinuations. Britons and Spaniards, he said, are votaries of the same Deity, and square their faith by the same precepts; their ideas are drawn from the same fountains of literature, and they speak dialects of the same tongue; their government and laws have more resemblances than differences; they were formerly provinces of the same civil, and till lately, of the same religious, Empire.

As to the motives which induce men to change the place of their abode, these must unavoidably be fleeting and mutable. If not bound to one spot by conjugal or parental ties, or by the nature of that employment to which we are indebted for subsistence, the inducements to change are far more numerous and powerful, than opposite inducements.

He spoke as if desirous of showing that he was not aware of the tendency of Pleyel's remarks; yet, certain tokens were apparent, that proved him by no means wanting in penetration. These tokens were to be read in his countenance, and not in his words. When anything was said, indicating curiosity in us, the gloom of his countenance was deepened, his eyes sunk to the ground, and his wonted air was not resumed without visible struggle. Hence, it was obvious to infer, that some incidents of his life were reflected on by him with regret; and that, since these incidents were carefully concealed, and even that regret which flowed from them laboriously stifled, they had not been merely disastrous. The secrecy that was observed appeared not designed to provoke or baffle the inquisitive, but was prompted by the shame, or by the prudence of guilt.

These ideas, which were adopted by Pleyel and my brother, as well as myself, hindered us from employing more direct means for accomplishing our wishes. Questions might have been put in such terms, that no room should be left for the pretence of misapprehension, and if modesty merely had been the obstacle, such questions would not have been wanting; but we considered, that, if the disclosure were productive of pain or disgrace, it was inhuman to extort it.

Amidst the various topics that were discussed in his presence, allusions were, of course, made to the inexplicable events that had lately happened. At those times, the words and looks of this man were objects of my particular attention. The subject was extraordinary; and any one whose experience or reflections could throw any light upon it, was entitled to my gratitude. As this man was enlightened by reading and travel, I listened with eagerness to the remarks which he should make.

At first, I entertained a kind of apprehension, that the tale would be heard by him with incredulity and secret ridicule. I had formerly heard stories that resembled this in some of their mysterious circumstances, but they were, commonly, heard by me with contempt. I was doubtful, whether the same impression would not now be made on the mind of our guest, but I was mistaken in my fears.

He heard them with seriousness, and without any marks either of surprize or incredulity. He pursued, with visible pleasure, that kind of disquisition which was naturally suggested by them. His fancy was eminently vigorous and prolific, and if he did not persuade us, that human beings are, sometimes, admitted to a feasible intercourse with the author of nature, he, at least, won over our inclination to the cause. He merely deduced, from his own reasonings, that such intercourse was probable; but confessed that, though he was acquainted with many instances somewhat similar to those which had been related by us, none of them were perfectly exempted from the suspicion of human agency.

On being requested to relate these instances, he amused us with many curious details. His narratives were constructed with so much skill, and rehearsed with so much energy, that all the effects of a dramatic exhibition were frequently produced by them. Those that were most coherent and most minute, and, of consequence, least entitled to credit, were yet rendered probable by the exquisite art of this rhetorician. For every difficulty that was suggested, a ready and plausible solution was furnished. Mysterious voices had always a share in producing the catastrophe, but they were always to be explained on some known principles, either as reflected into a focus, or communicated through a tube. I could not but remark that his narratives, however complex or marvellous, contained no instance sufficiently parallel to those that had befallen ourselves, and in which the solution was applicable to our own case.

My brother was a much more sanguine reasoner than our guest. Even in some of the facts which were related by Carwin, he maintained the probability of celestial interference, when the latter was disposed to deny it, and had found, as he imagined, footsteps of a human agent. Pleyel was by no means equally credulous. He scrupled not to deny faith to any testimony but that of his senses, and allowed the facts which had lately been supported by this testimony, not to mould his belief, but merely to give birth to doubts.

It was soon observed that Carwin adopted, in some degree, a similar distinction. A tale of this kind, related by others, he would believe, provided it was explicable upon known principles; but that such notices were actually communicated by beings of a higher order, he would believe only when his own ears were assailed in a manner which could not be otherwise accounted for. Civility forbade him to contradict my brother or myself, but his understanding refused to acquiesce in our testimony. Besides, he was disposed to question whether the voices heard in the temple, at the foot of the hill, and in my closet, were not really uttered by human organs. On this supposition he was desired to explain how the effect was produced.

He answered, that the power of mimicry was very common. Catharine's voice might easily be imitated by one at the foot of the hill, who would find no difficulty in eluding, by flight, the search of Wieland. The tidings of the death of the Saxon lady were uttered by one near at hand, who overheard the conversation, who conjectured her death, and whose conjecture happened to accord with the truth. That the voice appeared to come from the ceiling was to be considered as an illusion of the fancy. The cry for help, heard in the hall on the night of my adventure, was to be ascribed to a human creature, who actually stood in the hall when he uttered it. It was of no moment, he said, that we could not explain by what motives he that made the signal was led hither. How imperfectly acquainted were we with the condition and designs of the beings that surrounded us? The city was near at hand, and thousands might there exist whose powers and purposes might easily explain whatever was mysterious in this transaction. As to the closet dialogue, he was obliged to adopt one of two suppositions, and affirm either that it was fashioned in my own fancy, or that it actually took place between two persons in the closet.

Such was Carwin's mode of explaining these appearances. It is such, perhaps, as would commend itself as most plausible to the most sagacious minds, but it was insufficient to impart conviction to us. As to the treason that was meditated against me, it was doubtless just to conclude that it was either real or imaginary; but that it was real was attested by the mysterious warning in the summer-house, the secret of which I had hitherto locked up in my own breast.

A month passed away in this kind of intercourse. As to Carwin, our ignorance was in no degree enlightened respecting his genuine character and views. Appearances were uniform. No man possessed a larger store of knowledge, or a greater degree of skill in the communication of it to others: Hence he was regarded as an inestimable addition to our society. Considering the distance of my brother's house from the city, he was frequently prevailed upon to pass the night where he spent the evening. Two days seldom elapsed without a visit from him; hence he was regarded as a kind of intimate of the house. He entered and departed without ceremony. When he arrived he received an unaffected welcome, and when he chose to retire, no importunities were used to induce him to remain.

The temple was the principal scene of our social enjoyments; yet the felicity that we tasted when assembled in this asylum, was but the gleam of a former sun-shine. Carwin never parted with his gravity. The inscrutableness of his character, and the uncertainty whether his fellowship tended to good or to evil, were seldom absent from our minds. This circumstance powerfully contributed to sadden us.

My heart was the seat of growing disquietudes. This change in one who had formerly been characterized by all the exuberances of soul, could not fail to be remarked by my friends. My brother was always a pattern of solemnity. My sister was clay, moulded by the circumstances in which she happened to be placed. There was but one whose deportment remains to be described as being of importance to our happiness. Had Pleyel likewise dismissed his vivacity?

He was as whimsical and jestful as ever, but he was not happy. The truth, in this respect, was of too much importance to me not to make me a vigilant observer. His mirth was easily perceived to be the fruit of exertion. When his thoughts wandered from the company, an air of dissatisfaction and impatience stole across his features. Even the punctuality and frequency of his visits were somewhat lessened. It may be supposed that my own uneasiness was heightened by these tokens; but, strange as it may seem, I found, in the present state of my mind, no relief but in the persuasion that Pleyel was unhappy.

That unhappiness, indeed, depended, for its value in my eyes, on the cause that produced it. It did not arise from the death of the Saxon lady: it was not a contagious emanation from the countenances of Wieland or Carwin. There was but one other source whence it could flow. A nameless ecstacy thrilled through my frame when any new proof occurred that the ambiguousness of my behaviour was the cause.

CHAPTER IX.

My brother had received a new book from Germany. It was a tragedy, and the first attempt of a Saxon poet, of whom my brother had been taught to entertain the highest expectations. The exploits of Zisca, the Bohemian hero,[17] were woven into a dramatic series and connection. According to German custom, it was minute and diffuse, and dictated by an adventurous and lawless fancy. It was a chain of audacious acts, and unheard-of disasters. The moated fortress, and the thicket; the ambush and the battle; and the conflict of headlong passions, were pourtrayed in wild numbers, and with terrific energy. An afternoon was set apart to rehearse this performance. The language was familiar to all of us but Carwin, whose company, therefore, was tacitly dispensed with.

The morning previous to this intended rehearsal, I spent at home. My mind was occupied with reflections relative to my own situation. The sentiment which lived with chief energy in my heart, was connected with the image of Pleyel. In the midst of my anguish, I had not been destitute of consolation. His late deportment had given spring to my hopes. Was not the hour at hand, which should render me the happiest of human creatures? He suspected that I looked with favorable eyes upon Carwin. Hence arose disquietudes, which he struggled in vain to conceal. He loved me, but was hopeless that his love would be compensated. Is it not time, said I, to rectify this error? But by what means is this to be effected? It can only be done by a change of deportment in me; but how must I demean myself[18] for this purpose?

I must not speak. Neither eyes, nor lips, must impart the information. He must not be assured that my heart is his, previous to the tender of his own; but he must be convinced that it has not been given to another; he must be supplied with space whereon to build a doubt as to the true state of my affections; he must be prompted to avow himself. The line of delicate propriety; how hard it is, not to fall short, and not to overleap it!

This afternoon we shall meet at the temple. We shall not separate till late. It will be his province to accompany me home. The airy expanse is without a speck. This breeze is usually stedfast, and its promise of a bland and cloudless evening, may be trusted. The moon will rise at eleven, and at that hour, we shall wind along this bank. Possibly that hour may decide my fate. If suitable encouragement be given, Pleyel will reveal his soul to me; and I, ere I reach this threshold, will be made the happiest of beings. And is this good to be mine? Add wings to thy speed, sweet evening; and thou, moon, I charge thee, shroud thy beams at the moment when my Pleyel whispers love. I would not for the world, that the burning blushes, and the mounting raptures of that moment, should be visible.

But what encouragement is wanting? I must be regardful of insurmountable limits. Yet when minds are imbued with a genuine sympathy, are not words and looks superfluous? Are not motion and touch sufficient to impart feelings such as mine? Has he not eyed me at moments, when the pressure of his hand has thrown me into tumults, and was it possible that he mistook the impetuosities of love, for the eloquence of indignation?

But the hastening evening will decide. Would it were come! And yet I shudder at its near approach. An interview that must thus terminate, is surely to be wished for by me; and yet it is not without its terrors. Would to heaven it were come and gone!

I feel no reluctance, my friends to be thus explicit. Time was, when these emotions would be hidden with immeasurable solicitude, from every human eye. Alas! these airy and fleeting impulses of shame are gone. My scruples were preposterous and criminal. They are bred in all hearts, by a perverse and vicious education, and they would still have maintained their place in my heart, had not my portion been set in misery. My errors have taught me thus much wisdom; that those sentiments which we ought not to disclose, it is criminal to harbour.

It was proposed to begin the rehearsal at four o'clock; I counted the minutes as they passed; their flight was at once too rapid and too slow; my sensations were of an excruciating kind; I could taste no food, nor apply to any task, nor enjoy a moment's repose: when the hour arrived, I hastened to my brother's.

Pleyel was not there. He had not yet come. On ordinary occasions, he was eminent for punctuality. He had testified great eagerness to share in the pleasures of this rehearsal. He was to divide the task with my brother, and, in tasks like these, he always engaged with peculiar zeal. His elocution was less sweet than sonorous; and, therefore, better adapted than the mellifluences of his friend, to the outrageous vehemence of this drama.

What could detain him? Perhaps he lingered through forgetfulness. Yet this was incredible. Never had his memory been known to fail upon even more trivial occasions. Not less impossible was it, that the scheme had lost its attractions, and that he staid, because his coming would afford him no gratification. But why should we expect him to adhere to the minute?

An half hour elapsed, but Pleyel was still at a distance. Perhaps he had misunderstood the hour which had been proposed. Perhaps he had conceived that to-morrow, and not to-day, had been selected for this purpose: but no. A review of preceding circumstances demonstrated that such misapprehension was impossible; for he had himself proposed this day, and this hour. This day, his attention would not otherwise be occupied; but to-morrow, an indispensible engagement was foreseen, by which all his time would be engrossed: his detention, therefore, must be owing to some unforeseen and extraordinary event. Our conjectures were vague, tumultuous, and sometimes fearful. His sickness and his death might possibly have detained him.

Tortured with suspense, we sat gazing at each other, and at the path which led from the road. Every horseman that passed was, for a moment, imagined to be him. Hour succeeded hour, and the sun, gradually declining, at length, disappeared. Every signal of his coming proved fallacious, and our hopes were at length dismissed. His absence affected my friends in no insupportable degree. They should be obliged, they said, to defer this undertaking till the morrow; and, perhaps, their impatient curiosity would compel them to dispense entirely with his presence. No doubt, some harmless occurrence had diverted him from his purpose; and they trusted that they should receive a satisfactory account of him in the morning.

It may be supposed that this disappointment affected me in a very different manner. I turned aside my head to conceal my tears. I fled into solitude, to give vent to my reproaches, without interruption or restraint. My heart was ready to burst with indignation and grief. Pleyel was not the only object of my keen but unjust upbraiding. Deeply did I execrate my own folly. Thus fallen into ruins was the gay fabric which I had reared! Thus had my golden vision melted into air!

How fondly did I dream that Pleyel was a lover! If he were, would he have suffered any obstacle to hinder his coming? Blind and infatuated man! I exclaimed. Thou sportest with happiness. The good that is offered thee, thou hast the insolence and folly to refuse. Well, I will henceforth intrust my felicity to no one's keeping but my own.

The first agonies of this disappointment would not allow me to be reasonable or just. Every ground on which I had built the persuasion that Pleyel was not unimpressed in my favor, appeared to vanish. It seemed as if I had been misled into this opinion, by the most palpable illusions.

I made some trifling excuse, and returned, much earlier than I expected, to my own house. I retired early to my chamber, without designing to sleep. I placed myself at a window, and gave the reins to reflection.

The hateful and degrading impulses which had lately controuled me were, in some degree, removed. New dejection succeeded, but was now produced by contemplating my late behaviour. Surely that passion is worthy to be abhorred which obscures our understanding, and urges us to the commission of injustice. What right had I to expect his attendance? Had I not demeaned myself like one indifferent to his happiness, and as having bestowed my regards upon another? His absence might be prompted by the love which I considered his absence as a proof that he wanted. He came not because the sight of me, the spectacle of my coldness or aversion, contributed to his despair. Why should I prolong, by hypocrisy or silence, his misery as well as my own? Why not deal with him explicitly, and assure him of the truth?

You will hardly believe that, in obedience to this suggestion, I rose for the purpose of ordering a light, that I might instantly make this confession in a letter. A second thought shewed me the rashness of this scheme, and I wondered by what infirmity of mind I could be betrayed into a momentary approbation of it. I saw with the utmost clearness that a confession like that would be the most remediless and unpardonable outrage upon the dignity of my sex, and utterly unworthy of that passion which controuled me.

I resumed my seat and my musing. To account for the absence of Pleyel became once more the scope of my conjectures. How many incidents might occur to raise an insuperable impediment in his way? When I was a child, a scheme of pleasure, in which he and his sister were parties, had been, in like manner, frustrated by his absence; but his absence, in that instance, had been occasioned by his falling from a boat into the river, in consequence of which he had run the most imminent hazard of being drowned. Here was a second disappointment endured by the same persons, and produced by his failure. Might it not originate in the same cause? Had he not designed to cross the river that morning to make some necessary purchases in Jersey? He had preconcerted to return to his own house to dinner; but, perhaps, some disaster had befallen him. Experience had taught me the insecurity of a canoe, and that was the only kind of boat which Pleyel used: I was, likewise, actuated by an hereditary dread of water. These circumstances combined to bestow considerable plausibility on this conjecture; but the consternation with which I began to be seized was allayed by reflecting, that if this disaster had happened my brother would have received the speediest information of it. The consolation which this idea imparted was ravished from me by a new thought. This disaster might have happened, and his family not be apprized of it. The first intelligence of his fate may be communicated by the livid corpse which the tide may cast, many days hence, upon the shore.

Thus was I distressed by opposite conjectures: thus was I tormented by phantoms of my own creation. It was not always thus. I cannot ascertain the date when my mind became the victim of this imbecility; perhaps it was coeval with the inroad of a fatal passion; a passion that will never rank me in the number of its eulogists; it was alone sufficient to the extermination of my peace: it was itself a plenteous source of calamity, and needed not the concurrence of other evils to take away the attractions of existence, and dig for me an untimely grave.

The state of my mind naturally introduced a train of reflections upon the dangers and cares which inevitably beset an human being. By no violent transition was I led to ponder on the turbulent life and mysterious end of my father. I cherished, with the utmost veneration, the memory of this man, and every relique connected with his fate was preserved with the most scrupulous care. Among these was to be numbered a manuscript, containing memoirs of his own life. The narrative was by no means recommended by its eloquence; but neither did all its value flow from my relationship to the author. Its stile had an unaffected and picturesque simplicity. The great variety and circumstantial display of the incidents, together with their intrinsic importance, as descriptive of human manners and passions, made it the most useful book in my collection. It was late; but being sensible of no inclination to sleep, I resolved to betake myself to the perusal of it.

To do this it was requisite to procure a light. The girl had long since retired to her chamber: it was therefore proper to wait upon myself. A lamp, and the means of lighting it, were only to be found in the kitchen. Thither I resolved forthwith to repair; but the light was of use merely to enable me to read the book. I knew the shelf and the spot where it stood. Whether I took down the book, or prepared the lamp in the first place, appeared to be a matter of no moment. The latter was preferred, and, leaving my seat, I approached the closet in which, as I mentioned formerly, my books and papers were deposited.

Suddenly the remembrance of what had lately passed in this closet occurred. Whether midnight was approaching, or had passed, I knew not. I was, as then, alone, and defenceless. The wind was in that direction in which, aided by the deathlike repose of nature, it brought to me the murmur of the water-fall. This was mingled with that solemn and enchanting sound, which a breeze produces among the leaves of pines. The words of that mysterious dialogue, their fearful import, and the wild excess to which I was transported by my terrors, filled my imagination anew. My steps faultered, and I stood a moment to recover myself.

I prevailed on myself at length to move towards the closet. I touched the lock, but my fingers were powerless; I was visited afresh by unconquerable apprehensions. A sort of belief darted into my mind, that some being was concealed within, whose purposes were evil. I began to contend with these fears, when it occurred to me that I might, without impropriety, go for a lamp previously to opening the closet. I receded a few steps; but before I reached my chamber door my thoughts took a new direction. Motion seemed to produce a mechanical influence upon me. I was ashamed of my weakness. Besides, what aid could be afforded me by a lamp?

My fears had pictured to themselves no precise object. It would be difficult to depict, in words, the ingredients and hues of that phantom which haunted me. An hand invisible and of preternatural strength, lifted by human passions, and selecting my life for its aim, were parts of this terrific image. All places were alike accessible to this foe, or if his empire were restricted by local bounds, those bounds were utterly inscrutable by me. But had I not been told by some one in league with this enemy, that every place but the recess in the bank was exempt from danger?

I returned to the closet, and once more put my hand upon the lock. O! may my ears lose their sensibility, ere they be again assailed by a shriek so terrible! Not merely my understanding was subdued by the sound: it acted on my nerves like an edge of steel. It appeared to cut asunder the fibres of my brain, and rack every joint with agony.

The cry, loud and piercing as it was, was nevertheless human. No articulation was ever more distinct. The breath which accompanied it did not fan my hair, yet did every circumstance combine to persuade me that the lips which uttered it touched my very shoulder.

"Hold! Hold!" were the words of this tremendous prohibition, in whose tone the whole soul seemed to be rapt up, and every energy converted into eagerness and terror.

Shuddering, I dashed myself against the wall, and by the same involuntary impulse, turned my face backward to examine the mysterious monitor. The moon-light streamed into each window, and every corner of the room was conspicuous, and yet I beheld nothing!

The interval was too brief to be artificially measured, between the utterance of these words, and my scrutiny directed to the quarter whence they came. Yet if a human being had been there, could he fail to have been visible? Which of my senses was the prey of a fatal illusion? The shock which the sound produced was still felt in every part of my frame. The sound, therefore, could not but be a genuine commotion. But that I had heard it, was not more true than that the being who uttered it was stationed at my right ear; yet my attendant was invisible.

I cannot describe the state of my thoughts at that moment. Surprize had mastered my faculties. My frame shook, and the vital current was congealed. I was conscious only to the vehemence of my sensations. This condition could not be lasting. Like a tide, which suddenly mounts to an overwhelming height, and then gradually subsides, my confusion slowly gave place to order, and my tumults to a calm. I was able to deliberate and move. I resumed my feet, and advanced into the midst of the room. Upward, and behind, and on each side, I threw penetrating glances. I was not satisfied with one examination. He that hitherto refused to be seen, might change his purpose, and on the next survey be clearly distinguishable.

Solitude imposes least restraint upon the fancy. Dark is less fertile of images than the feeble lustre of the moon. I was alone, and the walls were chequered by shadowy forms. As the moon passed behind a cloud and emerged, these shadows seemed to be endowed with life, and to move. The apartment was open to the breeze, and the curtain was occasionally blown from its ordinary position. This motion was not unaccompanied with sound. I failed not to snatch a look, and to listen when this motion and this sound occurred. My belief that my monitor was posted near, was strong, and instantly converted these appearances to tokens of his presence, and yet I could discern nothing.

When my thoughts were at length permitted to revert to the past, the first idea that occurred was the resemblance between the words of the voice which I had just heard, and those which had terminated my dream in the summer-house. There are means by which we are able to distinguish a substance from a shadow, a reality from the phantom of a dream. The pit, my brother beckoning me forward, the seizure of my arm, and the voice behind, were surely imaginary. That these incidents were fashioned in my sleep, is supported by the same indubitable evidence that compels me to believe myself awake at present; yet the words and the voice were the same. Then, by some inexplicable contrivance, I was aware of the danger, while my actions and sensations were those of one wholly unacquainted with it. Now, was it not equally true that my actions and persuasions were at war? Had not the belief, that evil lurked in the closet, gained admittance, and had not my actions betokened an unwarrantable security? To obviate the effects of my infatuation, the same means had been used.

In my dream, he that tempted me to my destruction, was my brother. Death was ambushed in my path. From what evil was I now rescued? What minister or implement of ill was shut up in this recess? Who was it whose suffocating grasp I was to feel, should I dare to enter it? What monstrous conception is this? my brother!

No; protection, and not injury is his province. Strange and terrible chimera! Yet it would not be suddenly dismissed. It was surely no vulgar agency that gave this form to my fears. He to whom all parts of time are equally present, whom no contingency approaches, was the author of that spell which now seized upon me. Life was dear to me. No consideration was present that enjoined me to relinquish it. Sacred duty combined with every spontaneous sentiment to endear to me my being. Should I not shudder when my being was endangered? But what emotion should possess me when the arm lifted against me was Wieland's?

Ideas exist in our minds that can be accounted for by no established laws. Why did I dream that my brother was my foe? Why but because an omen of my fate was ordained to be communicated? Yet what salutary end did it serve? Did it arm me with caution to elude, or fortitude to bear the evils to which I was reserved? My present thoughts were, no doubt, indebted for their hue to the similitude existing between these incidents and those of my dream. Surely it was phrenzy that dictated my deed. That a ruffian was hidden in the closet, was an idea, the genuine tendency of which was to urge me to flight. Such had been the effect formerly produced. Had my mind been simply occupied with this thought at present, no doubt, the same impulse would have been experienced; but now it was my brother whom I was irresistably persuaded to regard as the contriver of that ill of which I had been forewarned. This persuasion did not extenuate my fears or my danger. Why then did I again approach the closet and withdraw the bolt? My resolution was instantly conceived, and executed without faultering.

The door was formed of light materials. The lock, of simple structure, easily forewent its hold. It opened into the room, and commonly moved upon its hinges, after being unfastened, without any effort of mine. This effort, however, was bestowed upon the present occasion. It was my purpose to open it with quickness, but the exertion which I made was ineffectual. It refused to open.

At another time, this circumstance would not have looked with a face of mystery. I should have supposed some casual obstruction, and repeated my efforts to surmount it. But now my mind was accessible to no conjecture but one. The door was hindered from opening by human force. Surely, here was new cause for affright. This was confirmation proper to decide my conduct. Now was all ground of hesitation taken away. What could be supposed but that I deserted the chamber and the house? that I at least endeavoured no longer to withdraw the door?

Have I not said that my actions were dictated by phrenzy? My reason had forborne, for a time, to suggest or to sway my resolves. I reiterated my endeavours. I exerted all my force to overcome the obstacle, but in vain. The strength that was exerted to keep it shut, was superior to mine.

A casual observer might, perhaps, applaud the audaciousness of this conduct. Whence, but from an habitual defiance of danger, could my perseverance arise? I have already assigned, as distinctly as I am able, the cause of it. The frantic conception that my brother was within, that the resistance made to my design was exerted by him, had rooted itself in my mind. You will comprehend the height of this infatuation, when I tell you, that, finding all my exertions vain, I betook myself to exclamations. Surely I was utterly bereft of understanding.

Now had I arrived at the crisis of my fate. "O! hinder not the door to open," I exclaimed, in a tone that had less of fear than of grief in it. "I know you well. Come forth, but harm me not. I beseech you come forth."

I had taken my hand from the lock, and removed to a small distance from the door. I had scarcely uttered these words, when the door swung upon its hinges, and displayed to my view the interior of the closet. Whoever was within, was shrouded in darkness. A few seconds passed without interruption of the silence. I knew not what to expect or to fear. My eyes would not stray from the recess. Presently, a deep sigh was heard. The quarter from which it came heightened the eagerness of my gaze. Some one approached from the farther end. I quickly perceived the outlines of a human figure. Its steps were irresolute and slow. I recoiled as it advanced.

By coming at length within the verge of the room, his form was clearly distinguishable. I had prefigured to myself a very different personage. The face that presented itself was the last that I should desire to meet at an hour, and in a place like this. My wonder was stifled by my fears. Assassins had lurked in this recess. Some divine voice warned me of danger, that at this moment awaited me. I had spurned the intimation, and challenged my adversary.

I recalled the mysterious countenance and dubious character of Carwin. What motive but atrocious ones could guide his steps hither? I was alone. My habit suited the hour, and the place, and the warmth of the season. All succour was remote. He had placed himself between me and the door. My frame shook with the vehemence of my apprehensions.

Yet I was not wholly lost to myself: I vigilantly marked his demeanour. His looks were grave, but not without perturbation. What species of inquietude it betrayed, the light was not strong enough to enable me to discover. He stood still; but his eyes wandered from one object to another. When these powerful organs were fixed upon me, I shrunk into myself. At length, he broke silence. Earnestness, and not embarrassment, was in his tone. He advanced close to me while he spoke.

"What voice was that which lately addressed you?"

He paused for an answer; but observing my trepidation, he resumed, with undiminished solemnity: "Be not terrified. Whoever he was, he hast done you an important service. I need not ask you if it were the voice of a companion. That sound was beyond the compass of human organs. The knowledge that enabled him to tell you who was in the closet, was obtained by incomprehensible means.

"You knew that Carwin was there. Were you not apprized of his intents? The same power could impart the one as well as the other. Yet, knowing these, you persisted. Audacious girl! but, perhaps, you confided in his guardianship. Your confidence was just. With succour like this at hand you may safely defy me.

"He is my eternal foe; the baffler of my best concerted schemes. Twice have you been saved by his accursed interposition. But for him I should long ere now have borne away the spoils of your honor."

He looked at me with greater stedfastness than before. I became every moment more anxious for my safety. It was with difficulty I stammered out an entreaty that he would instantly depart, or suffer me to do so. He paid no regard to my request, but proceeded in a more impassioned manner.

"What is it you fear? Have I not told you, you are safe? Has not one in whom you more reasonably place trust assured you of it? Even if I execute my purpose, what injury is done? Your prejudices will call it by that name, but it merits it not.

"I was impelled by a sentiment that does you honor; a sentiment, that would sanctify my deed; but, whatever it be you are safe. Be this chimera still worshipped; I will do nothing to pollute it." There he stopped.

The accents and gestures of this man left me drained of all courage. Surely, on no other occasion should I have been thus pusillanimous. My state I regarded as a hopeless one. I was wholly at the mercy of this being. Whichever way I turned my eyes, I saw no avenue by which I might escape. The resources of my personal strength, my ingenuity, and my eloquence, I estimated at nothing. The dignity of virtue, and the force of truth, I had been accustomed to celebrate; and had frequently vaunted of the conquests which I should make with their assistance.

I used to suppose that certain evils could never befall a being in possession of a sound mind; that true virtue supplies us with energy which vice can never resist; that it was always in our power to obstruct, by his own death, the designs of an enemy who aimed at less than our life. How was it that a sentiment like despair had now invaded me, and that I trusted to the protection of chance, or to the pity of my persecutor?

His words imparted some notion of the injury which he had meditated. He talked of obstacles that had risen in his way. He had relinquished his design. These sources supplied me with slender consolation. There was no security but in his absence. When I looked at myself, when I reflected on the hour and the place, I was overpowered by horror and dejection.

He was silent, museful, and inattentive to my situation, yet made no motion to depart. I was silent in my turn. What could I say? I was confident that reason in this contest would be impotent. I must owe my safety to his own suggestions. Whatever purpose brought him hither, he had changed it. Why then did he remain? His resolutions might fluctuate, and the pause of a few minutes restore to him his first resolutions.

Yet was not this the man whom we had treated with unwearied kindness? Whose society was endeared to us by his intellectual elevation and accomplishments? Who had a thousand times expatiated on the usefulness and beauty of virtue? Why should such a one be dreaded? If I could have forgotten the circumstances in which our interview had taken place, I might have treated his words as jests. Presently, he resumed:

"Fear me not: the space that severs us is small, and all visible succour is distant. You believe yourself completely in my power; that you stand upon the brink of ruin. Such are your groundless fears. I cannot lift a finger to hurt you. Easier it would be to stop the moon in her course than to injure you. The power that protects you would crumble my sinews, and reduce me to a heap of ashes in a moment, if I were to harbour a thought hostile to your safety.

"Thus are appearances at length solved. Little did I expect that they originated hence. What a portion is assigned to you? Scanned by the eyes of this intelligence, your path will be without pits to swallow, or snares to entangle you. Environed by the arms of this protection, all artifices will be frustrated, and all malice repelled."

Here succeeded a new pause. I was still observant of every gesture and look. The tranquil solemnity that had lately possessed his countenance gave way to a new expression. All now was trepidation and anxiety.

"I must be gone," said he in a faltering accent. "Why do I linger here? I will not ask your forgiveness. I see that your terrors are invincible. Your pardon will be extorted by fear, and not dictated by compassion. I must fly from you forever. He that could plot against your honor, must expect from you and your friends persecution and death. I must doom myself to endless exile."

Saying this, he hastily left the room. I listened while he descended the stairs, and, unbolting the outer door, went forth. I did not follow him with my eyes, as the moon-light would have enabled me to do. Relieved by his absence, and exhausted by the conflict of my fears, I threw myself on a chair, and resigned myself to those bewildering ideas which incidents like these could not fail to produce.

Chapter X.

Order could not readily be introduced into my thoughts. The voice still rung in my ears. Every accent that was uttered by Carwin was fresh in my remembrance. His unwelcome approach, the recognition of his person, his hasty departure, produced a complex impression on my mind which no words can delineate. I strove to give a slower motion to my thoughts, and to regulate a confusion which became painful; but my efforts were nugatory. I covered my eyes with my hand, and sat, I know not how long, without power to arrange or utter my conceptions.

I had remained for hours, as I believed, in absolute solitude. No thought of personal danger had molested my tranquillity. I had made no preparation for defence. What was it that suggested the design of perusing my father's manuscript? If, instead of this, I had retired to bed, and to sleep, to what fate might I not have been reserved? The ruffian, who must almost have suppressed his breathings to screen himself from discovery, would have noticed this signal, and I should have awakened only to perish with affright, and to abhor myself. Could I have remained unconscious of my danger? Could I have tranquilly slept in the midst of so deadly a snare?

And who was he that threatened to destroy me? By what means could he hide himself in this closet? Surely he is gifted with supernatural power. Such is the enemy of whose attempts I was forewarned. Daily I had seen him and conversed with him. Nothing could be discerned through the impenetrable veil of his duplicity. When busied in conjectures, as to the author of the evil that was threatened, my mind did not light, for a moment, upon his image. Yet has he not avowed himself my enemy? Why should he be here if he had not meditated evil?

He confesses that this has been his second attempt. What was the scene of his former conspiracy? Was it not he whose whispers betrayed him? Am I deceived; or was there not a faint resemblance between the voice of this man and that which talked of grasping my throat, and extinguishing my life in a moment? Then he had a colleague in his crime; now he is alone. Then death was the scope of his thoughts; now an injury unspeakably more dreadful. How thankful should I be to the power that has interposed to save me!

That power is invisible. It is subject to the cognizance of one of my senses. What are the means that will inform me of what nature it is? He has set himself to counterwork the machinations of this man, who had menaced destruction to all that is dear to me, and whose cunning had surmounted every human impediment. There was none to rescue me from his grasp. My rashness even hastened the completion of his scheme, and precluded him from the benefits of deliberation. I had robbed him of the power to repent and forbear. Had I been apprized of the danger, I should have regarded my conduct as the means of rendering my escape from it impossible. Such, likewise, seem to have been the fears of my invisible protector. Else why that startling intreaty to refrain from opening the closet? By what inexplicable infatuation was I compelled to proceed?

Yet my conduct was wise. Carwin, unable to comprehend my folly, ascribed my behaviour to my knowledge. He conceived himself previously detected, and such detection being possible to flow only from *my* heavenly friend, and *his* enemy, his fears acquired additional strength.

He is apprized of the nature and intentions of this being. Perhaps he is a human agent. Yet, on that supposition his atchievements are incredible. Why should I be selected as the object of his care; or, if a mere mortal, should I not recognize some one, whom, benefits imparted and received had prompted to love me? What were the limits and duration of his guardianship? Was the genius of my birth entrusted by divine benignity with this province? Are human faculties adequate to receive stronger proofs of the existence of unfettered and beneficent intelligences than I have received?

But who was this man's coadjutor? The voice that acknowledged an alliance in treachery with Carwin warned me to avoid the summerhouse. He assured me that there only my safety was endangered. His assurance, as it now appears, was fallacious. Was there not deceit in his admonition? Was his compact really annulled? Some purpose was, perhaps, to be accomplished by preventing my future visits to that spot. Why was I enjoined silence to others, on the subject of this admonition, unless it were for some unauthorized and guilty purpose?

No one but myself was accustomed to visit it. Backward, it was hidden from distant view by the rock, and in front, it was screened from all examination, by creeping plants, and the branches of cedars. What recess could be more propitious to secrecy? The spirit which haunted it formerly was pure and rapturous. It was a sane sacred to the memory of infantile days, and to blissful imaginations of the future! What a gloomy reverse had succeeded since the ominous arrival of this stranger! Now, perhaps, it is the scene of his meditations. Purposes fraught with horror, that shun the light, and contemplate the pollution of innocence, are here engendered, and fostered, and reared to maturity.

Such were the ideas that, during the night, were tumultuously revolved by me. I reviewed every conversation in which Carwin had borne a part. I studied to discover the true inferences deducible from his deportment and words with regard to his former adventures and actual views. I pondered on the comments which he made on the relation which I had given of the closet dialogue. No new ideas suggested themselves in the course of this review. My expectation had, from the first, been disappointed on the small degree of surprize which this narrative excited in him. He never explicitly declared his opinion as to the nature of those voices, or decided whether they were real or visionary. He recommended no measures of caution or prevention.

But what measures were now to be taken? Was the danger which threatened me at an end? Had I nothing more to fear? I was lonely, and without means of defence. I could not calculate the motives and regulate the footsteps of this person. What certainty was there, that he would not re-assume his purposes, and swiftly return to the execution of them?

This idea covered me once more with dismay. How deeply did I regret the solitude in which I was placed, and how ardently did I desire the return of day! But neither of these inconveniencies were susceptible of remedy. At first, it occurred to me to summon my servant, and make her spend the night in my chamber; but the inefficacy of this expedient to enhance my safety was easily seen. Once I resolved to leave the house, and retire to my brother's, but was deterred by reflecting on the unseasonableness of the hour, on the alarm which my arrival, and the account which I should be obliged to give, might occasion, and on the danger to which I might expose myself in the way thither. I began, likewise, to consider Carwin's return to molest me as exceedingly improbable. He had relinquished, of his own accord, his design, and departed without compulsion.

"Surely," said I, "there is omnipotence in the cause that changed the views of a man like Carwin. The divinity that shielded me from his attempts will take suitable care of my future safety. Thus to yield to my fears is to deserve that they should be realized."

Scarcely had I uttered these words, when my attention was startled by the sound of footsteps. They denoted some one stepping into the piazza in front of my house. My new-born confidence was extinguished in a moment. Carwin, I thought, had repented his departure, and was hastily returning. The possibility that his return was prompted by intentions consistent with my safety, found no place in my mind.

Images of violation and murder assailed me anew, and the terrors which succeeded almost incapacitated me from taking any measures for my defence. It was an impulse of which I was scarcely conscious, that made me fasten the lock and draw the bolts of my chamber door. Having done this, I threw myself on a seat; for I trembled to a degree which disabled me from standing, and my soul was so perfectly absorbed in the act of listening, that almost the vital motions were stopped.

The door below creaked on its hinges. It was not again thrust to, but appeared to remain open. Footsteps entered, traversed the entry, and began to mount the stairs. How I detested the folly of not pursuing the man when he withdrew, and bolting after him the outer door! Might he not conceive this omission to be a proof that my angel had deserted me, and be thereby fortified in guilt?

Every step on the stairs, which brought him nearer to my chamber, added vigor to my desperation. The evil with which I was menaced was to be at any rate eluded. How little did I preconceive the conduct which, in an exigence like this, I should be prone to adopt. You will suppose that deliberation and despair would have suggested the same course of action, and that I should have, unhesitatingly, resorted to the best means of personal defence within my power. A penknife lay open upon my table. I remembered that it was there, and seized it. For what purpose you will scarcely inquire. It will be immediately supposed that I meant it for my last refuge, and that if all other means should fail, I should plunge it into the heart of my ravisher.

I have lost all faith in the stedfastness of human resolves. It was thus that in periods of calm I had determined to act. No cowardice had been held by me in greater abhorrence than that which prompted an injured female to destroy, not her injurer ere the injury was perpetrated, but herself when it was without remedy. Yet now this penknife appeared to me of no other use than to baffle my assailant, and prevent the crime by destroying myself. To deliberate at such a time was impossible; but among the tumultuous suggestions of the moment, I do not recollect that it once occurred to me to use it as an instrument of direct defence.

The steps had now reached the second floor. Every footfall accelerated the completion, without augmenting the certainty of evil. The consciousness that the door was fast, now that nothing but that was interposed between me and danger, was a source of some consolation. I cast my eye towards the window. This, likewise, was a new suggestion. If the door should give way, it was my sudden resolution to throw myself from the window. Its height from the ground, which was covered beneath by a brick pavement, would insure my destruction; but I thought not of that.

When opposite to my door the footsteps ceased. Was he listening whether my fears were allayed, and my caution were asleep? Did he hope to take me by surprize? Yet, if so, why did he allow so many noisy signals to betray his approach? Presently the steps were again heard to approach the door. An hand was laid upon the lock, and the latch pulled back. Did he imagine it possible that I should fail to secure the door? A slight effort was made to push it open, as if all bolts being withdrawn, a slight effort only was required.

I no sooner perceived this, than I moved swiftly towards the window. Carwin's frame might be said to be all muscle. His strength and activity had appeared, in various instances, to be prodigious. A slight exertion of his force would demolish the door. Would not that exertion be made? Too surely it would; but, at the same moment that this obstacle should yield, and he should enter the apartment, my determination was formed to leap from the window. My senses were still bound to this object. I gazed at the door in momentary expectation that the assault would be made. The pause continued. The person without was irresolute and motionless.

Suddenly, it occurred to me that Carwin might conceive me to have fled. That I had not betaken myself to flight was, indeed, the least probable of all conclusions. In this persuasion he must have been confirmed on finding the lower door unfastened, and the chamber door locked. Was it not wise to foster this persuasion? Should I maintain deep silence, this, in addition to other circumstances, might encourage the belief, and he would once more depart. Every new reflection added plausibility to this reasoning. It was presently more strongly enforced, when I noticed footsteps withdrawing from the door. The blood once more flowed back to my heart, and a dawn of exultation began to rise: but my joy was short lived. Instead of descending the stairs, he passed to the door of the opposite chamber, opened it, and having entered, shut it after him with a violence that shook the house.

How was I to interpret this circumstance? For what end could he have entered this chamber? Did the violence with which he closed the door testify the depth of his vexation? This room was usually occupied by Pleyel. Was Carwin aware of his absence on this night? Could he be suspected of a design so sordid as pillage? If this were his view there were no means in my power to frustrate it. It behoved me to seize the first opportunity to escape; but if my escape were supposed by my enemy to have been already effected, no asylum was more secure than the present. How could my passage from the house be accomplished without noises that might incite him to pursue me?

Utterly at a loss to account for his going into Pleyel's chamber, I waited in instant expectation of hearing him come forth. All, however, was profoundly still. I listened in vain for a considerable period, to catch the sound of the door when it should again be opened. There was no other avenue by which he could escape, but a door which led into the girl's chamber. Would any evil from this quarter befall the girl?

Hence arose a new train of apprehensions. They merely added to the turbulence and agony of my reflections. Whatever evil impended over her, I had no power to avert it. Seclusion and silence were the only means of saving myself from the perils of this fatal night. What solemn vows did I put up, that if I should once more behold the light of day, I would never trust myself again within the threshold of this dwelling!

Minute lingered after minute, but no token was given that Carwin had returned to the passage. What, I again asked, could detain him in this room? Was it possible that he had returned, and glided, unperceived, away? I was speedily aware of the difficulty that attended an enterprize like this; and yet, as if by that means I were capable of gaining any information on that head, I cast anxious looks from the window.

The object that first attracted my attention was an human figure standing on the edge of the bank. Perhaps my penetration was assisted by my hopes. Be that as it will, the figure of Carwin was clearly distinguishable. From the obscurity of my station, it was impossible that I should be discerned by him, and yet he scarcely suffered me to catch a glimpse of him. He turned and went down the steep, which, in this part, was not difficult to be scaled.

My conjecture then had been right. Carwin has softly opened the door, descended the stairs, and issued forth. That I should not have overheard his steps, was only less incredible than that my eyes had deceived me. But what was now to be done? The house was at length delivered from this detested inmate. By one avenue might he again re-enter. Was it not wise to bar the lower door? Perhaps he had gone out by the kitchen door. For this end, he must have passed through Judith's chamber. These entrances being closed and bolted, as great security was gained as was compatible with my lonely condition.

The propriety of these measures was too manifest not to make me struggle successfully with my fears. Yet I opened my own door with the utmost caution, and descended as if I were afraid that Carwin had been still immured in Pleyel's chamber. The outer door was a-jar. I shut, with trembling eagerness, and drew every bolt that appended to it. I then passed with light and less cautious steps through the parlour, but was surprized to discover that the kitchen door was secure. I was compelled to acquiesce in the first conjecture that Carwin had escaped through the entry.

My heart was now somewhat eased of the load of apprehension. I returned once more to my chamber, the door of which I was careful to lock. It was no time to think of repose. The moon-light began already to fade before the light of the day. The approach of morning was betokened by the usual signals. I mused upon the events of this night, and determined to take up my abode henceforth at my brother's. Whether I should inform him of what had happened was a question which seemed to demand some consideration. My safety unquestionably required that I should abandon my present habitation.

As my thoughts began to flow with fewer impediments, the image of Pleyel, and the dubiousness of his condition, again recurred to me. I again ran over the possible causes of his absence on the preceding day. My mind was attuned to melancholy. I dwelt, with an obstinacy for which I could not account, on the idea of his death. I painted to myself his struggles with the billows, and his last appearance. I imagined myself a midnight wanderer on the shore, and to have stumbled on his corpse, which the tide had cast up. These dreary images affected me even to tears. I endeavoured not to restrain them. They imparted a relief which I had not anticipated. The more copiously they flowed, the more did my general sensations appear to subside into calm, and a certain restlessness give way to repose.

Perhaps, relieved by this effusion, the slumber so much wanted might have stolen on my senses, had there been no new cause of alarm.

Chapter XI.

I was aroused from this stupor by sounds that evidently arose in the next chamber. Was it possible that I had been mistaken in the figure which I had seen on the bank? or had Carwin, by some inscrutable means, penetrated once more into this chamber? The opposite door opened; footsteps came forth, and the person, advancing to mine, knocked.

So unexpected an incident robbed me of all presence of mind, and, starting up, I involuntarily exclaimed, "Who is there?" An answer was immediately given. The voice, to my inexpressible astonishment, was Pleyel's.

"It is I. Have you risen? If you have not, make haste; I want three minutes conversation with you in the parlour—I will wait for you there." Saying this he retired from the door.

Should I confide in the testimony of my ears? If that were true, it was Pleyel that had been hitherto immured in the opposite chamber: he whom my rueful fancy had depicted in so many ruinous and ghastly shapes: he whose footsteps had been listened to with such inquietude! What is man, that knowledge is so sparingly conferred upon him! that his heart should be wrung with distress, and his frame be exanimated with fear, though his safety be encompassed with impregnable walls! What are the bounds of human imbecility! He that warned me of the presence of my foe refused the intimation by which so many racking fears would have been precluded.

Yet who would have imagined the arrival of Pleyel at such an hour? His tone was desponding and anxious. Why this unseasonable summons? and why this hasty departure? Some tidings he, perhaps, bears of mysterious and unwelcome import.

My impatience would not allow me to consume much time in deliberation: I hastened down. Pleyel I found standing at a window, with eyes cast down as in meditation, and arms folded on his breast. Every line in his countenance was pregnant with sorrow. To this was added a certain wanness and air of fatigue. The last time I had seen him appearances had been the reverse of these. I was startled at the change. The first impulse was to question him as to the cause. This impulse was supplanted by some degree of confusion, flowing from a consciousness that love had too large, and, as it might prove, a perceptible share in creating this impulse. I was silent.

Presently he raised his eyes and fixed them upon me. I read in them an anguish altogether ineffable. Never had I witnessed a like demeanour in Pleyel. Never, indeed, had I observed an human countenance in which grief was more legibly inscribed. He seemed struggling for utterance; but his struggles being fruitless, he shook his head and turned away from me.

My impatience would not allow me to be longer silent: "What," said I, "for heaven's sake, my friend, what is the matter?"

He started at the sound of my voice. His looks, for a moment, became convulsed with an emotion very different from grief. His accents were broken with rage.

"The matter—O wretch!—thus exquisitely fashioned—on whom nature seemed to have exhausted all her graces; with charms so awful and so pure! how art thou fallen! From what height fallen! A ruin so complete—so unheard of!"

His words were again choaked by emotion. Grief and pity were again mingled in his features. He resumed, in a tone half suffocated by sobs:

"But why should I upbraid thee? Could I restore to thee what thou hast lost; efface this cursed stain; snatch thee from the jaws of this fiend; I would do it. Yet what will avail my efforts? I have not arms with which to contend with so consummate, so frightful a depravity.

"Evidence less than this would only have excited resentment and scorn. The wretch who should have breathed a suspicion injurious to thy honor, would have been regarded without anger; not hatred or envy could have prompted him; it would merely be an argument of madness. That my eyes, that my ears, should bear witness to thy fall! By no other way could detestible conviction be imparted.

"Why do I summon thee to this conference? Why expose myself to thy derision? Here admonition and entreaty are vain. Thou knowest him already, for a murderer and thief. I had thought to have been the first to disclose to thee his infamy; to have warned thee of the pit to which thou art hastening; but thy eyes are open in vain. O soul and insupportable disgrace!

"There is but one path. I know you will disappear together. In thy ruin, how will the felicity and honor of multitudes be involved! But it must come. This scene shall not be blotted by his presence. No doubt thou wilt shortly see thy detested paramour. This scene will be again polluted by a midnight assignation. Inform him of his danger; tell him that his crimes are known; let him fly far and instantly from this spot, if he desires to avoid the fate which menaced him in Ireland.

"And wilt thou not stay behind?—But shame upon my weakness. I know not what I would say.—I have done what I purposed. To stay longer, to expostulate, to beseech, to enumerate the consequences of thy act—what end can it serve but to blazon thy infamy and embitter our woes? And yet, O think, think ere it be too late, on the distresses which thy flight will entail upon us; on the base, grovelling, and atrocious character of the wretch to whom thou hast sold thy honor. But what is this? Is not thy effrontery impenetrable, and thy heart thoroughly cankered? O most specious, and most profligate of women!"

Saying this, he rushed out of the house. I saw him in a few moments hurrying along the path which led to my brother's. I had no power to prevent his going, or to recall, or to follow him. The accents I had heard were calculated to confound and bewilder. I looked around me to assure myself that the scene was real. I moved that I might banish the doubt that I was awake. Such enormous imputations from the mouth of Pleyel! To be stigmatized with the names of wanton and profligate! To be charged with the sacrifice of honor! with midnight meetings with a wretch known to be a murderer and thief! with an intention to fly in his company!

What I had heard was surely the dictate of phrenzy, or it was built upon some fatal, some incomprehensible mistake. After the horrors of the night, after undergoing perils so imminent from this man, to be summoned to an interview like this; to find Pleyel fraught with a belief that, instead of having chosen death as a refuge from the violence of this man, I had hugged his baseness to my heart, had sacrificed for him my purity, my spotless name, my friendships, and my fortune! that even madness could engender accusations like these was not to be believed.

What evidence could possibly suggest conceptions so wild? After the unlooked-for interview with Carwin in my chamber, he retired. Could Pleyel have observed his exit? It was not long after that Pleyel himself entered. Did he build on this incident, his odious conclusions? Could the long series of my actions and sentiments grant me no exemption from suspicions so foul? Was it not more rational to infer that Carwin's designs had been illicit; that my life had been endangered by the fury of one whom, by some means, he had discovered to be an assassin and robber; that my honor had been assailed, not by blandishments, but by violence?

He has judged me without hearing. He has drawn from dubious appearances, conclusions the most improbable and unjust. He has loaded me with all outrageous epithets. He has ranked me with prostitutes and thieves. I cannot pardon thee, Pleyel, for this injustice. Thy understanding must be hurt. If it be not, if thy conduct was sober and deliberate, I can never forgive an outrage so unmanly, and so gross.

These thoughts gradually gave place to others. Pleyel was possessed by some momentary phrenzy: appearances had led him into palpable errors. Whence could his sagacity have contracted this blindness? Was it not love? Previously assured of my affection for Carwin, distracted with grief and jealousy, and impelled hither at that late hour by some unknown instigation, his imagination transformed shadows into monsters, and plunged him into these deplorable errors.

This idea was not unattended with consolation. My soul was divided between indignation at his injustice, and delight on account of the source from which I conceived it to spring. For a long time they would allow admission to no other thoughts. Surprize is an emotion that enfeebles, not invigorates. All my meditations were accompanied with wonder. I rambled with vagueness, or clung to one image with an obstinacy which sufficiently testified the maddening influence of late transactions.

Gradually I proceeded to reflect upon the consequences of Pleyel's mistake, and on the measures I should take to guard myself against future injury from Carwin. Should I suffer this mistake to be detected by time? When his passion should subside, would he not perceive the flagrancy of his injustice, and hasten to atone for it? Did it not become my character to testify resentment for language and treatment so opprobrious? Wrapt up in the consciousness of innocence, and confiding in the influence of time and reflection to confute so groundless a charge, it was my province to be passive and silent.

As to the violences meditated by Carwin, and the means of eluding them, the path to be taken by me was obvious. I resolved to tell the tale to my brother, and regulate myself by his advice. For this end, when the morning was somewhat advanced, I took the way to his house. My sister was engaged in her customary occupations. As soon as I appeared, she remarked a change in my looks. I was not willing to alarm her by the information which I had to communicate. Her health was in that condition which rendered a disastrous tale particularly unsuitable. I forbore a direct answer to her inquiries, and inquired, in my turn, for Wieland.

"Why," said she, "I suspect something mysterious and unpleasant has happened this morning. Scarcely had we risen when Pleyel dropped among us. What could have prompted him to make us so early and so unseasonable a visit I cannot tell. To judge from the disorder of his dress, and his countenance, something of an extraordinary nature has occurred. He permitted me merely to know that he had slept none, nor even undressed, during the past night. He took your brother to walk with him. Some topic must have deeply engaged them, for Wieland did not return till the breakfast hour was passed, and returned alone. His disturbance was excessive; but he would not listen to my importunities, or tell me what had happened. I gathered from hints which he let fall, that your situation was, in some way, the cause: yet he assured me that you were at your own house, alive, in good health, and in perfect safety. He scarcely ate a morsel, and immediately after breakfast went out again. He would not inform me whither he was going, but mentioned that he probably might not return before night."

I was equally astonished and alarmed by this information. Pleyel had told his tale to my brother, and had, by a plausible and exaggerated picture, instilled into him unfavorable thoughts of me. Yet would not the more correct judgment of Wieland perceive and expose the fallacy of his conclusions? Perhaps his uneasiness might arise from some insight into the character of Carwin, and from apprehensions for my safety. The appearances by which Pleyel had been misled, might induce him likewise to believe that I entertained an indiscreet, though not dishonorable affection for Carwin. Such were the conjectures rapidly formed. I was inexpressibly anxious to change them into certainty. For this end an interview with my brother was desirable. He was gone, no one knew whither, and was not expected speedily to return. I had no clue by which to trace his footsteps.

My anxieties could not be concealed from my sister. They heightened her solicitude to be acquainted with the cause. There were many reasons persuading me to silence: at least, till I had seen my brother, it would be an act of inexcusable temerity to unfold what had lately passed. No other expedient for eluding her importunities occurred to me, but that of returning to my own house. I recollected my determination to become a tenant of this roof. I mentioned it to her. She joyfully acceded to this proposal, and suffered me, with less reluctance, to depart, when I told her that it was with a view to collect and send to my new dwelling what articles would be immediately useful to me.

Once more I returned to the house which had been the scene of so much turbulence and danger. I was at no great distance from it when I observed my brother coming out. On seeing me he stopped, and after ascertaining, as it seemed, which way I was going, he returned into the house before me. I sincerely rejoiced at this event, and I hastened to set things, if possible, on their right footing.

His brow was by no means expressive of those vehement emotions with which Pleyel had been agitated. I drew a favorable omen from this circumstance. Without delay I began the conversation.

"I have been to look for you," said I, "but was told by Catharine that Pleyel had engaged you on some important and disagreeable affair. Before his interview with you he spent a few minutes with me. These minutes he employed in upbraiding me for crimes and intentions with which I am by no means chargeable. I believe him to have taken up his opinions on very insufficient grounds. His behaviour was in the highest degree precipitate and unjust, and, until I receive some atonement, I shall treat him, in my turn, with that contempt which he justly merits: meanwhile I am fearful that he has prejudiced my brother against me. That is an evil which I most anxiously deprecate, and which I shall indeed exert myself to remove. Has he made me the subject of this morning's conversation?"

My brother's countenance testified no surprize at my address. The benignity of his looks were no wise diminished.

"It is true," said he, "your conduct was the subject of our discourse. I am your friend, as well as your brother. There is no human being whom I love with more tenderness, and whose welfare is nearer my heart. Judge then with what emotions I listened to Pleyel's story. I expect and desire you to vindicate yourself from aspersions so foul, if vindication be possible."

The tone with which he uttered the last words affected me deeply. "If vindication be possible!" repeated I. "From what you know, do you deem a formal vindication necessary? Can you harbour for a moment the belief of my guilt?"

He shook his head with an air of acute anguish. "I have struggled," said he, "to dismiss that belief. You speak before a judge who will profit by any pretence to acquit you: who is ready to question his own senses when they plead against you."

These words incited a new set of thoughts in my mind. I began to suspect that Pleyel had built his accusations on some foundation unknown to me. "I may be a stranger to the grounds of your belief. Pleyel loaded me with indecent and virulent invectives, but he withheld from me the facts that generated his suspicions. Events took place last night of which some of the circumstances were of an ambiguous nature. I conceived that these might possibly have fallen under his cognizance, and that, viewed through the mists of prejudice and passion, they supplied a pretence for his conduct, but believed that your more unbiassed judgment would estimate them at their just value. Perhaps his tale has been different from what I suspect it to be. Listen then to my narrative. If there be any thing in his story inconsistent with mine, his story is false."

I then proceeded to a circumstantial relation of the incidents of the last night. Wieland listened with deep attention. Having finished, "This," continued I, "is the truth; you see in what circumstances an interview took place between Carwin and me. He remained for hours in my closet, and for some minutes in my chamber. He departed without haste or interruption. If Pleyel marked him as he left the house, and it is not impossible that he did, inferences injurious to my character might suggest themselves to him. In admitting them, he gave proofs of less discernment and less candor than I once ascribed to him."

"His proofs," said Wieland, after a considerable pause, "are different. That he should be deceived, is not possible. That he himself is not the deceiver, could not be believed, if his testimony were not inconsistent with yours; but the doubts which I entertained are now removed. Your tale, some parts of it, is marvellous; the voice which exclaimed against your rashness in approaching the closet, your persisting notwithstanding that prohibition, your belief that I was the ruffian, and your subsequent conduct, are believed by me, because I have known you from childhood, because a thousand instances have attested your veracity, and because nothing less than my own hearing and vision would convince me, in opposition to her own assertions, that my sister had fallen into wickedness like this."

I threw my arms around him, and bathed his cheek with my tears. "That," said I, "is spoken like my brother. But what are the proofs?"

He replied—"Pleyel informed me that, in going to your house, his attention was attracted by two voices. The persons speaking sat beneath the bank out of sight. These persons, judging by their voices, were Carwin and you. I will not repeat the dialogue. If my sister was the female, Pleyel was justified in concluding you to be, indeed, one of the most profligate of women. Hence, his accusations of you, and his efforts to obtain my concurrence to a plan by which an eternal separation should be brought about between my sister and this man."

I made Wieland repeat this recital. Here, indeed, was a tale to fill me with terrible foreboding. I had vainly thought that my safety could be sufficiently secured by doors and bars, but this is a foe from whose grasp no power of divinity can save me! His artifices will ever lay my fame and happiness at his mercy. How shall I counterwork his plots, or detect his coadjutor? He has taught some vile and abandoned female to mimic my voice. Pleyel's ears were the witnesses of my dishonor. This is the midnight assignation to which he alluded. Thus is the silence he maintained when attempting to open the door of my chamber, accounted for. He supposed me absent, and meant, perhaps, had my apartment been accessible, to leave in it some accusing memorial.

Pleyel was no longer equally culpable. The sincerity of his anguish, the depth of his despair, I remembered with some tendencies to gratitude. Yet was he not precipitate? Was the conjecture that my part was played by some mimic so utterly untenable? Instances of this faculty are common. The wickedness of Carwin must, in his opinion, have been adequate to such contrivances, and yet the supposition of my guilt was adopted in preference to that.

But how was this error to be unveiled? What but my own assertion had I to throw in the balance against it? Would this be permitted to outweigh the testimony of his senses? I had no witnesses to prove my existence in another place. The real events of that night are marvellous. Few, to whom they should be related, would scruple to discredit them. Pleyel is sceptical in a transcendant degree. I cannot summon Carwin to my bar, and make him the attestor of my innocence, and the accuser of himself.

My brother saw and comprehended my distress. He was unacquainted, however, with the full extent of it. He knew not by how many motives I was incited to retrieve the good opinion of Pleyel. He endeavored to console me. Some new event, he said, would occur to disentangle the maze. He did not question the influence of my eloquence, if I thought proper to exert it. Why not seek an interview with Pleyel, and exact from him a minute relation, in which something may be met with serving to destroy the probability of the whole?

I caught, with eagerness, at this hope; but my alacrity was damped by new reflections. Should I, perfect in this respect, and unblemished as I was, thrust myself, uncalled, into his presence, and make my felicity depend upon his arbitrary verdict?

"If you chuse to seek an interview," continued Wieland, "you must make haste, for Pleyel informed me of his intention to set out this evening or to-morrow on a long journey."

No intelligence was less expected or less welcome than this. I had thrown myself in a window seat; but now, starting on my feet, I exclaimed, "Good heavens! what is it you say? a journey? whither? when?"

"I cannot say whither. It is a sudden resolution I believe. I did not hear of it till this morning. He promises to write to me as soon as he is settled."

I needed no further information as to the cause and issue of this journey. The scheme of happiness to which he had devoted his thoughts was blasted by the discovery of last night. My preference of another, and my unworthiness to be any longer the object of his adoration, were evinced by the same act and in the same moment. The thought of utter desertion originating in such a cause, was the prelude to distraction. That Pleyel should abandon me forever, because I was blind to his excellence, because I coveted pollution, and wedded infamy, when, on the contrary, my heart was the shrine of all purity, and beat only for his sake, was a destiny which, as long as my life was in my own hands, I would by no means consent to endure.

I remembered that this evil was still preventable; that this fatal journey it was still in my power to procrastinate, or, perhaps, to occasion it to be laid aside. There were no impediments to a visit: I only dreaded lest the interview should be too long delayed. My brother befriended my impatience, and readily consented to furnish me with a chaise and servant to attend me. My purpose was to go immediately to Pleyel's farm, where his engagements usually detained him during the day.

CHAPTER XII.

My way lay through the city. I had scarcely entered it when I was seized with a general sensation of sickness. Every object grew dim and swam before my sight. It was with difficulty I prevented myself from sinking to the bottom of the carriage. I ordered myself to be carried to Mrs. Baynton's, in hope that an interval of repose would invigorate and refresh me. My distracted thoughts would allow me but little rest. Growing somewhat better in the afternoon, I resumed my journey.

My contemplations were limited to a few objects. I regarded my success, in the purpose which I had in view, as considerably doubtful. I depended, in some degree, on the suggestions of the moment, and on the materials which Pleyel himself should furnish me. When I reflected on the nature of the accusation, I burned with disdain. Would not truth, and the consciousness of innocence, render me triumphant? Should I not cast from me, with irresistible force, such atrocious imputations?

What an entire and mournful change has been effected in a few hours! The gulf that separates man from insects is not wider than that which severs the polluted from the chaste among women. Yesterday and to-day I am the same. There is a degree of depravity to which it is impossible for me to sink; yet, in the apprehension of another, my ancient and intimate associate, the perpetual witness of my actions, and partaker of my thoughts, I had ceased to be the same. My integrity was tarnished and withered in his eyes. I was the colleague of a murderer, and the paramour of a thief!

His opinion was not destitute of evidence: yet what proofs could reasonably avail to establish an opinion like this? If the sentiments corresponded not with the voice that was heard, the evidence was deficient; but this want of correspondence would have been supposed by me if I had been the auditor and Pleyel the criminal. But mimicry might still more plausibly have been employed to explain the scene. Alas! it is the fate of Clara Wieland to fall into the hands of a precipitate and inexorable judge.

But what, O man of mischief! is the tendency of thy thoughts? Frustrated in thy first design, thou wilt not forego the immolation of thy victim. To exterminate my reputation was all that remained to thee, and this my guardian has permitted. To dispossess Pleyel of this prejudice may be impossible; but, if that be effected, it cannot be supposed that thy wiles are exhausted; thy cunning will discover innumerable avenues to the accomplishment of thy malignant purpose.

Why should I enter the lists against thee? Would to heaven I could disarm thy vengeance by my deprecations! When I think of all the resources with which nature and education have supplied thee; that thy form is a combination of steely fibres and organs of exquisite ductility and boundless compass, actuated by an intelligence gifted with infinite endowments, and comprehending all knowledge, I perceive that my doom is fixed. What obstacle will be able to divert thy zeal or repel thy efforts? That being who has hitherto protected me has borne testimony to the formidableness of thy attempts, since nothing less than supernatural interference could check thy career.

Musing on these thoughts, I arrived, towards the close of the day, at Pleyel's house. A month before, I had traversed the same path; but how different were my sensations! Now I was seeking the presence of one who regarded me as the most degenerate of human kind. I was to plead the cause of my innocence, against witnesses the most explicit and unerring, of those which support the fabric of human knowledge. The nearer I approached the crisis, the more did my confidence decay. When the chaise stopped at the door, my strength refused to support me, and I threw myself into the arms of an ancient female domestic. I had not courage to inquire whether her master was at home. I was tormented with fears that the projected journey was already undertaken. These fears were removed, by her asking me whether she should call her young master, who had just gone into his own room. I was somewhat revived by this intelligence, and resolved immediately to seek him there.

In my confusion of mind, I neglected to knock at the door, but entered his apartment without previous notice. This abruptness was altogether involuntary. Absorbed in reflections of such unspeakable moment, I had no leisure to heed the niceties of punctilio. I discovered him standing with his back towards the entrance. A small trunk, with its lid raised, was before him, in which it seemed as if he had been busy in packing his clothes. The moment of my entrance, he was employed in gazing at something which he held in his hand.

I imagined that I fully comprehended this scene. The image which he held before him, and by which his attention was so deeply engaged, I doubted not to be my own. These preparations for his journey, the cause to which it was to be imputed, the hopelessness of success in the undertaking on which I had entered, rushed at once upon my feelings, and dissolved me in a flood of tears.

Startled by this sound, he dropped the lid of the trunk and turned. The solemn sadness that previously overspread his countenance, gave sudden way to an attitude and look of the most vehement astonishment. Perceiving me unable to uphold myself, he stepped towards me without speaking, and supported me on his arm. The kindness of this action called forth a new effusion from my eyes. Weeping was a solace to which, at that time, I had not grown familiar, and which, therefore, was peculiarly delicious. Indignation was no longer to be read in the features of my friend. They were pregnant with a mixture of wonder and pity. Their expression was easily interpreted. This visit, and these tears, were tokens of my penitence. The wretch whom he had stigmatized as incurably and obdurately wicked, now showed herself susceptible of remorse, and had come to confess her guilt.

This persuasion had no tendency to comfort me. It only showed me, with new evidence, the difficulty of the task which I had assigned myself. We were mutually silent. I had less power and less inclination than ever to speak. I extricated myself from his hold, and threw myself on a sofa. He placed himself by my side, and appeared to wait with impatience and anxiety for some beginning of the conversation. What could I say? If my mind had suggested any thing suitable to the occasion, my utterance was suffocated by tears.

Frequently he attempted to speak, but seemed deterred by some degree of uncertainty as to the true nature of the scene. At length, in faltering accents he spoke:

"My friend! would to heaven I were still permitted to call you by that name. The image that I once adored existed only in my fancy; but though I cannot hope to see it realized, you may not be totally insensible to the horrors of that gulf into which you are about to plunge. What heart is forever exempt from the goadings of compunction and the influx of laudable propensities?

"I thought you accomplished and wise beyond the rest of women. Not a sentiment you uttered, not a look you assumed, that were not, in my apprehension, fraught with the sublimities of rectitude and the illuminations of genius. Deceit has some bounds. Your education could not be without influence. A vigorous understanding cannot be utterly devoid of virtue; but you could not counterfeit the powers of invention and reasoning. I was rash in my invectives. I will not, but with life, relinquish all hopes of you. I will shut out every proof that would tell me that your heart is incurably diseased.

"You come to restore me once more to happiness; to convince me that you have torn her mask from vice, and feel nothing but abhorrence for the part you have hitherto acted."

At these words my equanimity forsook me. For a moment I forgot the evidence from which Pleyel's opinions were derived, the benevolence of his remonstrances, and the grief which his accents bespoke; I was filled with indignation and horror at charges so black; I shrunk back and darted at him a look of disdain and anger. My passion supplied me with words.

"What detestable infatuation was it that led me hither! Why do I patiently endure these horrible insults! My offences exist only in your own distempered imagination: you are leagued with the traitor who assailed my life: you have vowed the destruction of my peace and honor. I deserve infamy for listening to calumnies so base!"

These words were heard by Pleyel without visible resentment. His countenance relapsed into its former gloom; but he did not even look at me. The ideas which had given place to my angry emotions returned, and once more melted me into tears. "O!" I exclaimed, in a voice broken by sobs, "what a task is mine! Compelled to hearken to charges which I feel to be false, but which I know to be believed by him that utters them; believed too not without evidence, which, though fallacious, is not unplausible.

"I came hither not to confess, but to vindicate, I know the source of your opinions. Wieland has informed me on what your suspicions are built. These suspicions are fostered by you as certainties; the tenor of my life, of all my conversations and letters, affords me no security; every sentiment that my tongue and my pen have uttered, bear testimony to the rectitude of my mind; but this testimony is rejected. I am condemned as brutally profligate: I am classed with the stupidly and sordidly wicked.

"And where are the proofs that must justify so foul and so improbable an accusation? You have overheard a midnight conference. Voices have saluted your ear, in which you imagine yourself to have recognized mine, and that of a detected villain. The sentiments expressed were not allowed to outweigh the casual or concerted resemblance of voice. Sentiments the reverse of all those whose influence my former life had attested, denoting a mind polluted by grovelling vices, and entering into compact with that of a thief and a murderer. The nature of these sentiments did not enable you to detect the cheat, did not suggest to you the possibility that my voice had been counterfeited by another.

"You were precipitate and prone to condemn. Instead of rushing on the impostors, and comparing the evidence of sight with that of hearing, you stood aloof, or you fled. My innocence would not now have stood in need of vindication, if this conduct had been pursued. That you did not pursue it, your present thoughts incontestibly prove. Yet this conduct might surely have been expected from Pleyel. That he would not hastily impute the blackest of crimes, that he would not couple my name with infamy, and cover me with ruin for inadequate or slight reasons, might reasonably have been expected." The sobs which convulsed my bosom would not suffer me to proceed.

Pleyel was for a moment affected. He looked at me with some expression of doubt; but this quickly gave place to a mournful solemnity. He fixed his eyes on the floor as in reverie, and spoke:

"Two hours hence I am gone. Shall I carry away with me the sorrow that is now my guest? or shall that sorrow be accumulated tenfold? What is she that is now before me? Shall every hour supply me with new proofs of a wickedness beyond example? Already I deem her the most abandoned and detestable of human creatures. Her coming and her tears imparted a gleam of hope, but that gleam has vanished."

He now fixed his eyes upon me, and every muscle in his face trembled. His tone was hollow and terrible—"Thou knowest that I was a witness of your interview, yet thou comest hither to upbraid me for injustice! Thou canst look me in the face and say that I am deceived!— An inscrutable providence has fashioned thee for some end. Thou wilt live, no doubt, to fulfil the purposes of thy maker, if he repent not of his workmanship, and send not his vengeance to exterminate thee, ere the measure of thy days be full. Surely nothing in the shape of man can vie with thee!

"But I thought I had stifled this fury. I am not constituted thy judge. My office is to pity and amend, and not to punish and revile. I deemed myself exempt from all tempestuous passions. I had almost persuaded myself to weep over thy fall; but I am frail as dust, and mutable as water; I am calm, I am compassionate only in thy absence.—Make this house, this room, thy abode as long as thou wilt, but forgive me if I prefer solitude for the short time during which I shall stay." Saying this, he motioned as if to leave the apartment.

The stormy passions of this man affected me by sympathy. I ceased to weep. I was motionless and speechless with agony. I sat with my hands clasped, mutely gazing after him as he withdrew. I desired to detain him, but was unable to make any effort for that purpose, till he had passed out of the room. I then uttered an involuntary and piercing cry—"Pleyel! Art thou gone? Gone forever?"

At this summons he hastily returned. He beheld me wild, pale, gasping for breath, and my head already sinking on my bosom. A painful dizziness seized me, and I fainted away.

When I recovered, I found myself stretched on a bed in the outer apartment, and Pleyel, with two female servants standing beside it. All the fury and scorn which the countenance of the former lately expressed, had now disappeared, and was succeeded by the most tender anxiety. As soon as he perceived that my senses were returned to me, he clasped his hands, and exclaimed, "God be thanked! you are once more alive. I had almost despaired of your recovery. I fear I have been precipitate and unjust. My senses must have been the victims of some inexplicable and momentary phrenzy. Forgive me, I beseech you, forgive my reproaches. I would purchase conviction of your purity, at the price of my existence here and hereafter."

He once more, in a tone of the most fervent tenderness, besought me to be composed, and then left me to the care of the women.

Chapter XIII.

Here was wrought a surprizing change in my friend. What was it that had shaken conviction so firm? Had any thing occurred during my fit, adequate to produce so total an alteration? My attendants informed me that he had not left my apartment; that the unusual duration of my fit, and the failure, for a time, of all the means used for my recovery, had filled him with grief and dismay. Did he regard the effect which his reproaches had produced as a proof of my sincerity?

In this state of mind, I little regarded my languors of body. I rose and requested an interview with him before my departure, on which I was resolved, notwithstanding his earnest solicitation to spend the night at his house. He complied with my request. The tenderness which he had lately betrayed, had now disappeared, and he once more relapsed into a chilling solemnity.

I told him that I was preparing to return to my brother's; that I had come hither to vindicate my innocence from the foul aspersions which he had cast upon it. My pride had not taken refuge in silence or distance. I had not relied upon time, or the suggestions of his cooler thoughts, to confute his charges. Conscious as I was that I was perfectly guiltless, and entertaining some value for his good opinion, I could not prevail upon myself to believe that my efforts to make my innocence manifest, would be fruitless. Adverse appearances might be numerous and specious, but they were unquestionably false. I was willing to believe him sincere, that he made no charges which he himself did not believe; but these charges were destitute of truth. The grounds of his opinion were fallacious; and I desired an opportunity of detecting their fallacy. I entreated him to be explicit, and to give me a detail of what he had heard, and what he had seen.

At these words, my companion's countenance grew darker. He appeared to be struggling with his rage. He opened his lips to speak, but his accents died away ere they were formed. This conflict lasted for some minutes, but his fortitude was finally successful. He spoke as follows:

"I would fain put an end to this hateful scene: what I shall say, will be breath idly and unprofitably consumed. The clearest narrative will add nothing to your present knowledge. You are acquainted with the grounds of my opinion, and yet you avow yourself innocent: Why then should I rehearse these grounds? You are apprized of the character of Carwin: why then should I enumerate the discoveries which I have made respecting him? Yet, since it is your request; since, considering the limitedness of human faculties, some error may possibly lurk in those appearances which I have witnessed, I will briefly relate what I know.

"Need I dwell upon the impressions which your conversation and deportment originally made upon me? We parted in childhood; but our intercourse, by letter, was copious and uninterrupted. How fondly did I anticipate a meeting with one whom her letters had previously taught me to consider as the first of women, and how fully realized were the expectations I had formed!

"Here, said I, is a being, after whom sages may model their transcendent intelligence, and painters, their ideal beauty. Here is exemplified, that union between intellect and form, which has hitherto existed only in the conceptions of the poet. I have watched your eyes; my attention has hung upon your lips. I have questioned whether the enchantments of your voice were more conspicuous in the intricacies of melody, or the emphasis of rhetoric. I have marked the transitions of your discourse, the felicities of your expression, your refined argumentation, and glowing imagery; and been forced to acknowledge, that all delights were meagre and contemptible, compared with those connected with the audience and sight of you. I have contemplated your principles, and been astonished at the solidity of their foundation, and the perfection of their structure. I have traced you to your home. I have viewed you in relation to your servants, to your family, to your neighbours, and to the world. I have seen by what skilful arrangements you facilitate the performance of the most arduous and complicated duties; what daily accessions of strength your judicious discipline bestowed upon your memory; what correctness and abundance of knowledge was daily experienced by your unwearied application to books, and to writing. If she that possesses so much in the bloom of youth, will go on accumulating her stores, what said I, is the picture she will display at a mature age?

"You know not the accuracy of my observation. I was desirous that others should profit by an example so rare. I therefore noted down, in writing, every particular of your conduct. I was anxious to benefit by an opportunity so seldom afforded us. I laboured not to omit the slightest shade, or the most petty line in your portrait. Here there was no other task incumbent on me but to copy; there was no need to exaggerate or overlook, in order to produce a more unexceptionable pattern. Here was a combination of harmonies and graces, incapable of dimunition or accession without injury to its completeness.

"I found no end and no bounds to my task. No display of a scene like this could be chargeable with redundancy or superfluity. Even the colour of a shoe, the knot of a ribband, or your attitude in plucking a rose, were of moment to be recorded. Even the arrangements of your breakfast-table and your toilet have been amply displayed.

"I know that mankind are more easily enticed to virtue by example than by precept. I know that the absoluteness of a model, when supplied by invention, diminishes its salutary influence, since it is useless, we think, to strive after that which we know to be beyond our reach. But the picture which I drew was not a phantom; as a model, it was devoid of imperfection; and to aspire to that height which had been really attained, was by no means unreasonable. I had another and more interesting object in view. One existed who claimed all my tenderness. Here, in all its parts, was a model worthy of assiduous study, and indefatigable imitation. I called upon her, as she wished to secure and enhance my esteem, to mould her thoughts, her words, her countenance, her actions, by this pattern.

"The task was exuberant of pleasure, and I was deeply engaged in it, when an imp of mischief was let loose in the form of Carwin. I admired his powers and accomplishments. I did not wonder that they were admired by you. On the rectitude of your judgment, however, I relied to keep this admiration within discreet and scrupulous bounds. I assured myself, that the strangeness of his deportment, and the obscurity of his life, would teach you caution. Of all errors, my knowledge of your character informed me that this was least likely to befall you.

"You were powerfully affected by his first appearance; you were bewitched by his countenance and his tones; your description was ardent and pathetic: I listened to you with some emotions of surprize. The portrait you drew in his absence, and the intensity with which you mused upon it, were new and unexpected incidents. They bespoke a sensibility somewhat too vivid; but from which, while subjected to the guidance of an understanding like yours, there was nothing to dread.

"A more direct intercourse took place between you. I need not apologize for the solicitude which I entertained for your safety. He that gifted me with perception of excellence, compelled me to love it. In the midst of danger and pain, my contemplations have ever been cheered by your image. Every object in competition with you, was worthless and trivial. No price was too great by which your safety could be purchased. For that end, the sacrifice of ease, of health, and even of life, would cheerfully have been made by me. What wonder then, that I scrutinized the sentiments and deportment of this man with ceaseless vigilance; that I watched your words and your looks when he was present; and that I extracted cause for deepest inquietudes, from every token which you gave of having put your happiness in this man's keeping?

"I was cautious in deciding. I recalled the various conversations in which the topics of love and marriage had been discussed. As a woman, young, beautiful, and independent, it behoved you to have fortified your mind with just principles on this subject. Your principles were eminently just. Had not their rectitude and their firmness been attested by your treatment of that specious seducer Dashwood? These principles, I was prone to believe, exempted you from danger in this new state of things. I was not the last to pay my homage to the unrivalled capacity, insinuation, and eloquence of this man. I have disguised, but could never stifle the conviction, that his eyes and voice had a witchcraft in them, which rendered him truly formidable: but I reflected on the ambiguous expression of his countenance—an ambiguity which you were the first to remark; on the cloud which obscured his character; and on the suspicious nature of that concealment which he studied; and concluded you to be safe. I denied the obvious construction to appearances. I referred your conduct to some principle which had not been hitherto disclosed, but which was reconcileable with those already known.

"I was not suffered to remain long in this suspense. One evening, you may recollect, I came to your house, where it was my purpose, as usual, to lodge, somewhat earlier than ordinary. I spied a light in your chamber as I approached from the outside, and on inquiring of Judith, was informed that you were writing. As your kinsman and friend, and fellow lodger, I thought I had a right to be familiar. You were in your chamber, but your employment and the time were such as to make it no infraction of decorum to follow you thither. The spirit of mischievous gaiety possessed me. I proceeded on tiptoe. You did not perceive my entrance; and I advanced softly till I was able to overlook your shoulder.

"I had gone thus far in error, and had no power to recede. How cautiously should we guard against the first inroads of temptation! I knew that to pry into your papers was criminal; but I reflected that no sentiment of yours was of a nature which made it your interest to conceal it. You wrote much more than you permitted your friends to peruse. My curiosity was strong, and I had only to throw a glance upon the paper, to secure its gratification. I should never have deliberately committed an act like this. The slightest obstacle would have repelled me; but my eye glanced almost spontaneously upon the paper. I caught only parts of sentences; but my eyes comprehended more at a glance, because the characters were short-hand. I lighted on the words *summer-house, midnight,* and made out a passage which spoke of the propriety and of the effects to be expected from *another* interview. All this passed in less than a moment. I then checked myself, and made myself known to you, by a tap upon your shoulder.

"I could pardon and account for some trifling alarm, but your trepidation and blushes were excessive. You hurried the paper out of sight, and seemed too anxious to discover whether I knew the contents to allow yourself to make any inquiries. I wondered at these appearances of consternation, but did not reason on them until I had retired. When alone, these incidents suggested themselves to my reflections anew.

"To what scene, or what interview, I asked, did you allude? Your disappearance on a former evening, my tracing you to the recess in the bank, your silence on my first and second call, your vague answers and invincible embarrassment, when you, at length, ascended the hill, I recollected with new surprize. Could this be the summer-house alluded to? A certain timidity and consciousness had generally attended you, when this incident and this recess had been the subjects of conversation. Nay, I imagined that the last time that adventure was mentioned, which happened in the presence of Carwin, the countenance of the latter betrayed some emotion. Could the interview have been with him?

"This was an idea calculated to rouse every faculty to contemplation. An interview at that hour, in this darksome retreat, with a man of this mysterious but formidable character; a clandestine interview, and one which you afterwards endeavoured with so much solicitude to conceal! It was a fearful and portentous occurrence. I could not measure his power, or fathom his designs. Had he rifled from you the secret of your love, and reconciled you to concealment and nocturnal meetings? I scarcely ever spent a night of more inquietude.

"I knew not how to act. The ascertainment of this man's character and views seemed to be, in the first place, necessary. Had he openly preferred his suit to you, we should have been impowered to make direct inquiries; but since he had chosen this obscure path, it seemed reasonable to infer that his character was exceptionable. It, at least, subjected us to the necessity of resorting to other means of information. Yet the improbability that you should commit a deed of such rashness, made me reflect anew upon the insufficiency of those grounds on which my suspicions had been built, and almost to condemn myself for harbouring them.

"Though it was mere conjecture that the interview spoken of had taken place with Carwin, yet two ideas occurred to involve me in the most painful doubts. This man's reasonings might be so specious, and his artifices so profound, that, aided by the passion which you had conceived for him, he had finally succeeded; or his situation might be such as to justify the secrecy which you maintained. In neither case did my wildest reveries suggest to me, that your honor had been forfeited.

"I could not talk with you on this subject. If the imputation was false, its atrociousness would have justly drawn upon me your resentment, and I must have explained by what facts it had been suggested. If it were true, no benefit would follow from the mention of it. You had chosen to conceal it for some reasons, and whether these reasons were true or false, it was proper to discover and remove them in the first place. Finally, I acquiesced in the least painful supposition, trammelled as it was with perplexities, that Carwin was upright, and that, if the reasons of your silence were known, they would be found to be just.

Chapter XIV.

"Three days have elapsed since this occurrence. I have been haunted by perpetual inquietude. To bring myself to regard Carwin without terror, and to acquiesce in the belief of your safety, was impossible. Yet to put an end to my doubts, seemed to be impracticable. If some light could be reflected on the actual situation of this man, a direct path would present itself. If he were, contrary to the tenor of his conversation, cunning and malignant, to apprize you of this, would be to place you in security. If he were merely unfortunate and innocent, most readily would I espouse his cause; and if his intentions were upright with regard to you, most eagerly would I sanctify your choice by my approbation.

"It would be vain to call upon Carwin for an avowal of his deeds. It was better to know nothing, than to be deceived by an artful tale. What he was unwilling to communicate, and this unwillingness had been repeatedly manifested, could never be extorted from him. Importunity might be appeased, or imposture effected by fallacious representations. To the rest of the world he was unknown. I had often made him the subject of discourse; but a glimpse of his figure in the street was the sum of their knowledge who knew most. None had ever seen him before, and received as new, the information which my intercourse with him in Valencia, and my present intercourse, enabled me to give.

"Wieland was your brother. If he had really made you the object of his courtship, was not a brother authorized to interfere and demand from him the confession of his views? Yet what were the grounds on which I had reared this supposition? Would they justify a measure like this? Surely not.

"In the course of my restless meditations, it occurred to me, at length, that my duty required me to speak to you, to confess the indecorum of which I had been guilty, and to state the reflections to which it had led me. I was prompted by no mean or selfish views. The heart within my breast was not more precious than your safety: most cheerfully would I have interposed my life between you and danger. Would you cherish resentment at my conduct? When acquainted with the motive which produced it, it would not only exempt me from censure, but entitle me to gratitude.

"Yesterday had been selected for the rehearsal of the newly-imported tragedy. I promised to be present. The state of my thoughts but little qualified me for a performer or auditor in such a scene; but I reflected that, after it was finished, I should return home with you, and should then enjoy an opportunity of discoursing with you fully on this topic. My resolution was not formed without a remnant of doubt, as to its propriety. When I left this house to perform the visit I had promised, my mind was full of apprehension and despondency. The dubiousness of the event of our conversation, fear that my interference was too late to secure your peace, and the uncertainty to which hope gave birth, whether I had not erred in believing you devoted to this man, or, at least, in imagining that he had obtained your consent to midnight conferences, distracted me with contradictory opinions, and repugnant emotions.

"I can assign no reason for calling at Mrs. Baynton's. I had seen her in the morning, and knew her to be well. The concerted hour had nearly arrived, and yet I turned up the street which leads to her house, and dismounted at her door. I entered the parlour and threw myself in a chair. I saw and inquired for no one. My whole frame was overpowered by dreary and comfortless sensations. One idea possessed me wholly; the inexpressible importance of unveiling the designs and character of Carwin, and the utter improbability that this ever would be effected. Some instinct induced me to lay my hand upon a newspaper. I had perused all the general intelligence it contained in the morning, and at the same spot. The act was rather mechanical than voluntary.

"I threw a languid glance at the first column that presented itself. The first words which I read, began with the offer of a reward of three hundred guineas for the apprehension of a convict under sentence of death, who had escaped from Newgate prison in Dublin. Good heaven! how every fibre of my frame tingled when I proceeded to read that the name of the criminal was Francis Carwin!

"The descriptions of his person and address were minute. His stature, hair, complexion, the extraordinary position and arrangement of his features, his aukward and disproportionate form, his gesture and gait, corresponded perfectly with those of our mysterious visitant. He had been found guilty in two indictments. One for the murder of the Lady Jane Conway, and the other for a robbery committed on the person of the honorable Mr. Ludloe.

"I repeatedly perused this passage. The ideas which flowed in upon my mind, affected me like an instant transition from death to life. The purpose dearest to my heart was thus effected, at a time and by means the least of all others within the scope of my foresight. But what purpose? Carwin was detected. Acts of the blackest and most sordid guilt had been committed by him. Here was evidence which imparted to my understanding the most luminous certainty. The name, visage, and deportment, were the same. Between the time of his escape, and his appearance among us, there was a sufficient agreement. Such was the man with whom I suspected you to maintain a clandestine correspondence. Should I not haste to snatch you from the talons of this vulture? Should I see you rushing to the verge of a dizzy precipice, and not stretch forth a hand to pull you back? I had no need to deliberate. I thrust the paper in my pocket, and resolved to obtain an immediate conference with you. For a time, no other image made its way to my understanding. At length, it occurred to me, that though the information I possessed was, in one sense, sufficient, yet if more could be obtained, more was desirable. This passage was copied from a British paper; part of it only, perhaps, was transcribed. The printer was in possession of the original.

"Towards his house I immediately turned my horse's head. He produced the paper, but I found nothing more than had already been seen. While busy in perusing it, the printer stood by my side. He noticed the object of which I was in search. 'Aye,' said he, 'that is a strange affair. I should never have met with it, had not Mr. Hallet sent to me the paper, with a particular request to republish that advertisement.'

"Mr. Hallet! What reasons could he have for making this request? Had the paper sent to him been accompanied by any information respecting the convict? Had he personal or extraordinary reasons for desiring its republication? This was to be known only in one way. I speeded to his house. In answer to my interrogations, he told me that Ludloe had formerly been in America, and that during his residence in this city, considerable intercourse had taken place between them. Hence a confidence arose, which has since been kept alive by occasional letters. He had lately received a letter from him, enclosing the newspaper from which this extract had been made. He put it into my hands, and pointed out the passages which related to Carwin.

"Ludloe confirms the facts of his conviction and escape; and adds, that he had reason to believe him to have embarked for America. He describes him in general terms, as the most incomprehensible and formidable among men; as engaged in schemes, reasonably suspected to be, in the highest degree, criminal, but such as no human intelligence is able to unravel: that his ends are pursued by means which leave it in doubt whether he be not in league with some infernal spirit: that his crimes have hitherto been perpetrated with the aid of some unknown but desperate accomplices: that he wages a perpetual war against the happiness of mankind, and sets his engines of destruction at work against every object that presents itself.

"This is the substance of the letter. Hallet expressed some surprize at the curiosity which was manifested by me on this occasion. I was too much absorbed by the ideas suggested by this letter, to pay attention to his remarks. I shuddered with the apprehension of the evil to which our indiscreet familiarity with this man had probably exposed us. I burnt with impatience to see you, and to do what in me lay to avert the calamity which threatened us. It was already five o'clock. Night was hastening, and there was no time to be lost. On leaving Mr. Hallet's house, who should meet me in the street, but Bertrand, the servant whom I left in Germany. His appearance and accoutrements bespoke him to have just alighted from a toilsome and long journey. I was not wholly without expectation of seeing him about this time, but no one was then more distant from my thoughts. You know what reasons I have for anxiety respecting scenes with which this man was conversant. Carwin was for a moment forgotten. In answer to my vehement inquiries, Bertrand produced a copious packet. I shall not at present mention its contents, nor the measures which they obliged me to adopt. I bestowed a brief perusal on these papers and having given some directions to Bertrand, resumed my purpose with regard to you. My horse I was obliged to resign to my servant, he being charged with a commission that required speed. The clock had struck ten, and Mettingen was five miles distant. I was to journey thither on foot. These circumstances only added to my expedition.

"As I passed swiftly along, I reviewed all the incidents accompanying the appearance and deportment of that man among us. Late events have been inexplicable and mysterious beyond any of which I have either read or heard. These events were coeval with Carwin's introduction. I am unable to explain their origin and mutual dependence; but I do not, on that account, believe them to have a supernatural origin. Is not this man the agent? Some of them seem to be propitious; but what should I think of those threats of assassination with which you were lately alarmed? Bloodshed is the trade, and horror is the element of this man. The process by which the sympathies of nature are extinguished in our hearts, by which evil is made our good, and by which we are made susceptible of no activity but in the infliction, and no joy but in the spectacle of woes, is an obvious process. As to an alliance with evil geniuses, the power and the malice of dæmons have been a thousand times exemplified in human beings. There are no devils but those which are begotten upon selfishness, and reared by cunning.

"Now, indeed, the scene was changed. It was not his secret poniard that I dreaded. It was only the success of his efforts to make you a confederate in your own destruction, to make your will the instrument by which he might bereave you of liberty and honor.

"I took, as usual, the path through your brother's ground. I ranged with celerity and silence upon the bank. I approached the fence, which divides Wieland's estate from yours. The recess in the bank being near this line, it being necessary for me to pass near it, my mind being tainted with inveterate suspicions concerning you; suspicions which were indebted for their strength to incidents connected with this spot; what wonder that it seized upon my thoughts?

"I leaped on the fence; but before I descended on the opposite side, I paused to survey the scene. Leaves dropping with dew, and glistening in the moon's rays, with no moving object to molest the deep repose, filled me with security and hope. I left the station at length, and tended forward. You were probably at rest. How should I communicate without alarming you, the intelligence of my arrival? An immediate interview was to be procured. I could not bear to think that a minute should be lost by remissness or hesitation. Should I knock at the door? or should I stand under your chamber windows, which I perceived to be open, and awaken you by my calls?

"These reflections employed me, as I passed opposite to the summerhouse. I had scarcely gone by, when my ear caught a sound unusual at this time and place. It was almost too faint and too transient to allow me a distinct perception of it. I stopped to listen; presently it was heard again, and now it was somewhat in a louder key. It was laughter; and unquestionably produced by a female voice. That voice was familiar to my senses. It was yours.

"Whence it came, I was at first at a loss to conjecture; but this uncertainty vanished when it was heard the third time. I threw back my eyes towards the recess. Every other organ and limb was useless to me. I did not reason on the subject. I did not, in a direct manner, draw my conclusions from the hour, the place, the hilarity which this sound betokened, and the circumstance of having a companion, which it no less incontestably proved. In an instant, as it were, my heart was invaded with cold, and the pulses of life at a stand.

"Why should I go further? Why should I return? Should I not hurry

to a distance from a sound, which, though formerly so sweet and de-
lectable, was now more hideous than the shrieks of owls?

"I had no time to yield to this impulse. The thought of approaching
and listening occurred to me. I had no doubt of which I was conscious.
Yet my certainty was capable of increase. I was likewise stimulated by
a sentiment that partook of rage. I was governed by a half-formed and
tempestuous resolution to break in upon your interview, and strike
you dead with my upbraiding.

"I approached with the utmost caution. When I reached the edge of
the bank immediately above the summer-house, I thought I heard
voices from below, as busy in conversation. The steps in the rock are
clear of bushy impediments. They allowed me to descend into a cavity
beside the building without being detected. Thus to lie in wait could
only be justified by the momentousness of the occasion."

Here Pleyel paused in his narrative, and fixed his eyes upon me.
Situated as I was, my horror and astonishment at this tale gave way to
compassion for the anguish which the countenance of my friend betrayed. I reflected on his force of understanding. I reflected on the
powers of my enemy. I could easily divine the substance of the conversation that was overheard. Carwin had constructed his plot in a
manner suited to the characters of those whom he had selected for his
victims. I saw that the convictions of Pleyel were immutable. I forbore
to struggle against the storm, because I saw that all struggles would be
fruitless. I was calm; but my calmness was the torpor of despair, and
not the tranquillity of fortitude. It was calmness invincible by any
thing that his grief and his fury could suggest to Pleyel. He resumed—

"Woman! wilt thou hear me further? Shall I go on to repeat the conversation? Is it shame that makes thee tongue-tied? Shall I go on? or art
thou satisfied with what has been already said?"

I bowed my head. "Go on," said I. "I make not this request in the
hope of undeceiving you. I shall no longer contend with my own
weakness. The storm is set loose, and I shall peaceably submit to
be driven by its fury. But go on. This conference will end only with
affording me a clearer foresight of my destiny; but that will be some
satisfaction, and I will not part without it."

Why, on hearing these words, did Pleyel hesitate? Did some

unlooked-for doubt insinuate itself into his mind? Was his belief suddenly shaken by my looks, or my words, or by some newly recollected circumstance? Whencesoever it arose, it could not endure the test of deliberation. In a few minutes the flame of resentment was again lighted up in his bosom. He proceeded with his accustomed vehemence—

"I hate myself for this folly. I can find no apology for this tale. Yet I am irresistibly impelled to relate it. She that hears me is apprized of every particular. I have only to repeat her own words. She will listen with a tranquil air, and the spectacle of her obduracy will drive me to some desperate act. Why then should I persist! yet persist I must."

Again he paused. "No," said he, "it is impossible to repeat your avowals of love, your appeals to former confessions of your tenderness, to former deeds of dishonor, to the circumstances of the first interview that took place between you. It was on that night when I traced you to this recess. Thither had he enticed you, and there had you ratified an unhallowed compact by admitting him—

"Great God! Thou witnessedst the agonies that tore my bosom at that moment! Thou witnessedst my efforts to repel the testimony of my ears! It was in vain that you dwelt upon the confusion which my unlooked-for summons excited in you, the tardiness with which a suitable excuse occurred to you; your resentment that my impertinent intrusion had put an end to that charming interview. A disappointment for which you endeavoured to compensate yourself, by the frequency and duration of subsequent meetings.

"In vain you dwelt upon incidents of which you only could be conscious; incidents that occurred on occasions on which none beside your own family were witnesses. In vain was your discourse characterized by peculiarities inimitable of sentiment and language. My conviction was effected only by an accumulation of the same tokens. I yielded not but to evidence which took away the power to withhold my faith.

"My sight was of no use to me. Beneath so thick an umbrage, the darkness was intense. Hearing was the only avenue to information, which the circumstances allowed to be open. I was couched within three feet of you. Why should I approach nearer? I could not contend with your betrayer. What could be the purpose of a contest? You stood in no need of a protector. What could I do, but retire from the spot overwhelmed with confusion and dismay? I sought my chamber, and endeavoured to regain my composure. The door of the house, which I found open, your subsequent entrance, closing, and fastening it, and going into your chamber, which had been thus long deserted, were only confirmations of the truth.

"Why should I paint the tempestuous fluctuation of my thoughts between grief and revenge, between rage and despair? Why should I repeat my vows of eternal implacability and persecution, and the speedy recantation of these vows?

"I have said enough. You have dismissed me from a place in your esteem. What I think, and what I feel, is of no importance in your eyes. May the duty which I owe myself enable me to forget your existence. In a few minutes I go hence. Be the maker of your fortune, and may adversity instruct you in that wisdom, which education was unable to impart to you."

Those were the last words which Pleyel uttered. He left the room, and my new emotions enabled me to witness his departure without any apparent loss of composure. As I sat alone, I ruminated on these incidents. Nothing was more evident than that I had taken an eternal leave of happiness. Life was a worthless thing, separate from that good which had now been wrested from me; yet the sentiment that now possessed me had no tendency to palsy my exertions, and overbear my strength. I noticed that the light was declining, and perceived the propriety of leaving this house. I placed myself again in the chaise, and returned slowly towards the city.

Chapter XV.

Before I reached the city it was dusk. It was my purpose to spend the night at Mettingen. I was not solicitous, as long as I was attended by a faithful servant, to be there at an early hour. My exhausted strength required me to take some refreshment. With this view, and in order to pay respect to one whose affection for me was truly maternal, I stopped at Mrs. Baynton's. She was absent from home; but I had scarcely entered the house when one of her domestics presented me a letter. I opened and read as follows:

"To Clara Wieland,

"What shall I say to extenuate the misconduct of last night? It is my duty to repair it to the utmost of my power, but the only way in which it can be repaired, you will not, I fear, be prevailed on to adopt. It is by granting me an interview, at your own house, at eleven o'clock this night. I have no means of removing any fears that you may entertain of my designs, but my simple and solemn declarations. These, after what has passed between us, you may deem unworthy of confidence. I cannot help it. My folly and rashness has left me no other resource. I will be at your door by that hour. If you chuse to admit me to a conference, provided that conference has no witnesses, I will disclose to you particulars, the knowledge of which is of the utmost importance to your happiness. Farewell.

CARWIN."

What a letter was this! A man known to be an assassin and robber; one capable of plotting against my life and my fame; detected lurking in my chamber, and avowing designs the most flagitious and dreadful, now solicits me to grant him a midnight interview! To admit him alone into my presence! Could he make this request with the expectation of my compliance? What had he seen in me, that could justify him in admitting so wild a belief? Yet this request is preferred with the utmost gravity. It is not accompanied by an appearance of uncommon earnestness. Had the misconduct to which he alludes been a slight incivility, and the interview requested to take place in the midst of my friends, there would have been no extravagance in the tenor of this letter; but, as it was, the writer had surely been bereft of his reason.

I perused this epistle frequently. The request it contained might be called audacious or stupid, if it had been made by a different person; but from Carwin, who could not be unaware of the effect which it must naturally produce, and of the manner in which it would unavoidably be treated, it was perfectly inexplicable. He must have counted on the success of some plot, in order to extort my assent. None of those motives by which I am usually governed would ever have persuaded me to meet any one of his sex, at the time and place which he had prescribed. Much less would I consent to a meeting with a man, tainted with the most detestable crimes, and by whose arts my own safety had been so imminently endangered, and my happiness irretrievably destroyed. I shuddered at the idea that such a meeting was possible. I felt some reluctance to approach a spot which he still visited and haunted.

Such were the ideas which first suggested themselves on the perusal of the letter. Meanwhile, I resumed my journey. My thoughts still dwelt upon the same topic. Gradually from ruminating on this epistle, I reverted to my interview with Pleyel. I recalled the particulars of the dialogue to which he had been an auditor. My heart sunk anew on viewing the inextricable complexity of this deception, and the inauspicious concurrence of events, which tended to confirm him in his error. When he approached my chamber door, my terror kept me mute. He put his ear, perhaps, to the crevice, but it caught the sound of nothing human. Had I called, or made any token that denoted some one to be within, words would have ensued: and as omnipresence was impossible, this discovery, and the artless narrative of what had just passed, would have saved me from his murderous invectives. He went into his chamber, and after some interval, I stole across the entry and down the stairs, with inaudible steps. Having secured the outer doors, I returned with less circumspection. He heard me not when I descended; but my returning steps were easily distinguished. Now, he thought, was the guilty interview at an end. In what other way was it possible for him to construe these signals?

How fallacious and precipitate was my decision! Carwin's plot owed its success to a coincidence of events scarcely credible. The balance was swayed from its equipoise by a hair. Had I even begun the conversation with an account of what befel me in my chamber, my previous interview with Wieland would have taught him to suspect me of imposture; yet, if I were discoursing with this ruffian, when Pleyel touched the lock of my chamber door, and when he shut his own door with so much violence, how, he might ask, should I be able to relate these incidents? Perhaps he had withheld the knowledge of these circumstances from my brother from whom, therefore, I could not obtain it, so that my innocence would have thus been irresistibly demonstrated.

The first impulse which flowed from these ideas was to return upon my steps, and demand once more an interview, but he was gone: his parting declarations were remembered.

Pleyel, I exclaimed, thou art gone for ever! Are thy mistakes beyond the reach of detection? Am I helpless in the midst of this snare? The plotter is at hand. He even speaks in the style of penitence. He solicits an interview which he promises shall end in the disclosure of something momentous to my happiness. What can he say which will avail to turn aside this evil? But why should his remorse be feigned? I have done him no injury. His wickedness is fertile only of despair; and the billows of remorse will some time overbear him. Why may not this event have already taken place? Why should I refuse to see him?

This idea was present, as it were, for a moment. I suddenly recoiled from it, confounded at that frenzy which could give even momentary harbour to such a scheme; yet presently it returned. At length I even conceived it to deserve deliberation. I questioned whether it was not proper to admit, at a lonely spot, in a sacred hour, this man of tremendous and inscrutable attributes, this performer of horrid deeds, and whose presence was predicted to call down unheard-of and unutterable horrors.

What was it that swayed me? I felt myself divested of the power to will contrary to the motives that determined me to seek his presence. My mind seemed to be split into separate parts, and these parts to have entered into furious and implacable contention. These tumults gradually subsided. The reasons why I should confide in that interposition which had hitherto defended me; in those tokens of compunction which this letter contained; in the efficacy of this interview to restore its spotlessness to my character, and banish all illusions from the mind of my friend, continually acquired new evidence and new strength.

What should I fear in his presence? This was unlike an artifice intended to betray me into his hands. If it were an artifice, what purpose would it serve? The freedom of my mind was untouched, and that freedom would defy the assaults of blandishments or magic. Force I was not able to repel. On the former occasion my courage, it is true, had failed at the imminent approach of danger; but then I had not enjoyed opportunities of deliberation; I had foreseen nothing; I was sunk into imbecility by my previous thoughts; I had been the victim of recent disappointments and anticipated ills: Witness my infatuation in opening the closet in opposition to divine injunctions.

Now, perhaps, my courage was the offspring of a no less erring principle. Pleyel was forever lost to me. I strove in vain to assume his person, and suppress my resentment; I strove in vain to believe in the assuaging influence of time, to look forward to the birth-day of new hopes, and the re-exaltation of that luminary, of whose effulgencies I had so long and liberally partaken.

What had I to suffer worse than was already inflicted?

Was not Carwin my foe? I owed my untimely fate to his treason. Instead of dying from his presence, ought I not to devote all my faculties to the gaining of an interview, and compel him to repair the ills of which he has been the author? Why should I suppose him impregnable to argument? Have I not reason on my side, and the power of imparting conviction? Cannot he be made to see the justice of unravelling the maze in which Pleyel is bewildered?

He may, at least, be accessible to fear. Has he nothing to fear from the rage of an injured woman? But suppose him inaccessible to such inducements, suppose him to persist in all his flagitious purposes; are not the means of defence and resistance in my power?

In the progress of such thoughts, was the resolution at last formed. I hoped that the interview was sought by him for a laudable end; but, be that as it would, I trusted that, by energy of reasoning or of action, I should render it auspicious, or, at least, harmless.

Such a determination must unavoidably fluctuate. The poet's chaos was no unapt emblem of my state of mind. A torment was awakened in my bosom, which I foresaw would end only when this interview was past, and its consequences fully experienced. Hence my impatience for the arrival of the hour prescribed by Carwin.

Meanwhile, my meditations were tumultuously active. New impediments to the execution of the scheme were speedily suggested. I had apprized Catharine of my intention to spend this and many future nights with her. Her husband was informed of this arrangement, and had zealously approved it. Eleven o'clock exceeded their hour of retiring. What excuse should I form for changing my plan? Should I shew this letter to Wieland, and submit myself to his direction? But I knew in what way he would decide. He would fervently dissuade me from going. Nay, would he not do more? He was apprized of the offences of Carwin, and of the reward offered for his apprehension. Would he not seize this opportunity of executing justice on a criminal?

This idea was new. I was plunged once more into doubt. Did not equity enjoin me thus to facilitate his arrest? No. I disdained the office of betrayer. Carwin was unapprized of his danger, and his intentions were possibly beneficent. Should I station guards about the house, and make an act, intended perhaps for my benefit, instrumental to his own destruction? Wieland might be justified in thus employing the knowledge which I should impart, but I, by imparting it, should pollute myself with more hateful crimes than those undeservedly imputed to me. This scheme, therefore, I unhesitatingly rejected. The views with which I should return to my own house, it would therefore be necessary to conceal. Yet some pretext must be invented. I had never been initiated into the trade of lying. Yet what but falshood was a deliberate suppression of the truth? To deceive by silence or by words is the same.

Yet what would a lie avail me? What pretext would justify this change in my plan? Would it not tend to confirm the imputations of Pleyel? That I should voluntarily return to an house in which honor and life had so lately been endangered, could be explained in no way favorable to my integrity.

These reflections, if they did not change, at least suspended my decision. In this state of uncertainty I alighted at the *Hut*. We gave this name to the house tenanted by the farmer and his servants, and which was situated on the verge of my brother's ground, and at a considerable distance from the mansion. The path to the mansion was planted by a double row of walnuts. Along this path I proceeded alone. I entered the parlour, in which a light was just expiring in the socket. There was no one in the room. I perceived by the clock that stood against the wall, that it was near eleven. The lateness of the hour startled me. What had become of the family? They were usually retired an hour before this; but the unextinguished taper, and the unbarred door were indications that they had not retired. I again returned to the hall, and passed from one room to another, but still encountered not a human being.

I imagined that, perhaps, the lapse of a few minutes would explain these appearances. Meanwhile I reflected that the preconcerted hour had arrived. Carwin was perhaps awaiting my approach. Should I immediately retire to my own house, no one would be apprized of my proceeding. Nay, the interview might pass, and I be enabled to return in half an hour. Hence no necessity would arise for dissimulation.

I was so far influenced by these views that I rose to execute this design; but again the unusual condition of the house occurred to me, and some vague solicitude as to the condition of the family. I was nearly certain that my brother had not retired; but by what motives he could be induced to desert his house thus unseasonably, I could by no means divine. Louisa Conway, at least, was at home, and had, probably, retired to her chamber; perhaps she was able to impart the information I wanted.

I went to her chamber and found her asleep.

She was delighted and surprized at my arrival, and told me with how much impatience and anxiety my brother and his wife had waited my coming. They were fearful that some mishap had befallen me, and had remained up longer than the usual period. Notwithstanding the lateness of the hour, Catharine would not resign the hope of seeing me. Louisa said she had left them both in the parlour, and she knew of no cause for their absence.

As yet I was not without solicitude on account of their personal safety. I was far from being perfectly at ease on that head, but entertained no distinct conception of the danger that impended over them. Perhaps to beguile the moments of my long protracted stay, they had gone to walk upon the bank. The atmosphere, though illuminated only by the star-light, was remarkably serene. Meanwhile the desireableness of an interview with Carwin again returned, and I finally resolved to seek it.

I passed with doubting and hasty steps along the path. My dwelling, seen at a distance, was gloomy and desolate. It had no inhabitant, for my servant, in consequence of my new arrangement, had gone to Mettingen. The temerity of this attempt began to shew itself in more vivid colours to my understanding. Whoever has pointed steel is not without arms; yet what must have been the state of my mind when I could meditate, without shuddering, on the use of a murderous weapon, and believe myself secure merely because I was capable of being made so by the death of another? Yet this was not my state. I felt as if I was rushing into deadly toils, without the power of pausing or receding.

Chapter XVI.

As soon as I arrived in sight of the front of the house, my attention was excited by a light from the window of my own chamber. No appearance could be less explicable. A meeting was expected with Carwin, but that he pre-occupied my chamber, and had supplied himself with light, was not to be believed. What motive could influence him to adopt this conduct? Could I proceed until this was explained? Perhaps, if I should proceed to a distance in front, some one would be visible. A sidelong but feeble beam from the window, fell upon the piny copse which skirted the bank. As I eyed it, it suddenly became mutable, and after flitting to and fro, for a short time, it vanished. I turned my eye again toward the window, and perceived that the light was still there; but the change which I had noticed was occasioned by a change in the position of the lamp or candle within. Hence, that some person was there was an unavoidable inference.

I paused to deliberate on the propriety of advancing. Might I not advance cautiously, and, therefore, without danger? Might I not knock at the door, or call, and be apprized of the nature of my visitant before I entered? I approached and listened at the door, but could hear nothing. I knocked at first timidly, but afterwards with loudness. My signals were unnoticed. I stepped back and looked, but the light was no longer discernible. Was it suddenly extinguished by a human agent? What purpose but concealment was intended? Why was the illumination produced, to be thus suddenly brought to an end? And why, since some one was there, had silence been observed?

These were questions, the solution of which may be readily supposed to be entangled with danger. Would not this danger, when measured by a woman's fears, expand into gigantic dimensions? Menaces of death; the stunning exertions of a warning voice; the known and unknown attributes of Carwin; our recent interview in this chamber; the pre-appointment of a meeting at this place and hour, all thronged into my memory. What was to be done?

Courage is no definite or stedfast principle. Let that man who shall purpose to assign motives to the actions of another, blush at his folly and forbear. Not more presumptuous would it be to attempt the classification of all nature, and the scanning of supreme intelligence. I gazed for a minute at the window, and fixed my eyes, for a second minute, on the ground. I drew forth from my pocket, and opened, a penknife. This, said I, be my safe-guard and avenger. The assailant shall perish, or myself shall fall.

I had locked up the house in the morning, but had the key of the kitchen door in my pocket. I, therefore, determined to gain access behind. Thither I hastened, unlocked and entered. All was lonely, darksome, and waste. Familiar as I was with every part of my dwelling, I easily found my way to a closet, drew forth a taper, a flint, tinder, and steel, and, in a moment as it were, gave myself the guidance and protection of light.

What purpose did I meditate? Should I explore my way to my chamber, and confront the being who had dared to intrude into this recess, and had laboured for concealment? By putting out the light did he seek to hide himself, or mean only to circumvent my incautious steps? Yet was it not more probable that he desired my absence by thus encouraging the supposition that the house was unoccupied? I would see this man in spite of all impediments; ere I died, I would see his face, and summon him to penitence and retribution; no matter at what cost an interview was purchased. Reputation and life might be wrested from me by another, but my rectitude and honor were in my own keeping, and were safe.

I proceeded to the foot of the stairs. At such a crisis my thoughts may be supposed at no liberty to range; yet vague images rushed into my mind, of the mysterious interposition which had been experienced on the last night. My case, at present, was not dissimilar; and, if my angel were not weary of fruitless exertions to save, might not a new warning be expected? Who could say whether his silence were ascribable to the absence of danger, or to his own absence?

In this state of mind, no wonder that a shivering cold crept through my veins; that my pause was prolonged; and, that a fearful glance was thrown backward.

Alas! my heart droops, and my fingers are enervated; my ideas are vivid, but my language is faint; now know I what it is to entertain incommunicable sentiments. The chain of subsequent incidents is drawn through my mind, and being linked with those which forewent, by turns rouse up agonies and sink me into hopelessness.

Yet I will persist to the end. My narrative may be invaded by inaccuracy and confusion; but if I live no longer, I will, at least, live to complete it. What but ambiguities, abruptnesses, and dark transitions, can be expected from the historian who is, at the same time, the sufferer of these disasters?

I have said that I cast a look behind. Some object was expected to be seen, or why should I have gazed in that direction? Two senses were at once assailed. The same piercing exclamation of *hold! hold!* was uttered within the same distance of my ear. This it was that I heard. The airy undulation, and the shock given to my nerves, were real. Whether the spectacle which I beheld existed in my fancy or without, might be doubted.

I had not closed the door of the apartment I had just left. The staircase, at the foot of which I stood, was eight or ten feet from the door, and attached to the wall through which the door led. My view, therefore, was sidelong, and took in no part of the room.

Through this aperture was an head thrust and drawn back with so much swiftness, that the immediate conviction was, that thus much of a form, ordinarily invisible, had been unshrouded. The face was turned towards me. Every muscle was tense; the forehead and brows were drawn into vehement expression; the lips were stretched as in the act of shrieking, and the eyes emitted sparks, which, no doubt, if I had been unattended by a light, would have illuminated like the corruscations of a meteor. The sound and the vision were present, and departed together at the same instant; but the cry was blown into my ear, while the face was many paces distant.

This face was well suited to a being whose performances exceeded the standard of humanity, and yet its features were akin to those I had before seen. The image of Carwin was blended in a thousand ways with the stream of my thoughts. This visage was, perhaps, pourtrayed by my fancy. If so, it will excite no surprize that some of his lineaments were now discovered. Yet affinities were few and unconspicuous, and were lost amidst the blaze of opposite qualities.

What conclusion could I form? Be the face human or not, the intimation was imparted from above. Experience had evinced the benignity of that being who gave it. Once he had interposed to shield me from harm, and subsequent events demonstrated the usefulness of that interposition. Now was I again warned to forbear. I was hurrying to the verge of the same gulf, and the same power was exerted to recall my steps. Was it possible for me not to obey? Was I capable of holding on in the same perilous career? Yes. Even of this I was capable!

The intimation was imperfect: it gave no form to my danger, and prescribed no limits to my caution. I had formerly neglected it, and yet escaped. Might I not trust to the same issue? This idea might possess, though imperceptibly, some influence. I persisted; but it was not merely on this account. I cannot delineate the motives that led me on. I now speak as if no remnant of doubt existed in my mind as to the supernal origin of these sounds; but this is owing to the imperfection of my language, for I only mean that the belief was more permanent, and visited more frequently my sober meditations than its opposite. The immediate effects served only to undermine the foundations of my judgment and precipitate my resolutions.

I must either advance or return. I chose the former, and began to ascend the stairs. The silence underwent no second interruption. My chamber door was closed, but unlocked, and, aided by vehement efforts of my courage, I opened and looked in.

No hideous or uncommon object was discernible. The danger, indeed, might easily have lurked out of sight, have sprung upon me as I entered, and have rent me with his iron talons; but I was blind to this fate, and advanced, though cautiously, into the room.

Still every thing wore its accustomed aspect. Neither lamp nor candle was to be found. Now, for the first time, suspicions were suggested as to the nature of the light which I had seen. Was it possible to have been the companion of that supernatural visage; a meteorous resulgence producible at the will or him to whom that visage belonged, and partaking of the nature of that which accompanied my father's death?

The closet was near, and I remembered the complicated horrors of which it had been productive. Here, perhaps, was inclosed the source of my peril, and the gratification of my curiosity. Should I adventure once more to explore its recesses? This was a resolution not easily formed. I was suspended in thought: when glancing my eye on a table, I perceived a written paper. Carwin's hand was instantly recognized, and snatching up the paper, I read as follows:—

"There was folly in expecting your compliance with my invitation. Judge how I was disappointed in finding another in your place. I have waited, but to wait any longer would be perilous. I shall still seek an interview, but it must be at a different time and place: meanwhile, I will write this—How will you bear—How inexplicable will be this transaction!—An event so unexpected—a sight so horrible."

Such was this abrupt and unsatisfactory script. The ink was yet moist, the hand was that of Carwin. Hence it was to be inferred that he had this moment left the apartment, or was still in it. I looked back, on the sudden expectation of seeing him behind me.

What other did he mean? What transaction had taken place adverse to my expectations? What sight was about to be exhibited? I looked around me once more, but saw nothing which indicated strangeness. Again I remembered the closet, and was resolved to seek in that the solution of these mysteries. Here, perhaps, was inclosed the scene destined to awaken my horrors and baffle my foresight.

I have already said, that the entrance into this closet was beside my bed, which, on two sides, was closely shrouded by curtains. On that side nearest the closet, the curtain was raised. As I passed along I cast my eye thither. I started, and looked again. I bore a light in my hand, and brought it nearer my eyes, in order to dispel any illusive mists that might have hovered before them. Once more I fixed my eyes upon the bed, in hope that this more stedfast scrutiny would annihilate the object which before seemed to be there.

This then was the sight which Carwin had predicted! This was the event which my understanding was to find inexplicable! This was the fate which had been reserved for me, but which, by some untoward chance, had befallen on another!

I had not been terrified by empty menaces. Violation and death awaited my entrance into this chamber. Some inscrutable chance had led *her* hither before me, and the merciless fangs of which I was designed to be the prey, had mistaken their victim, and had fixed themselves in *her* heart. But where was my safety? Was the mischief exhausted or flown? The steps of the assassin had just been here; they could not be far off; in a moment he would rush into my presence, and I should perish under the same polluting and suffocating grasp!

My frame shook, and my knees were unable to support me. I gazed alternately at the closet door and at the door of my room. At one of these avenues would enter the exterminator of my honor and my life. I was prepared for defence; but now that danger was imminent, my means of defence, and my power to use them were gone. I was not qualified, by education and experience, to encounter perils like these: or, perhaps, I was powerless because I was again assaulted by surprize, and had not fortified my mind by foresight and previous reflection against a scene like this.

Fears for my own safety again yielded place to reflections on the scene before me. I fixed my eyes upon her countenance. My sister's well-known and beloved features could not be concealed by convulsion or lividness. What direful illusion led thee hither? Bereft of thee, what hold on happiness remains to thy offspring and thy spouse? To lose thee by common fate would have been sufficiently hard; but thus suddenly to perish—to become the prey of this ghastly death! How will a spectacle like this be endured by Wieland? To die beneath his grasp would not satisfy thy enemy. This was mercy to the evils which he previously made thee suffer! After these evils death was a boon which thou besoughtest him to grant. He entertained no enmity against thee: I was the object of his treason; but by some tremendous mistake his fury was misplaced. But how camest thou hither? and where was Wieland in thy hour of distress?

I approached the corpse: I lifted the still flexible hand, and kissed the lips which were breathless. Her flowing drapery was discomposed. I restored it to order, and seating myself on the bed, again fixed stedfast eyes upon her countenance. I cannot distinctly recollect the ruminations of that moment. I saw confusedly, but forcibly, that every hope was extinguished with the life of *Catharine*. All happiness and dignity must henceforth be banished from the house and name of Wieland: all that remained was to linger out in agonies a short existence; and leave to the world a monument of blasted hopes and changeable fortune. Pleyel was already lost to me; yet, while Catharine lived life was not a detestable possession: but now, severed from the companion of my infancy, the partaker of all my thoughts, my cares, and my wishes, I was like one set afloat upon a stormy sea, and hanging his safety upon a plank; night was closing upon him, and an unexpected surge had torn him from his hold and overwhelmed him forever.

CHAPTER XVII.

I had no inclination nor power to move from this spot. For more than an hour, my faculties and limbs seemed to be deprived of all activity. The door below creaked on its hinges, and steps ascended the stairs. My wandering and confused thoughts were instantly recalled by these sounds, and dropping the curtain of the bed, I moved to a part of the room where any one who entered should be visible; such are the vibrations of sentiment, that notwithstanding the seeming fulfilment of my fears, and increase of my danger, I was conscious, on this occasion, to no turbulence but that of curiosity.

At length he entered the apartment, and I recognized my brother. It was the same Wieland whom I had ever seen. Yet his features were pervaded by a new expression. I supposed him unacquainted with the fate of his wife, and his appearance confirmed this persuasion. A brow expanding into exultation I had hitherto never seen in him, yet such a brow did he now wear. Not only was he unapprized of the disaster that had happened, but some joyous occurrence had betided. What a reverse was preparing to annihilate his transitory bliss! No husband ever doated more fondly, for no wife ever claimed so boundless a devotion.

I was not uncertain as to the effects to flow from the discovery of her fate. I confided not at all in the efforts of his reason or his piety. There were few evils which his modes of thinking would not disarm of their sting; but here, all opiates to grief, and all compellers of patience were vain. This spectacle would be unavoidably followed by the outrages of desperation, and a rushing to death.

For the present, I neglected to ask myself what motive brought him hither. I was only fearful of the effects to flow from the sight of the dead. Yet could it be long concealed from him? Some time and speedily he would obtain this knowledge. No stratagems could considerably or usefully prolong his ignorance. All that could be sought was to take away the abruptness of the change, and shut out the confusion of despair, and the inroads of madness: but I knew my brother, and knew that all exertions to console him would be fruitless.

What could I say? I was mute, and poured forth those tears on his account, which my own unhappiness had been unable to extort. In the midst of my tears, I was not unobservant of his motions. These were of a nature to rouse some other sentiment than grief, or, at least, to mix with it a portion of astonishment.

His countenance suddenly became troubled. His hands were clasped with a force that left the print of his nails in his flesh. His eyes were fixed on my feet. His brain seemed to swell beyond its continent. He did not cease to breathe, but his breath was stifled into groans. I had never witnessed the hurricane of human passions. My element had, till lately, been all sunshine and calm. I was unconversant with the altitudes and energies of sentiment, and was transfixed with inexplicable horror by the symptoms I now beheld.

After a silence and a conflict which I could not interpret, he lifted his eyes to heaven, and in broken accents exclaimed, "This is too much! Any victim but this, and thy will be done. Have I not sufficiently attested my faith and my obedience? She that is gone, they that have perished, were linked with my soul by ties which only thy command would have broken; but here is sanctity and excellence surpassing human. This workmanship is thine, and it cannot be thy will to heap it into ruins."

Here suddenly unclasping his hands, he struck one of them against his forehead, and continued—"Wretch! who made thee quicksighted in the councils of thy Maker? Deliverance from mortal fetters is awarded to this being, and thou art the minister of this decree."

So saying, Wieland advanced towards me. His words and his motions were without meaning, except on one supposition. The death of Catharine was already known to him, and that knowledge, as might have been suspected, had destroyed his reason. I had feared nothing less; but now that I beheld the extinction of a mind the most luminous and penetrating that ever dignified the human form, my sensations were fraught with new and insupportable anguish.

I had not time to reflect in what way my own safety would be affected by this revolution, or what I had to dread from the wild conceptions of a madman. He advanced towards me. Some hollow noises were wafted by the breeze. Confused clamours were succeeded by many feet traversing the grass, and then crowding into the piazza.

These sounds suspended my brother's purpose, and he stood to listen. The signals multiplied and grew louder; perceiving this, he turned from me, and hurried out of my sight. All about me was pregnant with motives to astonishment. My sister's corpse, Wieland's frantic demeanour, and, at length, this crowd of visitants so little accorded with my foresight, that my mental progress was stopped. The impulse had ceased which was accustomed to give motion and order to my thoughts.

Footsteps thronged upon the stairs, and presently many faces shewed themselves within the door of my apartment. These looks were full of alarm and watchfulness. They pryed into corners as if in search of some fugitive; next their gaze was fixed upon me, and betokened all the vehemence of terror and pity. For a time I questioned whether these were not shapes and faces like that which I had seen at the bottom of the stairs, creatures of my fancy or airy existences.

My eye wandered from one to another, till at length it fell on a countenance which I well knew. It was that of Mr. Hallet. This man was a distant kinsman of my mother, venerable for his age, his uprightness, and sagacity. He had long discharged the functions of a magistrate and good citizen. If any terrors remained, his presence was sufficient to dispel them.

He approached, took my hand with a compassionate air, and said in a low voice, "Where, my dear Clara, are your brother and sister?" I made no answer, but pointed to the bed. His attendants drew aside the curtain, and while their eyes glazed with horror at the spectacle which they beheld, those of Mr. Hallet overflowed with tears.

After considerable pause, he once more turned to me. "My dear girl, this sight is not for you. Can you confide in my care, and that of Mrs. Baynton's? We will see performed all that circumstances require."

I made strenuous opposition to this request. I insisted on remaining near her till she were interred. His remonstrances, however, and my own feelings, shewed me the propriety of a temporary dereliction. Louisa stood in need of a comforter, and my brother's children of a nurse. My unhappy brother was himself an object of solicitude and care. At length, I consented to relinquish the corpse, and go to my brother's, whose house, I said, would need a mistress, and his children a parent.

During this discourse, my venerable friend struggled with his tears, but my last intimation called them forth with fresh violence. Meanwhile, his attendants stood round in mournful silence, gazing on me and at each other. I repeated my resolution, and rose to execute it; but he took my hand to detain me. His countenance betrayed irresolution and reluctance. I requested him to state the reason of his opposition to this measure. I entreated him to be explicit. I told him that my brother had just been there, and that I knew his condition. This misfortune had driven him to madness, and his offspring must not want a protector. If he chose, I would resign Wieland to his care; but his innocent and helpless babes stood in instant need of nurse and mother, and these offices I would by no means allow another to perform while I had life.

Every word that I uttered seemed to augment his perplexity and distress. At last he said, "I think, Clara, I have entitled myself to some regard from you. You have professed your willingness to oblige me. Now I call upon you to confer upon me the highest obligation in your power. Permit Mrs. Baynton to have the management of your brother's house for two or three days; then it shall be yours to act in it as you please. No matter what are my motives in making this request: perhaps I think your age, your sex, or the distress which this disaster must occasion, incapacitates you for the office. Surely you have no doubt of Mrs. Baynton's tenderness or discretion."

New ideas now rushed into my mind. I fixed my eyes stedfastly on Mr. Hallet. "Are they well?" said I. "Is Louisa well? Are Benjamin, and William, and Constantine, and Little Clara, are they safe? Tell me truly, I beseech you!"

"They are well," he replied;[19] "they are perfectly safe."

"Fear no effeminate weakness in me: I can bear to hear the truth. Tell me truly, are they well?"

He again assured me that they were well.

"What then," resumed I, "do you fear? Is it possible for any calamity to disqualify me for performing my duty to these helpless innocents? I am willing to divide the care of them with Mrs. Baynton; I shall be grateful for her sympathy and aid; but what should I be to desert them at an hour like this!"

I will cut short this distressful dialogue. I still persisted in my purpose, and he still persisted in his opposition. This excited my suspicions anew; but these were removed by solemn declarations of their safety. I could not explain this conduct in my friend; but at length consented to go to the city, provided I should see them for a few minutes at present, and should return on the morrow.

Even this arrangement was objected to. At length he told me they were removed to the city. Why were they removed, I asked, and whither? My importunities would not now be eluded. My suspicions were roused, and no evasion or artifice was sufficient to allay them. Many of the audience began to give vent to their emotions in tears. Mr. Hallet himself seemed as if the conflict were too hard to be longer sustained. Something whispered to my heart that havoc had been wider than I now witnessed. I suspected this concealment to arise from apprehensions of the effects which a knowledge of the truth would produce in me. I once more entreated him to inform me truly of their state. To enforce my entreaties, I put on an air of insensibility. "I can guess," said I, "what has happened—They are indeed beyond the reach of injury, for they are dead! Is it not so?" My voice faltered in spite of my courageous efforts.

"Yes," said he, "they are dead! Dead by the same fate, and by the same hand, with their mother!"

"Dead!" replied I; "what, all?"

"All!" replied he: "he spared *not one*!"

Allow me, my friends, to close my eyes upon the after-scene. Why should I protract a tale which I already begin to feel is too long? Over this scene at least let me pass lightly. Here, indeed, my narrative would be imperfect. All was tempestuous commotion in my heart and in my brain. I have no memory for ought but unconscious transitions and rueful sights. I was ingenious and indefatigable in the invention of torments. I would not dispense with any spectacle adapted to exasperate my grief. Each pale and mangled form I crushed to my bosom. Louisa, whom I loved with so ineffable a passion, was denied me at first, but my obstinacy conquered their reluctance.

They led the way into a darkened hall. A lamp pendant from the ceiling was uncovered, and they pointed to a table. The assassin had defrauded me of my last and miserable consolation. I sought not in her visage, for the tinge of the morning, and the lustre of heaven. These had vanished with life; but I hoped for liberty to print a last kiss upon her lips. This was denied me; for such had been the merciless blow that destroyed her, that not a *lineament remained!*

I was carried hence to the city. Mrs. Hallet was my companion and my nurse. Why should I dwell upon the rage of fever, and the effusions of delirium? Carwin was the phantom that pursued my dreams, the giant oppressor under whose arm I was for ever on the point of being crushed. Strenuous muscles were required to hinder my flight, and hearts of steel to withstand the eloquence of my fears. In vain I called upon them to look upward, to mark his sparkling rage and scowling contempt. All I sought was to fly from the stroke that was lifted. Then I heaped upon my guards the most vehement reproaches, or betook myself to wailings on the haplessness of my condition.

This malady, at length, declined, and my weeping friends began to look for my restoration. Slowly, and with intermitted beams, memory revisited me. The scenes that I had witnessed were revived, became the theme of deliberation and deduction, and called forth the effusions of more rational sorrow.

Chapter XVIII.

I had imperfectly recovered my strength, when I was informed of the arrival of my mother's brother, Thomas Cambridge. Ten years since, he went to Europe, and was a surgeon in the British forces in Germany, during the whole of the late war. After its conclusion, some connection that he had formed with an Irish officer, made him retire into Ireland. Intercourse had been punctually maintained by letters with his sister's children, and hopes were given that he would shortly return to his native country, and pass his old age in our society. He was now in an evil hour arrived.

I desired an interview with him for numerous and urgent reasons. With the first returns of my understanding I had anxiously sought information of the fate of my brother. During the course of my disease I had never seen him; and vague and unsatisfactory answers were returned to all my inquiries. I had vehemently interrogated Mrs. Hallet and her husband, and solicited an interview with this unfortunate man; but they mysteriously insinuated that his reason was still unsettled, and that his circumstances rendered an interview impossible. Their reserve on the particulars of this destruction, and the author of it, was equally invincible.

For some time, finding all my efforts fruitless, I had desisted from direct inquiries and solicitations, determined, as soon as my strength was sufficiently renewed, to pursue other means of dispelling my uncertainty. In this state of things my uncle's arrival and intention to visit me were announced. I almost shuddered to behold the face of this man. When I reflected on the disasters that had befallen us, I was half unwilling to witness that dejection and grief which would be disclosed in his countenance. But I believed that all transactions had been thoroughly disclosed to him, and confided in my importunity to extort from him the knowledge that I sought.

I had no doubt as to the person of our enemy; but the motives that urged him to perpetrate these horrors, the means that he used, and his present condition, were totally unknown. It was reasonable to expect some information on this head, from my uncle. I therefore waited his coming with impatience. At length, in the dusk of the evening, and in my solitary chamber, this meeting took place.

This man was our nearest relation, and had ever treated us with the affection of a parent. Our meeting, therefore, could not be without overflowing tenderness and gloomy joy. He rather encouraged than restrained the tears that I poured out in his arms, and took upon himself the task of comforter. Allusions to recent disasters could not be long omitted. One topic facilitated the admission of another. At length, I mentioned and deplored the ignorance in which I had been kept respecting my brother's destiny, and the circumstances of our misfortunes. I entreated him to tell me what was Wieland's condition, and what progress had been made in detecting or punishing the author of this unheard-of devastation.

"The author," said he, "Do you know the author?"

"Alas!" I answered, "I am too well acquainted with him. The story of the grounds of my suspicions would be painful and too long. I am not apprized of the extent of your present knowledge. There are none but Weiland, Pleyel, and myself, who are able to relate certain facts."

"Spare yourself the pain," said he. "All that Wieland and Pleyel can communicate, I know already. If any thing of the moment has fallen within your own exclusive knowledge, and the relation be not too arduous for your present strength, I confess I am desirous of hearing it. Perhaps you allude to one by the name of Carwin. I will anticipate your curiosity by saying, that since these disasters, no one has seen or heard of him. His agency is, therefore, a mystery still unsolved."

I readily complied with his request, and related as distinctly as I could, though in general terms, the events transacted in the summer-house and my chamber. He listened without apparent surprize to the tale of Pleyel's errors and suspicions, and with augmented seriousness, to my narrative of the warnings and inexplicable vision, and the letter found on the table. I waited for his comments.

"You gather from this," said he, "that Carwin is the author of all this misery?"

"Is it not," answered I, "an unavoidable inference? But what know you respecting it? Was it possible to execute this mischief without witness or coadjutor? I beseech you to relate to me, when and why Mr. Hallet was summoned to the scene, and by whom this disaster was first suspected or discovered. Surely, suspicion must have fallen upon some one, and pursuit was made."

My uncle rose from his seat, and traversed the floor with hasty steps. His eyes were fixed upon the ground, and he seemed buried in perplexity. At length he paused, and said with an emphatic tone, "It is true; the instrument is known. Carwin may have plotted, but the execution was another's. That other is found, and his deed is ascertained."

"Good heaven!" I exclaimed, "what say you? Was not Carwin the assassin? Could any hand but his have carried into act this dreadful purpose?"

"Have I not said," returned he, "that the performance was another's? Carwin, perhaps, or heaven, or insanity, prompted the murderer; but Carwin is unknown. The actual performer has, long since, been called to judgment and convicted, and is, at this moment, at the bottom of a dungeon loaded with chains."

I lifted my hands and eyes. "Who then is this assassin? By what means, and whither was he traced? What is the testimony of his guilt?"

"His own, corroborated with that of a servant-maid who spied the murder of the children from a closet where she was concealed. The magistrate returned from your dwelling to your brother's. He was employed in hearing and recording the testimony of the only witness, when the criminal himself, unexpected, unsolicited, unsought, entered the hall, acknowledged his guilt, and rendered himself up to justice.

"He has since been summoned to the bar. The audience was composed of thousands whom rumours of this wonderful event had attracted from the greatest distance. A long and impartial examination was made, and the prisoner was called upon for his defence. In compliance with this call he delivered an ample relation of his motives and actions." There he stopped.

I besought him to say who this criminal was, and what the instigations that compelled him. My uncle was silent. I urged this inquiry with new force. I reverted to my own knowledge, and sought in this some basis to conjecture. I ran over the scanty catalogue of the men whom I knew; I lighted on no one who was qualified for ministering to malice like this. Again I resorted to importunity. Had I ever seen the criminal? Was it sheer cruelty, or diabolical revenge that produced this overthrow?

He surveyed me, for a considerable time, and listened to my interrogations in silence. At length he spoke: "Clara, I have known thee by report, and in some degree by observation. Thou art a being of no vulgar sort. Thy friends have hitherto treated thee as a child. They meant well, but, perhaps, they were unacquainted with thy strength. I assure myself that nothing will surpass thy fortitude.

"Thou art anxious to know the destroyer of thy family, his actions, and his motives. Shall I call him to thy presence, and permit him to confess before thee? Shall I make him the narrator of his own tale?"

I started on my feet, and looked round me with fearful glances, as if the murderer was close at hand. "What do you mean?" said I; "put an end, I beseech you, to this suspence."

"Be not alarmed; you will never more behold the face of this criminal, unless he be gifted with supernatural strength, and sever like threads the constraint of links and bolts. I have said that the assassin was arraigned at the bar, and that the trial ended with a summons from the judge to confess or to vindicate his actions. A reply was immediately made with significance of gesture, and a tranquil majesty, which denoted less of humanity than godhead. Judges, advocates and auditors were panic-struck and breathless with attention. One of the hearers faithfully recorded the speech. There it is," continued he, putting a roll of papers in my hand, "you may read it at your leisure."

With these words my uncle left me alone. My curiosity refused me a moment's delay. I opened the papers, and read as follows.

Chapter XIX.

"Theodore Wieland, the prisoner at the bar, was now called upon for his defence. He looked around him for some time in silence, and with a mild countenance. At length he spoke:

" 'It is strange; I am known to my judges and my auditors. Who is there present a stranger to the character of Wieland? who knows him not as an husband—as a father—as a friend? yet here am I arraigned as a criminal. I am charged with diabolical malice; I am accused of the murder of my wife and my children.

" 'It is true, they were slain by me; they all perished by my hand. The task of vindication is ignoble. What is it that I am called to vindicate? and before whom?

" 'You know that they are dead, and that they were killed by me. What more would you have? Would you extort from me a statement of my motives? Have you failed to discover them already? You charge me with malice; but your eyes are not shut; your reason is still vigorous; your memory has not forsaken you. You know whom it is that you thus charge. The habits of his life are known to you; his treatment of his wife and his offspring is known to you; the soundness of his integrity, and the unchangeableness of his principles, are familiar to your apprehension; yet you persist in this charge! You lead me hither manacled as a felon; you deem me worthy of a vile and tormenting death!

" 'Who are they whom I have devoted to death? My wife—the little ones, that drew their being from me—that creature who, as she surpassed them in excellence, claimed a larger affection than those whom natural affinities bound to my heart. Think ye that malice could have urged me to this deed? Hide your audacious fronts from the scrutiny of heaven. Take refuge in some cavern unvisited by human eyes. Ye may deplore your wickedness or folly, but ye cannot expiate it.

" 'Think not that I speak for your sakes. Hug to your hearts this detestable infatuation. Deem me still a murderer, and drag me to untimely death. I make not an effort to dispel your illusion: I utter not a word to cure you of your sanguinary folly: but there are probably some in this assembly who have come from far: for their sakes, whose distance has disabled them from knowing me, I will tell what I have done, and why.

" 'It is needless to say that God is the object of my supreme passion. I have cherished, in his presence, a single and upright heart. I have thirsted for the knowledge of his will. I have burnt with ardour to approve my faith and my obedience.

" 'My days have been spent in searching for the revelation of that will; but my days have been mournful, because my search failed. I solicited direction: I turned on every side where glimmerings of light could be discovered. I have not been wholly uninformed; but my knowledge had always stopped short of certainty. Dissatisfaction has insinuated itself into all my thoughts. My purposes have been pure; my wishes indefatigable; but not till lately were these purposes thoroughly accomplished, and these wishes fully gratified.

" 'I thank thee, my father, for thy bounty; that thou didst not ask a less sacrifice than this; that thou placedst me in a condition to testify my submission to thy will! What have I withheld which it was thy pleasure to exact? Now may I, with dauntless and erect eye, claim my reward, since I have given thee the treasure of my soul.

" 'I was at my own house: it was late in the evening: my sister had gone to the city, but proposed to return. It was in expectation of her return that my wife and I delayed going to bed beyond the usual hour; the rest of the family, however, were retired.

" 'My mind was contemplative and calm; not wholly devoid of apprehension on account of my sister's safety. Recent events, not easily explained, had suggested the existence of some danger; but this danger was without a distinct form in our imagination, and scarcely ruffled our tranquillity.

" 'Time passed, and my sister did not arrive; her house is at some distance from mine, and though her arrangements had been made with a view to residing with us, it was possible that, through forgetfulness, or the occurrence of unforeseen emergencies, she had returned to her own dwelling.

" 'Hence it was conceived proper that I should ascertain the truth by going thither. I went. On my way my mind was full of those ideas which related to my intellectual condition. In the torrent of fervid conceptions, I lost sight of my purpose. Some times I stood still; some times I wandered from my path, and experienced some difficulty, on recovering from my fit of musing, to regain it.

" 'The series of my thoughts is easily traced. At first every vein beat with raptures known only to the man whose parental and conjugal love is without limits, and the cup of whose desires, immense as it is, overflows with gratification. I know not why emotions that were perpetual visitants should now have recurred with unusual energy. The transition was not new from sensations of joy to a consciousness of gratitude. The author of my being was likewise the dispenser of every gift with which that being was embellished. The service to which a benefactor like this was entitled, could not be circumscribed. My social sentiments were indebted to their alliance with devotion for all their value. All passions are base, all joys feeble, all energies malignant, which are not drawn from this source.

" 'For a time, my contemplations soared above earth and its inhabitants. I stretched forth my hands; I lifted my eyes, and exclaimed, O! that I might be admitted to thy presence; that mine were the supreme delight of knowing thy will, and of performing it! The blissful privilege of direct communication with thee, and of listening to the audible enunciation of thy pleasure!

"What task would I not undertake, what privation would I not cheerfully endure, to testify my love of thee? Alas! thou hidest thyself from my view: glimpses only of thy excellence and beauty are afforded me. Would that a momentary emanation from thy glory would visit me! that some unambiguous token of thy presence would salute my senses!

" 'In this mood, I entered the house of my sister. It was vacant. Scarcely had I regained recollection of the purpose that brought me hither. Thoughts of a different tendency had such absolute possession of my mind, that the relations of time and space were almost obliterated from my understanding. These wanderings, however, were restrained, and I ascended to her chamber.

" 'I had no light, and might have known by external observation, that the house was without any inhabitant. With this, however, I was not satisfied. I entered the room, and the object of my search not appearing, I prepared to return.

" 'The darkness required some caution in descending the stair. I stretched my hand to seize the balustrade by which I might regulate my steps. How shall I describe the lustre, which, at that moment, burst upon my vision!

" 'I was dazzled. My organs were bereaved of their activity. My eyelids were half-closed, and my hands withdrawn from the balustrade. A nameless fear chilled my veins, and I stood motionless. This irradiation did not retire or lessen. It seemed as if some powerful effulgence covered me like a mantle.

" 'I opened my eyes and found all about me luminous and glowing. It was the element of heaven that flowed around. Nothing but a fiery stream was at first visible; but, anon, a shrill voice from behind called upon me to attend.

" 'I turned: It is forbidden to describe what I saw: Words, indeed, would be wanting to the task. The lineaments of that being, whose veil was now lifted, and whose visage beamed upon my sight, no hues of pencil or of language can pourtray.

" 'As it spoke, the accents thrilled to my heart. "Thy prayers are heard. In proof of thy faith, render me thy wife. This is the victim I chuse. Call her hither, and here let her fall."—The sound, and visage, and light vanished at once.

" 'What demand was this? The blood of Catharine was to be shed! My wife was to perish by my hand! I sought opportunity to attest my virtue. Little did I expect that a proof like this would have been demanded.

" 'My wife! I exclaimed: O God! substitute some other victim. Make me not the butcher of my wife. My own blood is cheap. This will I pour out before thee with a willing heart; but spare, I beseech thee, this precious life, or commission some other than her husband to perform the bloody deed.

" 'In vain. The conditions were prescribed; the decree had gone forth, and nothing remained but to execute it. I rushed out of the house and across the intermediate fields, and stopped not till I entered my own parlour.

" 'My wife had remained here during my absence, in anxious expectation of my return with some tidings of her sister. I had none to communicate. For a time, I was breathless with my speed: This, and the tremors that shook my frame, and the wildness of my looks, alarmed her. She immediately suspected some disaster to have happened to her friend, and her own speech was as much overpowered by emotion as mine.

" 'She was silent, but her looks manifested her impatience to hear what I had to communicate. I spoke, but with so much precipitation as scarcely to be understood; catching her, at the same time, by the arm, and forcibly pulling her from her seat.

" ' "Come along with me: fly: waste not a moment: time will be lost, and the deed will be omitted. Tarry not; question not; but fly with me!"

" 'This deportment added afresh to her alarms. Her eyes pursued mine, and she said, "What is the matter? For God's sake what is the matter? Where would you have me go?"

" 'My eyes were fixed upon her countenance while she spoke. I thought upon her virtues; I viewed her as the mother of my babes; as my wife: I recalled the purpose for which I thus urged her attendance. My heart faltered, and I saw that I must rouse to this work all my faculties. The danger of the least delay was imminent.

" 'I looked away from her, and again exerting my force, drew her towards the door—"You must go with me—indeed you must."

" 'In her fright she half-resisted my efforts, and again exclaimed, "Good heaven! what is it you mean? Where go? What has happened? Have you found Clara?"

" ' "Follow me, and you will see," I answered, still urging her reluctant steps forward.

" ' "What phrenzy has seized you? Something must needs have happened. Is she sick? Have you found her?"

" ' "Come and see. Follow me, and know for yourself."

" 'Still she expostulated and besought me to explain this mysterious behaviour. I could not trust myself to answer her; to look at her; but grasping her arm, I drew her after me. She hesitated, rather through confusion of mind than from unwillingness to accompany me. This confusion gradually abated, and she moved forward, but with irresolute footsteps, and continual exclamations of wonder and terror. Her interrogations of "what was the matter?" and "whither was I going?" were ceaseless and vehement.

" 'It was the scope of my efforts not to think; to keep up a conflict and uproar in my mind in which all order and distinctness should be lost; to escape from the sensations produced by her voice. I was, therefore, silent. I strove to abridge this interval by my haste, and to waste all my attention in furious gesticulations.

" 'In this state of mind we reached my sister's door. She looked at the windows and saw that all was desolate—"Why come we here? There is no body here. I will not go in."

" 'Still I was dumb; but opening the door, I drew her into the entry. This was the allotted scene: here she was to fall. I let go her hand, and pressing my palms against my forehead, made one mighty effort to work up my soul to the deed.

" 'In vain; it would not be; my courage was appalled; my arms nerveless: I muttered prayers that my strength might be aided from above. They availed nothing.

" 'Horror diffused itself over me. This conviction of my cowardice, my rebellion, fastened upon me, and I stood rigid and cold as marble. From this state I was somewhat relieved by my wife's voice, who renewed her supplications to be told why we came hither, and what was the fate of my sister.

" 'What could I answer? My words were broken and inarticulate. Her fears naturally acquired force from the observation of these symptoms; but these fears were misplaced. The only inference she deduced from my conduct was, that some terrible mishap had befallen Clara.

" 'She wrung her hands, and exclaimed in an agony, "O tell me, where is she? What has become of her? Is she sick? Dead? Is she in her chamber? O let me go thither and know the worst!"

" 'This proposal set my thoughts once more in motion. Perhaps what my rebellious heart refused to perform here, I might obtain strength enough to execute elsewhere.

" ' "Come then," said I, "let us go."

" ' "I will, but not in the dark. We must first procure a light."

" ' "Fly then and procure it; but I charge you, linger not. I will await for your return."

" 'While she was gone, I strode along the entry. The fellness of a gloomy hurricane but faintly resembled the discord that reigned in my mind. To omit this sacrifice must not be; yet my sinews had refused to perform it. No alternative was offered. To rebel against the mandate was impossible; but obedience would render me the executioner of my wife. My will was strong, but my limbs refused their office.

" 'She returned with a light; I led the way to the chamber; she looked round her; she lifted the curtain of the bed; she saw nothing.

" 'At length, she fixed inquiring eyes upon me. The light now enabled her to discover in my visage what darkness had hitherto concealed. Her cares were now transferred from my sister to myself, and she said in a tremulous voice, "Wieland! you are not well: What ails you? Can I do nothing for you?"

" 'That accents and looks so winning should disarm me of my resolution, was to be expected. My thoughts were thrown anew into anarchy. I spread my hand before my eyes that I might not see her, and answered only by groans. She took my other hand between her's, and pressing it to her heart, spoke with that voice which had ever swayed my will, and wasted away sorrow.

" ' "My friend! my soul's friend! tell me thy cause of grief. Do I not merit to partake with thee in thy cares? Am I not thy wife?"

" 'This was too much. I broke from her embrace, and retired to a corner of the room. In this pause, courage was once more infused into me. I resolved to execute my duty. She followed me, and renewed her passionate entreaties to know the cause of my distress.

" 'I raised my head and regarded her with stedfast looks. I muttered something about death, and the injunctions of my duty. At these words she shrunk back, and looked at me with a new expression of anguish. After a pause, she clasped her hands, and exclaimed—

" ' "O Wieland! Wieland! God grant that I am mistaken; but surely something is wrong. I see it: it is too plain: thou art undone—lost to me and to thyself." At the same time she gazed on my features with intensest anxiety, in hope that different symptoms would take place. I replied to her with vehemence—

" ' "Undone! No; my duty is known, and I thank my God that my cowardice is now vanquished, and I have power to fulfil it. Catharine! I pity the weakness of thy nature: I pity thee, but must not spare. Thy life is claimed from my hands: thou must die!"

" 'Fear was now added to her grief. "What mean you? Why talk you of death? Bethink yourself, Wieland: bethink yourself, and this fit will pass. O why came I hither! Why did you drag me hither?"

" ' "I brought thee hither to fulfil a divine command. I am appointed thy destroyer, and destroy thee I must." Saying this I seized her wrists. She shrieked aloud, and endeavoured to free herself from my grasp; but her efforts were vain.

" ' "Surely, surely Wieland, thou dost not mean it. Am I not thy wife? and wouldst thou kill me? Thou wilt not; and yet—I see—thou art Wieland no longer! A fury resistless and horrible possesses thee—Spare me—spare—help—help—"

" 'Till her breath was stopped she shrieked for help—for mercy. When she could speak no longer, her gestures, her looks appealed to my compassion. My accursed hand was irresolute and tremulous. I meant thy death to be sudden, thy struggles to be brief. Alas! my heart was infirm; my resolves mutable. Thrice I slackened my grasp, and life kept its hold, though in the midst of pangs. Her eye-balls started from their sockets. Grimness and distortion took place of all that used to bewitch me into transport, and subdue me into reverence.

" 'I was commissioned to kill thee, but not to torment thee[20] with the foresight of thy death; not to multiply thy fears, and prolong thy agonies. Haggard, and pale, and lifeless, at length thou ceasedst to contend with thy destiny.

" 'This was a moment of triumph. Thus had I successfully subdued the stubbornness of human passions: the victim which had been demanded was given: the deed was done past recal.

" 'I lifted the corpse in my arms and laid it on the bed. I gazed upon it with delight. Such was the elation of my thoughts, that I even broke into laughter. I clapped my hands and exclaimed, "It is done! My sacred duty is fulfilled! To that I have sacrificed, O my God! thy last and best gift, my wife!"

" 'For a while I thus soared above frailty. I imagined I had set myself forever beyond the reach of selfishness; but my imaginations were false. This rapture quickly subsided. I looked again at my wife. My joyous ebullitions vanished, and I asked myself who it was whom I saw? Methought it could not be Catharine. It could not be the woman who had lodged for years in my heart; who had slept, nightly, in my bosom; who had borne in her womb, who had fostered at her breast, the beings who called me father; whom I had watched with delight, and cherished with a fondness ever new and perpetually growing: it could not be the same.

" 'Where was her bloom! These deadly and blood-suffused orbs but ill resemble the azure and exstatic tenderness of her eyes. The lucid stream that meandered over that bosom, the glow of love that was wont to sit upon that cheek, are much unlike these livid stains and this hideous deformity. Alas! these were the traces of agony; the gripe of the assassin had been here!

" 'I will not dwell upon my lapse into desperate and outrageous sorrow. The breath of heaven that sustained me was withdrawn, and I sunk into *mere man*. I leaped from the floor: I dashed my head against the wall: I uttered screams of horror: I panted after torment and pain. Eternal fire, and the bickerings of hell, compared with what I felt, were music and a bed of roses.

" 'I thank my God that this degeneracy was transient, that he deigned once more to raise me aloft. I thought upon what I had done as a sacrifice to duty, and *was calm*. My wife was dead; but I reflected, that though this source of human consolation was closed, yet others were still open. If the transports of an husband were no more, the feelings of a father had still scope for exercise. When remembrance of their mother should excite too keen a pang, I would look upon them, and *be comforted*.

" 'While I revolved these ideas, new warmth flowed in upon my heart—I was wrong. These feelings were the growth of selfishness. Of this I was not aware, and to dispel the mist that obscured my perceptions, a new effulgence and a new mandate were necessary.

" 'From these thoughts I was recalled by a ray that was shot into the room. A voice spake like that which I had before heard—"Thou hast done well; but all is not done—the sacrifice is incomplete—thy children must be offered—they must perish with their mother!——" ' "

CHAPTER XX.

Will you wonder that I read no farther? Will you not rather be astonished that I read thus far? What power supported me through such a task I know not. Perhaps the doubt from which I could not disengage my mind, that the scene here depicted was a dream, contributed to my perseverance. In vain the solemn introduction of my uncle, his appeals to my fortitude, and allusions to something monstrous in the events he was about to disclose; in vain the distressful perplexity, the mysterious silence and ambiguous answers of my attendants, especially when the condition of my brother was the theme of my inquiries, were remembered. I recalled the interview with Wieland in my chamber, his preternatural tranquillity succeeded by bursts of passion and menacing actions. All these coincided with the tenor of this paper.

Catharine and her children, and Louisa were dead. The act that destroyed them was, in the highest degree, inhuman. It was worthy of savages trained to murder, and exulting in agonies.

Who was the performer of the deed? Wieland! My brother! The husband and the father! That man of gentle virtues and invincible benignity! placable and mild—an idolator of peace! Surely, said I, it is a dream. For many days have I been vexed with frenzy. Its dominion is still felt; but new forms are called up to diversify and augment my torments.

The paper dropped from my hand, and my eyes followed it. I shrunk back, as if to avoid some petrifying influence that approached me. My tongue was mute; all the functions of nature were at a stand, and I sunk upon the floor lifeless.

The noise of my fall, as I afterwards heard, alarmed my uncle, who was in a lower apartment, and whose apprehensions had detained him. He hastened to my chamber, and administered the assistance which my condition required. When I opened my eyes I beheld him before me. His skill as a reasoner as well as a physician, was exerted to obviate the injurious effects of this disclosure; but he had wrongly estimated the strength of my body or of my mind. This new shock brought me once more to the brink of the grave, and my malady was much more difficult to subdue than at first.

I will not dwell upon the long train of dreary sensations, and the hideous confusion of my understanding. Time slowly restored its customary firmness to my frame, and order to my thoughts. The images impressed upon my mind by this fatal paper were somewhat effaced by my malady. They were obscure and disjointed like the parts of a dream. I was desirous of freeing my imagination from this chaos. For this end I questioned my uncle, who was my constant companion. He was intimidated by the issue of his first experiment, and took pains to elude or discourage my inquiry. My impetuosity some times compelled him to have resort to misrepresentations and untruths.

Time effected that end, perhaps, in a more beneficial manner. In the course of my meditations the recollections of the past gradually became more distinct. I revolved them, however, in silence, and being no longer accompanied with surprize, they did not exercise a death-dealing power. I had discontinued the perusal of the paper in the midst of the narrative; but what I read, combined with information elsewhere obtained, threw, perhaps, a sufficient light upon these detestable transactions; yet my curiosity was not inactive. I desired to peruse the remainder.

My eagerness to know the particulars of this tale was mingled and abated by my antipathy to the scene which would be disclosed. Hence

I employed no means to effect my purpose. I desired knowledge, and, at the same time, shrunk back from receiving the boon.

One morning, being left alone, I rose from my bed, and went to a drawer where my finer clothing used to be kept. I opened it, and this fatal paper saluted my sight. I snatched it involuntarily, and withdrew to a chair. I debated, for a few minutes, whether I should open and read. Now that my fortitude was put to trial, it failed. I felt myself incapable of deliberately surveying a scene of so much horror. I was prompted to return it to its place, but this resolution gave way, and I determined to peruse some part of it. I turned over the leaves till I came near the conclusion. The narrative of the criminal was finished. The verdict of *guilty* reluctantly pronounced by the jury, and the accused interrogated why sentence of death should not pass. The answer was brief, solemn, and emphatical.

" 'No. I have nothing to say. My tale has been told. My motives have been truly stated. If my judges are unable to discern the purity of my intentions, or to credit the statement of them, which I have just made; if they see not that my deed was enjoined by heaven; that obedience was the test of perfect virtue, and the extinction of selfishness and error, they must pronounce me a murderer.

" 'They refuse to credit my tale; they impute my acts to the influence of dæmons; they account me an example of the highest wickedness of which human nature is capable; they doom me to death and infamy. Have I power to escape this evil? If I have, be sure I will exert it. I will not accept evil at their hand, when I am entitled to good; I will suffer only when I cannot elude suffering.

" 'You say that I am guilty. Impious and rash! thus to usurp the prerogatives of your Maker! to set up your bounded views and halting reason, as the measure of truth!

" 'Thou, Omnipotent and Holy! Thou knowest that my actions were conformable to thy will. I know not what is crime; what actions are evil in their ultimate and comprehensive tendency or what are good. Thy knowledge, as thy power, is unlimited. I have taken thee for my guide, and cannot err. To the arms of thy protection, I entrust my safety. In the awards of thy justice, I confide for my recompense.

" 'Come death when it will, I am safe. Let calumny and abhorrence pursue me among men; I shall not be defrauded of my dues. The peace of virtue, and the glory of obedience, will be my portion hereafter.' "

Here ended the speaker. I withdrew my eyes from the page; but before I had time to reflect on what I had read, Mr. Cambridge entered the room. He quickly perceived how I had been employed, and betrayed some solicitude respecting the condition of my mind.

His fears, however, were superfluous. What I had read, threw me into a state not easily described. Anguish and fury, however, had no part in it. My faculties were chained up in wonder and awe. Just then, I was unable to speak. I looked at my friend with an air of inquisitiveness, and pointed at the roll. He comprehended my inquiry, and answered me with looks of gloomy acquiescence. After some time, my thoughts found their way to my lips.

Such then were the acts of my brother. Such were his words. For this he was condemned to die: To die upon the gallows! A fate, cruel and unmerited! And is it so? continued I, struggling for utterance, which this new idea made difficult; is he—dead!

"No. He is alive. There could be no doubt as to the cause of these excesses. They originated in sudden madness; but that madness continues, and he is condemned to perpetual imprisonment."

"Madness, say you? Are you sure? Were not these sights, and these sounds, really seen and heard?"

My uncle was surprized at my question. He looked at me with apparent inquietude. "Can you doubt," said he, "that these were illusions? Does heaven, think you, interfere for such ends?"

"O no; I think it not. Heaven cannot stimulate to such unheard-of outrage. The agent was not good, but evil."

"Nay, my dear girl," said my friend, "lay aside these fancies. Neither angel nor devil had any part in this affair."

"You misunderstand me," I answered; "I believe the agency to be external and real, but not supernatural."

"Indeed!" said he, in an accent of surprize. "Whom do you then suppose to be the agent?"

"I know not. All is wildering conjecture. I cannot forget Carwin. I cannot banish the suspicion that he was the setter of these snares. But how can we suppose it to be madness? Did insanity ever before assume this form?"

"Frequently. The illusion, in this case, was more dreadful in its consequences, than any that has come to my knowledge; but, I repeat that similar illusions are not rare. Did you never hear of an instance which occurred in your mother's family?"

"No. I beseech you relate it. My grandfather's death I have understood to have been extraordinary, but I know not in what respect. A brother, to whom he was much attached, died in his youth, and this, as I have heard, influenced, in some remarkable way, the fate of my grandfather; but I am unacquainted with particulars."

"On the death of that brother," resumed my friend, "my father was seized with dejection, which was found to flow from two sources. He not only grieved for the loss of a friend, but entertained the belief that his own death would be inevitably consequent on that of his brother. He waited from day to day in expectation of the stroke which he predicted was speedily to fall upon him. Gradually, however, he recovered his cheerfulness and confidence. He married, and performed his part in the world with spirit and activity. At the end of twenty-one years it happened that he spent the summer with his family at an house which he possessed on the sea coast in Cornwall. It was at no great distance from a cliff which overhung the ocean, and rose into the air to a great height. The summit was level and secure, and easily ascended on the land side. The company frequently repaired hither in clear weather, invited by its pure airs and extensive prospects. One evening in June my father, with his wife and some friends, chanced to be on this spot. Every one was happy, and my father's imagination seemed particularly alive to the grandeur of the scenery.

"Suddenly, however, his limbs trembled and his features betrayed alarm. He threw himself into the attitude of one listening. He gazed earnestly in a direction in which nothing was visible to his friends. This lasted for a minute; then turning to his companions, he told them that his brother had just delivered to him a summons,[21] which must be instantly obeyed. He then took an hasty and solemn leave of each person, and, before their surprize would allow them to understand the scene, he rushed to the edge of the cliff, threw himself headlong, and was seen no more.

"In the course of my practice in the German army, many cases, equally remarkable, have occurred. Unquestionably the illusions were maniacal, though the vulgar thought otherwise. They are all reducible to one class,* and are not more difficult of explication and cure than most affections of our frame."

This opinion my uncle endeavoured, by various means, to impress upon me. I listened to his reasonings and illustrations with silent respect. My astonishment was great on finding proofs of an influence of which I had supposed there were no examples; but I was far from accounting for appearances in my uncle's manner. Ideas thronged into my mind which I was unable to disjoin or to regulate. I reflected that this madness, if madness it were, had affected Pleyel and myself as well as Wieland. Pleyel had heard a mysterious voice. I had seen and heard. A form had showed itself to me as well as to Wieland. The disclosure had been made in the same spot. The appearance was equally complete and equally prodigious in both instances. Whatever supposition I should adopt, had I not equal reason to tremble? What was my security against influences equally terrific and equally irresistible?

It would be vain to attempt to describe the state of mind which this idea produced. I wondered at the change which a moment had effected in my brother's condition. Now was I stupified with tenfold wonder in contemplating myself. Was I not likewise transformed from rational and human into a creature of nameless and fearful attributes? Was I not transported to the brink of the same abyss? Ere a new day should come, my hands might be embrued in blood, and my remaining life be consigned to a dungeon and chains.

With moral sensibility like mine, no wonder that this new dread was more insupportable than the anguish I had lately endured. Grief carries its own antidote along with it. When thought becomes merely a vehicle of pain, its progress must be stopped. Death is a cure which nature or ourselves must administer: To this cure I now looked forward with gloomy satisfaction.

* Mania Mutabilis. See Darwin's Zoonomia, vol. ii. Class III. 1. 2. where similar cases are stated.[22]

My silence could not conceal from my uncle the state of my thoughts. He made unwearied efforts to divert my attention from views so pregnant with danger. His efforts, aided by time, were in some measure successful. Confidence in the strength of my resolution, and in the healthful state of my faculties, was once more revived. I was able to devote my thoughts to my brother's state, and the causes of this disasterous proceeding.

My opinions were the sport of eternal change. Some times I conceived the apparition to be more than human. I had no grounds on which to build a disbelief. I could not deny faith to the evidence of my religion; the testimony of men was loud and unanimous: both these concurred to persuade me that evil spirits existed, and that their energy was frequently exerted in the system of the world.

These ideas connected themselves with the image of Carwin. Where is the proof, said I, that dæmons may not be subjected to the controul of men? This truth may be distorted and debased in the minds of the ignorant. The dogmas of the vulgar, with regard to this subject, are glaringly absurd; but though, these may justly be, neglected by the wise, we are scarcely justified in totally rejecting the possibility that men may obtain supernatural aid.

The dreams of superstition are worthy of contempt. Witchcraft, its instruments and miracles, the compact ratified by a bloody signature, the apparatus of sulpherous smells and thundering explosions, are monstrous and chimerical. These have no part in the scene over which the genius of Carwin presides. That conscious beings, dissimilar from human, but moral and voluntary agents as we are, some where exist, can scarcely be denied. That their aid may be employed to benign or malignant purposes, cannot be disproved.

Darkness rests upon the designs of this man. The extent of his power is unknown; but is there not evidence that it has been now exerted?

I recurred to my own experience. Here Carwin had actually appeared upon the stage; but this was in a human character. A voice and a form were discovered; but one was apparently exerted, and the other disclosed, not to befriend, but to counteract Carwin's designs. There were tokens of hostility, and not of alliance, between them. Carwin was the miscreant whose projects were resisted by a minister of heaven. How can this be reconciled to the stratagem which ruined my brother? There the agency was at once preternatural and malignant.

The recollection of this fact led my thoughts into a new channel. The malignity of that influence which governed my brother had hitherto been no subject of doubt. His wife and children were destroyed; they had expired in agony and fear; yet was it indisputably certain that their murderer was criminal? He was acquitted at the tribunal of his own conscience; his behaviour at his trial and since, was faithfully reported to me; appearances were uniform; not for a moment did he lay aside the majesty of virtue; he repelled all invectives by appealing to the deity, and to the tenor of his past life; surely there was truth in this appeal: none but a command from heaven could have swayed his will; and nothing but unerring proof of divine approbation could sustain his mind in its present elevation.

CHAPTER XXI.

Such, for some time, was the course of my meditations. My weakness, and my aversion to be pointed at as an object of surprize or compassion, prevented me from going into public. I studiously avoided the visits of those who came to express their sympathy, or gratify their curiosity. My uncle was my principal companion. Nothing more powerfully tended to console me than his conversation.

With regard to Pleyel, my feelings seemed to have undergone a total revolution. It often happens that one passion supplants another. Late disasters had rent my heart, and now that the wound was in some degree closed, the love which I had cherished for this man seemed likewise to have vanished.

Hitherto, indeed, I had had no cause for despair. I was innocent of that offence which had estranged him from my presence. I might reasonably expect that my innocence would at some time be irresistably demonstrated, and his affection for me be revived with his esteem. Now my aversion to be thought culpable by him continued, but was unattended with the same impatience. I desired the removal of his suspicions, not for the sake of regaining his love, but because I delighted in the veneration of so excellent a man, and because he himself would derive pleasure from conviction of my integrity.

My uncle had early informed me that Pleyel and he had seen each other, since the return of the latter from Europe. Amidst the topics of their conversation, I discovered that Pleyel had carefully omitted the mention of those events which had drawn upon me so much abhorrence. I could not account for his silence on this subject. Perhaps time or some new discovery had altered or shaken his opinion. Perhaps he was unwilling, though I were guilty, to injure me in the opinion of my venerable kinsman. I understood that he had frequently visited me during my disease, had watched many successive nights by my bedside, and manifested the utmost anxiety on my account.

The journey which he was preparing to take, at the termination of our last interview, the catastrophe of the ensuing night induced him to delay. The motives of this journey I had, till now, totally mistaken. They were explained to me by my uncle, whose tale excited my astonishment without awakening my regret. In a different state of mind, it would have added unspeakably to my distress, but now it was more a source of pleasure than pain. This, perhaps, is not the least extraordinary of the facts contained in this narrative. It will excite less wonder when I add, that my indifference was temporary, and that the lapse of a few days shewed me that my feelings were deadened for a time, rather than finally extinguished.

Theresa de Stolberg was alive. She had conceived the resolution of seeking her lover in America. To conceal her flight, she had caused the report of her death to be propagated. She put herself under the conduct of Bertrand, the faithful servant of Pleyel. The pacquet which the latter received from the hands of his servant, contained the tidings of her safe arrival at Boston, and to meet her there was the purpose of his journey.

This discovery had set this man's character in a new light. I had mistaken the heroism of friendship for the phrenzy of love. He who had gained my affections, may be supposed to have previously entitled himself to my reverence; but the levity which had formerly characterized the behaviour of this man, tended to obscure the greatness of his sentiments. I did not fail to remark, that since this lady was still alive, the voice in the temple which asserted her death, must either have been intended to deceive, or have been itself deceived. The latter supposition was inconsistent with the notion of a spiritual, and the former with that of a benevolent being.

When my disease abated, Pleyel had forborne his visits, and had lately set out upon this journey. This amounted to a proof that my guilt was still believed by him. I was grieved for his errors, but trusted that my vindication would, sooner or later, be made.

Meanwhile, tumultuous thoughts were again set afloat by a proposal made to me by my uncle. He imagined that new airs would restore my languishing constitution, and a varied succession of objects tend to repair the shock which my mind had received. For this end, he proposed to me to take up my abode with him in France or Italy.

At a more prosperous period, this scheme would have pleased for its own sake. Now my heart sickened at the prospect of nature. The world of man was shrowded in misery and blood, and constituted a loathsome spectacle. I willingly closed my eyes in sleep, and regretted that the respite it afforded me was so short. I marked with satisfaction the progress of decay in my frame, and consented to live, merely in the hope that the course of nature would speedily relieve me from the burthen. Nevertheless, as he persisted in his scheme, I concurred in it merely because he was entitled to my gratitude, and because my refusal gave him pain.

No sooner was he informed of my consent, than he told me I must make immediate preparation to embark, as the ship in which he had engaged a passage would be ready to depart in three days. This expedition was unexpected. There was an impatience in his manner when he urged the necessity of dispatch that excited my surprize. When I questioned him as to the cause of this haste, he generally stated reasons which, at that time, I could not deny to be plausible; but which, on the review, appeared insufficient. I suspected that the true motives were concealed, and believed that these motives had some connection with my brother's destiny.

I now recollected that the information respecting Wieland which had, from time to time, been imparted to me, was always accompanied with airs of reserve and mysteriousness. What had appeared sufficiently explicit at the time it was uttered, I now remembered to have been faltering and ambiguous. I was resolved to remove my doubts, by visiting the unfortunate man in his dungeon.

Heretofore the idea of this visit had occurred to me; but the horrors of his dwelling-place, his wild yet placid physiognomy, his neglected locks, the fetters which constrained his limbs, terrible as they were in description, how could I endure to behold!

Now, however, that I was preparing to take an everlasting farewell of my country, now that an ocean was henceforth to separate me from him, how could I part without an interview? I would examine his situation with my own eyes. I would know whether the representations which had been made to me were true. Perhaps the sight of the sister whom he was wont to love with a passion more than fraternal, might have an auspicious influence on his malady.

Having formed this resolution, I waited to communicate it to Mr. Cambridge. I was aware that, without his concurrence, I could not hope to carry it into execution, and could discover no objection to which it was liable. If I had not been deceived as to his condition, no inconvenience could arise from this proceeding. His consent, therefore, would be the test of his sincerity.

I seized this opportunity to state my wishes on this head. My suspicions were confirmed by the manner in which my request affected him. After some pause, in which his countenance betrayed every mark of perplexity, he said to me, "Why would you pay this visit? What useful purpose can it serve?"

"We are preparing," said I, "to leave the country forever: What kind of being should I be to leave behind me a brother in calamity without even a parting interview? Indulge me for three minutes in the sight of him. My heart will be much easier after I have looked at him, and shed a few tears in his presence."

"I believe otherwise. The sight of him would only augment your distress, without contributing, in any degree, to his benefit."

"I know not that," returned I. "Surely the sympathy of his sister, proofs that her tenderness is as lively as ever, must be a source of satisfaction to him. At present he must regard all mankind as his enemies and calumniators. His sister he, probably, conceives to partake in the general infatuation, and to join in the cry of abhorrence that is raised against him. To be undeceived in this respect, to be assured that, however I may impute his conduct to delusion, I still retain all my former affection for his person, and veneration for the purity of his motives, cannot but afford him pleasure. When he hears that I have left the country, without even the ceremonious attention of a visit, what will he think of me? His magnanimity may hinder him from repining, but he will surely consider my behaviour as savage and unfeeling. Indeed, dear Sir, I must pay this visit. To embark with you without paying it, will be impossible. It may be of no service to him, but will enable me to acquit myself of what I cannot but esteem a duty. Besides," continued I, "if it be a mere fit of insanity that has seized him, may not my presence chance to have a salutary influence? The mere sight of me, it is not impossible, may rectify his perceptions."

"Ay," said my uncle, with some eagerness; "it is by no means impossible that your interview may have that effect; and for that reason, beyond all others, would I dissuade you from it."

I expressed my surprize at this declaration. "Is it not to be desired that an error so fatal as this should be rectified?"

"I wonder at your question. Reflect on the consequences of this error. Has he not destroyed the wife whom he loved, the children whom he idolized? What is it that enables him to bear the remembrance, but the belief that he acted as his duty enjoined? Would you rashly bereave him of this belief? Would you restore him to himself, and convince him that he was instigated to this dreadful outrage by a perversion of his organs, or a delusion from hell?

"Now his visions are joyous and elate. He conceives himself to have reached a loftier degree of virtue, than any other human being. The merit of his sacrifice is only enhanced in the eyes of superior beings, by the detestation that pursues him here, and the sufferings to which he is condemned. The belief that even his sister has deserted him, and gone over to his enemies, adds to his sublimity of feelings, and his confidence in divine approbation and future recompense.

"Let him be undeceived in this respect, and what floods of despair and of horror will overwhelm him! Instead of glowing approbation and serene hope, will he not hate and torture himself? Self-violence, or a phrenzy far more savage and destructive than this, may be expected to succeed. I beseech you, therefore, to relinquish this scheme. If you calmly reflect upon it, you will discover that your duty lies in carefully shunning him."

Mr. Cambridge's reasonings suggested views to my understanding, that had not hitherto occurred. I could not but admit their validity, but they shewed, in a new light, the depth of that misfortune in which my brother was plunged. I was silent and irresolute.

Presently, I considered, that whether Wieland was a maniac, a faithful servant of his God, the victim of hellish illusions, or the dupe of human imposture, was by no means certain. In this state of my mind it became me to be silent during the visit that I projected. This visit should be brief: I should be satisfied merely to snatch a look at him. Admitting that a change in his opinions were not to be desired, there was no danger from the conduct which I should pursue, that this change should be wrought.

But I could not conquer my uncle's aversion to this scheme. Yet I persisted, and he found that to make me voluntarily relinquish it, it was necessary to be more explicit than he had hitherto been. He took both my hands, and anxiously examining my countenance as he spoke, "Clara," said he, "this visit must not be paid. We must hasten with the utmost expedition from this shore. It is folly to conceal the truth from you, and, since it is only by disclosing the truth that you can be prevailed upon to lay aside this project, the truth shall be told.

"O my dear girl!" continued he with increasing energy in his accent, "your brother's phrenzy is, indeed, stupendous and frightful. The soul that formerly actuated his frame has disappeared. The same form remains; but the wise and benevolent Wieland is no more. A fury that is rapacious of blood, that lifts his strength almost above that of mortals, that bends all his energies to the destruction of whatever was once dear to him, possesses him wholly.

"You must not enter his dungeon; his eyes will no sooner be fixed upon you, than an exertion of his force will be made. He will shake off his fetters in a moment, and rush upon you. No interposition will then be strong or quick enough to save you.

"The phantom that has urged him to the murder of Catharine and her children is not yet appeased. Your life, and that of Pleyel, are exacted from him by this imaginary being. He is eager to comply with this demand. Twice he has escaped from his prison. The first time, he no sooner found himself at liberty, than he hasted to Pleyel's house. It being midnight, the latter was in bed. Wieland penetrated unobserved to his chamber, and opened his curtain. Happily, Pleyel awoke at the critical moment, and escaped the fury of his kinsman, by leaping from his chamber window into the court. Happily, he reached the ground without injury. Alarms were given, and after diligent search, your brother was found in a chamber of your house, whither, no doubt, he had sought you.

"His chains, and the watchfulness of his guards, were redoubled; but again, by some miracle, he restored himself to liberty. He was now incautiously apprized of the place of your abode: and had not information of his escape been instantly given, your death would have been added to the number of his atrocious acts.

"You now see the danger of your project. You must not only forbear to visit him, but if you would save him from the crime of embruing his hands in your blood, you must leave the country. There is no hope that his malady will end but with his life, and no precaution will ensure your safety, but that of placing the ocean between you.

"I confess I came over with an intention to reside among you, but these disasters have changed my views. Your own safety and my happiness require that you should accompany me in my return, and I entreat you to give your cheerful concurrence to this measure."

After these representations from my uncle, it was impossible to retain my purpose. I readily consented to seclude myself from Wieland's presence. I likewise acquiesced in the proposal to go to Europe; not that I ever expected to arrive there, but because, since my principles forbad me to assail my own life, change had some tendency to make supportable the few days which disease should spare to me.

What a tale had thus been unfolded! I was hunted to death, not by one whom my misconduct had exasperated, who was conscious of illicit motives, and who fought his end by circumvention and surprize; but by one who deemed himself commissioned for this act by heaven; who regarded this career of horror as the last refinement of virtue; whose implacability was proportioned to the reverence and love which he felt for me, and who was inaccessible to the fear of punishment and ignominy!

In vain should I endeavour to stay his hand by urging the claims of a sister or friend: these were his only reasons for pursuing my destruction. Had I been a stranger to his blood; had I been the most worthless of human kind; my safety had not been endangered.

Surely, said I, my fate is without example. The phrenzy which is charged upon my brother, must belong to myself. My foe is manacled and guarded; but I derive no security from these restraints. I live not in a community of savages; yet, whether I sit or walk, go into crowds, or hide myself in solitude, my life is marked for a prey to inhuman violence; I am in perpetual danger of perishing; of perishing under the grasp of a brother!

I recollected the omens of this destiny; I remembered the gulf to which my brother's invitation had conducted me; I remembered that, when on the brink of danger, the author of my peril was depicted by my fears in his form: Thus realized, were the creatures of prophetic sleep, and of wakeful terror!

These images were unavoidably connected with that of Carwin. In this paroxysm of distress, my attention fastened on him as the grand deceiver; the author of this black conspiracy; the intelligence that governed in this storm.

Some relief is afforded in the midst of suffering, when its author is discovered or imagined; and an object found on which we may pour out our indignation and our vengeance. I ran over the events that had taken place since the origin of our intercourse with him, and reflected on the tenor of that description which was received from Ludloe. Mixed up with notions of supernatural agency, were the vehement suspicions which I entertained, that Carwin was the enemy whose machinations had destroyed us.

I thirsted for knowledge and for vengeance. I regarded my hasty departure with reluctance, since it would remove me from the means by which this knowledge might be obtained, and this vengeance gratified. This departure was to take place in two days. At the end of two days I was to bid an eternal adieu to my native country. Should I not pay a parting visit to the scene of these disasters? Should I not bedew with my tears the graves of my sister and her children? Should I not explore their desolate habitation, and gather from the sight of its walls and furniture food for my eternal melancholy?

This suggestion was succeeded by a secret shuddering. Some disastrous influence appeared to overhang the scene. How many memorials should I meet with serving to recall the images of those I had lost!

I was tempted to relinquish my design, when it occurred to me that I had left among my papers a journal of transactions in short-hand. I was employed in this manuscript on that night when Pleyel's incautious curiosity tempted him to look over my shoulder. I was then recording my adventure in *the recess*, an imperfect sight of which led him into such fatal errors.

I had regulated the disposition of all my property. This manuscript, however, which contained the most secret transactions of my life, I was desirous of destroying. For this end I must return to my house, and this I immediately determined to do.

I was not willing to expose myself to opposition from my friends, by mentioning my design; I therefore bespoke the use of Mr. Hallet's chaise, under pretence of enjoying an airing, as the day was remarkably bright.

This request was gladly complied with, and I directed the servant to conduct me to Mettingen. I dismissed him at the gate, intending to use, in returning, a carriage belonging to my brother.

Chapter XXII.

The inhabitants of the *Hut* received me with a mixture of joy and surprize. Their homely welcome, and their artless sympathy, were grateful to my feelings. In the midst of their inquiries, as to my health, they avoided all allusions to the source of my malady. They were honest creatures, and I loved them well. I participated in the tears which they shed when I mentioned to them my speedy departure for Europe, and promised to acquaint them with my welfare during my long absence.

They expressed great surprize when I informed them of my intention to visit my cottage. Alarm and foreboding overspread their features, and they attempted to dissuade me from visiting an house which they firmly believed to be haunted by a thousand ghastly apparitions.

These apprehensions, however, had no power over my conduct. I took an irregular path which led me to my own house. All was vacant and forlorn. A small enclosure, near which the path led, was the burying-ground belonging to the family. This I was obliged to pass. Once I had intended to enter it, and ponder on the emblems and inscriptions which my uncle had caused to be made on the tombs of Catharine and her children; but now my heart faltered as I approached, and I hastened forward, that distance might conceal it from my view.

When I approached the recess, my heart again sank. I averted my eyes, and left it behind me as quickly as possible. Silence reigned through my habitation, and a darkness which closed doors and shutters produced. Every object was connected with mine or my brother's history. I passed the entry, mounted the stair, and unlocked the door of my chamber. It was with difficulty that I curbed my fancy and smothered my fears. Slight movements and casual sounds were transformed into beckoning shadows and calling shapes.

I proceeded to the closet. I opened and looked round it with fearfulness. All things were in their accustomed order. I sought and found the manuscript where I was used to deposit it. This being secured, there was nothing to detain me; yet I stood and contemplated awhile the furniture and walls of my chamber. I remembered how long this apartment had been a sweet and tranquil asylum; I compared its former state with its present dreariness, and reflected that I now beheld it for the last time.

Here it was that the incomprehensible behaviour of Carwin was witnessed: this the stage on which that enemy of man shewed himself for a moment unmasked. Here the menaces of murder were wafted to my ear; and here these menaces were executed.

These thoughts had a tendency to take from me my self-command. My feeble limbs refused to support me, and I sunk upon a chair. Incoherent and half-articulate exclamations escaped my lips. The name of Carwin was uttered, and eternal woes, woes like that which his malice had entailed upon us, were heaped upon him. I invoked all-seeing heaven to drag to light and to punish this betrayer, and accused its providence for having thus long delayed the retribution that was due to so enormous a guilt.

I have said that the window shutters were closed. A feeble light, however, found entrance through the crevices. A small window illuminated the closet, and the door being closed, a dim ray streamed through the key-hole. A kind of twilight was thus created, sufficient for the purposes of vision; but, at the same time, involving all minuter objects in obscurity.

This darkness suited the colour of my thoughts. I sickened at the remembrance of the past. The prospect of the future excited my loathing. I muttered in a low voice, Why should I live longer? Why should I drag on a miserable being? All, for whom I ought to live, have perished. Am I not myself hunted to death?

At that moment, my despair suddenly became vigorous. My nerves were no longer unstrung. My powers, that had long been deadened, were revived. My bosom swelled with a sudden energy, and the conviction darted through my mind, that to end my torments was, at once, practicable and wise.

I knew how to find way to the recesses of life. I could use a lancet with some skill, and could distinguish between vein and artery. By piercing deep into the latter, I should shun the evils which the future had in store for me, and take refuge from my woes in quiet death.

I started on my feet, for my feebleness was gone, and hasted to the closet. A lancet and other small instruments were preserved in a case which I had deposited here. Inattentive as I was to foreign considerations, my ears were still open to any sound of mysterious import that should occur. I thought I heard a step in the entry. My purpose was suspended, and I cast an eager glance at my chamber door, which was open. No one appeared, unless the shadow which I discerned upon the floor, was the outline of a man. If it were, I was authorized to suspect that some one was posted close to the entrance, who possibly had overheard my exclamations.

My teeth chattered, and a wild confusion took place of my momentary calm. Thus it was when a terrific visage had disclosed itself on a former night. Thus it was when the evil destiny of Wieland assumed the lineaments of something human. What horrid apparition was preparing to blast my sight?

Still I listened and gazed. Not long, for the shadow moved; a foot, unshapely and huge, was thrust forward; a form advanced from its concealment, and stalked into the room. It was Carwin!

While I had breath I shrieked. While I had power over my muscles, I motioned with my hand that he should vanish. My exertions could not last long; I sunk into a fit.

O that this grateful oblivion had lasted for ever! Too quickly I recovered my senses. The power of distinct vision was no sooner restored to me, than this hateful form again presented itself, and I once more relapsed.

A second time, untoward nature recalled me from the sleep of death. I found myself stretched upon the bed. When I had power to look up, I remembered only that I had cause to fear. My distempered fancy fashioned to itself no distinguishable image. I threw a languid glance round me; once more my eyes lighted upon Carwin.

He was seated on the floor, his back rested against the wall, his knees were drawn up, and his face was buried in his hands. That his station was at some distance, that his attitude was not menacing, that his ominous visage was concealed, may account for my now escaping a shock, violent as those which were past. I withdrew my eyes, but was not again deferred by my senses.

On perceiving that I had recovered my sensibility, he lifted his head. This motion attracted my attention. His countenance was mild, but sorrow and astonishment sat upon his features. I averted my eyes and feebly exclaimed—"O! fly—fly far and for ever!—I cannot behold you and live!"

He did not rise upon his feet, but clasped his hands, and said in a tone of deprecation—"I will fly. I am become a fiend, the sight of whom destroys. Yet tell me my offence! You have linked curses with my name; you ascribe to me a malice monstrous and infernal. I look around; all is loneliness and desert! This house and your brother's are solitary and dismantled! You die away at the sight of me! My fear whispers that some deed of horror has been perpetrated; that I am the un-deigning cause."

What language was this? Had he not avowed himself a ravisher? Had not this chamber witnessed his atrocious purposes? I besought him with new vehemence to go.

He lifted his eyes—"Great heaven! what have I done? I think I know the extent of my offences. I have acted, but my actions have possibly effected more than I designed. This fear has brought me back from my retreat. I come to repair the evil of which my rashness was the cause, and to prevent more evil. I come to confess my errors."

"Wretch!" I cried when my suffocating emotions would permit me to speak, "the ghosts of my sister and her children, do they not rise to accuse thee? Who was it that blasted the intellects of Wieland? Who was it that urged him to fury, and guided him to murder? Who, but thou and the devil, with whom thou art confederated?"

At these words a new spirit pervaded his countenance. His eyes once more appealed to heaven. "If I have memory, if I have being, I am innocent. I intended no ill; but my folly, indirectly and remotely, may have caused it; but what words are these! Your brother lunatic! His children dead!"

What should I infer from this deportment? Was the ignorance which these words implied real or pretended?—Yet how could I imagine a mere human agency in these events? But if the influence was preternatural or maniacal in my brother's case, they must be equally so in my own. Then I remembered that the voice exerted, was to save me from Carwin's attempts. These ideas tended to abate my abhorrence of this man, and to detect the absurdity of my accusations.

"Alas!" said I, "I have no one to accuse. Leave me to my fate. Fly from a scene stained with cruelty; devoted to despair."

Carwin stood for a time musing and mournful. At length he said, "What has happened? I came to expiate my crimes: let me know them in their full extent. I have horrible forebodings! What has happened?"

I was silent; but recollecting the intimation given by this man when he was detected in my closet, which implied some knowledge of that power which interfered in my favor, I eagerly inquired, "What was that voice which called upon me to hold when I attempted to open the closet? What face was that which I saw at the bottom of the stairs? Answer me truly."

"I came to confess the truth. Your allusions are horrible and strange. Perhaps I have but faint conceptions of the evils which my infatuation has produced; but what remains I will perform. It was *my voice* that you heard! It was *my face* that you saw!"

For a moment I doubted whether my remembrance of events were not confused. How could he be at once stationed at my shoulder and shut up in my closet? How could he stand near me and yet be invisible? But if Carwin's were the thrilling voice and the fiery visage which I had heard and seen, then was he the prompter of my brother, and the author of these dismal outrages.

Once more I averted my eyes and struggled for speech. "Begone!

thou man of mischief! Remorseless and implacable miscreant! be-gone!"

"I will obey," said he in a disconsolate voice; "yet, wretch as I am, am I unworthy to repair the evils that I have committed? I came as a repentant criminal. It is you whom I have injured, and at your bar am I willing to appear, and confess and expiate my crimes. I have deceived you: I have sported with your terrors: I have plotted to destroy your reputation. I come now to remove your errors; to set you beyond the reach of similar fears; to rebuild your fame as far as I am able.

"This is the amount of my guilt, and this the fruit of my remorse. Will you not hear me? Listen to my confession, and then denounce punishment. All I ask is a patient audience."

"What!" I replied, "was not thine the voice that commanded my brother to imbrue his hands in the blood of his children—to strangle that angel of sweetness his wife? Has he not vowed my death, and the death of Pleyel, at thy bidding? Hast thou not made him the butcher of his family; changed him who was the glory of his species into worse than brute; robbed him of reason, and consigned the rest of his days to fetters and stripes?"

Carwin's eyes glared, and his limbs were petrified at this intelligence. No words were requisite to prove him guiltless of these enormities: at the time, however, I was nearly insensible to these exculpatory tokens. He walked to the farther end of the room, and having recovered some degree of composure, he spoke—

"I am not this villain; I have slain no one; I have prompted none to slay; I have handled a tool of wonderful efficacy without malignant in-tentions, but without caution; ample will be the punishment of my temerity, if my conduct has contributed to this evil." He paused.—

I likewise was silent. I struggled to command myself so far as to lis-ten to the tale which he should tell. Observing this, he continued—

"You are not apprized of the existence of a power which I possess. I know not by what name to call it.* It enables me to mimic exactly the

---

Biloquium, or ventrilocution. Sound is varied according to the variations of direction and distance. The art of the ventriloquist consists in modifying his voice according to all these variations, without changing his place. See the work of the Abbe de la Chappelle,[23] in which are accurately recorded the performances of one of these artists, and some ingenious, voice of another, and to modify the sound so that it shall appear to come from what quarter, and be uttered at what distance I please.

"I know not that every one possesses this power. Perhaps, though a casual position of my organs in my youth shewed me that I possessed it, it is an art which may be taught to all. Would to God I had died unknowing of the secret! It has produced nothing but degradation and calamity.

"For a time the possession of so potent and stupendous an endowment elated me with pride. Unfortified by principle, subjected to poverty, stimulated by headlong passions, I made this powerful engine subservient to the supply of my wants, and the gratification of my vanity. I shall not mention how diligently I cultivated this gift, which seemed capable of unlimited improvement; nor detail the various occasions on which it was successfully exerted to lead superstition, conquer avarice, or excite awe.

"I left America, which is my native soil, in my youth. I have been engaged in various scenes of life, in which my peculiar talent has been exercised with more or less success. I was finally betrayed by one who called himself my friend, into acts which cannot be justified, though they are susceptible of apology.

"The perfidy of this man compelled me to withdraw from Europe. I returned to my native country, uncertain whether silence and obscurity would save me from his malice. I resided in the purlieus of the city. I put on the garb and assumed the manners of a clown.

"My chief recreation was walking. My principal haunts were the lawns and gardens of Mettingen. In this delightful region the luxuri-

---

though unsatisfactory speculations are given on the means by which the effects are produced. This power is, perhaps, given by nature, but is doubtless improvable, if not acquirable, by art. It may, possibly, consist in an unusual flexibility or exertion of the bottom of the tongue and the uvula. That speech is producible by these alone must be granted, since anatomists mention two instances of persons speaking without a tongue. In one case, the organ was originally wanting, but its place was supplied by a small tubercle, and the uvula was perfect. In the other, the tongue was destroyed by disease, but probably a small part of it remained.

This power is difficult to explain, but the fact is undeniable. Experience shews that the human voice can imitate the voice of all men and of all inferior animals. The sound of musical instruments, and even noises from the contact of inanimate substances, have been accurately imitated. The mimicry of animals is notorious; and Dr. Burney (Musical Travels)[24] mentions one who imitated a flute and violin, so as to deceive even his ears.

ances of nature had been chastened by judicious art, and each successive contemplation unfolded new enchantments.

"I was studious of seclusion: I was satiated with the intercourse of mankind, and discretion required me to shun their intercourse. For these reasons I long avoided the observation of your family, and chiefly visited these precincts at night.

"I was never weary of admiring the position and ornaments of *the temple.* Many a night have I passed under its roof, revolving no pleasing meditations. When, in my frequent rambles, I perceived this apartment was occupied, I gave a different direction to my steps. One evening, when a shower had just passed, judging by the silence that no one was within, I ascended to this building. Glancing carelessly round, I perceived an open letter on the pedestal. To read it was doubtless an offence against politeness. Of this offence, however, I was guilty.

"Scarcely had I gone half through when I was alarmed by the approach of your brother. To scramble down the cliff on the opposite side was impracticable. I was unprepared to meet a stranger. Besides the aukwardness attending such an interview in these circumstances, concealment was necessary to my safety. A thousand times had I vowed never again to employ the dangerous talent which I possessed; but such was the force of habit and the influence of present convenience, that I used this method of arresting his progress and leading him back to the house, with his errand, whatever it was, unperformed. I had often caught parts, from my station below, of your conversation in this place, and was well acquainted with the voice of your sister.

"Some weeks after this I was again quietly seated in this recess. The lateness of the hour secured me, as I thought, from all interruption. In this, however, I was mistaken, for Wieland and Pleyel, as I judged by their voices, earnest in dispute, ascended the hill.

"I was not sensible that any inconvenience could possibly have flowed from my former exertion; yet it was followed with compunction, because it was a deviation from a path which I had assigned to myself. Now my aversion to this means of escape was enforced by an unauthorized curiosity, and by the knowledge of a bushy hollow on the edge of the hill, where I should be safe from discovery. Into this hollow I thrust myself.

propriety of removal to Europe was the question eagerly dis-
sed. Pleyel intimated that his anxiety to go was augmented by the
silence of Theresa de Stolberg. The temptation to interfere in this dispute was irresistible. In vain I contended with inveterate habits. I disguised to myself the impropriety of my conduct, by recollecting the
benefits which it might produce. Pleyel's proposal was unwise, yet it
was enforced with plausible arguments and indefatigable zeal. Your
brother might be puzzled and wearied, but could not be convinced. I
conceived that to terminate the controversy in favor of the latter was
conferring a benefit on all parties. For this end I profited by an opening in the conversation, and assured them of Catharine's irreconcilable aversion to the scheme, and of the death of the Saxon baroness.
The latter event was merely a conjecture, but rendered extremely
probable by Pleyel's representations. My purpose, you need not be
told, was effected.

"My passion for mystery, and a species of imposture, which I
deemed harmless, was thus awakened afresh. This second lapse into
error made my recovery more difficult. I cannot convey to you an adequate idea of the kind of gratification which I derived from these exploits; yet I meditated nothing. My views were bounded to the passing
moment, and commonly suggested by the momentary exigence.

"I must not conceal any thing. Your principles teach you to abhor a
voluptuous temper; but, with whatever reluctance, I acknowledge this
temper to be mine. You imagine your servant Judith to be innocent
as well as beautiful; but you took her from a family where hypocrisy, as
well as licentiousness, was wrought into a system. My attention was
captivated by her charms, and her principles were easily seen to be
flexible.

"Deem me not capable of the iniquity of seduction. Your servant is
not destitute of feminine and virtuous qualities; but she was taught
that the best use of her charms consists in the sale of them. My nocturnal visits to Mettingen were now prompted by a double view, and
my correspondence with your servant gave me, at all times, access to
your house.

"The second night after our interview, so brief and so little foreseen by either of us, some dæmon of mischief seized me. According

to my companion's report, your perfections were little less than divine. Her uncouth but copious narratives converted you into an object of worship. She chiefly dwelt upon your courage, because she herself was deficient in that quality. You held apparitions and goblins in contempt. You took no precautions against robbers. You were just as tranquil and secure in this lonely dwelling, as if you were in the midst of a crowd.

"Hence a vague project occurred to me, to put this courage to the test. A woman capable of recollection in danger, of warding off groundless panics, of discerning the true mode of proceeding, and profiting by her best resources, is a prodigy. I was desirous of ascertaining whether you were such an one.

"My expedient was obvious and simple: I was to counterfeit a murderous dialogue; but this was to be so conducted that another, and not yourself, should appear to be the object. I was not aware of the possibility that you should appropriate these menaces to yourself. Had you been still and listened, you would have heard the struggles and prayers of the victim, who would likewise have appeared to be shut up in the closet, and whose voice would have been Judith's. This scene would have been an appeal to your compassion; and the proof of cowardice or courage which I expected from you, would have been your remaining inactive in your bed, or your entering the closet with a view to assist the sufferer. Some instances which Judith related of your fearlessness and promptitude made me adopt the latter supposition with some degree of confidence.

"By the girl's direction I found a ladder, and mounted to your closet window. This is scarcely large enough to admit the head, but it answered my purpose too well.

"I cannot express my confusion and surprize at your abrupt and precipitate flight. I hastily removed the ladder; and, after some pause, curiosity and doubts of your safety induced me to follow you. I found you stretched on the turf before your brother's door, without sense or motion. I felt the deepest regret at this unlooked-for consequence of my scheme. I knew not what to do to procure you relief. The idea of awakening the family naturally presented itself. This emergency was critical, and there was no time to deliberate. It was a sudden thought that occurred. I put my lips to the key-hole, and sounded an alarm which effectually roused the sleepers. My organs were naturally forcible, and had been improved by long and assiduous exercise.

"Long and bitterly did I repent of my scheme. I was somewhat consoled by reflecting that my purpose had not been evil, and renewed my fruitless vows never to attempt such dangerous experiments. For some time I adhered, with laudable forbearance, to this resolution.

"My life has been a life of hardship and exposure. In the summer I prefer to make my bed of the smooth turf, or, at most, the shelter of a summer-house suffices. In all my rambles I never found a spot in which so many picturesque beauties and rural delights were assembled as at Mettingen. No corner of your little domain unites fragrance and secrecy in so perfect a degree as the recess in the bank. The odour of its leaves, the coolness of its shade, and the music of its water-fall, had early attracted my attention. Here my sadness was converted into peaceful melancholy—here my slumbers were found, and my pleasures enhanced.

"As most free from interruption, I chose this as the scene of my midnight interviews with Judith. One evening, as the sun declined, I was seated here, when I was alarmed by your approach. It was with difficulty that I effected my escape unnoticed by you.

"At the customary hour, I returned to your habitation, and was made acquainted by Judith, with your unusual absence. I half suspected the true cause, and felt uneasiness at the danger there was that I should be deprived of my retreat; or, at least, interrupted in the possession of it. The girl, likewise, informed me, that, among your other singularities, it was not uncommon for you to leave your bed, and walk forth for the sake of night-airs and starlight contemplations.

"I desired to prevent this inconvenience. I found you easily swayed by fear. I was influenced, in my choice of means, by the facility and certainty of that to which I had been accustomed. All that I forsaw was, that, in future, this spot would be cautiously shunned by you.

"I entered the recess with the utmost caution, and discovered, by your breathings, in what condition you were. The unexpected interpretation which you placed upon my former proceeding, suggested my conduct on the present occasion. The mode in which heaven is said by the poet, to interfere for the prevention of crimes,* was somewhat analogous to my province, and never failed to occur to me at seasons like this. It was requisite to break your slumbers, and for this end I uttered the powerful monosyllable, 'hold! hold!' My purpose was not prescribed by duty, yet surely it was far from being atrocious and inexpiable. To effect it, I uttered what was false, but it was well suited to my purpose. Nothing less was intended than to injure you. Nay, the evil resulting from my former act, was partly removed by assuring you that in all places but this you were safe.

*——Peeps through the blanket of the dark, and cries
Hold! Hold!——[25]   SHAKESPEARE.

Chapter XXIII.

"My morals will appear to you far from rigid, yet my conduct will fall short of your suspicions. I am now to confess actions less excusable, and yet surely they will not entitle me to the name of a desperate or sordid criminal.

"Your house was rendered, by your frequent and long absences, easily accessible to my curiosity. My meeting with Pleyel was the prelude to direct intercourse with you. I had seen much of the world, but your character exhibited a specimen of human powers that was wholly new to me. My intercourse with your servant furnished me with curious details of your domestic management. I was of a different sex: I was not your husband; I was not even your friend; yet my knowledge of you was of that kind, which conjugal intimacies can give, and, in some respects, more accurate. The observation of your domestic was guided by me.

"You will not be surprised that I should sometimes profit by your absence, and adventure to examine with my own eyes, the interior of your chamber. Upright and sincere, you used no watchfulness, and practiced no precautions. I scrutinized every thing, and pried every where. Your closet was usually locked, but it was once my fortune to find the key on a bureau. I opened and found new scope for my curiosity in your books. One of these was manuscript, and written in characters which essentially agreed with a short-hand system which I had learned from a Jesuit missionary.

"I cannot justify my conduct, yet my only crime was curiosity. I perused this volume with eagerness. The intellect which it unveiled, was brighter than my limited and feeble organs could bear. I was naturally inquisitive as to your ideas respecting my deportment, and the mysteries that had lately occurred.

"You know what you have written. You know that in this volume the key to your inmost soul was contained. If I had been a profound and malignant impostor, what plenteous materials were thus furnished me of stratagems and plots!

"The coincidence of your dream in the summer-house with my exclamation, was truly wonderful. The voice which warned you to forbear was, doubtless, mine; but mixed by a common process of the fancy, with the train of visionary incidents.

"I saw in a stronger light than ever, the dangerousness of that instrument which I employed, and renewed my resolutions to abstain from the use of it in future; but I was destined perpetually to violate my resolutions. By some perverse fate, I was led into circumstances in which the exertion of my powers was the sole or the best means of escape.

"On that memorable night on which our last interview took place, I came as usual to Mettingen. I was apprized of your engagement at your brother's, from which you did not expect to return till late. Some incident suggested the design of visiting your chamber. Among your books which I had not examined, might be something tending to illustrate your character, or the history of your family. Some intimation had been dropped by you in discourse, respecting a performance of your father, in which some important transaction in his life was recorded.

"I was desirous of seeing this book; and such was my habitual attachment to mystery, that I preferred the clandestine perusal of it. Such were the motives that induced me to make this attempt. Judith had disappeared, and finding the house unoccupied, I supplied myself with a light, and proceeded to your chamber.

"I found it easy, on experiment, to lock and unlock your closet door without the aid of a key. I shut myself in this recess, and was busily exploring your shelves, when I heard some one enter the room below. I was at a loss who it could be, whether you or your servant. Doubtful, however, as I was, I conceived it prudent to extinguish the light. Scarcely was this done, when some one entered the chamber. The footsteps were easily distinguished to be yours.

"My situation was now full of danger and perplexity. For some time, I cherished the hope that you would leave the room so long as to afford me an opportunity of escaping. As the hours passed, this hope gradually deserted me. It was plain that you had retired for the night.

"I knew not how soon you might find occasion to enter the closet. I was alive to all the horrors of detection, and ruminated without ceasing, on the behaviour which it would be proper, in case of detection, to adopt. I was unable to discover any consistent method of accounting for my being thus immured.

"It occurred to me that I might withdraw you from your chamber for a few minutes, by counterfeiting a voice from without. Some message from your brother might be delivered, requiring your presence at his house. I was deterred from this scheme by reflecting on the resolution I had formed, and on the possible evils that might result from it. Besides, it was not improbable that you would speedily retire to bed, and then, by the exercise of sufficient caution, I might hope to escape unobserved.

"Meanwhile I listened with the deepest anxiety to every motion from without. I discovered nothing which betokened preparation for sleep. Instead of this I heard deep-drawn sighs, and occasionally an half-expressed and mournful ejaculation. Hence I inferred that you were unhappy. The true state of your mind with regard to Pleyel your own pen had disclosed; but I supposed you to be framed of such materials, that, though a momentary sadness might affect you, you were impregnable to any permanent and heartfelt grief. Inquietude for my own safety was, for a moment, suspended by sympathy with your distress.

"To the former consideration I was quickly recalled by a motion of yours which indicated I knew not what. I fostered the persuasion that you would now retire to bed; but presently you approached the closet, and detection seemed to be inevitable. You put your hand upon the lock. I had formed no plan to extricate myself from the dilemma in which the opening of the door would involve me. I felt an irreconcilable aversion to detection. Thus situated, I involuntarily seized the door with a resolution to resist your efforts to open it.

"Suddenly you receded from the door. This deportment was inexplicable, but the relief it afforded me was quickly gone. You returned, and I once more was thrown into perplexity. The expedient that suggested itself was precipitate and inartificial. I exerted my organs and called upon you *to hold*.

"That you should persist in spite of this admonition, was a subject of astonishment. I again resisted your efforts; for the first expedient having failed, I knew not what other to resort to. In this state, how was my astonishment increased when I heard your exclamations!

"It was now plain that you knew me to be within. Further resistance was unavailing and useless. The door opened, and I shrunk backward. Seldom have I felt deeper mortification, and more painful perplexity. I did not consider that the truth would be less injurious than any lie which I could hastily frame. Conscious as I was of a certain degree of guilt, I conceived that you would form the most odious suspicions. The truth would be imperfect, unless I were likewise to explain the mysterious admonition which had been given; but that explanation was of too great moment, and involved too extensive consequences to make me suddenly resolve to give it.

"I was aware that this discovery would associate itself in your mind, with the dialogue formerly heard in this closet. Thence would your suspicions be aggravated, and to escape from these suspicions would be impossible. But the mere truth would be sufficiently opprobrious, and deprive me for ever of your good opinion.

"Thus was I rendered desperate, and my mind rapidly passed to the contemplation of the use that might be made of previous events. Some good genius would appear to you to have interposed to save you from injury intended by me. Why, I said, since I must sink in her opinion, should I not cherish this belief? Why not personate an enemy, and pretend that celestial interference has frustrated my schemes? I must fly, but let me leave wonder and fear behind me. Elucidation of the mystery will always be practicable. I shall do no injury, but merely talk of evil that was designed, but is now past.

"Thus I extenuated my conduct to myself, but I scarcely expect that this will be to you a sufficient explication of the scene that followed. Those habits which I have imbibed, the rooted passion which possesses me for scattering around me amazement and fear, you enjoy no opportunities of knowing. That a man should wantonly impute to himself the most flagitious designs, will hardly be credited, even though you reflect that my reputation was already, by my own folly, irretrievably ruined; and that it was always in my power to communicate the truth, and rectify the mistake.

"I left you to ponder on this scene. My mind was full of rapid and incongruous ideas. Compunction, self-upbraiding, hopelessness, satisfaction at the view of those effects likely to flow from my new scheme, misgivings as to the beneficial result of this scheme, took possession of my mind, and seemed to struggle for the mastery.

"I had gone too far to recede. I had painted myself to you as an assassin and a ravisher, withheld from guilt only by a voice from heaven. I had thus reverted into the path of error, and now, by having gone thus far, my progress seemed to be irrevocable. I said to myself, I must leave these precincts for ever. My acts have blasted my fame in the eyes of the Wielands. For the sake of creating a mysterious dread, I have made myself a villain. I may complete this mysterious plan by some new imposture, but I cannot aggravate my supposed guilt.

"My resolution was formed, and I was swiftly ruminating on the means for executing it, when Pleyel appeared in sight. This incident decided my conduct. It was plain that Pleyel was a devoted lover, but he was, at the same time, a man of cold resolves and exquisite sagacity. To deceive him would be the sweetest triumph I had ever enjoyed. The deception would be momentary, but it would likewise be complete. That his delusion would so soon be rectified, was a recommendation to my scheme, for I esteemed him too much to desire to entail upon him lasting agonies.

"I had no time to reflect further, for he proceeded, with a quick step, towards the house. I was hurried onward involuntarily and by a mechanical impulse. I followed him as he passed the recess in the bank, and shrowding myself in that spot, I counterfeited sounds which I knew would arrest his steps.

"He stopped, turned, listened, approached, and overheard a dialogue whose purpose was to vanquish his belief in a point where his belief was most difficult to vanquish. I exerted all my powers to imitate your voice, your general sentiments, and your language. Being master, by means of your journal, of your personal history and most secret thoughts, my efforts were the more successful. When I reviewed the tenor of this dialogue, I cannot believe but that Pleyel was deluded. When I think of your character, and of the inferences which this dialogue was intended to suggest, it seems incredible that this delusion should be produced.

"I spared not myself. I called myself murderer, thief, guilty of innumerable perjuries and misdeeds: that you had debased yourself to the level of such an one, no evidence, methought, would suffice to convince him who knew you so thoroughly as Pleyel; and yet the imposture amounted to proof which the most jealous scrutiny would find to be unexceptionable.

"He left his station precipitately and resumed his way to the house. I saw that the detection of his error would be instantaneous, since, not having gone to bed, an immediate interview would take place between you. At first this circumstance was considered with regret; but as time opened my eyes to the possible consequences of this scene, I regarded it with pleasure.

"In a short time the infatuation which had led me thus far began to subside. The remembrance of former reasonings and transactions was renewed. How often I had repented this kind of exertion; how many evils were produced by it which I had not foreseen; what occasions for the bitterest remorse it had administered, now passed through my mind. The black catalogue of stratagems was now increased. I had inspired you with the most vehement terrors: I had filled your mind with faith in shadows and confidence in dreams: I had depraved the imagination of Pleyel: I had exhibited you to his understanding as devoted to brutal gratifications and consummate in hypocrisy. The evidence which accompanied this delusion would be irresistible to one whose passion had perverted his judgment, whose jealousy with regard to me had already been excited, and who, therefore, would not fail to overrate the force of this evidence. What fatal act of despair or of vengeance might not this error produce?

"With regard to myself, I had acted with a phrenzy that surpassed belief. I had warred against my peace and my fame: I had banished myself from the fellowship of vigorous and pure minds: I was self-expelled from a scene which the munificence of nature had adorned with unrivalled beauties, and from haunts in which all the muses and humanities had taken refuge.

"I was thus torn by conflicting fears and tumultuous regrets. The night passed away in this state of confusion; and next morning in the gazette left at my obscure lodging, I read a description and an offer of reward for the apprehension of my person. I was said to have escaped from an Irish prison, in which I was confined as an offender convicted of enormous and complicated crimes.

"This was the work of an enemy, who, by falsehood and stratagem, had procured my condemnation. I was, indeed, a prisoner, but escaped, by the exertion of my powers, the fate to which I was doomed, but which I did not deserve. I had hoped that the malice of my foe was exhausted; but I now perceived that my precautions had been wise, for that the intervention of an ocean was insufficient for my security.

"Let me not dwell on the sensations which this discovery produced. I need not tell by what steps I was induced to seek an interview with you, for the purpose of disclosing the truth, and repairing, as far as possible, the effects of my misconduct. It was unavoidable that this gazette would fall into your hands, and that it would tend to confirm every erroneous impression.

"Having gained this interview, I purposed to seek some retreat in the wilderness, inaccessible to your inquiry and to the malice of my foe, where I might henceforth employ myself in composing a faithful narrative of my actions. I designed it as my vindication from the aspersions that had rested on my character, and as a lesson to mankind on the evils of credulity on the one hand, and of imposture on the other.

"I wrote you a billet, which was left at the house of your friend, and which I knew would, by some means, speedily come to your hands. I entertained a faint hope that my invitation would be complied with. I knew not what use you would make of the opportunity which this proposal afforded you of procuring the seizure of my person; but this fate I was determined to avoid, and I had no doubt but due circumspection, and the exercise of the faculty which I possessed, would enable me to avoid it.

"I lurked, through the day, in the neighbourhood of Mettingen: I approached your habitation of the appointed hour: I entered it in silence, by a trap-door which led into the cellar. This had formerly been bolted on the inside, but Judith had, at an early period in our intercourse, removed this impediment. I ascended to the first floor, but met with no one, nor any thing that indicated the presence of an human being.

"I crept softly up stairs, and at length perceived your chamber door to be opened, and a light to be within. It was of moment to discover by whom this light was accompanied. I was sensible of the inconveniencies to which my being discovered at your chamber door by any one within would subject me; I therefore called out in my own voice, but so modified that it should appear to ascend from the court below, 'Who is in the chamber? Is it Miss Wieland?'

"No answer was returned to this summons. I listened, but no motion could be heard. After a pause I repeated my call, but no less ineffectually.

"I now approached nearer the door, and adventured to look in. A light stood on the table, but nothing human was discernible. I entered cautiously, but all was solitude and stillness.

"I knew not what to conclude. If the house were inhabited, my call would have been noticed; yet some suspicion insinuated itself that silence was studiously kept by persons who intended to surprize me. My approach had been wary, and the silence that ensued my call had likewise preceded it; a circumstance that tended to dissipate my fears.

"At length it occurred to me that Judith might possibly be in her own room. I turned my steps thither; but she was not to be found. I passed into other rooms, and was soon convinced that the house was totally deserted. I returned to your chamber, agitated by vain surmises and opposite conjectures. The appointed hour had passed, and I dismissed the hope of an interview.

"In this state of things I determined to leave a few lines on your toilet, and prosecute my journey to the mountains. Scarcely had I taken the pen when I laid it aside, uncertain in what manner to address you. I rose from the table and walked across the floor. A glance thrown upon the bed acquainted me with a spectacle to which my conceptions of horror had not yet reached.

"In the midst of shuddering and trepidation, the signal of your presence in the court below recalled me to myself. The deed was newly done: I only was in the house: what had lately happened justified any suspicions, however enormous. It was plain that this catastrophe was unknown to you. I thought upon the wild commotion which the discovery would awaken in your breast: I found the confusion of my own thoughts unconquerable, and perceived that the end for which I sought an interview was not now to be accomplished.

"In this state of things it was likewise expedient to conceal my being within. I put out the light and hurried down stairs. To my unspeakable surprize, notwithstanding every motive to fear, you lighted a candle and proceeded to your chamber.

"I retired to that room below from which a door leads into the cellar. This door concealed me from your view as you passed. I thought upon the spectacle which was about to present itself. In an exigence so abrupt and so little foreseen, I was again subjected to the empire of mechanical and habitual impulses. I dreaded the effects which this shocking exhibition, bursting on your unprepared senses, might produce.

"Thus actuated, I stept swiftly to the door, and thrusting my head forward, once more pronounced the mysterious interdiction. At that moment, by some untoward fate, your eyes were cast back, and you saw me in the very act of utterance. I fled through the darksome avenue at which I entered, covered with the shame of this detection.

"With diligence, stimulated by a thousand ineffable emotions, I pursued my intended journey. I have a brother whose farm is situated in the bottom of a fertile desert, near the sources of the Leheigh, and thither I now repaired.

Chapter XXIV.

"Deeply did I ruminate on the occurrences that had just passed. Nothing excited my wonder so much as the means by which you discovered my being in the closet. This discovery appeared to be made at the moment when you attempted to open it. How could you have otherwise remained so long in the chamber apparently fearless and tranquil? And yet, having made this discovery, how could you persist in dragging me forth: persist in defiance of an interdiction so emphatical and solemn?

"But your sister's death was an event detestable and ominous. She had been the victim of the most dreadful species of assassination. How, in a state like yours, the murderous intention could be generated, was wholly inconceivable.

"I did not relinquish my design of confessing to you the part which I had sustained in your family, but I was willing to defer it till the task which I had set myself was finished. That being done, I resumed the resolution. The motives to incite me to this continually acquired force. The more I revolved the events happening at Mettingen, the more insupportable and ominous my terrors became. My waking hours and my sleep were vexed by dismal presages and frightful intimations.

"Catharine was dead by violence. Surely my malignant fears had not made me the cause of her death; yet had I not rashly set in motion a machine over whose progress I had no controul, and which experience had shewn me was infinite in power? Every day might add to the catalogue of horrors of which this was the source, and a seasonable disclosure of the truth might prevent numberless ills.

"Fraught with this conception, I have turned my steps hither. I find your brother's house desolate: the furniture removed, and the walls stained with damps. Your own is in the same situation. Your chamber is dismantled and dark, and you exhibit an image of incurable grief, and of rapid decay.

"I have uttered the truth. This is the extent of my offences. You tell me an horrid tale of Wieland being led to the destruction of his wife and children, by some mysterious agent. You charge me with the guilt of this agency; but I repeat that the amount of my guilt has been truly stated. The perpetrator of Catharine's death was unknown to me till now; nay, it is still unknown to me."

At that moment, the closing of a door in the kitchen was distinctly heard by us. Carwin started and paused. "There is some one coming. I must not be found here by my enemies, and need not, since my purpose is answered."

I had drunk in, with the most vehement attention, every word that he had uttered. I had no breath to interrupt his tale by interrogations or comments. The power that he spoke of was hitherto unknown to me: its existence was incredible, it was susceptible of no direct proof.

He owns that his were the voice and face which I heard and saw. He attempts to give an human explanation of these phantasms; but it is enough that he owns himself to be the agent; his tale is a lie, and his nature devilish. As he deceived me, he likewise deceived my brother, and now do I behold the author of all our calamities!

Such were my thoughts when his pause allowed me to think. I should have had him begone if the silence had not been interrupted; but now I feared no more for myself; and the milkiness of my nature was curdled into hatred and rancour. Some one was near, and this enemy of God and man might possibly be brought to justice. I reflected not that the preternatural power which he had hitherto exerted, would avail to rescue him from any toils in which his feet might be entangled. Meanwhile, looks, and not words of menace and abhorrence, were all that I could bestow.

He did not depart. He seemed dubious, whether, by passing out of the house, or by remaining somewhat longer where he was, he should most endanger his safety. His confusion increased when steps of one barefoot were heard upon the stairs. He threw anxious glances sometimes at the closet, sometimes at the window, and sometimes at the chamber door, yet he was detained by some inexplicable fascination. He stood as if rooted to the spot.

As to me, my soul was bursting with detestation and revenge. I had no room for surmises and tears respecting him that approached. It was doubtless a human being, and would befriend me so far as to aid me in arresting this offender.

The stranger quickly entered the room. My eyes and the eyes of Carwin were, at the same moment, darted upon him. A second glance was not needed to inform us who he was. His locks were tangled, and fell confusedly over his forehead and ears. His shirt was of coarse stuff, and open at the neck and breast. His coat was once of bright and fine texture, but now torn and tarnished with dust. His feet, his legs, and his arms were bare. His features were the seat of a wild and tranquil solemnity, but his eyes bespoke inquietude and curiosity.

He advanced with firm step, and looking as in search of some one. He saw me and stopped. He bent his sight on the floor, and clenching his hands, appeared suddenly absorbed in meditation. Such were the figure and deportment of Wieland! Such, in his fallen state, were the aspect and guise of my brother!

Carwin did not fail to recognize the visitant. Care for his own safety was apparently swallowed up in the amazement which this spectacle produced. His station was conspicuous, and he could not have escaped the roving glances of Wieland; yet the latter seemed totally unconscious of his presence.

Grief at this scene of ruin and blast was at first the only sentiment of which I was conscious. A fearful stillness ensued. At length Wieland, lifting his hands, which were locked in each other, to his breast, exclaimed, "Father! I thank thee. This is thy guidance. Hither thou hast led me, that I might perform thy will: yet let me not err: let me hear again thy messenger!"

He stood for a minute as if listening; but recovering from his attitude, he continued—"It is not needed. Dastardly wretch! thus eternally questioning the behests of thy Maker! weak in resolution! wayward in faith!"

He advanced to me, and, after another pause, resumed: "Poor girl! a dismal fate has set its mark upon thee. Thy life is demanded as a sacrifice. Prepare thee to die. Make not my office difficult by fruitless opposition. Thy prayers might subdue stones; but none but he who enjoined my purpose can shake it."

These words were a sufficient explication of the scene. The nature of his phrenzy, as described by my uncle, was remembered. I who had sought death, was now thrilled with horror because it was near. Death in this form, death from the hand of a brother, was thought upon with undescribable repugnance.

In a state thus verging upon madness, my eye glanced upon Carwin. His astonishment appeared to have struck him motionless and dumb. My life was in danger, and my brother's hand was about to be embrued in my blood. I firmly believed that Carwin's was the instigation. I could rescue me from this abhorred fate; I could dissipate this tremendous illusion; I could save my brother from the perpetration of new horrors, by pointing out the devil who seduced him; to hesitate a moment was to perish. These thoughts gave strength to my limbs, and energy to my accents: I started on my feet.

"O brother! spare me, spare thyself: There is thy betrayer. He counterfeited the voice and face of an angel, for the purpose of destroying thee and me. He has this moment confessed it. He is able to speak where he is not. He is leagued with hell, but will not avow it; yet he confesses that the agency was his."

My brother turned slowly his eyes, and fixed them upon Carwin. Every joint in the frame of the latter trembled. His complexion was paler than a ghost's. His eye dared not meet that of Wieland, but wandered with an air of distraction from one space to another.

"Man," said my brother, in a voice totally unlike that which he had used to me, "what art thou? The charge has been made. Answer it. The visage—the voice—at the bottom of these stairs—at the hour of eleven—To whom did they belong? To thee?"

Twice did Carwin attempt to speak, but his words died away upon his lips. My brother resumed in a tone of greater vehemence—

"Thou falterest; faltering is ominous; say yes or no: one word will suffice; but beware of falsehood. Was it a stratagem of hell to overthrow my family? Wast thou the agent?"

I now saw that the wrath which had been prepared for me was to be heaped upon another. The tale that I heard from him, and his present trepidations, were abundant testimonies of his guilt. But what if Wieland should be undeceived! What if he shall find his acts to have proceeded not from an heavenly prompter, but from human treachery! Will not his rage mount into whirlwind? Will not he tear limb from limb this devoted wretch?

Instinctively I recoiled from this image, but it gave place to another. Carwin may be innocent, but the impetuosity of his judge may misconstrue his answers into a confession of guilt. Wieland knows not that mysterious voices and appearances were likewise witnessed by me. Carwin may be ignorant of those which misled my brother. Thus may his answers unwarily betray himself to ruin.

Such might be the consequences of my frantic precipitation, and these, it was necessary, if possible, to prevent. I attempted to speak, but Wieland, turning suddenly upon me, commanded silence, in a tone furious and terrible. My lips closed, and my tongue refused its office.

"What art thou?" he resumed, addressing himself to Carwin. "Answer me; whose form—whose voice—was it thy contrivance? Answer me."

The answer was now given, but confusedly and fearedly articulated. "I meant nothing—I intended no ill—if I understand—if I do not mistake you—it is too true—I did appear—in the entry—did speak. The contrivance was mine, but—"

These words were no sooner uttered, than my brother ceased to wear the same aspect. His eyes were downcast: he was motionless: his respiration became hoarse like that of a man in the agonies of death. Carwin seemed unable to say more. He might have easily escaped, but the thought which occupied him related to what was horrid and unintelligible in this scene, and not to his own danger.

Presently the faculties of Wieland, which, for a time, were chained up, were seized with restlessness and trembling. He broke silence. The stoutest heart would have been appalled by the tone in which he spoke. He addressed himself to Carwin.

"Why art thou here? Who detains thee? Go and learn better. I will meet thee, but it must be at the bar of thy Maker. There shall I bear witness against thee."

Perceiving that Carwin did not obey, he continued, "Dost thou wish me to complete the catalogue by thy death? Thy life is a worthless thing. Tempt me no more. I am but a man, and thy presence may awaken a fury which may spurn my controul. Begone!"

Carwin, irresolute, striving in vain for utterance, his complexion pallid as death, his knees beating one against another, slowly obeyed the mandate and withdrew.

Chapter XXV.

A few words more and I lay aside the pen for ever. Yet why should I not relinquish it now? All that I have said is preparatory to this scene, and my fingers, tremulous and cold as my heart, refuse any further exertion. This must not be. Let my last energies support me in the finishing of this task. Then will I lay down my head in the lap of death. Hushed will be all my murmurs in the sleep of the grave.

Every sentiment has perished in my bosom. Even friendship is extinct. Your love for me has prompted me to this task; but I would not have complied if it had not been a luxury thus to feast upon my woes. I have justly calculated upon my remnant of strength. When I lay down the pen the taper of life will expire: my existence will terminate with my tale.

Now that I was left alone with Wieland, the perils of my situation presented themselves to my mind. That this paroxysm should terminate in havock and rage it was reasonable to predict. The first suggestion of my fears had been disproved by my experience. Carwin had acknowledged his offences, and yet had escaped. The vengeance which I had harboured had not been admitted by Wieland, and yet the evils which I had endured, compared with those inflicted on my brother, were as nothing. I thirsted for his blood, and was tormented with an insatiable appetite for his destruction; yet my brother was unmoved, and had dismissed him in safety. Surely thou wast more than man, while I am sunk below the beasts.

Did I place a right construction on the conduct of Wieland? Was the error that misled him so easily rectified? Were views so vivid and faith so strenuous thus liable to fading and to change? Was there not reason to doubt the accuracy of my perceptions? With images like these was my mind thronged, till the deportment of my brother called away my attention.

I saw his lips move and his eyes cast up to heaven. Then would he listen and look back, as if in expectation of some one's appearance. Thrice he repeated these gesticulations and this inaudible prayer. Each time the mist of confusion and doubt seemed to grow darker and to settle on his understanding. I guessed at the meaning of these tokens. The words of Carwin had shaken his belief, and he was employed in summoning the messenger who had formerly communed with him, to attest the value of these new doubts. In vain the summons was repeated, for his eye met nothing but vacancy, and not a sound saluted his ear.

He walked to the bed, gazed with eagerness at the pillow which had sustained the head of the breathless Catharine, and then returned to the place where I sat. I had no power to lift my eyes to his face: I was dubious of his purpose: this purpose might aim at my life.

Alas! nothing but subjection to danger, and exposure to temptation, can show us what we are. By this test I was now tried, and found to be cowardly and rash. Men can deliberately untie the thread of life, and of this I had deemed myself capable; yet now that I stood upon the brink of fate, that the knife of the sacrificer was aimed at my heart, I shuddered and betook myself to any means of escape, however monstrous.

Can I bear to think—can I endure to relate the outrage which my heart meditated? Where were my means of safety? Resistance was vain. Not even the energy of despair could set me on a level with that strength which his terrific prompter had bestowed upon Wieland. Terror enables us to perform incredible feats; but terror was not then the state of my mind: where then were my hopes of rescue?

Methinks it is too much. I stand aside, as it were, from myself; I estimate my own deservings; a hatred, immortal and inexorable, is my due. I listen to my own pleas, and find them empty and false: yes, I acknowledge that my guilt surpasses that of all mankind: I confess that the curses of a world, and the frowns of a deity, are inadequate to my demerits. Is there a thing in the world worthy of infinite abhorrence? It is I.

What shall I say! I was menaced, as I thought, with death, and, to elude this evil, my hand was ready to inflict death upon the menacer. In visiting my house, I had made provision against the machinations of Carwin. In a fold of my dress an open penknife was concealed. This I now seized and drew forth. It lurked out of view; but I now see that my state of mind would have rendered the deed inevitable if my brother had lifted his hand. This instrument of my preservation would have been plunged into his heart.

O, insupportable remembrance! hide thee from my view for a time; hide it from me that my heart was black enough to meditate the stabbing of a brother! a brother thus supreme in misery; thus towering in virtue!

He was probably unconscious of my design, but presently drew back. This interval was sufficient to restore me to myself. The madness, the iniquity of that act which I had purposed rushed upon my apprehension. For a moment I was breathless with agony. At the next moment I recovered my strength, and threw the knife with violence on the floor.

The sound awoke my brother from his reverie. He gazed alternately at me and at the weapon. With a movement equally solemn he stooped and took it up. He placed the blade in different positions, scrutinizing it accurately, and maintaining, at the same time, a profound silence.

Again he looked at me, but all that vehemence and loftiness of spirit which had so lately characterized his features, were flown. Fallen muscles, a forehead contracted into folds, eyes dim with unbidden drops, and a ruefulness of aspect which no words can describe, were now visible.

His looks touched into energy the same sympathies in me, and I poured forth a flood of tears. This passion was quickly checked by fear, which had now, no longer, my own, but his safety for their object. I watched his deportment in silence. At length he spoke:

"Sister," said he, in an accent mournful and mild, "I have acted poorly my part in this world. What thinkest thou? Shall I not do better in the next?"

I could make no answer. The mildness of his tone astonished and encouraged me. I continued to regard him with wistful and anxious looks.

"I think," resumed he, "I will try. My wife and my babes have gone before. Happy wretches! I have sent you to repose, and ought not to linger behind."

These words had a meaning sufficiently intelligible. I looked at the open knife in his hand and shuddered, but knew not how to prevent the deed which I dreaded. He quickly noticed my fears, and comprehended them. Stretching towards me his hand, with an air of increasing mildness: "Take it," said he: "Fear not for thy own sake, nor for mine. The cup is gone by, and its transient inebriation is succeeded by the soberness of truth.

"Thou angel whom I was wont to worship! fearest thou, my sister, for thy life? Once it was the scope of my labours to destroy thee, but I was prompted to the deed by heaven; such, at least, was my belief. Thinkest thou that thy death was sought to gratify malevolence? No. I am pure from all stain. I believed that my God was my mover!

"Neither thee nor myself have I cause to injure. I have done my duty, and surely there is merit in having sacrificed to that, all that is dear to the heart of man. If a devil has deceived me, he came in the habit of an angel. If I erred, it was not my judgment that deceived me, but my senses. In thy sight, being of beings! I am still pure. Still will I look for my reward in thy justice!"

Did my ears truly report these sounds? If I did not err, my brother was restored to just perceptions. He knew himself to have been betrayed to the murder of his wife and children, to have been the victim of infernal artifice; yet he found consolation in the rectitude of his motives. He was not devoid of sorrow, for this was written on his countenance; but his soul was tranquil and sublime.

Perhaps this was merely a transition of his former madness into a new shape. Perhaps he had not yet awakened to the memory of the horrors which he had perpetrated. Infatuated wretch that I was! To set myself up as a model by which to judge of my heroic brother! My reason taught me that his conclusions were right; but conscious of the impotence of reason over my own conduct; conscious of my cowardly rashness and my criminal despair, I doubted whether any one could be stedfast and wise.

Such was my weakness, that even in the midst of these thoughts, my mind glided into abhorrence of Carwin, and I uttered in a low voice, O! Carwin! Carwin! What hast thou to answer for?

My brother immediately noticed the involuntary exclamation; "Clara!" said he, "be thyself. Equity used to be a theme for thy eloquence. Reduce its lessons to practice, and be just to that unfortunate man. The instrument has done its work, and I am satisfied.

"I thank thee, my God, for this last illumination! My enemy is thine also. I deemed him to be man, the man with whom I have often communed; but now thy goodness has unveiled to me his true nature. As the performer of thy behests, he is my friend."

My heart began now to misgive me. His mournful aspect had gradually yielded place to a serene brow. A new soul appeared to actuate his frame, and his eyes to beam with preternatural lustre. These symptoms did not abate, and he continued:

"Clara! I must not leave thee in doubt. I know not what brought about thy interview with the being whom thou callest Carwin. For a time, I was guilty of thy error, and deduced from his incoherent confessions that I had been made the victim of human malice. He left us at my bidding, and I put up a prayer that my doubts should be removed. Thy eyes were shut, and thy ears sealed to the vision that answered my prayer.

"I was indeed deceived. The form thou hast seen was the incarnation of a dæmon. The visage and voice which urged me to the sacrifice of my family, were his. Now he personates a human form: then he was invironed with the lustre of heaven.—

"Clara," he continued, advancing closer to me, "thy death must come. This minister is evil, but he from whom his commission was received is God. Submit then with all thy wonted resignation to a decree that cannot be reversed or resisted. Mark the clock. Three minutes are allowed to thee, in which to call up thy fortitude, and prepare thee for thy doom." There he stopped.

Even now, when this scene exists only in memory, when life and all its functions have sunk into torpor, my pulse throbs, and my hairs uprise: my brows are knit, as then; and I gaze around me in distraction. I was unconquerably averse to death; but death, imminent and full of agony as that which was threatened, was nothing. This was not the only or chief inspirer of my fears.

For him, not for myself, was my soul tormented. I might die, and no crime, surpassing the reach of mercy, would pursue me to the presence of my Judge; but my assassin would survive to contemplate his deed, and that assassin was Wieland!

Wings to bear me beyond his reach I had not. I could not vanish with a thought. The door was open, but my murderer was interposed between that and me. Of self-defence I was incapable. The phrenzy that lately prompted me to blood was gone; my state was desperate; my rescue was impossible.

The weight of these accumulated thoughts could not be borne. My sight became confused; my limbs were seized with convulsion; I spoke, but my words were half-formed:—

"Spare me, my brother! Look down, righteous Judge! snatch me from this fate! take away this fury from him, or turn it elsewhere!"

Such was the agony of my thoughts, that I noticed not steps entering my apartment. Supplicating eyes were cast upward, but when my prayer was breathed, I once more wildly gazed at the door. A form met my sight: I shuddered as if the God whom I invoked were present. It was Carwin that again intruded, and who stood before me, erect in attitude, and stedfast in look!

The sight of him awakened new and rapid thoughts. His recent tale was remembered: his magical transitions and mysterious energy of voice: Whether he were infernal or miraculous, or human, there was no power and no need to decide. Whether the contriver or not of this spell, he was able to unbind it, and to check the fury of my brother. He had ascribed to himself intentions not malignant. Here now was afforded a test of his truth. Let him interpose, as from above; revoke the savage decree which the madness of Wieland has assigned to heaven, and extinguish for ever this passion for blood!

My mind detected at a glance this avenue to safety. The recommendations it possessed thronged as it were together, and made but one impression on my intellect. Remoter effects and collateral dangers I saw not. Perhaps the pause of an instant had sufficed to call them up. The improbability that the influence which governed Wieland was external or human; the tendency of this stratagem to sanction so fatal an error, or substitute a more destructive rage in place of this; the sufficiency of Carwin's mere muscular forces to counteract the efforts, and restrain the fury of Wieland, might, at a second glance, have been discovered; but no second glance was allowed. My first thought hurried me to action, and, fixing my eyes upon Carwin I exclaimed—

"O wretch! once more hast thou come? Let it be to abjure thy malice; to counterwork this hellish stratagem; to turn from me and from my brother, this desolating rage!

"Testify thy innocence or thy remorse: exert the powers which pertain to thee, whatever they be, to turn aside this ruin. Thou art the author of these horrors! What have I done to deserve thus to die? How have I merited this unrelenting persecution? I adjure thee, by that God whose voice thou hast dared to counterfeit, to save my life!

"Wilt thou then go? leave me! Succourless!"

Carwin listened to my intreaties unmoved, and turned from me. He seemed to hesitate a moment; then glided through the door. Rage and despair stifled my utterance. The interval of respite was passed; the pangs reserved for me by Wieland, were not to be endured; my thoughts rushed again into anarchy. Having received the knife from his hand, I held it loosely and without regard; but now it seized again my attention, and I grasped it with force.

He seemed to notice not the entrance or exit of Carwin. My gesture and the murderous weapon appeared to have escaped his notice. His silence was unbroken; his eye, fixed upon the clock for a time, was now withdrawn; fury kindled in every feature; all that was human in his face gave way to an expression supernatural and tremendous. I felt my left arm within his grasp.—

Even now I hesitated to strike. I shrunk from his assault, but in vain.—

Here let me desist. Why should I rescue this event from oblivion? Why should I paint this detestable conflict? Why not terminate at once this series of horrors?—Hurry to the verge of the precipice, and cast myself for ever beyond remembrance and beyond hope?

Still I live: with this load upon my breast; with this phantom to pursue my steps; with adders lodged in my bosom, and stinging me to madness: still I consent to live!

Yes, I will rise above the sphere of mortal passions: I will spurn at the cowardly remorse that bids me seek impunity in silence, or comfort in forgetfulness. My nerves shall be new strung to the task. Have I not resolved? I will die. The gulph before me is inevitable and near. I will die, but then only when my tale is at an end.

Chapter XXVI.

My right hand, grasping the unseen knife, was still disengaged. It was lifted to strike. All my strength was exhausted, but what was sufficient to the performance of this deed. Already was the energy awakened, and the impulse given, that should bear the fatal steel to his heart, when——Wieland shrunk back: his hand was withdrawn. Breathless with affright and desperation, I stood, freed from his grasp; unassailed; untouched.

Thus long had the power which controuled the scene forborne to interfere; but now his might was irresistible, and Wieland in a moment was disarmed of all his purposes. A voice, louder than human organs could produce, shriller than language can depict, burst from the ceiling, and commanded him—*to hold*!

Trouble and dismay succeeded to the stedfastness that had lately been displayed in the looks of Wieland. His eyes roved from one quarter to another, with an expression of doubt. He seemed to wait for a further intimation.

Carwin's agency was here easily recognized. I had besought him to interpose in my defence. He had flown. I had imagined him deaf to my prayer, and resolute to see me perish: yet he disappeared merely to devise and execute the means of my relief.

Why did he not forbear when this end was accomplished? Why did his misjudging zeal and accursed precipitation overpass that limit? Or meant he thus to crown the scene, and conduct his inscrutable plots to this consummation?

Such ideas were the fruit of subsequent contemplation. This moment was pregnant with fate. I had no power to reason. In the career of my tempestuous thoughts, rent into pieces, as my mind was, by accumulating horrors, Carwin was unseen and unsuspected. I partook of Wieland's credulity, shook with his amazement, and panted with his awe.

Silence took place for a moment; so much as allowed the attention to recover its post. Then new sounds were uttered from above.

"Man of errors! cease to cherish thy delusion: not heaven or hell, but thy senses have misled thee to commit these acts. Shake off thy phrenzy, and ascend into rational and human. Be lunatic no longer."

My brother opened his lips to speak. His tone was terrific and faint. He muttered an appeal to heaven. It was not difficult to comprehend the theme of his inquiries. They implied doubt as to the nature of the impulse that hitherto had guided him, and questioned whether he had acted in consequence of insane perceptions.

To these interrogatories the voice, which now seemed to hover at his shoulder, loudly answered in the affirmative. Then uninterrupted silence ensued.

Fallen from his lofty and heroic station; now finally restored to the perception of truth; weighed to earth by the recollection of his own deeds; consoled no longer by a consciousness of rectitude, for the loss of offspring and wife—a loss for which he was indebted to his own misguided hand; Wieland was transformed at once into the *man of sorrows*![26]

He reflected not that credit should be as reasonably denied to the last, as to any former intimation; that one might as justly be ascribed to erring or diseased senses as the other. He saw not that this discovery in no degree affected the integrity of his conduct; that his motives had lost none of their claims to the homage of mankind; that the preference of supreme good, and the boundless energy of duty, were undiminished in his bosom.

It is not for me to pursue him through the ghastly changes of his countenance. Words he had none. Now he sat upon the floor, motionless in all his limbs, with his eyes glazed and fixed; a monument of woe.

Anon a spirit of tempestuous but undesigning activity seized him. He rose from his place and strode across the floor, tottering and at random. His eyes were without moisture, and gleamed with the fire that consumed his vitals. The muscles of his face were agitated by convulsion. His lips moved, but no sound escaped him.

That nature should long sustain this conflict was not to be believed. My state was little different from that of my brother. I entered, as it were, into his thought. My heart was visited and rent by his pangs— Oh that thy phrenzy had never been cured! that thy madness, with its blissful visions, would return! or, if that must not be, that thy scene would hasten to a close! that death would cover thee with his oblivion!

What can I wish for thee? Thou who hast vied with the great preacher of thy faith in sanctity of motives, and in elevation above sensual and selfish! Thou whom thy fate has changed into paricide and savage! Can I wish for the continuance of thy being? No.

For a time his movements seemed destitute of purpose. If he walked; if he turned; if his fingers were entwined with each other; if his hands were pressed against opposite sides of his head with a force sufficient to crush it into pieces; it was to tear his mind from self-contemplation; to waste his thoughts on external objects.

Speedily this train was broken. A beam appeared to be darted into his mind, which gave a purpose to his efforts. An avenue to escape presented itself; and now he eagerly gazed about him: when my thoughts became engaged by his demeanour, my fingers were stretched as by a mechanical force, and the knife, no longer heeded or of use, escaped from my grasp, and fell unperceived on the floor. His eye now lighted upon it; he seized it with the quickness of thought.

I shrieked aloud, but it was too late. He plunged it to the hilt in his neck; and his life instantly escaped with the stream that gushed from the wound. He was stretched at my feet; and my hands were sprinkled with his blood as he fell.

Such was thy last deed, my brother! For a spectacle like this was it my fate to be reserved! Thy eyes were closed—thy face ghastly with death—thy arms, and the spot where thou liedest, floated in thy life's blood! These images have not, for a moment, forsaken me. Till I am breathless and cold, they must continue to hover in my sight.

Carwin, as I said, had left the room, but he still lingered in the house. My voice summoned him to my aid, but I scarcely noticed his re-entrance, and now faintly recollect his terrified looks, his broken exclamations, his vehement avowals of innocence, the effusions of his pity for me, and his offers of assistance.

I did not listen—I answered him not—I ceased to upbraid or accuse. His guilt was a point to which I was indifferent. Ruffian or devil, black as hell or bright as angels, thenceforth he was nothing to me. I was incapable of sparing a look or a thought from the ruin that was spread at my feet.

When he left me, I was scarcely conscious of any variation in the scene. He informed the inhabitants of the *Hut* of what had passed, and they flew to the spot. Careless of his own safety, he hastened to the city to inform my friends of my condition.

My uncle speedily arrived at the house. The body of Wieland was removed from my presence, and they supposed that I would follow it; but no, my home is ascertained; here I have taken up my rest, and never will I go hence, till, like Wieland, I am borne to my grave.

Importunity was tried in vain: they threatened to remove me by violence—nay, violence was used; but my soul prizes too dearly this little roof to endure to be bereaved of it. Force should not prevail when the hoary looks and supplicating tears of my uncle were ineffectual. My repugnance to move gave birth to ferociousness and phrenzy when force was employed, and they were obliged to consent to my return.

They besought me—they remonstrated—they appealed to every duty that connected me with him that made me, and with my fellow-men—in vain. While I live I will not go hence. Have I not fulfilled my destiny?

Why will ye torment me with your reasonings and reproofs? Can ye restore to me the hope of my better days? Can ye give me back Catharine and her babes? Can ye recall to life him who died at my feet?

I will eat—I will drink—I will lie down and rise up at your bidding—all I ask is the choice of my abode. What is there unreasonable in this demand? Shortly will I be at peace. This is the spot which I have chosen in which to breathe my last sigh. Deny me not, I beseech you, so slight a boon.

Talk not to me, O my revered friend! of Carwin. He has told thee his tale, and thou exculpatest him from all direct concern in the fate of Wieland. This scene of havock was produced by an illusion of the senses. Be it so: I care not from what source these disasters have flowed; it suffices that they have swallowed up our hopes and our existence.

What his agency began, his agency conducted to a close. He intended, by the final effort of his power, to rescue me and to banish his illusions from my brother. Such is his tale, concerning the truth of which I care not. Henceforth I foster but one wish—I ask only quick deliverance from life and all the ills that attend it.—

Go wretch! torment me not with thy presence and thy prayers.—Forgive thee? Will that avail thee when thy fateful hour shall arrive? Be thou acquitted at thy own tribunal, and thou needest not fear the verdict of others. If thy guilt be capable of blacker hues, if hitherto thy conscience be without stain, thy crime will be made more flagrant by thus violating my retreat. Take thyself away from my sight if thou wouldest not behold my death!

Thou art gone! murmuring and reluctant! And now my repose is coming—my work is done!

Chapter XXVII.

[Written three years after the foregoing, and dated at Montpellier.]

I imagined that I had forever laid aside the pen; and that I should take up my abode in this part of the world, was of all events the least probable. My destiny I believed to be accomplished, and I looked forward to a speedy termination of my life with the fullest confidence.

Surely I had reason to be weary of existence, to be impatient of every tie which held me from the grave. I experienced this impatience in its fullest extent. I was not only enamoured of death, but conceived, from the condition of my frame, that to shun it was impossible, even though I had ardently desired it; yet here am I, a thousand leagues from my native soil, in full possession of life and of health, and not destitute of happiness.

Such is man. Time will obliterate the deepest impressions. Grief the most vehement and hopeless, will gradually decay and wear itself out. Arguments may be employed in vain: every moral prescription may be ineffectually tried: remonstrances, however cogent or pathetic, shall have no power over the attention, or shall be repelled with disdain; yet, as day follows day, the turbulence of our emotions shall subside, and our fluctuations be finally succeeded by a calm.

Perhaps, however, the conquest of despair was chiefly owing to an accident which rendered my continuance in my own house impossible. At the conclusion of my long, and, as I then supposed, my last letter to you, I mentioned my resolution to wait for death in the very spot which had been the principal scene of my misfortunes. From this resolution my friends exerted themselves with the utmost zeal and perseverance to make me depart. They justly imagined that to be thus surrounded by memorials of the fate of my family, would tend to foster my disease. A swift succession of new objects, and the exclusion of every thing calculated to remind me of my loss, was the only method of cure.

I refused to listen to their exhortations. Great as my calamity was, to be torn from this asylum was regarded by me as an aggravation of it. By a perverse constitution of mind, he was considered as my greatest enemy who sought to withdraw me from a scene which supplied eternal food to my melancholy, and kept my despair from languishing.

In relating the history of these disasters I derived a similar species of gratification. My uncle earnestly dissuaded me from this task; but his remonstrances were as fruitless on this head as they had been on others. They would have withheld from me the implements of writing; but they quickly perceived that to withstand would be more injurious than to comply with my wishes. Having finished my tale, it seemed as if the scene were closing. A fever lurked in my veins, and my strength was gone. Any exertion, however slight, was attended with difficulty, and, at length, I refused to rise from my bed.

I now see the infatuation and injustice of the conduct in its true colours. I reflect upon the sensations and reasonings of that period with wonder and humiliation. That I should be insensible to the claims and tears of my friends; that I should overlook the suggestions of duty, and fly from that post in which only I could be instrumental to the benefit of others; that the exercise of the social and beneficent affections, the contemplation of nature and the acquisition of wisdom should not be seen to be means of happiness still within my reach, is, at this time, scarcely credible.

It is true that I am now changed; but I have not the consolation to reflect that my change was owing to my fortitude or to my capacity for instruction. Better thoughts grew up in my mind imperceptibly. I cannot but congratulate myself on the change, though, perhaps, it merely argues a fickleness of temper, and a defect of sensibility.

After my narrative was ended I betook myself to my bed, in the full belief that my career in this world was on the point of finishing. My uncle took up his abode with me, and performed for me every office of nurse, physician and friend. One night, after some hours of restlessness and pain, I sunk into deep sleep. Its tranquillity, however, was of no long duration. My fancy became suddenly distempered, and my brain was turned into a theatre of uproar and confusion. It would not be easy to describe the wild and phantastical incongruities that pestered me. My uncle, Wieland, Pleyel and Carwin were successively and momently discerned amidst the storm. Sometimes I was swallowed up by whirlpools, or caught up in the air by half-seen and gigantic forms, and thrown upon pointed rocks, or cast among the billows. Sometimes gleams of light were shot into a dark abyss, on the verge of which I was standing, and enabled me to discover, for a moment, its enormous depth and hideous precipices. Anon, I was transported to some ridge of Ætna, and made a terrified spectator of its fiery torrents and its pillars of smoke.

However strange it may seem, I was conscious, even during my dream, of my real situation. I knew myself to be asleep, and struggled to break the spell, by muscular exertions. These did not avail, and I continued to suffer these abortive creations till a loud voice, at my bed side, and some one shaking me with violence, put an end to my reverie. My eyes were unsealed, and I started from my pillow.

My chamber was filled with smoke, which, though in some degree luminous, would permit me to see nothing, and by which I was nearly suffocated. The crackling of flames, and the deafening clamour of voices without, burst upon my ears. Stunned as I was by this hubbub, scorched with heat, and nearly choaked by the accumulating vapours, I was unable to think or act for my own preservation; I was incapable, indeed, of comprehending my danger.

I was caught up, in an instant, by a pair of sinewy arms, borne to the window, and carried down a ladder which had been placed there. My uncle stood at the bottom and received me. I was not fully aware of my situation till I found myself sheltered in the *Hut,* and surrounded by its inhabitants.

By neglect of the servant, some unextinguished embers had been placed in a barrel in the cellar of the building. The barrel had caught fire; this was communicated to the beams of the lower floor, and thence to the upper part of the structure. It was first discovered by some persons at a distance, who hastened to the spot and alarmed my uncle and the servants. The flames had already made considerable progress, and my condition was overlooked till my escape was rendered nearly impossible.

My danger being known, and a ladder quickly procured, one of the spectators ascended to my chamber, and effected my deliverance in the manner before related.

This incident, disastrous as it may at first seem, had, in reality, a beneficial effect upon my feelings. I was, in some degree, roused from the stupor which had seized my faculties. The monotonous and gloomy series of my thoughts was broken. My habitation was levelled with the ground, and I was obliged to seek a new one. A new train of images, disconnected with the fate of my family, forced itself on my attention, and a belief insensibly sprung up, that tranquillity, if not happiness, was still within my reach. Notwithstanding the shocks which my frame had endured, the anguish of my thoughts no sooner abated than I recovered my health.

I now willingly listened to my uncle's solicitations to be the companion of his voyage. Preparations were easily made, and after a tedious passage, we set our feet on the shore of the ancient world. The memory of the past did not forsake me; but the melancholy which it generated, and the tears with which it filled my eyes, were not unprofitable. My curiosity was revived, and I contemplated, with ardour, the spectacle of living manners and the monuments of past ages.

In proportion as my heart was reinstated in the possession of its ancient tranquillity, the sentiment which I had cherished with regard to Pleyel returned. In a short time he was united to the Saxon woman, and made his residence in the neighbourhood of Boston. I was glad that circumstances would not permit an interview to take place between us. I could not desire their misery; but I reaped no pleasure from reflecting on their happiness. Time, and the exertions of my fortitude, cured me, in some degree, of this folly. I continued to love him, but my passion was diguised to myself; I considered it merely as a more tender species of friendship, and cherished it without compunction.

Through my uncle's exertions a meeting was brought about between Carwin and Pleyel, and explanations took place which restored me at once to the good opinion of the latter. Though separated so widely our correspondence was punctual and frequent, and paved the way for that union which can only end with the death of one of us.

In my letters to him I made no secret of my former sentiments. This was a theme on which I could talk without painful, though not without delicate emotions. That knowledge which I should never have imparted to a lover, I felt little scruple to communicate to a friend.

A year and an half elapsed when Theresa was snatched from him by death, in the hour in which she gave him the first pledge of their mutual affection. This event was borne by him with his customary fortitude. It induced him, however, to make a change in his plans. He disposed of his property in America, and joined my uncle and me, who had terminated the wanderings of two years at Montpellier, which will henceforth, I believe, be our permanent abode.

If you reflect upon that entire confidence which had subsisted from our infancy between Pleyel and myself; on the passion that I had contracted, and which was merely smothered for a time; and on the esteem which was mutual, you will not, perhaps, be surprized that the renovation of our intercourse should give birth to that union which at present subsists. When the period had elapsed necessary to weaken the remembrance of Theresa, to whom he had been bound by ties more of honor than of love, he tendered his affections to me. I need not add that the tender was eagerly accepted.

Perhaps you are somewhat interested in the fate of Carwin. He saw, when too late, the danger of imposture. So much affected was he by the catastrophe to which he was a witness, that he laid aside all regard to his own safety. He sought my uncle, and confided to him the tale which he had just related to me. He found a more impartial and indulgent auditor in Mr. Cambridge, who imputed to maniacal illusion the conduct of Wieland, though he conceived the previous and unseen agency of Carwin, to have indirectly but powerfully predisposed him to this deplorable perversion of mind.

It was easy for Carwin to elude the persecutions of Ludloe. It was merely requisite to hide himself in a remote district of Pennsylvania. This, when he parted from us, he determined to do. He is now probably engaged in the harmless pursuits of agriculture, and may come to think, without insupportable remorse, on the evils to which his fatal talents have given birth. The innocence and usefulness of his future life may, in some degree, atone for the miseries so rashly or so thoughtlessly inflicted.

More urgent considerations hindered me from mentioning, in the course of my former mournful recital, any particulars respecting the unfortunate father of Louisa Conway. That man surely was reserved to be a monument of capricious fortune. His southern journies being finished, he returned to Philadelphia. Before he reached the city he left the highway, and alighted at my brother's door. Contrary to his expectation, no one came forth to welcome him, or hail his approach. He attempted to enter the house, but bolted doors, barred windows, and a silence broken only by unanswered calls, shewed him that the mansion was deserted.

He proceeded thence to my habitation, which he found, in like manner, gloomy and tenantless. His surprize may be easily conceived. The rustics who occupied the *Hut* told him an imperfect and incredible tale. He hasted to the city, and extorted from Mrs. Baynton a full disclosure of late disasters.

He was inured to adversity, and recovered, after no long time, from the shocks produced by this disappointment of his darling scheme. Our intercourse did not terminate with his departure from America. We have since met with him in France, and light has at length been thrown upon the motives which occasioned the disappearance of his wife, in the manner which I formerly related to you.

I have dwelt upon the ardour of their conjugal attachment, and mentioned that no suspicion had ever glanced upon her purity. This, though the belief was long cherished, recent discoveries have shewn to be questionable. No doubt her integrity would have survived to the present moment, if an extraordinary fate had not befallen her.

Major Stuart had been engaged, while in Germany, in a contest of honor with an Aid de Camp of the Marquis of Granby.[27] His adversary had propagated a rumour injurious to his character. A challenge was sent; a meeting ensued, and Stuart wounded and disarmed the calumniator. The offence was atoned for, and his life secured by suitable concessions.

Maxwell, that was his name, shortly after, in consequence of succeeding to a rich inheritance, sold his commission and returned to London. His fortune was speedily augmented by an opulent marriage. Interest was his sole inducement to this marriage, though the lady had been swayed by a credulous affection. The true state of his heart was quickly discovered, and a separation, by mutual consent, took place. The lady withdrew to an estate in a distant county, and Maxwell continued to consume his time and fortune in the dissipation of the capital.

Maxwell, though deceitful and sensual, possessed great force of mind and specious accomplishments. He contrived to mislead the generous mind of Stuart, and to regain the esteem which his misconduct, for a time, had forfeited. He was recommended by her husband to the confidence of Mrs. Stuart. Maxwell was stimulated by revenge, and by a lawless passion, to convert this confidence into a source of guilt.

The education and capacity of this woman, the worth of her husband, the pledge of their alliance which time had produced, her maturity in age and knowledge of the world—all combined to render this attempt hopeless. Maxwell, however, was not easily discouraged. The most perfect being, he believed, must owe his exemption from vice to the absence of temptation. The impulses of love are so subtile and the influence of false reasoning, when enforced by eloquence and passion, so unbounded, that no human virtue is secured from degeneracy. All arts being tried, every temptation being summoned to his aid, dissimulation being carried to its utmost bound, Maxwell, at length, nearly accomplished his purpose. The lady's affections were withdrawn from her husband and transferred to him. She could not, as yet, be reconciled to dishonor. All efforts to induce her to elope with him were ineffectual. She permitted herself to love, and to avow her love; but at this limit she stopped, and was immoveable.

Hence this revolution in her sentiments was productive only of despair. Her rectitude of principle preserved her from actual guilt, but could not restore to her her ancient affection, or save her from being the prey of remorseful and impracticable wishes. Her husband's absence produced a state of suspense. This, however, approached to a period, and she received tidings of his intended return. Maxwell, being likewise apprized of this event, and having made a last and unsuccessful effort to conquer her reluctance to accompany him in a journey to Italy, whither he pretended an invincible necessity of going, left her to pursue the measures which despair might suggest. At the same time she received a letter from the wife of Maxwell, unveiling the true character of this man, and revealing facts which the artifices of her seducer had hitherto concealed from her. Mrs. Maxwell had been prompted to this disclosure by a knowledge of her husband's practices, with which his own impetuosity had made her acquainted.

This discovery, joined to the delicacy of her scruples and the anguish of remorse, induced her to abscond. This scheme was adopted in haste, but effected with consummate prudence. She fled, on the eve of her husband's arrival, in the disguise of a boy, and embarked at Falmouth in a packet bound for America.

The history of her disastrous intercourse with Maxwell, the motives inducing her to forsake her country, and the measures she had taken to effect her design, were related to Mrs. Maxwell, in reply to her communication. Between these women an ancient intimacy and considerable similitude of character subsisted. This disclosure was accompanied with solemn injunctions of secrecy, and these injunctions were, for a long time, faithfully observed.

Mrs. Maxwell's abode was situated on the banks of the Wey. Stuart was her kinsman; their youth had been spent together; and Maxwell was in some degree indebted to the man whom he betrayed, for his alliance with this unfortunate lady. Her esteem for the character of Stuart had never been diminished. A meeting between them was occasioned by a tour which the latter had undertaken, in the year after his return from America, to Wales, and the western counties. This interview produced pleasure and regret in each. Their own transactions naturally became the topics of their conversation; and the untimely fate of his wife and daughter was related by the guest.

Mrs. Maxwell's regard for her friend, as well as for the safety of her husband, persuaded her to concealment; but the former being dead, and the latter being out of the kingdom, she ventured to produce Mrs. Stuart's letter, and to communicate her knowledge of the treachery of Maxwell. She had previously extorted from her guest a promise not to pursue any scheme of vengeance; but this promise was made while ignorant of the full extent of Maxwell's depravity, and his passion refused to adhere to it.

At this time my uncle and I resided at Avignon. Among the English resident there, and with whom we maintained a social intercourse, was Maxwell. This man's talents and address rendered him a favorite both with my uncle and myself. He had even tendered me his hand in marriage; but this being refused, he had sought and obtained permission to continue with us the intercourse of friendship. Since a legal marriage was impossible, no doubt, his views were flagitious. Whether he had relinquished these views I was unable to judge. *wicked*

He was one in a large circle at a villa in the environs, to which I had likewise been invited, when Stuart abruptly entered the apartment. He was recognized with genuine satisfaction by me, and with seeming pleasure by Maxwell. In a short time, some affair of moment being pleaded, which required an immediate and exclusive interview, Maxwell and he withdrew together. Stuart and my uncle had been known to each other in the German army; and the purpose contemplated by the former in this long and hasty journey, was confided to his old friend.

A defiance was given and received, and the banks of a rivulet, about a league from the city, was selected as the scene of this contest. My uncle, having exerted himself in vain to prevent an hostile meeting, consented to attend them as a surgeon.—Next morning, at sun-rise, was the time chosen.

I returned early in the evening to my lodgings. Preliminaries being settled between the combatants, Stuart had consented to spend the evening with us, and did not retire till late. On the way to his hotel he was exposed to no molestation, but just as he stepped within the portico, a swarthy and malignant figure started from behind a and plunged a stiletto into his body.

The author of this treason could not certainly be discovered; but the details communicated by Stuart, respecting the history of Maxwell, naturally pointed him out as an object of suspicion. No one expressed more concern, on account of this disaster, than he; and he pretended an ardent zeal to vindicate his character from the aspersions that were cast upon it. Thenceforth, however, I denied myself to his visits; and shortly after he disappeared from this scene.

 Few possessed more estimable qualities, and a better title to happiness and the tranquil honors of long life, than the mother and father of Louisa Conway: yet they were cut off in the bloom of their days; and their destiny was thus accomplished by the same hand. Maxwell was the instrument of their destruction, though the instrument was applied to this end in so different a manner.

I leave you to moralize on this tale. That virtue should become the victim of treachery is, no doubt, a mournful consideration; but it will not escape your notice, that the evils of which Carwin and Maxwell were the authors, owed their existence to the errors of the sufferers. All efforts would have been ineffectual to subvert the happiness or shorten the existence of the Stuarts, if their own frailty had not seconded these efforts. If the lady had crushed her disastrous passion in the bud, and driven the seducer from her presence, when the tendency of his artifices was seen; if Stuart had not admitted the spirit of absurd revenge, we should not have had to deplore this catastrophe. If Wieland had framed juster notions of moral duty, and of the divine attributes; or if I had been gifted with ordinary equanimity or foresight, the double-tongued deceiver would have been baffled and repelled.

Memoirs of Carwin the Biloquist

I was the second son of a farmer, whose place of residence was a western district of Pennsylvania. My eldest brother seemed fitted by nature for the employment to which he was destined. His wishes never led him astray from the hay-stack and the furrow. His ideas never ranged beyond the sphere of his vision, or suggested the possibility that to-morrow could differ from to-day. He could read and write, because he had no alternative between learning the lesson prescribed to him, and punishment. He was diligent, as long as fear urged him forward, but his exertions ceased with the cessation of this motive. The limits of his acquirements consisted in signing his name, and spelling out a chapter in the bible.

My character was the reverse of his. My thirst of knowledge was augmented in proportion as it was supplied with gratification. The more I heard or read, the more restless and unconquerable my curiosity became. My senses were perpetually alive to novelty, my fancy teemed with visions of the future, and my attention fastened upon every thing mysterious or unknown.

My father intended that my knowledge should keep pace with that of my brother, but conceived that all beyond the mere capacity to write and read was useless or pernicious. He took as much pains to keep me within these limits, as to make the acquisitions of my brother come up to them, but his efforts were not equally successful in both cases. The most vigilant and jealous scrutiny was exerted in vain: Reproaches and blows, painful privations and ignominious penances had no power to slacken my zeal and abate my perseverance. He might enjoin upon me the most laborious tasks, set the envy of my brother to watch me during the performance, make the most diligent search after my books, and destroy them without mercy, when they were found; but he could not outroot my darling propensity. I exerted all my powers to elude his watchfulness. Censures and stripes were sufficiently unpleasing to make me strive to avoid them. To effect this desirable end, I was incessantly employed in the invention of stratagems and the execution of expedients.

My passion was surely not deserving of blame, and I have frequently lamented the hardships to which it subjected me; yet, perhaps, the claims which were made upon my ingenuity and fortitude were not without beneficial effects upon my character.

This contention lasted from the sixth to the fourteenth year of my age. My father's opposition to my schemes was incited by a sincere though unenlightened desire for my happiness. That all his efforts were secretly eluded or obstinately repelled, was a source of the bitterest regret. He has often lamented, with tears, what he called my incorrigible depravity, and encouraged himself to perseverance by the notion of the ruin that would inevitably overtake me if I were allowed to persist in my present career. Perhaps the sufferings which arose to him from the disappointment, were equal to those which he inflicted on me.

In my fourteenth year, events happened which ascertained my future destiny. One evening I had been sent to bring cows from a meadow, some miles distant from my father's mansion. My time was limited, and I was menaced with severe chastisement if, according to my custom, I should stay beyond the period assigned.

For some time these menaces rung in my ears, and I went on my way with speed. I arrived at the meadow, but the cattle had broken the fence and escaped. It was my duty to carry home the earliest tidings of this accident, but the first suggestion was to examine the cause and manner of this escape. The field was bounded by cedar railing. Five of these rails were laid horizontally from post to post. The upper one had been broken in the middle, but the rest had merely been drawn out of the holes on one side, and rested with their ends on the ground. The means which had been used for this end, the reason why one only was broken, and that one the uppermost, how a pair of horns could be so managed as to effect that which the hands of man would have found difficult, supplied a theme of meditation.

Some accident recalled me from this reverie, and reminded me how much time had thus been consumed. I was terrified at the consequences of my delay, and sought with eagerness how they might be obviated. I asked myself if there were not a way back shorter than that by which I had come. The beaten road was rendered circuitous by a precipice that projected into a neighbouring stream, and closed up a passage by which the length of the way would have been diminished one half: at the foot of the cliff the water was of considerable depth, and agitated by an eddy. I could not estimate the danger which I should incur by plunging into it, but I was resolved to make the attempt. I have reason to think, that this experiment, if it had been tried, would have proved fatal, and my father, while he lamented my untimely fate, would have been wholly unconscious that his own unreasonable demands had occasioned it.

I turned my steps towards the spot. To reach the edge of the stream was by no means an easy undertaking, so many abrupt points and gloomy hollows were interposed. I had frequently skirted and penetrated this tract, but had never been so completely entangled in the maze as now: hence I had remained unacquainted with a narrow pass, which, at the distance of an hundred yards from the river, would conduct me, though not without danger and toil, to the opposite side of the ridge.

This glen was now discovered, and this discovery induced me to change my plan. If a passage could be here effected, it would be shorter and safer than that which led through the stream, and its practicability was to be known only by experiment. The path was narrow, steep, and overshadowed by rocks. The sun was nearly set, and the shadow of the cliff above, obscured the passage almost as much as midnight would have done: I was accustomed to despise danger when it presented itself in a sensible form, but, by a defect common in every one's education, goblins and spectres were to me the objects of the most violent apprehensions. These were unavoidably connected with solitude and darkness, and were present to my fears when I entered this gloomy recess.

These terrors are always lessened by calling the attention away to some indifferent object. I now made use of this expedient, and began to amuse myself by hallowing as loud as organs of unusual compass and vigour would enable me. I uttered the words which chanced to occur to me, and repeated in the shrill tones of a Mohock[1] savage . . . "Cow! cow! come home! home!" . . . These notes were of course reverberated from the rocks which on either side towered aloft, but the echo was confused and indistinct.

I continued, for some time, thus to beguile the way, till I reached a space more than commonly abrupt, and which required all my attention. My rude ditty was suspended till I had surmounted this impediment. In a few minutes I was at leisure to renew it. After finishing the strain, I paused. In a few seconds a voice, as I then imagined, uttered the same cry from the point of a rock some hundred feet behind me; the same words, with equal distinctness and deliberation, and in the same tone, appeared to be spoken. I was startled by this incident, and cast a fearful glance behind, to discover by whom it was uttered. The spot where I stood was buried in dusk, but the eminences were still invested with a luminous and vivid twilight. The speaker, however, was concealed from my view.

I had scarcely begun to wonder at this occurrence, when a new occasion for wonder, was afforded me. A few seconds, in like manner, elapsed, when my ditty was again rehearsed, with a no less perfect imitation, in a different quarter. . . . To this quarter I eagerly turned my eyes, but no one was visible. . . . The station, indeed, which this new speaker seemed to occupy, was inaccessible to man or beast.

If I were surprized at this second repetition of my words, judge how much my surprize must have been augmented, when the same calls were a third time repeated, and coming still in a new direction. Five times was this ditty successively resounded, at intervals nearly equal, always from a new quarter, and with little abatement of its original distinctness and force.

A little reflection was sufficient to shew that this was no more than an echo of an extraordinary kind. My terrors were quickly supplanted by delight. The motives to dispatch were forgotten, and I amused myself for an hour, with talking to these cliffs: I placed myself in new positions, and exhausted my lungs and my invention in new clamours.

The pleasures of this new discovery were an ample compensation for the ill treatment which I expected on my return. By some caprice in my father I escaped merely with a few reproaches. I seized the first opportunity of again visiting this recess, and repeating my amusement; time, and incessant repetition, could scarcely lessen its charms or exhaust the variety produced by new tones and new positions.

The hours in which I was most free from interruption and restraint were those of moonlight. My brother and I occupied a small room above the kitchen, disconnected, in some degree, with the rest of the house. It was the rural custom to retire early to bed and to anticipate the rising of the sun. When the moonlight was strong enough to permit me to read, it was my custom to escape from bed, and hie with my book to some neighbouring eminence, where I would remain stretched on the mossy rock, till the sinking or beclouded moon, forbade me to continue my employment. I was indebted for books to a friendly person in the neighbourhood, whose compliance with my solicitations was prompted partly by benevolence and partly by enmity to my father, whom he could not more egregiously offend than by gratifying my perverse and pernicious curiosity.

In leaving my chamber I was obliged to use the utmost caution to avoid rousing my brother, whose temper disposed him to thwart me in the least of my gratifications. My purpose was surely laudable, and yet on leaving the house and returning to it, I was obliged to use the vigilance and circumspection of a thief.

One night I left my bed with this view. I posted first to my vocal glen, and thence scrambling up a neighbouring steep, which overlooked a wide extent of this romantic country, gave myself up to contemplation, and the perusal of Milton's Comus.[2]

My reflections were naturally suggested by the singularity of this echo. To hear my own voice speak at a distance would have been formerly regarded as prodigious. To hear too, that voice, not uttered by another, by whom it might easily be mimicked, but by myself! I cannot now recollect the transition which led me to the notion of sounds, similar to these, but produced by other means than reverberation. Could I not so dispose my organs as to make my voice appear at a distance?

From speculation I proceeded to experiment. The idea of a distant voice, like my own, was intimately present to my fancy. I exerted myself with a most ardent desire, and with something like a persuasion that I should succeed. I started with surprise, for it seemed as if success had crowned my attempts. I repeated the effort, but failed. A certain position of the organs took place on the first attempt, altogether new, unexampled and as it were, by accident, for I could not attain it on the second experiment.

You will not wonder that I exerted myself with indefatigable zeal to regain what had once, though for so short a space, been in my power. Your own ears have witnessed the success of these efforts. By perpetual exertion I gained it a second time, and now was a diligent observer of the circumstances attending it. Gradually I subjected these finer and more subtle motions to the command of my will. What was at first difficult, by exercise and habit, was rendered easy. I learned to accommodate my voice to all the varieties of distance and direction.

It cannot be denied that this faculty is wonderful and rare, but when we consider the possible modifications of muscular motion, how few of these are usually exerted, how imperfectly they are subjected to the will, and yet that the will is capable of being rendered unlimited and absolute, will not our wonder cease?

We have seen men who could hide their tongues so perfectly that even an Anatomist, after the most accurate inspection that a living subject could admit, has affirmed the organ to be wanting, but this was effected by the exertion of muscles unknown and incredible to the greater part of mankind.

The concurrence of teeth, palate and tongue, in the formation of speech should seem to be indispensable, and yet men have spoken distinctly though wanting a tongue, and to whom, therefore, teeth and palate were superfluous. The tribe of motions requisite to this end, are wholly latent and unknown, to those who possess that organ.

I mean not to be more explicit. I have no reason to suppose a peculiar conformation or activity in my own organs, or that the power which I possess may not, with suitable directions and by steady efforts, be obtained by others, but I will do nothing to facilitate the acquisition. It is by far, too liable to perversion for a good man to desire to possess it, or to teach it to another.

There remained but one thing to render this instrument as powerful in my hands as it was capable of being. From my childhood, I was remarkably skilful at imitation. There were few voices whether of men or birds or beasts which I could not imitate with success. To add my ancient, to my newly acquired skill, to talk from a distance, and at the same time, in the accents of another, was the object of my endeavours, and this object, after a certain number of trials, I finally obtained.

In my present situation every thing that denoted intellectual exertion was a crime, and exposed me to invectives if not stripes. This circumstance induced me to be silent to all others, on the subject of my discovery. But, added to this, was a confused belief, that it might be made, in some way instrumental to my relief from the hardships and restraints of my present condition. For some time I was not aware of the mode in which it might be rendered subservient to this end.

My father's sister was an ancient lady, resident in Philadelphia, the relict of a merchant, whose decease left her the enjoyment of a frugal competence. She was without children, and had often expressed her desire that her nephew Frank, whom she always considered as a sprightly and promising lad, should be put under her care. She offered to be at the expense of my education, and to bequeath to me at her death her slender patrimony.

This arrangement was obstinately rejected by my father, because it was merely fostering and giving scope to propensities, which he considered as hurtful, and because his avarice desired that this inheritance should fall to no one but himself. To me, it was a scheme of ravishing felicity, and to be debarred from it was a source of anguish known to few. I had too much experience of my father's pertinaciousness ever to hope for a change in his views; yet the bliss of living with my aunt, in a new and busy scene, and in the unbounded indulgence of my literary passion, continually occupied my thoughts: for a long time these thoughts were productive only of despondency and tears.

Time only enhanced the desirableness of this scheme; my new faculty would naturally connect itself with these wishes, and the question could not fail to occur whether it might not aid me in the execution of my favourite plan.

A thousand superstitious tales were current in the family. Apparitions had been seen, and voices had been heard on a multitude of occasions. My father was a confident believer in supernatural tokens. The voice of his wife, who had been many years dead, had been twice heard at midnight whispering at his pillow. I frequently asked myself whether a scheme favourable to my views might not be built upon these foundations. Suppose (thought I) my mother should be made to enjoin upon him compliance with my wishes?

This idea bred in me a temporary consternation. To imitate the voice of the dead, to counterfeit a commission from heaven, bore the aspect of presumption and impiety. It seemed an offence which could not fail to draw after it the vengeance of the deity. My wishes for a time yielded to my fears, but this scheme in proportion as I meditated on it, became more plausible; no other occurred to me so easy and so efficacious. I endeavoured to persuade myself that the end proposed, was, in the highest degree praiseworthy, and that the excellence of my purpose would justify the means employed to attain it.

My resolutions were, for a time, attended with fluctuations and misgivings. These gradually disappeared, and my purpose became firm; I was next to devise the means of effecting my views; this did not demand any tedious deliberation. It was easy to gain access to my father's chamber without notice or detection; cautious footsteps and the suppression of breath would place me, unsuspected and unthought of, by his bed side. The words I should use, and the mode of utterance were not easily settled, but having at length selected these, I made myself by much previous repetition, perfectly familiar with the use of them.

I selected a blustering and inclement night, in which the darkness was augmented by a veil of the blackest clouds. The building we inhabited was slight in its structure, and full of crevices through which the gale found easy way, and whistled in a thousand cadencies. On this night the elemental music was remarkably sonorous, and was mingled not unfrequently with *thunder heard remote*.[3]

I could not divest myself of secret dread. My heart faultered with a consciousness of wrong. Heaven seemed to be present and to disapprove my work; I listened to the thunder and the wind, as to the stern voice of this disapprobation. Big drops stood on my forehead, and my tremors almost incapacitated me from proceeding.

These impediments however I surmounted; I crept up stairs at midnight, and entered my father's chamber. The darkness was intense and I sought with outstretched hands for his bed. The darkness, added to the trepidation of my thoughts, disabled me from making a right estimate of distances: I was conscious of this, and when I advanced within the room, paused.

I endeavoured to compare the progress I had made with my knowledge of the room, and governed by the result of this comparison, proceeded cautiously and with hands still outstretched in search of the foot of the bed. At this moment lightning flashed into the room: the brightness of the gleam was dazzling, yet it afforded me an exact knowledge of my situation. I had mistaken my way, and discovered that my knees nearly touched the bedstead, and that my hands at the next step, would have touched my father's cheek. His closed eyes and every line in his countenance, were painted, as it were, for an instant on my sight.

The flash was accompained with a burst of thunder, whose vehemence was stunning. I always entertained a dread of thunder, and now recoiled, overborne with terror. Never had I witnessed so luminous a gleam and so tremendous a shock, yet my father's slumber appeared not to be disturbed by it.

I stood irresolute and trembling; to prosecute my purpose in this state of mind was impossible. I resolved for the present to relinquish it, and turned with a view of exploring my way out of the chamber. Just then a light seen through the window, caught my eye. It was at first weak but speedily increased; no second thought was necessary to inform me that the barn, situated at a small distance from the house, and newly stored with hay, was in flames, in consequence of being struck by the lightning.

My terror at this spectacle made me careless of all consequences relative to myself. I rushed to the bed and throwing myself on my father, awakened him by loud cries. The family were speedily roused, and were compelled to remain impotent spectators of the devastation. Fortunately the wind blew in a contrary direction, so that our habitation was not injured.

The impression that was made upon me by the incidents of that night is indelible. The wind gradually rose into an hurricane; the largest branches were torn from the trees, and whirled aloft into the air; others were uprooted and laid prostrate on the ground. The barn was a spacious edifice, consisting wholly of wood, and filled with a plenteous harvest. Thus supplied with fuel, and fanned by the wind, the fire raged with incredible fury; meanwhile clouds rolled above, whose blackness was rendered more conspicuous by reflection from the flames; the vast volumes of smoke were dissipated in a moment by the storm, while glowing fragments and cinders were borne to an immense hight, and tossed everywhere in wild confusion. Ever and anon the sable canopy that hung around us was streaked with lightning, and the peals, by which it was accompained, were deafning, and with scarcely any intermission.

It was, doubtless, absurd to imagine any connexion between this portentous scene and the purpose that I had meditated, yet a belief of this connexion, though wavering and obscure, lurked in my mind; something more than a coincidence merely casual, appeared to have subsisted between my situation, at my father's bed side, and the flash that darted through the window, and diverted me from my design. It palsied my courage, and strengthened my conviction, that my scheme was criminal.

After some time had elapsed, and tranquility was, in some degree, restored in the family, my father reverted to the circumstances in which I had been discovered on the first alarm of this event. The truth was impossible to be told. I felt the utmost reluctance to be guilty of a falsehood, but by falsehood only could I elude detection. That my guilt was the offspring of a fatal necessity, that the injustice of others gave it birth and made it unavoidable, afforded me slight consolation. Nothing can be more injurous than a lie, but its evil tendency chiefly respects our future conduct. Its direct consequences may be transient and few, but it facilitates a repetition, strengthens temptation, and grows into habit. I pretended some necessity had drawn me from my bed, and that discovering the condition of the barn, I hastened to inform my father.

Some time after this, my father summoned me to his presence. I had been previously guilty of disobedience to his commands, in a matter about which he was usually very scrupulous. My brother had been privy to my offence, and had threatened to be my accuser. On this occasion I expected nothing but arraignment and punishment. Weary of oppression, and hopeless of any change in my father's temper and views, I had formed the resolution of eloping from his house, and of trusting, young as I was, to the caprice of fortune. I was hesitating whether to abscond without the knowledge of the family, or to make my resolutions known to them, and while I avowed my resolution, to adhere to it in spite of opposition and remonstrances, when I received this summons.

I was employed at this time in the field; night was approaching, and I had made no preparation for departure; all the preparation in my power to make, was indeed small; a few clothes made into a bundle, was the sum of my possessions. Time would have little influence in improving my prospects, and I resolved to execute my scheme immediately.

I left my work intending to seek my chamber, and taking what was my own, to disappear forever. I turned a stile that led out of the field into a bye path, when my father appeared before me, advancing in an opposite direction; to avoid him was impossible, and I summoned my fortitude to a conflict with his passion.

As soon as we met, instead of anger and upbraiding, he told me, that he had been reflecting on my aunt's proposal, to take me under her protection, and had concluded that the plan was proper; if I still retained my wishes on that head, he would readily comply with them, and that, if I chose, I might set off for the city next morning, as a neighbour's waggon was preparing to go.

I shall not dwell on the rapture with which this proposal was listened to: it was with difficulty that I persuaded myself that he was in earnest in making it, nor could I divine the reasons, for so sudden and unexpected a change in his maxims. . . . These I afterwards discovered. Some one had instilled into him fears, that my aunt exasperated at his opposition to her request, respecting the unfortunate Frank, would bequeath her property to strangers; to obviate this evil, which his avarice prompted him to regard as much greater than any mischief, that would accrue to me, from the change of my abode, he embraced her proposal.

I entered with exultation and triumph on this new scene; my hopes were by no means disappointed. Detested labour was exchanged for luxurious idleness. I was master of my time, and the chuser of my occupations. My kinswoman on discovering that I entertained no relish for the drudgery of colleges, and was contented with the means of intellectual gratification, which I could obtain under her roof, allowed me to pursue my own choice.

Three tranquil years passed away, during which, each day added to my happiness, by adding to my knowledge. My biloquial faculty was not neglected. I improved it by assiduous exercise; I deeply reflected on the use to which it might be applied. I was not destitute of pure intentions; I delighted not in evil; I was incapable of knowingly contributing to another's misery, but the sole or principal end of my endeavours was not the happiness of others.

I was actuated by ambition. I was delighted to possess superior power; I was prone to manifest that superiority, and was satisfied if this were done, without much solicitude concerning consequences. I sported frequently with the apprehensions of my associates, and threw out a bait for their wonder, and supplied them with occasions for the structure of theories. It may not be amiss to enumerate one or two adventures in which I was engaged.

I had taken much pains to improve the sagacity of a favourite Spaniel. It was my purpose, indeed, to ascertain to what degree of improvement the principles of reasoning and imitation could be carried in a dog. There is no doubt that the animal affixes distinct ideas to sounds. What are the possible limits of his vocabulary no one can tell. In conversing with my dog I did not use English words, but selected simple monosyllables. Habit likewise enabled him to comprehend my gestures. If I crossed my hands on my breast he understood the signal and laid down behind me. If I joined my hands and lifted them to my breast, he returned home. If I grasped one arm above the elbow he ran before me. If I lifted my hand to my forehead he trotted composedly behind. By one motion I could make him bark; by another I could reduce him to silence. He would howl in twenty different strains of mournfulness, at my bidding. He would fetch and carry with undeviating faithfulness.

His actions being thus chiefly regulated by gestures, that to a stranger would appear indifferent or casual, it was easy to produce a belief that the animal's knowledge was much greater than in truth, it was.

One day, in a mixed company, the discourse turned upon the unrivaled abilities of *Damon*. Damon had, indeed, acquired in all the circles which I frequented, an extraordinary reputation. Numerous instances of his sagacity were quoted and some of them exhibited on the spot. Much surprise was excited by the readiness with which he appeared to comprehend sentences of considerable abstraction and complexity, though, he in reality, attended to nothing but the movements of hand or fingers with which I accompanied my words. I enhanced the astonishment of some and excited the ridicule of others, by observing that my dog not only understood English when spoken by others, but actually spoke the language himself, with no small degree of precision.

This assertion could not be admitted without proof; proof, therefore, was readily produced. At a known signal, Damon began a low interrupted noise, in which the astonished hearers clearly distinguished English words. A dialogue began between the animal and his master, which was maintained, on the part of the former, with great vivacity and spirit. In this dialogue the dog asserted the dignity of his species and capacity of intellectual improvement. The company separated lost in wonder, but perfectly convinced by the evidence that had been produced.

On a subsequent occasion a select company was assembled at a garden, at a small distance from the city. Discourse glided through a variety of topics, till it lighted at length on the subject of invisible beings. From the speculations of philosophers we proceeded to the creations of the poet. Some maintained the justness of Shakspear's delineations of aerial beings, while others denied it. By no violent transition, Ariel and his songs were introduced, and a lady, celebrated for her musical skill, was solicited to accompany her pedal harp with the song of "Five fathom deep thy father lies."[4] . . . She was known to have set, for her favourite instrument, all the songs of Shakspeare.

My youth made me little more than an auditor on this occasion. I sat apart from the rest of the company, and carefully noted every thing.

The track which the conversation had taken, suggested a scheme which was not thoroughly digested when the lady began her enchanting strain.

She ended and the audience were mute with rapture. The pause continued, when a strain was wafted to our ears from another quarter. The spot where we sat was embowered by a vine. The verdant arch was lofty and the area beneath was spacious.

The sound proceeded from above. At first it was faint and scarcely audible; presently it reached a louder key, and every eye was cast up in expectation of beholding a face among the pendant clusters. The strain was easily recognized, for it was no other than that which Ariel is made to sing when finally absolved from the service of the wizard.

> In the Cowslip's bell I lie,[5]
> On the Bat's back I do fly . . .
> After summer merrily, &c.

Their hearts palpitated as they listened: they gazed at each other for a solution of the mystery. At length the strain died away at distance, and an interval of silence was succeeded by an earnest discussion of the cause of this prodigy. One supposition only could be adopted, which was, that the strain was not uttered by human organs. That the songster was stationed on the roof of the arbour, and having finished his melody had risen into the viewless fields of air.

I had been invited to spend a week at this house: this period was nearly expired when I received information that my aunt was suddenly taken sick, and that her life was in imminent danger. I immediately set out on my return to the city, but before my arrival she was dead.

This lady was entitled to my gratitude and esteem; I had received the most essential benefits at her hand. I was not destitute of sensibility, and was deeply affected by this event: I will own, however, that my grief was lessened by reflecting on the consequences of her death, with regard to my own condition. I had been ever taught to consider myself as her heir, and her death, therefore, would free me from certain restraints.

My aunt had a female servant, who had lived with her for twenty years: she was married, but her husband, who was an artizan, lived apart from her: I had no reason to suspect the woman's sincerity and disinterestedness; but my aunt was no sooner consigned to the grave than a will was produced, in which Dorothy was named her sole and universal heir.

It was in vain to urge my expectations and my claims . . . the instrument was legibly and legally drawn up. . . . Dorothy was exasperated by my opposition and surmises, and vigorously enforced her title. In a week after the decease of my kinswoman, I was obliged to seek a new dwelling. As all my property consisted in my clothes and my papers, this was easily done.

My condition was now calamitous and forlorn. Confiding in the acquisition of my aunt's patrimony, I had made no other provision for the future; I hated manual labour, or any task of which the object was gain. To be guided in my choice of occupations by any motive but the pleasure which the occupation was qualified to produce, was intolerable to my proud, indolent, and restive temper.

This resource was now cut off; the means of immediate subsistence were denied me: If I had determined to acquire the knowledge of some lucrative art, the acquisition would demand time, and, meanwhile, I was absolutely destitute of support. My father's house was, indeed, open to me, but I preferred to stifle myself with the filth of the kennel, rather than to return to it.

Some plan it was immediately necessary to adopt. The exigence of my affairs, and this reverse of fortune, continually occupied my thoughts; I estranged myself from society and from books, and devoted myself to lonely walks and mournful meditation.

One morning as I ranged along the bank of Schuylkill, I encountered a person, by name Ludloe, of whom I had some previous knowledge. He was from Ireland; was a man of some rank and apparently rich: I had met with him before, but in mixed companies, where little direct intercourse had taken place between us. Our last meeting was in the arbour where Ariel was so unexpectedly introduced.

Our acquaintance merely justified a transient salutation; but he did not content himself with noticing me as I passed, but joined me in my walk and entered into conversation. It was easy to advert to the occasion on which we had last met, and to the mysterious incident which then occurred. I was solicitous to dive into his thoughts upon this head and put some questions which tended to the point that I wished.

I was somewhat startled when he expressed his belief, that the performer of this mystic strain was one of the company then present, who exerted, for this end, a faculty not commonly possessed. Who this person was he did not venture to guess, and I could not discover, by the tokens which he suffered to appear, that his suspicions glanced at me. He expatiated with great profoundness and fertility of ideas, on the uses to which a faculty like this might be employed. No more powerful engine, he said, could be conceived, by which the ignorant and credulous might be moulded to our purposes; managed by a man of ordinary talents, it would open for him the straightest and surest avenues to wealth and power.

His remarks excited in my mind a new strain of thoughts. I had not hitherto considered the subject in this light, though vague ideas of the importance of this art could not fail to be occasionally suggested: I ventured to inquire into his ideas of the mode, in which an art like this could be employed, so as to effect the purposes he mentioned.

He dealt chiefly in general representations. Men, he said, believed in the existence and energy of invisible powers, and in the duty of discovering and conforming to their will. This will was supposed to be sometimes made known to them through the medium of their senses. A voice coming from a quarter where no attendant form could be seen would, in most cases, be ascribed to supernal agency, and a command imposed on them, in this manner, would be obeyed with religious scrupulousness. Thus men might be imperiously directed in the disposal of their industry, their property, and even of their lives. Men, actuated by a mistaken sense of duty, might, under this influence, be led to the commission of the most flagitious, as well as the most heroic acts: If it were his desire to accumulate wealth, or institute a new sect, he should need no other instrument.

I listened to this kind of discourse with great avidity, and regretted when he thought proper to introduce new topics. He ended by requesting me to visit him, which I eagerly consented to do. When left alone, my imagination was filled with the images suggested by this conversation. The hopelessness of better fortune, which I had lately harboured, now gave place to cheering confidence. Those motives of rectitude which should deter me from this species of imposture, had never been vivid or stable, and were still more weakened by the artifices of which I had already been guilty. The utility or harmlessness of the end, justified, in my eyes, the means.

No event had been more unexpected, by me, than the bequest of my aunt to her servant. The will, under which the latter claimed, was dated prior to my coming to the city. I was not surprised, therefore, that it had once been made, but merely that it had never been cancelled or superseded by a later instrument. My wishes inclined me to suspect the existence of a later will, but I had conceived that, to ascertain its existence, was beyond my power.

Now, however, a different opinion began to be entertained. This woman like those of her sex and class was unlettered and superstitious. Her faith in spells and apparitions, was of the most lively kind. Could not her conscience be awakened by a voice from the grave! Lonely and at midnight, my aunt might be introduced, upbraiding her for her injustice, and commanding her to attone for it by acknowledging the claim of the rightful proprietor.

True it was, that no subsequent will might exist, but this was the fruit of mistake, or of negligence. She probably intended to cancel the old one, but this act might, by her own weakness, or by the artifices of her servant, be delayed till death had put it out of her power. In either case a mandate from the dead could scarcely fail of being obeyed.

I considered this woman as the usurper of my property. Her husband as well as herself, were laborious and covetous; their good fortune had made no change in their mode of living, but they were as frugal and as eager to accumulate as ever. In their hands, money was inert and sterile, or it served to foster their vices. To take it from them would, therefore, be a benefit both to them and to myself; not even an imaginary injury would be inflicted. Restitution, if legally compelled to it, would be reluctant and painful, but if enjoined by Heaven would be voluntary, and the performance of a seeming duty would carry with it, its own reward.

These reasonings, aided by inclination, were sufficient to determine me. I have no doubt but their fallacy would have been detected in the sequel, and my scheme have been productive of nothing but confusion and remorse. From these consequences, however, my fate interposed, as in the former instance, to save me.

Having formed my resolution, many preliminaries to its execution were necessary to be settled. These demanded deliberation and delay; meanwhile I recollected my promise to Ludloe, and paid him a visit. I met a frank and affectionate reception. It would not be easy to paint the delight which I experienced in this man's society. I was at first oppressed with the sense of my own inferiority in age, knowledge and rank. Hence arose numberless reserves and incapacitating diffidences; but these were speedily dissipated by the fascinations of this man's address. His superiority was only rendered, by time, more conspicuous, but this superiority, by appearing never to be present to his own mind, ceased to be uneasy to me. My questions required to be frequently answered, and my mistakes to be rectified; but my keenest scrutiny, could detect in his manner, neither arrogance nor contempt. He seemed to talk merely from the overflow of his ideas, or a benevolent desire of imparting information.

My visits gradually became more frequent. Meanwhile my wants increased, and the necessity of some change in my condition became daily more urgent. This incited my reflections on the scheme which I had formed. The time and place suitable to my design, were not selected without much anxious inquiry and frequent waverings of purpose. These being at length fixed, the interval to elapse, before the carrying of my design into effect, was not without perturbation and suspense. These could not be concealed from my new friend and at length prompted him to inquire into the cause.

It was not possible to communicate the whole truth; but the warmth of his manner inspired me with some degree of ingenuousness. I did not hide from him my former hopes and my present destitute condition. He listened to my tale with no expressions of sympathy, and when I had finished, abruptly inquired whether I had any objection to a voyage to Europe? I answered in the negative. He then said that he was preparing to depart in a fortnight and advised me to make up my mind to accompany him.

This unexpected proposal gave me pleasure and surprize, but the want of money occurred to me as an insuperable objection. On this being mentioned, Oho! said he, carelessly, that objection is easily removed, I will bear all expenses of your passage myself.

The extraordinary beneficence of this act as well as the air of uncautiousness attending it, made me doubt the sincerity of his offer, and when new declarations removed this doubt, I could not forbear expressing at once my sense of his generosity and of my own unworthiness.

He replied that generosity had been expunged from his catalogue as having no meaning or a vicious one.[6] It was the scope of his exertions to be just. This was the sum of human duty, and he that fell short, ran beside, or outstripped justice was a criminal. What he gave me was my due or not my due. If it were my due, I might reasonably demand it from him and it was wicked to withhold it. Merit on one side or gratitude on the other, were contradictory and unintelligible.

If I were fully convinced that this benefit was not my due and yet received it, he should hold me in contempt. The rectitude of my principles and conduct would be the measure of his approbation, and no benefit should he ever bestow which the receiver was not entitled to claim, and which it would not be criminal in him to refuse.

These principles were not new from the mouth of Ludloe, but they had, hitherto, been regarded as the fruits of a venturous speculation in my mind. I had never traced them into their practical consequences, and if his conduct on this occasion had not squared with his maxims, I should not have imputed to him inconsistency. I did not ponder on these reasonings at this time: objects of immediate importance engrossed my thoughts.

One obstacle to this measure was removed. When my voyage was performed how should I subsist in my new abode? I concealed not my perplexity and he commented on it in his usual manner. How did I mean to subsist, he asked, in my own country? The means of living would be, at least, as much within my reach there as here. As to the pressure of immediate and absolute want, he believed I should be exposed to little hazard. With talents such as mine, I must be hunted by a destiny peculiarly malignant, if I could not provide myself with necessaries wherever my lot were cast.

He would make allowances, however, for my diffidence and self-distrust, and would obviate my fears by expressing his own intentions with regard to me. I must be apprized, however, of his true meaning. He laboured to shun all hurtful and vitious things, and therefore carefully abstained from making or confiding *in promises.*[7] It was just to assist me in this voyage, and it would probably be equally just to continue to me similar assistance when it was finished. That indeed was a subject, in a great degree, within my own cognizance. His aid would be proportioned to my wants and to my merits, and I had only to take care that my claims were just, for them to be admitted.

This scheme could not but appear to me eligible. I thirsted after an acquaintance with new scenes; my present situation could not be changed for a worse; I trusted to the constancy of Ludloe's friendship; to this at least it was better to trust than to the success of my imposture on Dorothy, which was adopted merely as a desperate expedient: finally I determined to embark with him.

In the course of this voyage my mind was busily employed. There were no other passengers beside ourselves, so that my own condition and the character of Ludloe, continually presented themselves to my reflections. It will be supposed that I was not a vague or indifferent observer.

There were no vicissitudes in the deportment or lapses in the discourse of my friend. His feelings appeared to preserve an unchangeable tenor, and his thoughts and words always to flow with the same rapidity. His slumber was profound and his wakeful hours serene. He was regular and temperate in all his exercises and gratifications. Hence were derived his clear perceptions and exuberant health.

His treatment of me, like all his other mental and corporal operations, was modelled by one inflexible standard. Certain scruples and delicacies were incident to my situation. Of the existence of these he seemed to be unconscious, and yet nothing escaped him inconsistent with a state of absolute equality.

I was naturally inquisitive as to his fortune and the collateral circumstances of his condition. My notions of politeness hindered me from making direct inquiries. By indirect means I could gather nothing but that his state was opulent and independent, and that he had two sisters whose situation resembled his own.

Though, in conversation, he appeared to be governed by the utmost candour; no light was let in upon the former transactions of his life. The purpose of his visit to America I could merely guess to be the gratification of curiosity.

My future pursuits must be supposed chiefly to occupy my attention. On this head I was destitute of all stedfast views. Without profession or habits of industry or sources of permanent revenue, the world appeared to me an ocean on which my bark was set afloat, without compass or sail. The world into which I was about to enter, was untried and unknown, and though I could consent to profit by the guidance, I was unwilling to rely on the support of others.

This topic, being nearest my heart, I frequently introduced into conversation with my friend; but on this subject he always allowed himself to be led by me, while on all others, he was zealous to point the way. To every scheme that I proposed he was sure to cause objections. All the liberal professions were censured as perverting the understanding, by giving scope to the sordid motive of gain, or embuing the mind with erroneous principles. Skill was slowly obtained, and success, though integrity and independence must be given for it, dubious and instable. The mechanical trades were equally obnoxious; they were vitious by contributing to the spurious gratifications of the rich and multiplying the objects of luxury; they were destructive to the intellect and vigour of the artizan; they enervated his frame and brutalized his mind.

When I pointed out to him the necessity of some species of labour, he tacitly admitted that necessity, but refused to direct me in the choice of a pursuit, which though not free from defect should yet have the fewest inconveniences. He dwelt on the fewness of our actual wants, the temptations which attend the possession of wealth, the benefits of seclusion and privacy, and the duty of unfettering our minds from the prejudices which govern the world.

His discourse tended merely to unsettle my views and increase my perplexity. This effect was so uniform that I at length desisted from all allusions to this theme and endeavoured to divert my own reflections from it. When our voyage should be finished, and I should actually tread this new stage, I believed that I should be better qualified to judge of the measures to be taken by me.

At length we reached Belfast. From thence we immediately re-paired to Dublin. I was admitted as a member of his family. When I expressed my uncertainty as to the place to which it would be proper for me to repair, he gave me a blunt but cordial invitation to his house. My circumstances allowed me no option and I readily complied. My attention was for a time engrossed by a diversified succession of new objects. Their novelty, however, disappearing left me at liberty to turn my eyes upon myself and my companion, and here my reflections were supplied with abundant food.

His house was spacious and commodious, and furnished with profusion and elegance. A suit of apartments was assigned to me, in which I was permitted to reign uncontrouled and access was permitted to a well furnished library. My food was furnished in my own room, prepared in the manner which I had previously directed. Occasionally Ludloe would request my company to breakfast, when an hour was usually consumed in earnest or sprightly conversation. At all other times he was invisible, and his apartments being wholly separate from mine, I had no opportunity of discovering in what way his hours were employed.

He defended this mode of living as being most compatible with liberty. He delighted to expatiate on the evils of cohabitation. Men, subjected to the same regimen, compelled to eat and sleep and associate at certain hours, were strangers to all rational independence and liberty. Society would never be exempt from servitude and misery, till those artificial ties which held human beings together under the same roof[8] were dissolved. He endeavoured to regulate his own conduct in pursuance of these principles, and to secure to himself as much freedom as the present regulations of society would permit. The same independence which he claimed for himself he likewise extended to me. The distribution of my own time, the selection of my own occupations and companions should belong to myself.

But these privileges, though while listening to his arguments I could not deny them to be valuable, I would have willingly dispensed with. The solitude in which I lived became daily more painful. I ate and drank, enjoyed clothing and shelter, without the exercise of forethought or industry; I walked and sat, went out and returned for as long and at what seasons I thought proper, yet my condition was a fertile source of discontent.

I felt myself removed to a comfortless and chilling distance from Ludloe. I wanted to share in his occupations and views. With all his ingenuousness of aspect and overflow of thoughts, when he allowed me his company, I felt myself painfully bewildered with regard to his genuine condition and sentiments.

He had it in his power to introduce me to society, and without an introduction, it was scarcely possible to gain access to any social circle or domestic fireside. Add to this, my own obscure prospects and dubious situation. Some regular intellectual pursuit would render my state less irksome, but I had hitherto adopted no scheme of this kind.

Time tended, in no degree, to alleviate my dissatisfaction. It increased till the determination became at length formed of opening my thoughts to Ludloe. At the next breakfast interview which took place, I introduced the subject, and expatiated without reserve, on the state of my feelings. I concluded with intreating him to point out some path in which my talents might be rendered useful to himself or to mankind.

After a pause of some minutes, he said, What would you do? You forget the immaturity of your age. If you are qualified to act a part in the theatre of life, step forth; but you are not qualified. You want knowledge, and with this you ought previously to endow yourself. . . . Means, for this end, are within your reach. Why should you waste your time in idleness, and torment yourself with unprofitable wishes? Books are at hand . . . books from which most sciences and languages can be learned. Read, analise, digest; collect facts, and investigate theories: ascertain the dictates of reason, and supply yourself with the inclination and the power to adhere to them. You will not, legally speaking, be a man in less than three years. Let this period be devoted to the acquisition of wisdom. Either stay here, or retire to an house I have on the banks of Killarney, where you will find all the conveniences of study.

I could not but reflect with wonder at this man's treatment of me. I could plead none of the rights of relationship; yet I enjoyed the privileges of a son. He had not imparted to me any scheme, by pursuit of which I might finally compensate him for the expense to which my maintainance and education would subject him. He gave me reason to hope for the continuance of his bounty. He talked and acted as if my fortune were totally disjoined from his; yet was I indebted to him for the morsel which sustained my life. Now it was proposed to withdraw myself to studious leisure, and romantic solitude. All my wants, personal and intellectual, were to be supplied gratuitously and copiously. No means were prescribed by which I might make compensation for all these benefits. In conferring them he seemed to be actuated by no view to his own ultimate advantage. He took no measures to secure my future services.

I suffered these thoughts to escape me, on this occasion, and observed that to make my application successful, or useful, it was necessary to pursue some end. I must look forward to some post which I might hereafter occupy beneficially to myself or others; and for which all the efforts of my mind should be bent to qualify myself.

These hints gave him visible pleasure; and now, for the first time, he deigned to advise me on this head. His scheme, however, was not suddenly produced. The way to it was circuitous and long. It was his business to make every new step appear to be suggested by my own reflections. His own ideas were the seeming result of the moment, and sprung out of the last idea that was uttered. Being hastily taken up, they were, of course, liable to objection. These objections, sometimes occurring to me and sometimes to him, were admitted or contested with the utmost candour. One scheme went through numerous modifications before it was proved to be ineligible, or before it yielded place to a better. It was easy to perceive, that books alone were insufficient to impart knowledge: that men must be examined with our own eyes to make us acquainted with their nature: that ideas collected from observation and reading, must correct and illustrate each other: that the value of all principles, and their truth, lie in their practical effects. Hence, gradually arose, the usefulness of travelling, of inspecting the habits and manners of a nation, and investigating, on the spot, the causes of their happiness and misery. Finally, it was determined that Spain was more suitable than any other, to the views of a judicious traveller.

My language, habits, and religion were mentioned as obstacles to close and extensive views; but these difficulties successively and slowly vanished. Converse with books, and natives of Spain, a steadfast purpose and unwearied diligence would efface all differences between me and a Castilian with respect to speech. Personal habits, were changeable, by the same means. The bars to unbounded intercourse, rising from the religion of Spain being irreconcilably opposite to mine, cost us no little trouble to surmount, and here the skill of Ludloe was eminently displayed.

I had been accustomed to regard as unquestionable, the fallacy of the Romish faith. This persuasion was habitual and the child of prejudice, and was easily shaken by the artifices of this logician. I was first led to bestow a kind of assent on the doctrines of the Roman church; but my convictions were easily subdued by a new species of argumentation, and, in a short time, I reverted to my ancient disbelief, so that, if an exterior conformity to the rites of Spain were requisite to the attainment of my purpose, that conformity must be dissembled.

My moral principles had hitherto been vague and unsettled. My circumstances had led me to the frequent practice of insincerity; but my transgressions, as they were slight and transient, did not much excite my previous reflections, or subsequent remorse. My deviations, however, though rendered easy by habit, were by no means sanctioned by my principles. Now an imposture, more profound and deliberate, was projected; and I could not hope to perform well my part, unless steadfastly and thoroughly persuaded of its rectitude.

My friend was the eulogist of sincerity.[9] He delighted to trace its influence on the happiness of mankind; and proved that nothing but the universal practice of this virtue was necessary to the perfection of human society. His doctrine was splendid and beautiful. To detect its imperfections was no easy task; to lay the foundations of virtue in utility, and to limit, by that scale, the operation of general principles; to see that the value of sincerity, like that of every other mode of action, consisted in its tendency to good, and that, therefore the obligation to speak truth was not paramount or intrinsical; that my duty is modelled on a knowledge and foresight of the conduct of others; and that, since men in their actual state, are infirm and deceitful, a just estimate of consequences may sometimes make dissimulation my duty were truths that did not speedily occur. The discovery, when made, appeared to be a joint work. I saw nothing in Ludloe but proofs of candour, and a judgment incapable of bias.

The means which this man employed to fit me for his purpose, perhaps owed their success to my youth and ignorance. I may have given you exaggerated ideas of his dexterity and address. Of that I am unable to judge. Certain it is, that no time or reflection has abated my astonishment at the profoundness of his schemes, and the perseverance with which they were pursued by him. To detail their progress would expose me to the risk of being tedious, yet none but minute details would sufficiently display his patience and subtlety.

It will suffice to relate, that after a sufficient period of preparation and arrangements being made for maintaining a copious intercourse with Ludloe, I embarked for Barcelona. A restless curiosity and vigorous application have distinguished my character in every scene. Here was spacious field for the exercise of all my energies. I sought out a preceptor in my new religion. I entered into the hearts of priests and confessors, the *hidalgo* and the peasant, the monk and the prelate, the austere and voluptuous devotee were scrutinized in all their forms.

Man was the chief subject of my study, and the social sphere that in which I principally moved; but I was not inattentive to inanimate nature, nor unmindful of the past. If the scope of virtue were to maintain the body in health, and to furnish its highest enjoyments to every sense, to increase the number, and accuracy, and order of our intellectual stores, no virtue was ever more unblemished than mine. If to act upon our conceptions of right, and to acquit ourselves of all prejudice and selfishness in the formation of our principles, entitle us to the testimony of a good conscience, I might justly claim it.

I shall not pretend to ascertain my rank in the moral scale. Your notions of duty differ widely from mine. If a system of deceit, pursued merely from the love of truth; if voluptuousness, never gratified at the expense of health, may incur censure, I am censurable. This, indeed, was not the limit of my deviations. Deception was often unnecessarily practised, and my biloquial faculty did not lie unemployed. What has happened to yourselves may enable you, in some degree, to judge of the scenes in which my mystical exploits engaged me. In none of them, indeed, were the effects equally disastrous, and they were, for the most part, the result of well digested projects.

To recount these would be an endless task. They were designed as mere specimens of power, to illustrate the influence of superstition: to give sceptics the consolation of certainty: to annihilate the scruples of a tender female, or facilitate my access to the bosoms of courtiers and monks.

The first achievement of this kind took place in the convent of the Escurial.[10] For some time the hospitality of this brotherhood allowed me a cell in that magnificent and gloomy fabric. I was drawn hither chiefly by the treasures of Arabian literature, which are preserved here in the keeping of a learned Maronite, from Lebanon. Standing one evening on the steps of the great altar, this devout friar expatiated on the miraculous evidences of his religion; and, in a moment of enthusiasm, appealed to San Lorenzo, whose martyrdom was displayed before us. No sooner was the appeal made than the saint, obsequious to the summons, whispered his responses from the shrine, and commanded the heretic to tremble and believe. This event was reported to the convent. With whatever reluctance, I could not refuse my testimony to its truth, and its influence on my faith was clearly shewn in my subsequent conduct.

A lady of rank, in Seville, who had been guilty of many unauthorized indulgences, was, at last, awakened to remorse, by a voice from Heaven, which she imagined had commanded her to expiate her sins by an abstinence from all food for thirty days. Her friends found it impossible to outroot this persuasion, or to overcome her resolution even by force. I chanced to be one in a numerous company where she was present. This fatal illusion was mentioned, and an opportunity afforded to the lady of defending her scheme. At a pause in the discourse, a voice was heard from the ceiling, which confirmed the truth of her tale; but, at the same time revoked the command, and, in consideration of her faith, pronounced her absolution. Satisfied with this proof, the auditors dismissed their unbelief, and the lady consented to eat.

In the course of a copious correspondence with Ludloe, the observations I had collected were given. A sentiment, which I can hardly describe, induced me to be silent on all adventures connected with my bivocal projects. On other topics, I wrote fully, and without restraint. I painted, in vivid hues, the scenes with which I was daily conversant, and pursued, fearlessly, every speculation on religion and government that occurred. This spirit was encouraged by Ludloe, who failed not to comment on my narrative, and multiply deductions from my principles.

He taught me to ascribe the evils that infest society to the errors of opinion. The absurd and unequal distribution of power and property gave birth to poverty and riches, and these were the sources of luxury and crimes. These positions were readily admitted; but the remedy for these ills, the means of rectifying these errors were not easily discovered. We have been inclined to impute them to inherent defects in the moral constitution of men: that oppression and tyranny grow up by a sort of natural necessity, and that they will perish only when the human species is extinct. Ludloe laboured to prove that this was, by no means, the case: that man is the creature of circumstances: that he is capable of endless improvement: that his progress has been stopped by the artificial impediment of government: that by the removal of this, the fondest dreams of imagination will be realized.

From detailing and accounting for the evils which exist under our present institutions, he usually proceeded to delineate some scheme of Utopian felicity, where the empire of reason should supplant that of force;[11] where justice should be universally understood and practised; where the interest of the whole and of the individual should be seen by all to be the same; where the public good should be the scope of all activity; where the tasks of all should be the same, and the means of subsistence equally distributed.

No one could contemplate his pictures without rapture. By their comprehensiveness and amplitude they filled the imagination. I was unwilling to believe that in no region of the world, or at no period could these ideas be realized. It was plain that the nations of Europe were tending to greater depravity, and would be the prey of perpetual vicissitude. All individual attempts at their reformation would be fruitless. He therefore who desired the diffusion of right principles, to make a just system be adopted by a whole community, must pursue some extraordinary method.

In this state of mind I recollected my native country, where a few colonists from Britain had sown the germe of populous and mighty empires. Attended, as they were, into their new abode, by all their prejudices, yet such had been the influence of new circumstances, of consulting for their own happiness, of adopting simple forms of government, and excluding nobles and kings from their system, that they enjoyed a degree of happiness far superior to their parent state.

To conquer the prejudices and change the habits of millions, are impossible. The human mind, exposed to social influences, inflexibly adheres to the direction that is given to it; but for the same reason why men who begin in error will continue, those who commence in truth, may be expected to persist. Habit and example will operate with equal force in both instances.

Let a few, sufficiently enlightened and disinterested, take up their abode in some unvisited region. Let their social scheme be founded in equity, and how small soever their original number may be, their growth into a nation is inevitable. Among other effects of national justice, was to be ranked the swift increase of numbers. Exempt from servile obligations and perverse habits, endowed with property, wisdom, and health, hundreds will expand, with inconceivable rapidity into thousands, and thousands into millions; and a new race, tutored in truth, may, in a few centuries, overflow the habitable world.

Such were the visions of youth! I could not banish them from my mind. I knew them to be crude; but believed that deliberation would bestow upon them solidity and shape. Meanwhile I imparted them to Ludloe.

In answer to the reveries and speculations which I sent to him respecting this subject, Ludloe informed me, that they had led his mind into a new sphere of meditation. He had long and deeply considered in what way he might essentially promote my happiness. He had entertained a faint hope that I would one day be qualified for a station like that to which he himself had been advanced. This post required an elevation and stability of views which human beings seldom reach, and which could be attained by me only by a long series of heroic labours. Hitherto every new stage in my intellectual progress had added vigour to his hopes, and he cherished a stronger belief than formerly that my career would terminate auspiciously. This, however, was necessarily distant. Many preliminaries must first be settled; many arduous accomplishments be first obtained; and my virtue be subjected to severe trials. At present it was not in his power to be more explicit; but if my reflections suggested no better plan, he advised me to settle my affairs in Spain, and return to him immediately. My knowledge of this country would be of the highest use, on the supposition of my ultimately arriving at the honours to which he had alluded; and some of these preparatory measures could be taken only with his assistance, and in his company.

This intimation was eagerly obeyed, and, in a short time, I arrived at Dublin. Meanwhile my mind had copious occupation in commenting on my friend's letter. This scheme, whatever it was, seemed to be suggested by my mention of a plan of colonization, and my preference of that mode of producing extensive and permanent effects on the condition of mankind. It was easy therefore to conjecture that this mode had been pursued under some mysterious modifications and conditions.

It had always excited my wonder that so obvious an expedient had been overlooked. The globe which we inhabit was very imperfectly known. The regions and nations unexplored, it was reasonable to believe, surpassed in extent, and perhaps in populousness, those with which we were familiar. The order of Jesuits had furnished an example of all the errors and excellencies of such a scheme. Their plan was founded on erroneous notions of religion and policy, and they had absurdly chosen a scene* within reach of the injustice and ambition of an European tyrant.

It was wise and easy to profit by their example. Resting on the two props of fidelity and zeal, an association might exist for ages in the heart of Europe, whose influence might be felt, and might be boundless, in some region of the southern hemisphere; and by whom a moral and political structure might be raised, the growth of pure wisdom,

---

*Paraguay.[12]

and totally unlike those fragments of Roman and Gothic barbarism, which cover the face of what are called the civilized nations. The belief now rose in my mind that some such scheme had actually been prosecuted, and that Ludloe was a coadjutor. On this supposition, the caution with which he approached to his point, the arduous probation which a candidate for a part on this stage must undergo, and the rigours of that test by which his fortitude and virtue must be tried, were easily explained. I was too deeply imbued with veneration for the effects of such schemes, and too sanguine in my confidence in the rectitude of Ludloe, to refuse my concurrence in any scheme by which my qualifications might at length be raised to a due point.

Our interview was frank and affectionate. I found him situated just as formerly. His aspect, manners, and deportment were the same. I entered once more on my former mode of life, but our intercourse became more frequent. We constantly breakfasted together, and our conversation was usually prolonged through half the morning.

For a time our topics were general. I thought proper to leave to him the introduction of more interesting themes: this, however, he betrayed no inclination to do. His reserve excited some surprise, and I began to suspect that whatever design he had formed with regard to me, had been laid aside. To ascertain this question, I ventured, at length, to recall his attention to the subject of his last letter, and to enquire whether subsequent reflection had made any change in his views.

He said that his views were too momentous to be hastily taken up, or hastily dismissed; the station, my attainment of which depended wholly on myself, was high above vulgar heads, and was to be gained by years of solicitude and labour. This, at least, was true with regard to minds ordinarily constituted; I, perhaps, deserved to be regarded as an exception, and might be able to accomplish in a few months that for which others were obliged to toil during half their lives.

Man, continued he, is the slave of habit. Convince him to-day that his duty leads straight forward: he shall advance, but at every step his belief shall fade; habit will resume its empire, and to-morrow he shall turn back, or betake himself to oblique paths.

We know not our strength till it be tried. Virtue, till confirmed by habit, is a dream. You are a man imbued by errors, and vincible by slight temptations. Deep enquiries must bestow light on your opinions, and the habit of encountering and vanquishing temptation must inspire you with fortitude. Till this be done, you are unqualified for that post, in which you will be invested with divine attributes, and prescribe the condition of a large portion of mankind.

Confide not in the firmness of your principles, or the stedfastness of your integrity. Be always vigilant and fearful. Never think you have enough of knowledge, and let not your caution slumber for a moment, for you know not when danger is near.

I acknowledged the justice of his admonitions, and professed myself willing to undergo any ordeal which reason should prescribe. What, I asked, were the conditions, on the fulfilment of which depended my advancement to the station he alluded to? Was it necessary to conceal from me the nature and obligations of this rank?

These enquiries sunk him more profoundly into meditation than I had ever before witnessed. After a pause, in which some perplexity was visible, he answered:

I scarcely know what to say. As to promises, I claim them not from you. We are now arrived at a point, in which it is necessary to look around with caution, and that consequences should be fully known. A number of persons are leagued together for an end of some moment.[13] To make yourself one of these is submitted to your choice. Among the conditions of their alliance are mutual fidelity and secrecy.

Their existence depends upon this: their existence is known only to themselves. This secrecy must be obtained by all the means which are possible. When I have said thus much, I have informed you, in some degree, of their existence, but you are still ignorant of the purpose contemplated by this association, and of all the members, except myself. So far no dangerous disclosure is yet made: but this degree of concealment is not sufficient. Thus much is made known to you, because it is unavoidable. The individuals which compose this fraternity are not immortal, and the vacancies occasioned by death must be supplied from among the living. The candidate must be instructed and prepared, and they are always at liberty to recede. Their reason must approve the obligations and duties of their station, or they are unfit for it.

If they recede, one duty is still incumbent upon them: they must observe an inviolable silence. To this they are not held by any promise. They must weigh consequences, and freely decide; but they must not fail to number among these consequences their own death.

Their death will not be prompted by vengeance. The executioner will say, he that has once revealed the tale is likely to reveal it a second time; and, to prevent this, the betrayer must die. Nor is this the only consequence: to prevent the further revelation, he, to whom the secret was imparted, must likewise perish. He must not console himself with the belief that his trespass will be unknown. The knowledge cannot, by human means, be withheld from this fraternity. Rare, indeed, will it be that his purpose to disclose is not discovered before it can be effected, and the disclosure prevented by his death.

Be well aware of your condition. What I now, or may hereafter mention, mention not again. Admit not even a doubt as to the propriety of hiding it from all the world. There are eyes who will discern this doubt amidst the closest folds of your heart, and your life will instantly be sacrificed.

At present be the subject dismissed. Reflect deeply on the duty which you have already incurred. Think upon your strength of mind, and be careful not to lay yourself under impracticable obligations. It will always be in your power to recede. Even after you are solemnly enrolled a member, you may consult the dictates of your own understanding, and relinquish your post; but while you live, the obligation to be silent will perpetually attend you.

We seek not the misery or death of any one, but we are swayed by an immutable calculation. Death is to be abhorred, but the life of the betrayer is productive of more evil than his death: his death, therefore, we chuse, and our means are instantaneous and unerring.

I love you. The first impulse of my love is to dissuade you from seeking to know more. Your mind will be full of ideas; your hands will be perpetually busy to a purpose into which no human creature, beyond the verge of your brotherhood, must pry. Believe me, who have made the experiment, that compared with this task, the task of inviolable secrecy, all others are easy. To be dumb will not suffice; never to know any remission in your zeal or your watchfulness will not suffice.

If the sagacity of others detect your occupations, however strenuously you may labour for concealment, your doom is ratified, as well as that of the wretch whose evil destiny led him to pursue you.

Yet if your fidelity fail not, great will be your recompence. For all your toils and self-devotion, ample will be the retribution. Hitherto you have been wrapt in darkness and storm; then will you be exalted to a pure and unruffled element. It is only for a time that temptation will environ you, and your path will be toilsome. In a few years you will be permitted to withdraw to a land of sages, and the remainder of your life will glide away in the enjoyments of beneficence and wisdom.

Think deeply on what I have said. Investigate your own motives and opinions, and prepare to submit them to the test of numerous hazards and experiments.

Here my friend passed to a new topic. I was desirous of reverting to this subject, and obtaining further information concerning it, but he assiduously repelled all my attempts, and insisted on my bestowing deep and impartial attention on what had already been disclosed. I was not slow to comply with his directions. My mind refused to admit any other theme of contemplation than this.

As yet I had no glimpse of the nature of this fraternity. I was permitted to form conjectures, and previous incidents bestowed but one form upon my thoughts. In reviewing the sentiments and deportment of Ludloe, my belief continually acquired new strength. I even recollected hints and ambiguous allusions in his discourse, which were easily solved, on the supposition of the existence of a new model of society, in some unsuspected corner of the world.

I did not fully perceive the necessity of secrecy; but this necessity perhaps would be rendered apparent, when I should come to know the connection that subsisted between Europe and this imaginary colony. But what was to be done? I was willing to abide by these conditions. My understanding might not approve of all the ends proposed by this fraternity, and I had liberty to withdraw from it, or to refuse to ally myself with them. That the obligation of secrecy should still remain, was unquestionably reasonable.

It appeared to be the plan of Ludloe rather to damp than to stimulate my zeal. He discouraged all attempts to renew the subject in conversation. He dwelt upon the arduousness of the office to which I aspired, the temptations to violate my duty with which I should be continually beset, the inevitable death with which the slightest breach of my engagements would be followed, and the long apprenticeship which it would be necessary for me to serve, before I should be fitted to enter into this conclave.

Sometimes my courage was depressed by these representations.... My zeal, however, was sure to revive; and at length Ludloe declared himself willing to assist me in the accomplishment of my wishes. For this end, it was necessary, he said, that I should be informed of a second obligation, which every candidate must assume. Before any one could be deemed qualified, he must be thoroughly known to his associates. For this end, he must determine to disclose every fact in his history, and every secret of his heart. I must begin with making these confessions, with regard to my past life, to Ludloe, and must continue to communicate, at stated seasons, every new thought, and every new occurrence, to him. This confidence was to be absolutely limitless: no exceptions were to be admitted, and no reserves to be practised; and the same penalty attended the infraction of this rule as of the former. Means would be employed, by which the slightest deviation, in either case, would be detected, and the deathful consequence would follow with instant and inevitable expedition. If secrecy were difficult to practise, sincerity, in that degree in which it was here demanded, was a task infinitely more arduous, and a period of new deliberation was necessary before I should decide. I was at liberty to pause: nay, the longer was the period of deliberation which I took, the better; but, when I had once entered this path, it was not in my power to recede. After having solemnly avowed my resolution to be thus sincere in my confession, any particle of reserve or duplicity would cost me my life.

This indeed was a subject to be deeply thought upon. Hitherto I had been guilty of concealment with regard to my friend. I had entered into no formal compact, but had been conscious to a kind of tacit obligation to hide no important transaction of my life from him. This consciousness was the source of continual anxiety. I had exerted, on numerous occasions, my bivocal faculty, but, in my intercourse with

Ludloe, had suffered not the slightest intimation to escape me with regard to it. This reserve was not easily explained. It was, in a great degree, the product of habit; but I likewise considered that the efficacy of this instrument depended upon its existence being unknown. To confide the secret to one, was to put an end to my privilege: how widely the knowledge would thenceforth be diffused, I had no power to foresee.

Each day multiplied the impediments to confidence. Shame hindered me from acknowledging my past reserves. Ludloe, from the nature of our intercourse, would certainly account my reserve, in this respect, unjustifiable, and to excite his indignation or contempt was an unpleasing undertaking. Now, if I should resolve to persist in my new path, this reserve must be dismissed: I must make him master of a secret which was precious to me beyond all others; by acquainting him with past concealments, I must risk incurring his suspicion and his anger. These reflections were productive of considerable embarrassment.

There was, indeed, an avenue by which to escape these difficulties, if it did not, at the same time, plunge me into greater. My confessions might, in other respects, be unbounded, but my reserves, in this particular, might be continued. Yet should I not expose myself to formidable perils? Would my secret be for ever unsuspected and undiscovered?

When I considered the nature of this faculty, the impossibility of going farther than suspicion, since the agent could be known only by his own confession, and even this confession would not be believed by the greater part of mankind, I was tempted to conceal it.

In most cases, if I had asserted the possession of this power, I should be treated as a liar; it would be considered as an absurd and audacious expedient to free myself from the suspicion of having entered into compact with a dæmon, or of being myself an emissary of the grand foe. Here, however, there was no reason to dread a similar imputation, since Ludloe had denied the preternatural pretensions of these airy sounds.

My conduct on this occasion was nowise influenced by the belief of any inherent sanctity in truth. Ludloe had taught me to model myself in this respect entirely with a view to immediate consequences. If my genuine interest, on the whole, was promoted by veracity, it was proper to adhere to it; but, if the result of my investigation were opposite, truth was to be sacrificed without scruple.

Meanwhile, in a point of so much moment, I was not hasty to determine. My delay seemed to be, by no means, unacceptable to Ludloe, who applauded my discretion, and warned me to be circumspect. My attention was chiefly absorbed by considerations connected with this subject, and little regard was paid to any foreign occupation or amusement.

One evening, after a day spent in my closet, I sought recreation by walking forth. My mind was chiefly occupied by the review of incidents which happened in Spain. I turned my face towards the fields, and recovered not from my reverie, till I had proceeded some miles on the road to Meath. The night had considerably advanced, and the darkness was rendered intense, by the setting of the moon. Being somewhat weary, as well as undetermined in what manner next to proceed, I seated myself on a grassy bank beside the road. The spot which I had chosen was aloof from passengers, and shrouded in the deepest obscurity.

Some time elapsed, when my attention was excited by the slow approach of an equipage. I presently discovered a coach and six horses, but unattended, except by coachman and postillion, and with no light to guide them on their way. Scarcely had they passed the spot where I rested, when some one leaped from beneath the hedge, and seized the head of the fore-horses. Another called upon the coachman to stop, and threatened him with instant death if he disobeyed. A third drew open the coach-door, and ordered those within to deliver their purses. A shriek of terror showed me that a lady was within, who eagerly consented to preserve her life by the loss of her money.

To walk unarmed in the neighbourhood of Dublin, especially at night, has always been accounted dangerous. I had about me the usual instruments of defence. I was desirous of rescuing this person from the danger which surrounded her, but was somewhat at a loss how to effect my purpose. My single strength was insufficient to contend with three ruffians. After a moment's debate, an expedient was suggested, which I hastened to execute.

Time had not been allowed for the ruffian who stood beside the carriage to receive the plunder, when several voices, loud, clamorous, and eager, were heard in the quarter whence the traveller had come. By trampling with quickness, it was easy to imitate the sound of many feet. The robbers were alarmed, and one called upon another to attend. The sounds increased, and, at the next moment, they betook themselves to flight, but not till a pistol was discharged. Whether it was aimed at the lady in the carriage, or at the coachman, I was not permitted to discover, for the report affrighted the horses, and they set off at full speed.

I could not hope to overtake them: I knew not whither the robbers had fled, and whether, by proceeding, I might not fall into their hands.... These considerations induced me to resume my feet, and retire from the scene as expeditiously as possible. I regained my own habitation without injury.

I have said that I occupied separate apartments from those of Ludloe. To these there were means of access without disturbing the family. I hasted to my chamber, but was considerably surprized to find, on entering my apartment, Ludloe seated at a table, with a lamp before him.

My momentary confusion was greater than his. On discovering who it was, he assumed his accustomed looks, and explained appearances, by saying, that he wished to converse with me on a subject of importance, and had therefore sought me at this secret hour, in my own chamber. Contrary to his expectation, I was absent. Conceiving it possible that I might shortly return, he had waited till now. He took no further notice of my absence, nor manifested any desire to know the cause of it, but proceeded to mention the subject which had brought him hither. These were his words.

You have nothing which the laws permit you to call your own. Justice entitles you to the supply of your physical wants, from those who are able to supply them; but there are few who will acknowledge your claim, or spare an atom of their superfluity to appease your cravings. That which they will not spontaneously give, it is not right to wrest from them by violence. What then is to be done?

Property is necessary to your own subsistence. It is useful, by enabling you to supply the wants of others. To give food, and clothing,
and shelter, is to give life, to annihilate temptation, to unshackle virtue,
and propagate felicity. How shall property be gained?

You may set your understanding or your hands at work. You may
weave stockings, or write poems, and exchange them for money; but
these are tardy and meager schemes. The means are disproportioned
to the end, and I will not suffer you to pursue them. My justice will
supply your wants.

But dependance on the justice of others is a precarious condition.
To be the object is a less ennobling state than to be the bestower of
benefit. Doubtless you desire to be vested with competence and riches,
and to hold them by virtue of the law, and not at the will of a benefactor. . . . He paused as if waiting for my assent to his positions. I readily
expressed my concurrence, and my desire to pursue any means compatible with honesty. He resumed.

There are various means, besides labour, violence, or fraud. It is
right to select the easiest within your reach. It happens that the easiest
is at hand. A revenue of some thousands a year, a stately mansion in
the city, and another in Kildare, old and faithful domestics, and magnificent furniture, are good things. Will you have them?

A gift like that, replied I, will be attended by momentous conditions. I cannot decide upon its value, until I know these conditions.

The sole condition is your consent to receive them. Not even the
airy obligation of gratitude will be created by acceptance. On the contrary, by accepting them, you will confer the highest benefit upon
another.

I do not comprehend you. Something surely must be given in
return.

Nothing. It may seem strange that, in accepting the absolute controul of so much property, you subject yourself to no conditions;
that no claims of gratitude or service will accrue; but the wonder
is greater still. The law equitably enough fetters the gift with no
restraints, with respect to you that receive it; but not so with regard
to the unhappy being who bestows it. That being must part, not only
with property but liberty. In accepting the property, you must consent

to enjoy the services of the present possessor. They cannot be disjoined.

Of the true nature and extent of the gift, you should be fully apprized. Be aware, therefore, that, together with this property, you will receive absolute power over the liberty and person of the being who now possesses it. That being must become your domestic slave; be governed, in every particular, by your caprice.

Happily for you, though fully invested with this power, the degree and mode in which it will be exercised will depend upon yourself.... You may either totally forbear the exercise, or employ it only for the benefit of your slave. However injurious, therefore, this authority may be to the subject of it, it will, in some sense, only enhance the value of the gift to you.

The attachment and obedience of this being will be chiefly evident in one thing. Its duty will consist in conforming, in every instance, to your will. All the powers of this being are to be devoted to your happiness; but there is one relation between you, which enables you to confer, while exacting, pleasure.... This relation is *sexual*. Your slave is a woman; and the bond, which transfers her property and person to you, is ... *marriage*.[14]

My knowledge of Ludloe, his principles, and reasonings, ought to have precluded that surprise which I experienced at the conclusion of his discourse. I knew that he regarded the present institution of marriage as a contract of servitude, and the terms of it unequal and unjust. When my surprise had subsided, my thoughts turned upon the nature of his scheme. After a pause of reflection, I answered:

Both law and custom have connected obligations with marriage, which, though heaviest on the female, are not light upon the male. Their weight and extent are not immutable and uniform; they are modified by various incidents, and especially by the mental and personal qualities of the lady.

I am not sure that I should willingly accept the property and person of a woman decrepid with age, and enslaved by perverse habits and evil passions: whereas youth, beauty, and tenderness would be worth accepting, even for their own sake, and disconnected with fortune.

As to altar vows, I believe they will not make me swerve from equity. I shall exact neither service nor affection from my spouse. The value of these, and indeed, not only the value, but the very existence, of the latter depends upon its spontaneity. A promise to love tends rather to loosen than strengthen the tie.

As to myself, the age of illusion is past. I shall not wed, till I find one whose moral and physical constitution will make personal fidelity easy. I shall judge without mistiness or passion, and habit will come in aid of an enlightened and deliberate choice.

I shall not be fastidious in my choice. I do not expect, and scarcely desire, much intellectual similitude between me and my wife. Our opinions and pursuits cannot be in common. While women are formed by their education, and their education continues in its present state, tender hearts and misguided understandings are all that we can hope to meet with.

What are the character, age, and person of the woman to whom you allude? and what prospect of success would attend my exertions to obtain her favour?

I have told you she is rich. She is a widow, and owes her riches to the liberality of her husband, who was a trader of great opulence, and who died while on a mercantile adventure to Spain. He was not unknown to you. Your letters from Spain often spoke of him. In short, she is the widow of Bennington, whom you met at Barcelona. She is still in the prime of life; is not without many feminine attractions; has an ardent and credulent temper; and is particularly given to devotion. This temper it would be easy to regulate according to your pleasure and your interest, and I now submit to you the expediency of an alliance with her.

I am a kinsman, and regarded by her with uncommon deference; and my commendations, therefore, will be of great service to you, and shall be given.

I will deal ingenuously with you. It is proper you should be fully acquainted with the grounds of this proposal. The benefits of rank, and property, and independence, which I have already mentioned as likely to accrue to you from this marriage, are solid and valuable benefits; but these are not the sole advantages, and to benefit you, in these respects, is not my whole view.

No. My treatment of you henceforth will be regulated by one principle. I regard you only as one undergoing a probation or apprenticeship; as subjected to trials of your sincerity and fortitude. The
marriage I now propose to you is desirable, because it will make you
independent of me. Your poverty might create an unsuitable bias in
favour of proposals, one of whose effects would be to set you beyond
fortune's reach. That bias will cease, when you cease to be poor and
dependent.

Love is the strongest of all human delusions. That fortitude, which
is not subdued by the tenderness and blandishments of woman, may
be trusted; but no fortitude, which has not undergone that test, will be
trusted by us.

This woman is a charming enthusiast. She will never marry but him
whom she passionately loves. Her power over the heart that loves her
will scarcely have limits. The means of prying into your transactions,
of suspecting and sifting your thoughts, which her constant society
with you, while sleeping and waking, her zeal and watchfulness for
your welfare, and her curiosity, adroitness, and penetration will afford
her, are evident. Your danger, therefore, will be imminent. Your fortitude will be obliged to have recourse, not to flight, but to vigilance.
Your eye must never close.

Alas! what human magnanimity can stand this test! How can I persuade myself that you will not fail? I waver between hope and fear.
Many, it is true, have fallen, and dragged with them the author of their
ruin, but some have soared above even these perils and temptations,
with their fiery energies unimpaired, and great has been, as great
ought to be, their recompence.

But you are doubtless aware of your danger. I need not repeat the
consequences of betraying your trust, the rigour of those who will
judge your fault, the unerring and unbounded scrutiny to which your
actions, the most secret and indifferent, will be subjected.

Your conduct, however, will be voluntary. At your own option be it,
to see or not to see this woman. Circumspection, deliberation, fore-
thought, are your sacred duties and highest interest.

Ludloe's remarks on the seductive and bewitching powers of
women, on the difficulty of keeping a secret which they wish to know,

and to gain which they employ the soft artillery of tears and prayers, and blandishments and menaces, are familiar to all men, but they had little weight with me, because they were unsupported by my own experience. I had never had any intellectual or sentimental connection with the sex. My meditations and pursuits had all led a different way, and a bias had gradually been given to my feelings, very unfavourable to the refinements of love. I acknowledge, with shame and regret, that I was accustomed to regard the physical and sensual consequences of the sexual relation as realities, and every thing intellectual, disinterested, and heroic, which enthusiasts connect with it, as idle dreams. Besides, said I, I am yet a stranger to the secret, on the preservation of which so much stress is laid, and it will be optional with me to receive it or not. If, in the progress of my acquaintance with Mrs. Benington, I should perceive any extraordinary danger in the gift, cannot I refuse, or at least delay to comply with any new conditions from Ludloe? Will not his candour and his affection for me rather commend than disapprove my diffidence? In fine, I resolved to see this lady.

She was, it seems, the widow of Benington, whom I knew in Spain. This man was an English merchant settled at Barcelona, to whom I had been commended by Ludloe's letters, and through whom my pecuniary supplies were furnished. . . . Much intercourse and some degree of intimacy had taken place between us, and I had gained a pretty accurate knowledge of his character. I had been informed, through different channels, that his wife was much his superior in rank, that she possessed great wealth in her own right, and that some disagreement of temper or views occasioned their separation. She had married him for love, and still doated on him: the occasions for separation having arisen, it seems, not on her side but on his. As his habits of reflection were nowise friendly to religion, and as hers, according to Ludloe, were of the opposite kind, it is possible that some jarring had arisen between them from this source. Indeed, from some casual and broken hints of Benington, especially in the latter part of his life, I had long since gathered this conjecture. . . . Something, thought I, may be derived from my acquaintance with her husband favourable to my views.

I anxiously waited for an opportunity of acquainting Ludloe with my resolution. On the day of our last conversation, he had made a short excursion from town, intending to return the same evening, but had continued absent for several days. As soon as he came back, I hastened to acquaint him with my wishes.

Have you well considered this matter, said he. Be assured it is of no trivial import. The moment at which you enter the presence of this woman will decide your future destiny. Even putting out of view the subject of our late conversations, the light in which you shall appear to her will greatly influence your happiness, since, though you cannot fail to love her, it is quite uncertain what return she may think proper to make. Much, doubtless, will depend on your own perseverance and address, but you will have many, perhaps insuperable obstacles to encounter on several accounts, and especially in her attachment to the memory of her late husband. As to her devout temper, this is nearly allied to a warm imagination in some other respects, and will operate much more in favour of an ardent and artful lover, than against him.

I still expressed my willingness to try my fortune with her.

Well, said he, I anticipated your consent to my proposal, and the visit I have just made was to her. I thought it best to pave the way, by informing her that I had met with one for whom she had desired me to look out. You must know that her father was one of these singular men who set a value upon things exactly in proportion to the difficulty of obtaining or comprehending them. His passion was for antiques, and his favourite pursuit during a long life was monuments in brass, marble, and parchment, of the remotest antiquity. He was wholly indifferent to the character or conduct of our present sovereign and his ministers, but was extremely solicitous about the name and exploits of a king of Ireland that lived two or three centuries before the flood. He felt no curiosity to know who was the father of his wife's child, but would travel a thousand miles, and consume months, in investigating which son of Noah it was that first landed on the coast of Munster. He would give a hundred guineas from the mint for a piece of old decayed copper no bigger than his nail, provided it had aukward characters upon it, too much defaced to be read. The whole stock of a great bookseller was, in his eyes, a cheap exchange for a shred of parchment, containing half a homily written by St. Patrick. He would have gratefully given all his patrimonial domains to one who should inform him what pendragon[15] or druid it was who set up the first stone on Salisbury plain.[16]

This spirit, as you may readily suppose, being seconded by great wealth and long life, contributed to form a very large collection of venerable lumber, which, though beyond all price to the collector himself, is of no value to his heiress but so far as it is marketable. She designs to bring the whole to auction, but for this purpose a catalogue and description are necessary. Her father trusted to a faithful memory, and to vague and scarcely legible memorandums, and has left a very arduous task to any one who shall be named to the office. It occurred to me, that the best means of promoting your views was to recommend you to this office.

You are not entirely without the antiquarian frenzy yourself. The employment, therefore, will be somewhat agreeable to you for its own sake. It will entitle you to become an inmate of the same house, and thus establish an incessant intercourse between you, and the nature of the business is such, that you may perform it in what time, and with what degree of diligence and accuracy you please.

I ventured to insinuate that, to a woman of rank and family, the character of a hireling was by no means a favourable recommendation.

He answered, that he proposed, by the account he should give of me, to obviate every scruple of that nature. Though my father was no better than a farmer, it is not absolutely certain but that my remoter ancestors had princely blood in their veins: but as long as proofs of my low extraction did not impertinently intrude themselves, my silence, or, at most, equivocal surmises, seasonably made use of, might secure me from all inconveniences on the score of birth. He should represent me, and I was such, as his friend, favourite, and equal, and my passion for antiquities should be my principal inducement to undertake this office, though my poverty would make no objection to a reasonable pecuniary recompense.

Having expressed my acquiescence in his measures, he thus proceeded: My visit was made to my kinswoman, for the purpose, as I just now told you, of paving your way into her family; but, on my arrival at her house, I found nothing but disorder and alarm. Mrs. Benington, it seems, on returning from a longer ride than customary, last Thursday evening, was attacked by robbers. Her attendants related an imperfect tale of somebody advancing at the critical moment to her rescue. It seems, however, they did more harm than good; for the horses took to flight and overturned the carriage, in consequence of which Mrs. Benington was severely bruised. She has kept her bed ever since, and a fever was likely to ensue, which has only left her out of danger to-day.

As the adventure before related, in which I had so much concern, occurred at the time mentioned by Ludloe, and as all other circumstances were alike, I could not doubt that the person whom the exertion of my mysterious powers had relieved was Mrs. Benington: but what an ill-omened interference was mine! The robbers would probably have been satisfied with the few guineas in her purse, and, on receiving these, would have left her to prosecute her journey in peace and security, but, by absurdly offering a succour, which could only operate upon the fears of her assailants, I endangered her life, first by the desperate discharge of a pistol, and next by the fright of the horses. . . . My anxiety, which would have been less if I had not been, in some degree, myself the author of the evil, was nearly removed by Ludloe's proceeding to assure me that all danger was at an end, and that he left the lady in the road to perfect health. He had seized the earliest opportunity of acquainting her with the purpose of his visit, and had brought back with him her cheerful acceptance of my services. The next week was appointed for my introduction.

With such an object in view, I had little leisure to attend to any indifferent object. My thoughts were continually bent upon the expected introduction, and my impatience and curiosity drew strength, not merely from the character of Mrs. Benington, but from the nature of my new employment. Ludloe had truly observed, that I was infected with somewhat of this antiquarian mania myself, and I now remembered that Benington had frequently alluded to this collection in possession of his wife. My curiosity had then been more than once excited by his representations, and I had formed a vague resolution of making myself acquainted with this lady and her learned treasure, should I ever return to Ireland.... Other incidents had driven this matter from my mind.

Meanwhile, affairs between Ludloe and myself remained stationary. Our conferences, which were regular and daily, related to general topics, and though his instructions were adapted to promote my improvement in the most useful branches of knowledge, they never afforded a glimpse towards that quarter where my curiosity was most active.

The next week now arrived, but Ludloe informed me that the state of Mrs. Benington's health required a short excursion into the country, and that he himself proposed to bear her company. The journey was to last about a fortnight, after which I might prepare myself for an introduction to her.

This was a very unexpected and disagreeable trial to my patience. The interval of solitude that now succeeded would have passed rapidly and pleasantly enough, if an event of so much moment were not in suspense. Books, of which I was passionately fond, would have afforded me delightful and incessant occupation, and Ludloe, by way of reconciling me to unavoidable delays, had given me access to a little closet, in which his rarer and more valuable books were kept.

All my amusements, both by inclination and necessity, were centered in myself and at home. Ludloe appeared to have no visitants, and though frequently abroad, or at least secluded from me, had never proposed my introduction to any of his friends, except Mrs. Benington. My obligations to him were already too great to allow me to lay claim to new favours and indulgences, nor, indeed, was my disposition such as to make society needful to my happiness. My character had been, in some degree, modelled by the faculty which I possessed. This deriving all its supposed value from impenetrable secrecy, and Ludloe's admonitions tending powerfully to impress me with the necessity of wariness and circumspection in my general intercourse with mankind, I had gradually fallen into sedate, reserved, mysterious, and unsociable habits. My heart wanted not a friend.

In this temper of mind, I set myself to examine the novelties which Ludloe's private book-cases contained. 'Twill be strange, thought I, if his favourite volumes do not show some marks of my friend's character. To know a man's favourite or most constant studies cannot fail of letting in some little light upon his secret thoughts, and though he would not have given me the reading of these books, if he had thought them capable of unveiling more of his concerns than he wished, yet possibly my ingenuity may go one step farther than he dreams of. You shall judge whether I was right in my conjectures.

The books which composed this little library were chiefly the voyages and travels of the missionaries of the sixteenth and seventeenth centuries. Added to these were some works upon political economy and legislation. Those writers who have amused themselves with reducing their ideas to practice, and drawing imaginary pictures of nations or republics, whose manners or government came up to their standard of excellence, were, all of whom I had ever heard, and some I had never heard of before, to be found in this collection. A translation of Aristotle's republic, the political romances of sir Thomas Moore, Harrington, and Hume,[17] appeared to have been much read, and Ludloe had not been sparing of his marginal comments. In these writers he appeared to find nothing but error and absurdity; and his notes were introduced for no other end than to point out groundless principles and false conclusions. . . . The style of these remarks was already familiar to me. I saw nothing new in them, or different from the strain of those speculations with which Ludloe was accustomed to indulge himself in conversation with me.

After having turned over the leaves of the printed volumes, I at length lighted on a small book of maps, from which, of course, I could reasonably expect no information, on that point about which I was most curious. It was an atlas, in which the maps had been drawn by the pen. None of them contained any thing remarkable, so far as I, who was indeed a smatterer in geography, was able to perceive, till I came to the end, when I noticed a map, whose prototype I was wholly unacquainted with. It was drawn on a pretty large scale, representing two islands, which bore some faint resemblance, in their relative proportions, at least, to Great Britain and Ireland. In shape they were widely different, but as to size there was no scale by which to measure them. From the great number of subdivisions, and from signs, which apparently represented towns and cities, I was allowed to infer, that the country was at least as extensive as the British isles. This map was apparently unfinished, for it had no names inscribed upon it.

I have just said, my geographical knowledge was imperfect. Though I had not enough to draw the outlines of any country by memory, I had still sufficient to recognize what I had before seen, and to discover that none of the larger islands in our globe resembled the one before me. Having such and so strong motives to curiosity, you may easily imagine my sensations on surveying this map. Suspecting, as I did, that many of Ludloe's intimations alluded to a country well known to him, though unknown to others, I was, of course, inclined to suppose that this country was now before me.

In search of some clue to this mystery, I carefully inspected the other maps in this collection. In a map of the eastern hemisphere I soon observed the outlines of islands, which, though on a scale greatly diminished, were plainly similar to that of the land above described.

It is well known that the people of Europe are strangers to very nearly one half of the surface of the globe.* From the south pole up to the equator, it is only the small space occupied by southern Africa and by South America with which we are acquainted. There is a vast extent, sufficient to receive a continent as large as North America, which our ignorance has filled only with water. In Ludloe's maps nothing was still to be seen, in these regions, but water, except in that spot where the transverse parallels of the southern tropic and the 150th degree east longitude intersect each other. On this spot were Ludloe's islands placed, though without any name or inscription whatever.

I needed not to be told that this spot had never been explored by any European voyager, who had published his adventures. What authority had Ludloe for fixing a habitable land in this spot? and why did he give us nothing but the courses of shores and rivers, and the scite of towns and villages, without a name?

As soon as Ludloe had set out upon his proposed journey of a fortnight, I unlocked his closet, and continued rummaging among these

*The reader must be reminded that the incidents of this narrative are supposed to have taken place before the voyages of Bougainville and Cook.[18]—EDITOR.

books and maps till night. By that time I had turned over every book and almost every leaf in this small collection, and did not open the closet again till near the end of that period. Meanwhile I had many reflections upon this remarkable circumstance. Could Ludloe have intended that I should see this atlas? It was the only book that could be styled a manuscript on these shelves, and it was placed beneath several others, in a situation far from being obvious and forward to the eye or the hand. Was it an oversight in him to leave it in my way, or could he have intended to lead my curiosity and knowledge a little farther onward by this accidental disclosure? In either case how was I to regulate my future deportment toward him? Was I to speak and act as if this atlas had escaped my attention or not? I had already, after my first examination of it, placed the volume exactly where I found it. On every supposition I thought this was the safest way, and unlocked the closet a second time, to see that all was precisely in the original order. . . . How was I dismayed and confounded on inspecting the shelves to perceive that the atlas was gone. This was a theft, which, from the closet being under lock and key, and the key always in my own pocket, and which, from the very nature of the thing stolen, could not be imputed to any of the domestics. After a few moments a suspicion occurred, which was soon changed into certainty by applying to the housekeeper, who told me that Ludloe had returned, apparently in much haste, the evening of the day on which he had set out upon his journey, and just after I had left the house, that he had gone into the room where this closet of books was, and, after a few minutes' stay, came out again and went away. She told me also, that he had made general enquiries after me, to which she had answered, that she had not seen me during the day, and supposed that I had spent the whole of it abroad. From this account it was plain, that Ludloe had returned for no other purpose but to remove this book out of my reach. But if he had a double key to this door, what should hinder his having access, by the same means, to every other locked up place in the house?

This suggestion made me start with terror. Of so obvious a means for possessing a knowledge of every thing under his roof, I had never been till this moment aware. Such is the infatuation which lays our most secret thoughts open to the world's scrutiny. We are frequently in most danger when we deem ourselves most safe, and our fortress is taken sometimes through a point, whose weakness nothing, it should seem, but the blindest stupidity could overlook.

My terrors, indeed, quickly subsided when I came to recollect that there was nothing in any closet or cabinet of mine which could possibly throw light upon subjects which I desired to keep in the dark. The more carefully I inspected my own drawers, and the more I reflected on the character of Ludloe, as I had known it, the less reason did there appear in my suspicions; but I drew a lesson of caution from this circumstance, which contributed to my future safety.

From this incident I could not but infer Ludloe's unwillingness to let me so far into his geographical secret, as well as the certainty of that suspicion, which had very early been suggested to my thoughts, that Ludloe's plans of civilization had been carried into practice in some unvisited corner of the world. It was strange, however, that he should betray himself by such an inadvertency. One who talked so confidently of his own powers, to unveil any secret of mine, and, at the same time, to conceal his own transactions, had surely committed an unpardonable error in leaving this important document in my way. My reverence, indeed, for Ludloe was such, that I sometimes entertained the notion that this seeming oversight was, in truth, a regular contrivance to supply me with a knowledge, of which, when I came maturely to reflect, it was impossible for me to make any ill use. There is no use in relating what would not be believed; and should I publish to the world the existence of islands in the space allotted by Ludloe's maps to these *incognitæ,* what would the world answer? That whether the space described was sea or land was of no importance. That the moral and political condition of its inhabitants was the only topic worthy of rational curiosity. Since I had gained no information upon this point; since I had nothing to disclose but vain and fantastic surmises; I might as well be ignorant of every thing. Thus, from secretly condemning Ludloe's imprudence, I gradually passed to admiration of his policy. This discovery had no other effect than to stimulate my curiosity; to keep up my zeal to prosecute the journey I had commenced under his auspices.

I had hitherto formed a resolution to stop where I was in Ludloe's confidence: to wait till the success should be ascertained of my projects with respect to Mrs. Benington, before I made any new advance in the perilous and mysterious road into which he had led my steps. But, before this tedious fortnight had elapsed, I was grown extremely impatient for an interview, and had nearly resolved to undertake whatever obligation he should lay upon me.

This obligation was indeed a heavy one, since it included the confession of my vocal powers. In itself the confession was little. To possess this faculty was neither laudable nor culpable, nor had it been exercised in a way which I should be very much ashamed to acknowledge. It had led me into many insincerities and artifices, which, though not justifiable by any creed, was entitled to some excuse, on the score of youthful ardour and temerity. The true difficulty in the way of these confessions was the not having made them already. Ludloe had long been entitled to this confidence, and, though the existence of this power was venial or wholly innocent, the obstinate concealment of it was a different matter, and would certainly expose me to suspicion and rebuke. But what was the alternative? To conceal it. To incur those dreadful punishments awarded against treason in this particular. Ludloe's menaces still rung in my ears, and appalled my heart. How should I be able to shun them? By concealing from every one what I concealed from him? How was my concealment of such a faculty to be suspected or proved? Unless I betrayed myself, who could betray me?

In this state of mind, I resolved to confess myself to Ludloe in the way that he required, reserving only the secret of this faculty. Awful, indeed, said I, is the crisis of my fate. If Ludloe's declarations are true, a horrid catastrophe awaits me: but as fast as my resolutions were shaken, they were confirmed anew by the recollection—Who can betray me but myself? If I deny, who is there can prove? Suspicion can never light upon the truth. If it does, it can never be converted into certainty. Even my own lips cannot confirm it, since who will believe my testimony?

By such illusions was I fortified in my desperate resolution. Ludloe returned at the time appointed. He informed me that Mrs. Benington expected me next morning. She was ready to depart for her country residence, where she proposed to spend the ensuing summer, and would carry me along with her. In consequence of this arrangement, he said, many months would elapse before he should see me again. You will indeed, continued he, be pretty much shut up from all society. Your books and your new friend will be your chief, if not only companions. Her life is not a social one, because she has formed extravagant notions of the importance of lonely worship and devout solitude. Much of her time will be spent in meditation upon pious books in her closet. Some of it in long solitary rides in her coach, for the sake of exercise. Little will remain for eating and sleeping, so that unless you can prevail upon her to violate her ordinary rules for your sake, you will be left pretty much to yourself. You will have the more time to reflect upon what has hitherto been the theme of our conversations. You can come to town when you want to see me. I shall generally be found in these apartments.

In the present state of my mind, though impatient to see Mrs. Benington, I was still more impatient to remove the veil between Ludloe and myself. After some pause, I ventured to enquire if there was any impediment to my advancement in the road he had already pointed out to my curiosity and ambition.

He replied, with great solemnity, that I was already acquainted with the next step to be taken in this road. If I was prepared to make him my confessor, as to the past, the present, and the future, *without exception or condition,* but what arose from defect of memory, he was willing to receive my confession.

I declared myself ready to do so.

I need not, he returned, remind you of the consequences of concealment or deceit. I have already dwelt upon these consequences. As to the past, you have already told me, perhaps, all that is of any moment to know. It is in relation to the future that caution will be chiefly necessary. Hitherto your actions have been nearly indifferent to the ends of your future existence. Confessions of the past are required, because they are an earnest of the future character and conduct. Have you then—but this is too abrupt. Take an hour to reflect and deliberate. Go by yourself; take yourself to severe task, and make up your mind with a full, entire, and unfailing resolution; for the moment in which you assume this new obligation will make you a new being. Perdition or felicity will hang upon that moment.

This conversation was late in the evening. After I had consented to postpone this subject, we parted, he telling me that he would leave his chamber door open, and as soon as my mind was made up I might come to him.

I retired accordingly to my apartment, and spent the prescribed hour in anxious and irresolute reflections. They were no other than had hitherto occurred, but they occurred with more force than ever. Some fatal obstinacy, however, got possession of me, and I persisted in the resolution of concealing *one thing*. We become fondly attached to objects and pursuits, frequently for no conceivable reason but the pain and trouble they cost us. In proportion to the danger in which they involve us do we cherish them. Our darling potion is the poison that scorches our vitals.

After some time, I went to Ludloe's apartment. I found him solemn, and yet benign, at my entrance. After intimating my compliance with the terms prescribed, which I did, in spite of all my labour for composure, with accents half faultering, he proceeded to put various questions to me, relative to my early history.

I knew there was no other mode of accomplishing the end in view, but by putting all that was related in the form of answers to questions; and when meditating on the character of Ludloe, I experienced excessive uneasiness as to the consummate art and penetration which his questions would manifest. Conscious of a purpose to conceal, my fancy invested my friend with the robe of a judicial inquisitor, all whose questions should aim at extracting the truth, and entrapping the liar.

In this respect, however, I was wholly disappointed. All his inquiries were general and obvious.—They betokened curiosity, but not suspicion; yet there were moments when I saw, or fancied I saw, some dissatisfaction betrayed in his features; and when I arrived at that period of my story which terminated with my departure, as his companion, for Europe, his pauses were, I thought, a little longer and more museful than I liked. At this period, our first conference ended. After a talk, which had commenced at a late hour, and had continued many hours, it was time to sleep, and it was agreed that next morning the conference should be renewed.

On retiring to my pillow, and reviewing all the circumstances of this interview, my mind was filled with apprehension and disquiet. I seemed to recollect a thousand things, which showed that Ludloe was not fully satisfied with my part in this interview. A strange and nameless mixture of wrath and of pity appeared, on recollection, in the glances which, from time to time, he cast upon me. Some emotion played upon his features, in which, as my fears conceived, there was a tincture of resentment and ferocity. In vain I called my usual sophistries to my aid. In vain I pondered on the inscrutable nature of my peculiar faculty. In vain I endeavoured to persuade myself, that, by telling the truth, instead of entitling myself to Ludloe's approbation, I should only excite his anger, by what he could not but deem an attempt to impose upon his belief an incredible tale of impossible events. I had never heard or read of any instance of this faculty. I supposed the case to be absolutely singular, and I should be no more entitled to credit in proclaiming it, than if I should maintain that a certain billet of wood possessed the faculty of articulate speech. It was now, however, too late to retract. I had been guilty of a solemn and deliberate concealment. I was now in the path in which there was no turning back, and I must go forward.

The return of day's encouraging beams in some degree quieted my nocturnal terrors, and I went, at the appointed hour, to Ludloe's presence. I found him with a much more cheerful aspect than I expected, and began to chide myself, in secret, for the folly of my late apprehensions.

After a little pause, he reminded me, that he was only one among many, engaged in a great and arduous design. As each of us, continued he, is mortal, each of us must, in time, yield his post to another.—Each of us is ambitious to provide himself a successor, to have his place filled by one selected and instructed by himself. All our personal feelings and affections are by no means intended to be swallowed up by a passion for the general interest; when they can be kept alive and be brought into play, in subordination and subservience to the *great end*, they are cherished as useful, and revered as laudable; and whatever austerity and rigour you may impute to my character, there are few more susceptible of personal regards than I am.

You cannot know, till *you* are what *I* am, what deep, what all-absorbing interest I have in the success of my tutorship on this occasion. Most joyfully would I embrace a thousand deaths, rather than that you should prove a recreant. The consequences of any failure in your integrity will, it is true, be fatal to yourself: but there are some minds, of a generous texture, who are more impatient under ills they have inflicted upon others, than of those they have brought upon themselves; who had rather perish, themselves, in infamy, than bring infamy or death upon a benefactor.

Perhaps of such noble materials is your mind composed. If I had not thought so, you would never have been an object of my regard, and therefore, in the motives that shall impel you to fidelity, sincerity, and perseverance, some regard to my happiness and welfare will, no doubt, have place.

And yet I exact nothing from you on this score. If your own safety be insufficient to controul you, you are not fit for us. There is, indeed, abundant need of all possible inducements to make you faithful. The task of concealing nothing from me must be easy. That of concealing every thing from others must be the only arduous one. The *first* you can hardly fail of performing, when the exigence requires it, for what motive can you possibly have to practice evasion or disguise with me? You have surely committed no crime; you have neither robbed, nor murdered, nor betrayed. If you have, there is no room for the fear of punishment or the terror of disgrace to step in, and make you hide your guilt from me. You cannot dread any further disclosure, because I can have no interest in your ruin or your shame: and what evil could ensue the confession of the foulest murder, even before a bench of magistrates, more dreadful than that which will inevitably follow the practice of the least concealment to me, or the least undue disclosure to others?

You cannot easily conceive the emphatical solemnity with which this was spoken. Had he fixed piercing eyes on me while he spoke; had I perceived him watching my looks, and labouring to penetrate my secret thoughts, I should doubtless have been ruined: but he fixed his eyes upon the floor, and no gesture or look indicated the smallest suspicion of my conduct. After some pause, he continued, in a more pathetic tone, while his whole frame seemed to partake of his mental agitation.

I am greatly at a loss by what means to impress you with a full conviction of the truth of what I have just said. Endless are the sophistries by which we seduce ourselves into perilous and doubtful paths. What we do not see, we disbelieve, or we heed not. The sword may descend upon our infatuated head from above, but we who are, meanwhile, busily inspecting the ground at our feet, or gazing at the scene around us, are not aware or apprehensive of its irresistible coming. In this case, it must not be seen before it is felt, or before that time comes when the danger of incurring it is over. I cannot withdraw the veil, and disclose to your view the exterminating angel. All must be vacant and blank, and the danger that stands armed with death at your elbow must continue to be totally invisible, till that moment when its vengeance is provoked or unprovokable. I will do my part to encourage you in good, or intimidate you from evil. I am anxious to set before you all the motives which are fitted to influence your conduct; but how shall I work on your convictions?

Here another pause ensued, which I had not courage enough to interrupt. He presently resumed.

Perhaps you recollect a visit which you paid, on Christmas day, in the year ——, to the cathedral church at Toledo. Do you remember?

A moment's reflection recalled to my mind all the incidents of that day. I had good reason to remember them. I felt no small trepidation when Ludloe referred me to that day, for, at the moment, I was doubtful whether there had not been some bivocal agency exerted on that occasion. Luckily, however, it was almost the only similar occasion in which it had been wholly silent.

I answered in the affirmative: I remember them perfectly.

And yet, said Ludloe, with a smile that seemed intended to disarm this declaration of some of its terrors, I suspect your recollection is not as exact as mine, nor, indeed, your knowledge as extensive. You met there, for the first time, a female, whose nominal uncle, but real father, a dean of that ancient church, resided in a blue stone house, the third from the west angle of the square of St. Jago.

All this was exactly true.

This female, continued he, fell in love with you. Her passion made her deaf to all the dictates of modesty and duty, and she gave you sufficient intimations, in subsequent interviews at the same place, of this passion; which, she being fair and enticing, you were not slow in comprehending and returning. As not only the safety of your intercourse, but even of both your lives, depended on being shielded even from suspicion, the utmost wariness and caution was observed in all your proceedings. Tell me whether you succeeded in your efforts to this end.

I replied, that, at the time, I had no doubt but I had.

And yet, said he, drawing something from his pocket, and putting it into my hand, there is the slip of paper, with the preconcerted emblem inscribed upon it, which the infatuated girl dropped in your sight, one evening, in the left aisle of that church. That paper you imagined you afterwards burnt in your chamber lamp. In pursuance of this token, you deferred your intended visit, and next day the lady was accidentally drowned, in passing a river. Here ended your connexion with her, and with her was buried, as you thought, all memory of this transaction.

I leave you to draw your own inference from this disclosure. Meditate upon it when alone. Recal all the incidents of that drama, and labour to conceive the means by which my sagacity has been able to reach events that took place so far off, and under so deep a covering. If you cannot penetrate these means, learn to reverence my assertions, that I cannot be deceived; and let sincerity be henceforth the rule of your conduct towards me, not merely because it is right, but because concealment is impossible.

We will stop here. There is no haste required of us. Yesterday's discourse will suffice for to-day, and for many days to come. Let what has already taken place be the subject of profound and mature reflection. Review, once more, the incidents of your early life, previous to your introduction to me, and, at our next conference, prepare to supply all those deficiences occasioned by negligence, forgetfulness, or design on our first. There must be some. There must be many. The whole truth can only be disclosed after numerous and repeated conversations. These must take place at considerable intervals, and when *all* is told, then shall you be ready to encounter the final ordeal, and load yourself with heavy and terrific sanctions.

I shall be the proper judge of the completeness of your confession.—Knowing previously, and by unerring means, your whole history, I shall be able to detect all that is deficient, as well as all that is redundant. Your confessions have hitherto adhered to the truth, but deficient they are, and they must be, for who, at a single trial can detail the secrets of his life? whose recollection can fully serve him at an instant's notice? who can free himself, by a single effort, from the dominion of fear and shame? We expect no miracles of fortitude and purity from our disciples. It is our discipline, our wariness, our laborious preparation that creates the excellence we have among us. We find it not ready made.

I counsel you to join Mrs. Bennington without delay. You may see me when and as often as you please. When it is proper to renew the present topic, it shall be renewed. Till then we will be silent.— Here Ludloe left me alone, but not to indifference or vacuity. Indeed I was overwhelmed with the reflections that arose from this conversation. So, said I, I am still saved, if I have wisdom enough to use the opportunity, from the consequences of past concealments. By a distinction which I had wholly overlooked, but which could not be missed by the sagacity and equity of Ludloe, I have praise for telling the truth, and an excuse for withholding some of the truth. It was, indeed, a praise to which I was entitled, for I have made no *additions* to the tale of my early adventures. I had no motive to exaggerate or dress out in false colours. What I sought to conceal, I was careful to exclude entirely, that a lame or defective narrative might awaken no suspicions.

The allusion to incidents at Toledo confounded and bewildered all my thoughts. I still held the paper he had given me. So far as memory could be trusted, it was the same which, an hour after I had received it, I burnt, as I conceived, with my own hands. How Ludloe came into possession of this paper; how he was apprised of incidents, to which only the female mentioned and myself were privy, which she had too good reason to hide from all the world, and which I had taken infinite pains to bury in oblivion, I vainly endeavoured to conjecture.

THESSALONICA: A ROMAN STORY

Thessalonica, in consequence of its commercial situation, was populous and rich. Its fortifications and numerous garrison had preserved it from injury during the late commotions,* and the number of inhabitants was greatly increased, at the expense of the defenceless districts and cities. Its place, with relation to Dalmatia, the Peloponnesus, and the Danube, was nearly centrical. Its security had been uninterrupted for ages, and no city in the empire of Theodosius[2] exhibited so many monuments of its ancient prosperity. It had been, for many years, the residence of the prince, and had thence become the object of a kind of filial affection. He had laboured to render it impregnable, by erecting bulwarks, and guarding it with the bravest of his troops; he had endowed the citizens with new revenues and privileges, had enhanced the frequency of their shows, and the magnificence of their halls and avenues, and made it the seat of government of Illyria and Greece.

Its defence was intrusted to Botheric,[3] whom he had selected for his valour, fidelity, and moderation; and he commended, with equal zeal to this officer, the defence of the city from external enemies, and the maintenance of justice and order within its walls.

The temper of Botheric was generous and impetuous. He was unacquainted with civil forms, and refrained, as much as possible, from encroaching on the functions of the magistrate. His education and genius were military, and he conceived that his commission required from him nothing but unwearied attention to his soldiers. His vigilance was bent to maintain order and obedience among them, and to prevent or to stifle dissentions between them and the citizens. For this end he multiplied their duties and exercises, so as to leave no room for intercourse with the people. Their time was constantly occupied with attendance at their stations, or performance of some personal duty in their quarters.

*At the conclusion of the Gothic war, A.D. 390.[1]

By these means, the empire of order was, for some time, maintained, but no diligence or moderation can fully restrain the passions of the multitude. Quarrels sometimes arose between the spectators at the theatre and circus, and the centinels who were planted in the avenues. The General was always present at the public shows; clamour and riot instantly attracted his attention, and if a soldier was a party in the fray, he hasted to terminate the contest, by examination and punishment.

You need not be told, that the populace of Roman cities are actuated by a boundless passion for public shows. The bounty of the prince cannot be more acceptably exerted than in pecuniary donations for this purpose, and by making exhibitions more frequent and magnificent. The gratitude of this people is proportioned, not to the efficacy of edicts to restrain crimes, alleviate cares, or diminish the price of provisions; but to the commodiousness and cheapness of seats in a theatre, or to the number and beauty of the horses which are provided for the circus.

The prince had manifested his attachment to this city in the usual manner. The finest horses were procured, at his expense, from Africa and Spain; new embellishments were added to the chariots, and a third set of characters, distinguished by a crimson uniform,[4] was added to the former. Once a month, the people were amused by races, at the expense of their sovereign.

At one of these exhibitions, a citizen, by name Macro,[5] attempted to enter a gate by which the Senators passed to their seats. Order had long since established distinctions in this respect, and every class of the people enjoyed their peculiar seats and entrances. Macro was therefore denied admission, by two soldiers stationed in the passage. He persisted in his efforts to enter, and the soldiers persisted in their opposition, till, at length, a scuffle ensued, in which the citizen was slightly wounded.

The games not having begun, many from within and without were attracted to the spot. The crowd insensibly increased, and the spectators seemed willing to discountenance the claims of Macro. The sight of his blood, however, changed the tide in his favour. The soldiers were believed to have proceeded to this extremity without necessity, and to have exercised their power wantonly.

Clamours of disapprobation were succeeded by attempts to disarm the centinels, and conduct them before the tribunal of their General. This was usually held in an upper porch of the edifice. Botheric was momently expected, and the persons who urged the seizure of the culprits, were governed by pacific intentions. The soldiers were supposed to have transgressed their duty, and redress was sought in a lawful manner. Botheric was the only judge of their conduct, and confidence was placed in the equity of his decision.

The soldiers maintained the rectitude of their proceeding, and refused to resign their arms, or leave the post. Some endeavoured to gain their end by expostulation and remonstrance. The greater number were enraged, and their menaces being ineffectual, were quickly succeeded by violence. The interior passages were wide, but the entrance was narrow, and the soldiers profited by their situation, to repel the assaults that were made upon them. The wounds which they inflicted in their own defence augmented the fury of their assailants. They fought with desperate resolution, and were not overpowered till they had killed five of the citizens.

At length the soldiers sought their safety in flight. The mob poured into the passages. One of the fugitives was overtaken in a moment. The pursuers were unarmed, but the victim was dashed against the pavement, and his limbs were torn from each other by the furious hands that were fastened upon him. While his lifeless and bleeding trunk was dragged along the ground, and thrown to and fro by some, others were engaged in searching for him that escaped.

While roaming from place to place, they met a soldier whom his officer had dispatched upon some message. They staid not to inquire whether this was he of whom they were in search, but seizing him, they dragged him to the midst of the square, and dispatched him with a thousand blows.

The tumult was by no means appeased by these executions. Numbers flocked to the scene. The sight of the dead bodies of the citizens, imperfect and exaggerated rumours of the cruelty of the centinels, the execrations and example of those who had been leaders in the tumult, conspired to engage them in the same outrages.

The pursuit of the fugitive soldier did not slacken. The galleries and vaults were secured, and every place resounded with uproar and menace. Meanwhile, the seats of the Senators were filled with a per-miscuous crowd, who gladly seized this opportunity of engrossing places more convenient than any other.

At this moment, Botheric and his officers arrived. The entrance was inaccessible, by reason of the crowd stationed without, and the num-bers that were struggling in the passages to gain the senatorial benches. In this contest, the weaker were overpowered, and scores were trodden to death or suffocated. The General and his officers were no sooner known to be arrived, than they were greeted on all hands, by threaten-ing gestures and insolent clamours. The heads of the slaughtered sol-diers were placed upon pikes. Botheric was compelled to gaze upon their gory visages, and listen to the outcries for vengeance which as-cended from a thousand mouths.

This unwonted spectacle, and the confusion which surrounded him, threw him into temporary panic. It was requisite to ascertain the causes of this tumult, to prevent its progress, and to punish its authors; but his own safety was to be, in the first place, consulted. How far that was endangered by the fury of the populace it was impossible to fore-see.

His retinue consisted of twenty officers, who were armed, as usual, with daggers. Recovering from their first astonishment, they involun-tarily drew their weapons, and crowded round their General. This movement seemed by no means to intimidate the populace, whose outcries and menaces became more vehement than ever. As their numbers and fury increased, they pressed more closely and auda-ciously upon this slender band, whose weapons pointed at the bosoms of those who were nearest, and who could scarcely preserve them-selves from being overwhelmed.

Botheric's surprize quickly yielded to a just view of the perils that surrounded him. The cause of this tumult was unknown; but it was evi-dent that the temper of the people was revengeful and sanguinary. The slightest incident was sufficient to set them free from restraint. The first blood that should be shed would be the signal for outrage, and nei-ther he nor his officers could hope to escape with their lives.

His first care, therefore, was to inculcate forbearance on his officers. This, indeed, would avail them but little, since the foremost of the crowd would be irresistibly impelled by those who were behind, and whose numbers incessantly increased. In a moment they would be pressed together; their arms would be useless; and secret enemies, by whom he vaguely suspected that this tumult had been excited, would seize that opportunity for wreaking their vengeance.

To escape to the neighbouring portico was an obvious expedient; but the galleries, above and below, were already filled with a clamorous multitude, whose outcries and gesticulations prompted those below to the commission of violence. His troops were either dispersed in their quarters, or stationed on the walls. The few whose duty required their attendance at the circus could afford no protection. Those at a distance could not be seasonably apprized of the danger of their leader; and if they were apprized, would be at a loss, in the absence of their officers, in what manner to act. To endeavour to restore tranquillity by persuasion or remonstrance was chimerical. No single voice could be heard amidst the uproar.

In this part of the square there had formerly been erected an equestrian statue of Constantius.[6] It had been overthrown and broken to pieces in a popular sedition. The pedestal still remained. The advantage of a lofty station, for the sake either of defence or of being heard, was apparent. Botheric, and two of his officers, leaped upon it, and stretched forth their hands in an attitude commanding silence.

This station, by rendering the person of Botheric distinguishable at a distance, only enhanced his danger. A soldier, by name Eustace, who had, a few days before, been punished for some infraction of discipline, by stripes and ignominious dismission from the service, chanced to be one of those who were gazing at the scene from the upper portico. The treatment he had suffered could not fail to excite resentment, but the means of vengeance were undigested and impracticable. His cowardice and narrow understanding equally conspired to render his malice impotent. He intended, the next day, to set out for his native country, Syria, and, meanwhile, mixed with the rabble which infested the circus.

Botheric had extorted, by his equity and firmness, the esteem of the magistrates and better class of the people. The vile populace were influenced by no sentiment but fear. Botheric had done nothing to excite their hatred; and his person would probably have been uninjured till the alarm had reached the citadel, and the troops had hastened to his rescue, had not Eustace unhappily espied him, as he stood upon the pedestal.

The soldier had an heavy stone in his hand, with which he had armed himself, from a general propensity to mischief, and a vague conception that it might be useful to his own defence. The person of his enemy was no sooner distinctly seen, than a sudden impulse to seize this opportunity for the gratification of his vengeance was felt by him. He threw the stone towards the spot where the General stood.

Botheric was exerting his voice to obtain audience, when the stone struck upon his breast. The blood gushed from his mouth and nostrils, his speech and strength failed, and he sunk upon the ground.

This outrage was observed with grief, rage and consternation by his retinue. Their own safety required the most desperate exertions. Two of them lifted the General in their arms, while the rest, with one accord, brandished their weapons, and rushed upon the crowd. They determined to open a way by killing all that opposed them.

Men, crowded together in a narrow space, are bereft of all power over their own motions. Their exertions contribute merely to destroy their weaker neighbours, without extricating themselves. Those whom chance exposed to the swords of the officers were unable to fly. Their condition was no less desperate; and the blood that flowed around them insensibly converted their terror into rage.

The contest was unequal, and a dreadful carnage ensued before the weapons were wrested from their owners. A thousand hands were eager to partake in the work of vengeance. The father had seen the death of his son, and the son had witnessed the agonies of his father. The execution appeared to be needless and wanton; and the swords, after being stained with the blood of their kinsmen, were aimed at their own breasts. This was no time to speculate upon causes and consequences. All around them was anarchy and uproar, and passion was triumphant in all hearts.

Botheric and his train were thrown to the ground, mangled by numberless wounds, or trampled into pieces. The assassins contended for the possession of the dismembered bodies, and threw the limbs, yet palpitating, into the air, which was filled with shouts and imprecations.

All this passed in a few minutes. Few were acquainted with the cause of the tumult. Still fewer were acquainted with the deplorable issue to which it had led. The immediate actors and witnesses were fully occupied. The distant crowd, whose numbers were increased by the arrival of those who, from all quarters, were hastening to the circus, could only indulge their wonder and panic, and make fruitless inquiries of their neighbours.

In this state of things a rumour was hatched, and propagated with infinite rapidity, that the soldiers had received orders to massacre the people, and that the execution had already begun. All was commotion and flight. The crowd melted away in a moment. The avenues were crowded with the fugitives, who overturned those whom they met, or communicated to them their belief and their terror. Every one fled to his house, and imparted to his family the dreadful tidings. Distraction and lamentation seized upon the women and domestics. They barred their doors, and prepared to avoid or resist the fate which impended over them.

Meanwhile, those who had rushed through the unguarded passages, and occupied the senatorial seats, were alarmed, and prompted to return, by the continuance of the uproar without. In their haste to issue forth they incumbered and impeded each other, and the passage was choked. Some one appeared in an upper gallery, and called upon the people to provide for their safety, for that Botheric had directed a general massacre.

This intelligence operated more destructively than a thousand swords. In the universal eagerness to escape, the avenues were made impassable, and numbers were overthrown and trampled to death.

The magistrates had taken their places when the tumult began. Some were infected with the general panic, and made ineffectual efforts to escape. My duty, as chief magistrate, required me to apply all my endeavours to the checking of the evil. I waited, in anxious suspense, for information as to the nature and extent of the mischief. In my present situation nothing could reach me but a disjointed and mutilated tale. I heard outcries, and witnessed the commotion, but was wholly at a loss as to their cause or tendency.

After a time the tumult began to subside. The passages were gradually cleared by the suffocation of the weaker, and the multitude rushed over the bodies of their fellow citizens into the square. The timorous hastened to their homes, and spread the alarm to the most distant quarters of the city. Others, more courageous or inquisitive, lingered on the spot, gazed upon the mangled and disfigured bodies, which were strewed around the pedestal, and listened to the complaints of the wounded, and the relations of those who had been active in the fray.

Those whose passions had not been previously excited, no sooner recognized the visages of Botheric and some of his retinue among the slain, than terrors of a new kind were awakened. The murder of one of the most illustrious men in the empire, and one who possessed, beyond all others, the affections of the prince, was an event pregnant with disastrous consequences. That his death would call down some signal punishment, in which themselves, though innocent, might be involved, was justly to be dreaded. That the resentment of the soldiery would stimulate them to some sudden outrage was no less probable. There was imminent peril in being found near the spot. The spectators gradually withdrew, and solitude and silence succeeded. The uproar was hushed, the circus was deserted, and a panic stillness seemed to hover over the city.

As soon as obstructions were removed, in my character as prefect of the city, and attended by civil officers, I ascended a tribunal in an hall near the circus. Some of my attendants were immediately dispatched to examine the scene of the conflict, to arrest all who should be found near it, and collect all the information that offered.

Those charged with this commission speedily returned, leading two men, whose wounds did not disable them from walking when supported by others. These persons were questioned as to their knowledge of this disaster. One of them related that when the officers were encompassed by the mob, it was his ill fortune to be placed near them. He was a stranger to the cause of the tumult, and endeavoured, with his utmost strength, to extricate himself from his perilous situation. The populace were loud in their clamours, the officers seemed resolute in their own defence, and he dreaded that the scene would terminate in bloodshed. His temper was pacific and timid, and he desired nothing more than to remove to a safe distance.

While making efforts for this purpose, the officers assailed the crowd, and he was the first to fall by their swords. His senses deserted him, and he did not revive till the mob was entirely dispersed. His companion told a tale nearly similar, and the attendants informed the magistrate that Botheric and his tribunes had perished, their scattered remains being found upon the spot.

I was startled and confounded by this incident. To what excesses the soldiers might be suddenly transported when freed from the restraints of discipline, it was easy to foresee. No other expedient suggested itself, than to summon the municipal body, and request their counsel in this urgent danger.

The members of the senate were preparing to go to the circus. This was commonly done with equipage and pompous train. The hour of assembling was arrived, and they were preparing to set out, when rumours of sedition and massacre assailed them. Messengers were by some dispatched to obtain more distinct information, some of whom returned with the tidings gleaned from the fugitives whom they encountered in the way. Others, more intrepid, ventured to approach the circus, and examine objects with their own eyes. They brought back the tidings that Botheric and his officers were slain by the people.

The most courageous were deeply apprehensive of the consequences which would grow out of his untimely death. They were alternately perplexed with wonder respecting the cause of so memorable a catastrophe, and with dread of the vengeance which it would excite in the bosom; not only of the soldiers, but of the prince. They were recalled from their mournful reveries, by loud signals at their gate, and the entrance of an herald, who, in the name of the prefect, summoned them to council. The summons was gladly obeyed.

Some time had now elapsed. The citizens, immured in their houses, darted fearful glances from their balconies and windows, anxious to hear tidings. The passing Senators were recognized, and their progress attended with importunate inquiries into the nature of the threatened evil, and with supplications that their zeal should be exerted to preclude it.

Many, encouraged by the presence of their magistrates, joined the cavalcade, and the Senate house was quickly surrounded by an immense, but trembling multitude. The Senate being, at length, convened, I laid before them all the intelligence which I had been able to procure respecting the late tumult. I expatiated on the enormity of the deed that had been perpetrated in the murder of Botheric and his officers, and enumerated its probable effects on the minds of the soldiers, and of the prince. I pointed out the necessity of ascertaining the genuine circumstances of the case, of detecting and punishing the criminals, and of appeasing the resentment of the sovereign and the troops.

While engaged in consultation, the wrath which we so justly dreaded, was already excited in the soldiers. Affrighted at the fate of their companions, the centinels posted in the circus fled with precipitation to the military quarter. The rumour was at first indistinct, and as affrays of this kind were not uncommon, the soldiers trusted to the equity of their leader for the vindication of their wrongs. Presently a messenger arrived, informing them that their General was surrounded and likely to be slain by the populace.

At this news, many ran together, and intreated the subaltern officers to lead them to the rescue of their General. As no orders were transmitted from their superiors, the Centurions hesitated to comply. Their reluctance to interpose was increased by the incredibility of the danger. The clamours of the soldiers, however, who threatened to march without permission, conquered this reluctance, and five hundred men were called out.

The general consternation which they witnessed on their march, excited their fears. The few persons who remained in the square, vanished at their approach, and they were left to learn the fate of their officers from the view of their lifeless remains.

The soldiers of Botheric were his friends, countrymen, and family. They had devoted themselves to his honour, and followed his standard, in the service of Theodosius, with invincible fidelity. Many of them had bound themselves by oaths to die with him.

The mangled and dishonoured corpse of this adored leader, now presented itself to their eyes. Every sentiment was absorbed, for a time, in astonishment and grief. They inquired of each other, if the spectacle which they beheld was real; if these, indeed, were the members and features of their beloved chief. They held up his remains to view, bathed his disfigured face with their tears, and burst, at length, into a cry of universal lamentation.

Many, in pursuance of their vow not to survive their leader, stabbed themselves, and died upon the spot. Others exclaimed that their vows to that effect, should be performed only when the funeral honours and the vengeance due to their chief, were fully paid. They collected his remains, and wrapping them in his mantle, set out on their return to the citadel, in a solemn procession. On their way they sung wild and melancholy dirges, in the fashion of their country, and mingled with their music fits of passionate weeping. In the streets which they passed, every one fled before them, and all around was lonely and desolate.

Intelligence of their approach was quickly received by their comrades at the citadel, who came out in great numbers, and joined the procession. Indignation and fury appeared to be suspended in a superior passion.

Meanwhile, the subaltern officers were no sooner fully apprized of the havoc which had taken place, than they assembled in a kind of counsel. They were aware of the necessity of subordination, and they did not mean that their vengeance should be less sure because it was delayed. One of their number, by name Walimer, an hoary veteran, was unanimously chosen their leader.

Walimer concealed, under a savage aspect, all the qualities of a judicious commander. His grief for the fate of Botheric was tempered by prudence and foresight. As soon as the choice was known, he leaped into the midst of the assembly, and devoted himself, with solemn imprecations, to the task of avenging their late chief. At the same time, he enlarged upon the benefits of circumspection and delay. The first measure he proposed was to dispatch a messenger to Theodosius, with an account of this transaction. He questioned not that the Emperor would authorize a signal retribution to be inflicted on the guilty city, and that they would be appointed the ministers of his justice. It was easy to convince his hearers of the advantage of proceeding in the business of revenge with the sanction or connivance of the government. If the Emperor should refuse justice, it would then be time enough to extort it. The arms and fortifications were still in their possession, and these it would be wise to guard with the utmost vigilance. In this counsel the new tribunes readily concurred, and suitable remonstrances convinced the soldiers of the propriety of the choice that had been made, and the proceedings adopted. Three horsemen, charged with the delivery of a message to the Emperor, were immediately dispatched to *Mediolanum*.[7]

To communicate information of these events to the monarch, to deprecate his anger, and convince him of the innocence of the magistrates and the greater part of the people, were likewise suggested to the Senate by one of its members. The wisdom of this counsel was obvious. I was authorized, as prefect, to draw up a statement of the truth, from such information as I had already received, or should speedily obtain. This was to be done with all possible expedition, in order to prevent the propagation of rumours.

Meanwhile, a deputation was appointed to visit the citadel, to declare to the soldiers the sincere regret of the Senate for the unhappy event that had befallen, to exhort them to moderation and peace, and assure them that the most strenuous exertions should be made to detect the authors of the tumult, on whom the most signal punishment should be inflicted.

The deputies were astonished to observe the order which reigned in the soldiers' quarters. No clamours or menaces were heard. They were conducted to the hall, where Walimer and his officers were seated, and their exhortations and pleas were listened to with sullen and mournful silence.

Walimer, in answer to their message, informed them of the choice which the soldiers had made of a new chief, declared his implicit reliance on the justice of the Emperor, to whose decrees he and his troops were determined to conform, and admonished them to execute, without delay, the justice which they promised. He told them that discipline should be as rigidly maintained as formerly, and that things should remain in their present state till the will of their common sovereign was known. The Senate waited, in eager suspense, the return of their deputies. The pacific deportment and professions of Walimer being communicated to them, they retired, with their fears considerably allayed, to their houses.

Heralds were dispatched to all quarters to acquaint the people with the result of this conference, and to exhort them to observe a cautious and peaceable behaviour; punishments were denounced against any who should be detected in any riotous act, and all persons were enjoined to repair to the tribunal of the chief magistrate, and give what information they possessed relative to this transaction.

The ensuing night was passed by the prefect in receiving and comparing depositions of real or pretended witnesses. Macro was traced to his home. He was, by trade, an armourer, and lived with his family, in an obscure corner. His wounds were of no great moment, and the officers of justice found him at supper, in his hovel. He was hurried to the tribunal, followed by his wife and immediate kindred, who trembled for his safety.

As he was the author of this tumult, he could expect little mercy from his audience. Those whose relations or friends had fallen were deeply exasperated at him whose folly and rashness had given birth to the evil. Others, who reflected on future calamities, likely to flow from the same source, pursued him with the utmost rancour.

In spite of proclamations and menaces, curiosity and fear attracted great numbers to the hall of justice. Their panic stillness was succeeded by commotion and rage. The steps of Macro were accompanied by hootings and execrations, and they clamoured loudly for his punishment.

I was sensible of the danger that attended this unlawful meeting. I showed myself to the people from a balcony, and endeavoured to harangue them into moderation and patience. I pointed out the enormous evils which their turbulent concourse had already produced, and urged every topic likely to influence their fears, to induce them to disperse.

The effects of these remonstrances were partial and temporary. My promises that the culprits should not escape the most condign punishment, gratified their sanguinary appetites, and their murmurs were hushed.

The threats of torment extorted from Macro a confession of his offences. It seems that when he came to the circus, he was intoxicated with wine, and had mistaken one entrance for another. In the confusion of his intellects, he neither listened to, nor understood the objections of the centinels, and he persisted in claiming a privilege which he regarded as justly his due. The consequences have been already related, and afford a memorable proof from what slight causes the most disastrous and extensive effects may flow.

Macro's offence was venial and slight; but it was considered that, even if he were innocent, his life was a necessary sacrifice. Neither the soldiers nor the people, whose judgments were always fettered by prejudice and passion, would consent to dismiss him in safety. Neither would they be satisfied by the infliction of a slight or tardy penalty. Macro, besides, was a depraved and worthless individual, whose life or death was, in the eyes of his judges, of the most trivial moment. Influenced by these considerations, the magistrates, with some reluctance, condemned Macro to have his arms and legs cut off, and afterwards to be beheaded on the spot where Botheric had fallen, and which was dyed with the blood of those who owed their untimely fate to his temerity.

This sentence was heard by the friends of the criminal with groans of despair, and by the rest of the audience, with shouts of applause. The criminal was loaded with chains, and led away to prison. Being aware that the fury of the people might betray them into some outrage, I addressed them anew from the balcony, and admonished them to retire.

Some symptoms of compliance appeared in part of the assembly, who began to separate. A multitude, however, crowded round Macro, as he came forth from the hall, and greeted him with insults and curses.

This unhappy man was not destitute of courage; but he was willing to avoid that lingering and dreadful death to which he was doomed. He was, besides, penetrated with indignation at the injustice of his sentence. He, therefore, retorted the curses that were heaped upon him, both because he conceived them to be unmerited, and because he wished to exasperate the mob to inflict a speedy death.

Those who followed him were the vilest of the vile; base, sanguinary and impetuous, delighting in tumult, prone to violence, and stimulated by revenge for those who had been stifled in the press, or slain by the tribunes. Macro had not gone many steps before the officers who guarded him were driven to a distance. The mob, enraged by his taunts, took the work of justice into their own hands, and Macro received from their pikes and clubs that death which he sought.

The magistrates were quickly informed of this event. They had been accustomed, on similar cases, to vindicate their authority by the aid of the soldiers. This expedient was now impracticable or hazardous, and they sat in powerless inactivity, consoling themselves with the hope that the popular indignation would be appeased by this victim.

Relieved from the dread of military execution, multitudes, though the night was somewhat advanced, resorted from the senate house, and hall of justice, to the circus. The kindred and friends of the dead hastened to ascertain their true condition, and to bestow upon them funeral rites.

The circus and its avenues quickly overflowed with inquisitive or anxious spectators. Innumerable torches were borne to and fro; women hung over the bodies of their husbands, fathers and sons, and filled the air with outcries and wailings; some explored the courts and passages, in search of those who were missing, while others, lifting corpses in their arms, bent homeward their steps, in tumultuous procession, and with far-heared laments.

Meanwhile, several witnesses informed the magistrates of the stone which had been thrown at Botheric, and at length the name, and character, and guilt of Eustace were detected. Eustace was justly regarded as the immediate author of this calamity. He was likewise a soldier, and his detection and punishment might be expected eminently to gratify the military. It would transfer, in some degree, the guilt of this sedition from the people to their own order.

Officers were quickly dispersed, throughout the city, in search of the fugitive. Eustace had seen his enemy fall. Momentary exultation was followed by terror, and he made haste to shroud himself from inquiry and suspicion in an obscure habitation near the port.

He had secured his passage in a barque, which designed to set sail, next morning, for Ptolemais, in Syria. He meant to go on board at the dawn of day, and hoped, meanwhile, to be unthought of and unknown.

It was peculiarly unfortunate for this wretch, that a mariner belonging to this vessel happened to be stationed at his elbow when the stone was thrown. The mariner had been present when Eustace had contracted for his passage with the master of the barque; hence arose his knowledge of Eustace. He was a way-farer; had been attracted, by a natural curiosity, to the circus; had gazed, with wandering eyes and beating heart, upon the tumult; and, in the fluctuations of the mob, had undesignedly been placed by the side of the assassin.

He had afterwards listened to the voice of the herald, summoning before the magistrate all who possessed any knowledge of the author and circumstances of the insurrection. His timidity, the child of inexperience, deterred him from disclosing his knowledge, till he himself became, by a concurrence of events not necessary to be mentioned, the object of suspicion, and was dragged by public officers to the tribunal of the prefect. He then explained his knowledge of Eustace, and pointed him out as the only agent.

This tale, though insufficient to rescue the mariner from danger, occasioned diligent search to be made for Eustace. The master of the barque was acquainted with the past condition and present views of the soldier, and his evidence suggested to the magistrate the expedient of placing officers on board the vessel, who, if the assassin should not be previously detected, might seize him as he entered the ship, in pursuance of his contract with the captain.

This expedient was successful. Eustace ventured from his recess in the dusk of morning, proceeded unmolested to the port, and put himself on board the vessel, which was anchored at some distance from the quays. At the moment when he began to exult in his escape, he was seized, pinioned, and conducted, without delay, to the presence of the judge. The testimony of the mariner, and his own confession, extorted by the fear of torment, established his guilt. The prefect lost no time in informing Walimer and his tribunes of the measures which had been adopted; and offered to deliver Eustace into their hands, to be treated in what manner they thought proper. The offer was readily, though ungraciously accepted.

Eustace had been detained in the hall, the magistrate fearing that the same outrage would be perpetrated by the people, on this criminal, if he were placed within their reach, of which Macro had already been the victim. A band of soldiers from the citadel received him at the door of the hall, and surrounding him with sullen visages and drawn swords, returned, in hostile array, to their quarters. The windows and galleries that overlooked their march, were filled with silent and astonished gazers.

The succeeding day passed in a state of general suspense. Men had leisure to ruminate upon the consequences that impended, and to wonder at the change that had so abruptly taken place in their condition. Fear and hope struggled in their bosoms. All customary occupations and pursuits were laid aside. Neighbours assembled to communicate to each other the story of what themselves had witnessed or endured, to recount their imminent danger in the press, and their hair-breadth escapes, to expatiate on the movements of the soldiery, and propagate their terrors of the future.

Upwards of three hundred citizens perished on this occasion. The cemeteries were opened, and funeral processions were every where seen. Though the streets were crowded, and the whole city was in motion, appearances exhibited a powerful contrast to the impetuosities and clamours of the preceding day. The pavements were beaten by numberless feet; but every movement was grave and slow. Discourse was busy, but was carried on in whispers, and, instead of horrid uproar, nothing but murmurs, indistinct and doubtful, assailed the ear. The very children partook of the general consternation and awe.

At noon-day, a messenger from the citadel demanded admission to the prefect,[8] whom he acquainted with the intention of the soldiers to celebrate, on the ensuing evening, and at the spot where they fell, the obsequies of Botheric and his officers. This intention, however hazardous or inconvenient to the city, could not be thwarted or changed. This ceremony was likely to exasperate the grief of the soldiers, all of whom would be present and partake in it. Some fatal impulse of indignation, some inauspicious rumour or groundless alarm, might unseasonably start into birth. The night would lend its cloak to purposes of cruelty, and, before a new day, the city might be wrapt in flames, and ten thousand victims might be offered to the shade of Botheric.

In this emergency the Senate were once more convened, and their counsel required. They deputed one of their members to the citadel, in order to gain from Walimer, a clear explanation of his purposes. This officer maintained a stately reserve and ambiguous silence. His demeanour plunged them deeper into uncertainty. Many put the blackest construction on his words, and forboded, that the coming night would be signalized by indiscriminate massacre and havoc.

How to avert this evil was a subject of fruitless deliberation. One measure was obviously prudent. The people were informed of the ceremony that was about to take place, were exhorted to stay in their houses, and assured, that nothing was intended by the soldiers, but honour to their chiefs. The danger of tumultuous concourse, or panic apprehensions, at such a time, was evident.

The Senators, however, were destitute of that confidence which they endeavoured to instil into the people. Some, at the approach of night, secretly withdrew from the city. The guards, posted at the gates, suffered all to pass without question or hindrance. Others, more irresolute, or less timorous, remained; but they armed their domestics, and closed their doors, or made preparation to fly or conceal themselves on the first alarm. Spies were directed to hover round the circus, or were posted on the turrets of the houses, to watch the first glimmering of torches, or the remotest sound of footsteps.

The people were sufficiently aware of the danger of crowding to a spectacle like this. The assurance of the magistrates suppressed all but nameless and indefinable terrors. They withdrew to their homes, when several trumpets from the ramparts announced, at the appointed hour, that the military procession was begun.

By various avenues which led to the circus, the army repaired thither, and forming a circle round the pile, on which the remains of the officers were laid, they silently beheld them consumed. Eustace was stabbed by the hands of Walimer; and many of the soldiers could not be restrained from pouring out their blood at this altar. The flames that ascended from this pile were seen to a great distance. It was watched, with unspeakable solicitude, by those that remained in the city. Those at a distance were left in uncertainty whether it was from a funeral pile, or indicated the commencement of a general conflagration.

The flame and the light attendant on it gradually disappeared. An interval of ominous repose succeeded. The troops peaceably returned to their quarters. Those only who dwelt in the streets through which their march lay, were conscious of their movements. The rest of the city was hushed in profound and uninterrupted repose.

Next day, the tumult of consternation and suspense somewhat subsided. Still, however, all classes were penetrated with dread. The sentence of the prince was yet unknown. To what measures his indignation would hurry him, was a topic of foreboding.

In pursuance of the directions of the Senate, the prefect had dispatched, early in the morning, a messenger to *Mediolanum*. A faithful narrative of this transaction had been drawn up, in which the partial, abrupt, and unpremeditated nature of the tumult was copiously displayed. The messenger was charged to deliver this statement to Acilius, one of the Imperial ministers, of whom the prefect was a kinsman, and on whose good offices with the prince there was the utmost reason to rely.

The horsemen whom Walimer had sent upon the same errand, were better mounted, pursued their journey with more diligence, and had set out several hours sooner than the herald of the Senate. In fifteen days they arrived at the capital, and hastened to communicate their tiding to Rufinus,[9] a minister who had long enjoyed the highest place in the Emperor's favour.

Rufinus and Botheric had contracted a political alliance, the purpose of which was, to secure the former the civil administration, and to the latter the highest military authority in the empire. This unexpected catastrophe blasted the hopes of Rufinus. His efforts had been directed to remove and destroy all his competitors in favour, and to place the whole power of the state in the hands of himself and of his creatures. Theodosius regarded Botheric with singular and almost paternal affection. Rufinus had married the sister of the chief, and embarked his fortunes in the same cause.

The messengers had delivered their message to Rufinus in a secret audience; but his wife recognizing her countrymen, and the soldiers of her brother, took measures to obtain from them the substance of their tidings. Her grief gave place to revenge, and she used the most powerful means to stimulate the zeal of her husband in what she deemed the cause of justice. Rufinus was sufficiently disposed to avenge the blood of her kinsman, in that of the rebellious city.

The monarch was sitting at a banquet when his minister rushed into his presence, and, with every symptom of grief, communicated the fatal news, that Botheric, his faithful soldier, the support of his throne, and the guardian of his children, had been murdered, with every circumstance of wanton cruelty, by the people of Thessalonica.

The Emperor, starting from his seat, expressed, at the same time, his incredulity and horror at this news. The former sentiment was overpowered by the arts of the minister, who produced the letter that had just been received, and the men who had brought it. The horsemen, on being interrogated, gave a minute, though exaggerated and fallacious picture of the tumult. The messengers were unacquainted with its true causes, and the most accurate statement which it was in their power to make, would have left the hearers in astonishment at the savage ferocity of the Thessalonians.

Incredulity at length gave place to rage. In the first transport of his fury he vowed to obliterate the offending city from the face of the earth. The cholerick temper of Theodosius was capable of transporting him to the wildest excesses. These excesses, when reason resumed its power, were beheld in their genuine deformity, and were productive of exquisite remorse.[10] Rufinus, therefore, was eager to improve the opportunity, and before the paroxysm of passion should subside, to extort from him a sanguinary edict.

It was not possible, indeed, for malice to contrive an higher provocation than this. There was little danger that his passion should subside, if it were not assailed by the lenient counsels and remonstrances of others. This, however, would certainly happen as soon as the disaster was publicly known, and was, therefore, to be prevented by dispatch.

Rufinus assumed the specious office of asswaging his master's resentment. He perceived the folly of demolishing towers, and walls, and habitations, on account of an offence committed by those who resided within them. It was just to punish the guilty people; but to slay them on the very stage of their crimes was all that equity demanded.

The punishment could not follow too soon upon the heel of the offence, and the soldiers of Botheric were the suitable ministers of vengeance. There was no danger that their hands would be tied up by scruples or commiseration. The death of the people was, indeed, claimed by the justice of the soldiers as well as of the prince, and should that justice be refused by the monarch, the troops would not fail, being in possession of fortifications and arms, to execute it of their own accord. The punishment could not be prevented, and if his sanction should be refused, their deed would constitute them rebels to his authority, and the fairest city in his empire would thus be torn from his possession.

These motives were artfully, tho' needlessly insinuated. The Emperor eagerly affixed his seal and his signature to the warrant which condemned the people of the most illustrious and populous of Roman cities to military execution.

Rufinus knew, that to complete the execution of this sentence, it was necessary that the preliminary measures should be secret. A knowledge of their fate would impel numbers to flight, and others, urged by despair, would rush into rebellion, and oppose force by force. There was likewise but one method in which justice could be fully executed. By assembling the whole body of the people in the circus, the task imposed on their assassins would be with more facility executed, and the theatre of their offences would be made, as justice required, the scene of their punishment.

With these views, the horsemen, a few hours after their arrival, set out on their return, with secret directions to Walimer, under the Emperor's own seal, to collect the people in the circus, under pretence of an equestrian exhibition, and slay them to a man.

The number of the people did not fall short of three hundred thousand. Rufinus laid claim to the praise of clemency, in withstanding the fury of his master, whose revenge reluctantly consented to spare one. The criminals were naturally supposed chiefly to consist of males of mature age, and justice was thought to be satisfied with the destruction of one third of this number. The circus usually contained between twenty and thirty thousand spectators.

These messengers were, likewise charged with letters to Julius

Malchus, the prefect, in which he was informed, that the prince had received the tidings of what had lately happened. Much regret was expressed for the fate of Botheric, and the magistrate was charged to execute speedy and condign justice on the authors of the tumult. To show, however, that Theodosius confided in the zeal of the civil magistrates, that he discriminated between the innocent and guilty, and that, notwithstanding these outrages, he had not withdrawn his affection from this people, he authorized the magistrates to publish his forgiveness, and in testimony of his sincerity, to invite them to a splendid exhibition of the public games.

A tedious interval elapsed between the departure and return of Walimer's messengers. This interval was big with anxiety and suspense. The popular disquiet and impatience increased as the day approached which was to decide their fate. Antioch, which three years before had committed a less atrocious offence,[11] and which had escaped with the utmost difficulty, a sentence of extermination, was universally remembered, and was the parent of rueful prognostics.

The attention which regular pursuits and sober duties required, was swallowed up by this growing fear. Ears were open to nothing but rumours and conjectures, and the popular mind was alternately agonized with terror, and elated with hope. Sleep was harassed with terrific dreams, and, in many, even the appetite for food was suspended by their mournful presages.

If there be any proportion between evils inflicted and suffered, the death of Botheric was *retributed,* a thousand fold, in a single day after its occurrence; but twenty-eight days elapsed, and each hour added to the weight of apprehension which oppressed the last.

The distance by land, and round the head of the Hadriatic, from Thessalonica to the Imperial residence, was eight hundred and seventy five miles. The journey, therefore, though pursued with little intermission, by means of post horses, and covered litters, could not be effected in less than fourteen days. One day would be consumed in deliberation, and an equal period of fourteen days would elapse, before letters could be received from Mediolanum by the public carriers.

The messengers, dispatched by Malchus, were outstripped, on expedition, by those of Walimer, and the Emperor's letters were delivered to the prefect one day sooner than was expected by him. He dreaded to unclose the packet, perceiving, that the information received by the ministers had gone through the hands of the soldiers, by whom the truth would unavoidably be perverted. The Senate was convened, and the dispatches laid before them.

Intimations of this event reached the people. A Senatorial meeting, at an uncustomary hour, was prolific of conjecture and alarm. Multitudes hastened to the Senate house, and the members of that body forced their way, with difficulty, through the crowd which besieged the entrances. The tumult and clamour became so great, that the prefect was obliged to postpone the opening of the packets till a Senator had exhorted the multitude to order and forbearance, and explained the purport of the meeting, promising to return as soon as the decision of the Emperor were known, and impart to them the tidings.

This assurance was followed by a general pause. Every murmur was hushed. Every eye was fixed, in anxious gaze, upon the door through which the Speaker had withdrawn from their sight, and at which he was momently expected to re-appear. The uproar of a troubled sea was succeeded by portentous calm, and the silence of death.

At length the magistrate came forth. The joy, indicated by his countenance, did not escape the general observation. Their hopes were elated, and exultation spoke forth from every mouth, as soon as the forgiveness and gracious condescention of the prince were made known. He was heard, distinctly, by few; but the rapturous exclamations of those conveyed the import of the speech to the most distant spectators.

The joyous tidings were diffused with unspeakable celerity. Pleasure was proportioned to the dread that had lately prevailed. Fire and the sword were ready to involve them in a common ruin; but these evils were averted, and not only their pristine security returned, but their darling sports, with new embellishments, were to be renewed. The exhibitions of the circus were ordered to take place on the next day.

The streets resounded with mutual congratulations. Laughter and song, and dance, and feasting, and magnificent illuminations, and processions to the churches, to pour forth the praises of God and of

Theodosius, the father of his people, and the darling of mankind, occupied the people during the succeeding night.

The Senators, after the first emotions of their joy had subsided, began to look upon this circumstance with eyes of some suspicion. The choleric and impetuous temper of Theodosius was well known. A much more trivial offence, in the inhabitants of Antioch, had excited his wrath, and prompted him to decree the destruction of the guilty city.

The crime of Thessalonica had been reported by the soldiers. No deprecation had been used. The cause of the tumult and the punishment of its authors, were unknown at the time when Walimer dismissed his messengers. Time for the interposition of beneficent counsellers, or for rage to be displaced by equanimity, had not been allowed.

It was, indeed, remembered that Antioch had fewer claims upon the affection of Theodosius, that the dictates of his hasty indignation, with regard to that city, had been to himself a topic of humiliation and regret, and that he might now be guarded against the impulse of choler. It was likewise known that the genuine intentions of the monarch had not, at any time, been concealed from the Antiochians; and no motives could be imagined by which the prince might be induced to conceal his anger, or counterfeit forgiveness.

These opposite considerations were anxiously revolved by the prefect Malchus. He was unable to divest his mind wholly of inquietude and doubt. The acquiescence of the soldiers, in a sentence like this, was incredible. Macro and Eustace had not dipped their hands in the blood of Botheric and his retinue. Search was made for those who had been active in the bloody fray; but the evidence obtained was doubtful and contradictory, and the populace began to view their deportment as justified by necessity and self-defence. The officers were known by all to be, with regard to the crowd surrounding them, the first assailants.

The secret, if any secret existed, was reposited with Walimer. A careful observation of his conduct might detect the truth. For this purpose an interview was necessary. To invite him and his tribunes to a banquet was an obvious expedient to detect the truth, if his purposes were hostile, or to confirm his intentions, if they were amicable and pacific.

The senators and officers were therefore invited to a feast. Malchus selected the most sagacious of his servants, and directed them to treat the military followers in a cordial and bounteous manner, and to watch their looks and discourse. Some unguarded expression, it was thought, would escape them in the midst of their carousals, betraying their designs.

This scheme was partly frustrated by the precaution of Walimer, who at once testified his confidence in Malchus, and precluded the hazard of impetuosity or babbling in his soldiers, by coming to the palace of the prefect unattended except by his tribunes. The carousals were prolonged till midnight, and every proof of a sincere reconciliation was given by the guests.

The next day was ushered in as a solemn and joyous festival. It happened that this day was sacred to Demetrius, the saint or tutelary genius of the city, and to whose divine influence the people fondly ascribed the clemency of Theodosius.

It was usual for centinels to be posted at the avenues of the hippodrome. This was a customary duty, and, to omit it on this occasion, would have bred suspicion. No alarm, therefore, was excited by the march, at noon-day, of a detachment from the citadel for this purpose.

On the preceding night, Malchus had imparted his doubts and apprehensions to some of the senators. A secret consultation had been held. No measures sufficiently conducive to their safety could be adopted. Whatever evil was meditated by the soldiers, it was impossible to avert or elude it. The towers and gates were in their hands. Circumspection or disguise, would avail nothing. If the danger had assumed any known form, suitable precautions could scarcely be discovered; but now, when all was uncertain and inscrutable, a frank and fearless deportment was most proper.

The presence of the senate and magistrates was necessary at the public shows. My mind was actuated by inexplicable fears, and I would willingly have forborne to attend; but reflection convinced me that my life was equally in the power of the soldiers, in the recesses of my palace, and in the courts of the citadel.

Noon arrived, thousands hurried to the hippodrome; the concourse was uncommonly large, as numbers from the neighbouring villages and districts flocked to the spectacle; all benches were quickly filled and galleries crowded; I proceeded thither at the head of the senatorial order, and was received with low obeisance by the guards, and with loud acclamations by the people. The games only waited the arrival of the general and tribunes to begin.

His approach was quickly announced by the sound of military music. At that moment a civil officer, whose face was pale with affright, thrust himself amidst the crowd, and whispered something in the ear of a senator who sat near me. The senator was observed to start; and inquiry being made into the cause of his alarm, he replied, that Walimer was followed, not by the usual retinue, but by a formidable brigade, who surrounded the circus and seemed to meditate violence.

Walimer and his officers now entered and placed themselves on an elevated platform assigned for his use, and which was ascended by a narrow staircase. His entrance was greeted by grateful acclamations, and he was observed to bow his head in token of his satisfaction. In a moment after the trumpet, whose note was a signal for the chariots to start from their goal, was sounded.

Before the signal was obeyed, a dart, thrown by an unknown hand and with inconceivable force, struck the breast of a charioteer, who fell headlong from his seat. His horses were alarmed, and swerving from their true direction, threw all into disorder. This event was noticed by the people with amazement.

Their attention was speedily recalled from this object by troops of soldiers rushing through the various passages, and brandishing their swords. No time was allowed to question their purpose or elude it. They fell upon those who were nearest and hewed them to pieces.

Every avenue poured forth a destroying band. Few, therefore, were allowed to be mere spectators of the danger. Every one witnessed the butchery of his neighbour, and shrunk from the swords, which, in a few moments, would be steeped in his own blood.

The multitude rose, with one consent, from their seats. The extent of the evil that threatened them was fully apprehended by none. They were far from imagining that this havoc was directed or sanctioned by the prince. They did not conceive that the soldiers had acted by the orders of Walimer; but that a conspiracy was formed against them by the military order was apparent.

Those who were near the station of Walimer, stretched their hands towards him in supplication, and uttered the most piercing cries of distress. His sullen and immoveable air convinced them that he was an accomplice in their fate.

Some vainly flattered themselves that the sword would be weary of its task before it reached them. They sheltered themselves behind their neighbours, and in their eagerness to put themselves in the midst of the crowd, were bereaved of breath, or trampled under foot.

Those whose situation exposed them to the first assault, struggled to gain the passages. Such as escaped the edge of the sabre and passed into the square, were transfixed by darts. The soldiers were drawn up in firm array, and extending themselves on all sides, rendered escape impossible.

To expatiate on the scene that followed, and which did not terminate till midnight; to count up the victims, to describe the various circumstances of their death, is a task to which I am unequal. Language sinks under the enormity and complication of these ills. I was a witness and partaker; the images exist in my imagination as vividly as when they were presented to my senses; my blood is still chilled, my dreams are still agonized by dire remembrance; but my eloquence is too feeble to impart to others the conceptions of my own mind.

The woes of my country are not past. Hundreds who escaped the bounds of this devoted city, are, like me, in the full fruition of melancholy or despair. The images of wife and offspring, of friends and neighbours, mangled by the sword, or perishing by lingering torments, pursue them to their retreats, and deny them a momentary respite. Some have lost their terror only by the extinction of their reason; and the phantoms of the past have disappeared in the confusion of insanity. Others, whose heroic or fortunate efforts set them beyond the reach of the soldiers, were no sooner at liberty to review the past, and contemplate their condition, than they inflicted on themselves that death which had been, with so much difficulty avoided, when menaced by others. Their misery was too abrupt, and too enormous, to be forgotten or endured.

I envy the lot of such, but it will quickly be my lot. The period of forgetfulness, or of tranquil existence in another scene, is hastening to console me. Meanwhile, my task shall be, to deliver to you, and to posterity, a faithful narrative. The horrors of this scene are only portions of the evil that has overspread the Roman world, which has been inflicted by the cavalry of Scythia,[12] and which will end only in the destruction of the empire, and the return of the human species to their original barbarity.

WALSTEIN'S SCHOOL OF HISTORY.
FROM THE GERMAN OF
KRANTS OF GOTHA

Walstein was professor of history at Jena, and, of course, had several pupils. Nine of them were more assiduous in their attention to their tutor than the others. This circumstance came at length to be noticed by each other, as well as by Walstein, and naturally produced good-will and fellowship among them. They gradually separated themselves from the negligent and heedless crowd, cleaved to each other, and frequently met to exchange and compare ideas. Walstein was prepossessed in their favour by their studious habits, and their veneration for him. He frequently admitted them to exclusive interviews, and, laying aside his professional dignity, conversed with them on the footing of a friend and equal.

Walstein's two books were read by them with great attention. These were justly to be considered as exemplifications of his rules, as specimens of the manner in which history was to be studied and written.

No wonder that they found few defects in the model; that they gradually adopted the style and spirit of his composition, and, from admiring and contemplating, should, at length, aspire to imitate. It could not but happen, however, that the criterion of excellence would be somewhat modified in passing through the mind of each; that each should have his peculiar modes of writing and thinking.

All observers, indeed, are, at the first and transient view, more affected by resemblances than differences. The works of Walstein and his disciples were hastily ascribed to the same hand. The same minute explication of motives, the same indissoluble and well-woven tissue of causes and effects, the same unity and coherence of design, the same power of engrossing the attention, and the same felicity, purity, and compactness of style, are conspicuous in all.

There is likewise evidence, that each had embraced the same scheme of accounting for events, and the same notions of moral and political duty. Still, however, there were marks of difference in the different nature of the themes that were adopted, and of the purpose which the productions of each writer seemed most directly to promote.

We may aim to exhibit the influence of some moral or physical cause, to enforce some useful maxim, or illustrate some momentous truth. This purpose may be more or less simple, capable of being diffused over the surface of an empire or a century, or of shrinking into the compass of a day, and the bounds of a single thought.

The elementary truths of morals and politics may merit the preference: our theory may adapt itself to, and derive confirmation from whatever is human. Newton and Xavier, Zengis and William Tell,[1] may bear close and manifest relation to the system we adopt, and their fates be linked, indissolubly, in a common chain.

The physician may be attentive to the constitution and diseases of man in all ages and nations. Some opinions, on the influence of a certain diet, may make him eager to investigate the physical history of every human being. No fact, falling within his observation, is useless or anomalous. All sensibly contribute to the symmetry and firmness of some structure which he is anxious to erect. Distances of place and time, and diversities of moral conduct, may, by no means, obstruct their union into one homogeneous mass.

I am apt to think, that the moral reasoner may discover principles equally universal in their application, and giving birth to similar co-incidence and harmony among characters and events. Has not this been effected by WALSTEIN?

Walstein composed two works. One exhibited, with great minuteness, the life of Cicero; the other, that of the Marquis of Pombal.[2] What link did his reason discover, or his fancy create between times, places, situations, events, and characters so different? He reasoned thus:—

Human society is powerfully modified by individual members. The authority of individuals sometimes flows from physical incidents; birth, or marriage, for example. Sometimes it springs, independently of physical relation, and, in defiance of them, from intellectual vigour. The authority of kings and nobles exemplifies the first species of influence. Birth and marriage, physical, and not moral incidents, entitle them to rule.

The second kind of influence, that flowing from intellectual vigour, is remarkably exemplified in Cicero and Pombal. In this respect they are alike.

The mode in which they reached eminence, and in which they exercised power, was different, in consequence of different circumstances. One lived in a free, the other in a despotic state. One gained it from the prince, the other from the people. The end of both, for their degree of virtue was the same, was the general happiness. They promoted this end by the best means which human wisdom could suggest. One cherished, the other depressed the aristocracy. Both were right in their means as in their end; and each, had he exchanged conditions with the other, would have acted like that other.

Walstein was conscious of the uncertainty of history. Actions and motives cannot be truly described. We can only make approaches to the truth. The more attentively we observe mankind, and study ourselves, the greater will this uncertainty appear, and the farther shall we find ourselves from truth.

This uncertainty, however, has some bounds. Some circumstances of events, and some events, are more capable of evidence than others. The same may be said of motives. Our guesses as to the motives of some actions are more probable than the guesses that relate to other actions. Though no one can state the motives from which any action has flowed, he may enumerate motives from which it is quite certain, that the action did *not* flow.

The lives of Cicero and Pombal are imperfectly related by historians. An impartial view of that which history has preserved makes the belief of their wisdom and virtue more probable than the contrary belief.

Walstein desired the happiness of mankind. He imagined that the exhibition of virtue and talents, forcing its way to sovereign power, and employing that power for the national good, was highly conducive to their happiness.

By exhibiting a virtuous being in opposite conditions, and pursuing his end by means suited to his own condition, he believes himself displaying a model of right conduct, and furnishing incitements to imitate that conduct, supplying men not only with knowledge of just ends and just means, but with the love and the zeal of virtue.

How men might best promote the happiness of mankind in given situations, was the problem that he desired to solve. The more portraits of human excellence he was able to exhibit the better; but his power in this respect was limited. The longer his life and his powers endured the more numerous would his portraits become. Futurity, however, was precarious, and, therefore, it behoved him to select, in the first place, the most useful theme.

His purpose was not to be accomplished by a brief or meagre story. To illuminate the understanding, to charm curiosity, and sway the passions, required that events should be copiously displayed and artfully linked, that motives should be vividly depicted, and scenes made to pass before the eye. This has been performed. Cicero is made to compose the story of his political and private life from his early youth to his flight from Astura, at the coalition of Antony and Octavius.[3] It is addressed to Atticus,[4] and meant to be the attestor of his virtue, and his vindicator with posterity.

The style is energetic, and flows with that glowing impetuosity which was supposed to actuate the writer. Ardent passions, lofty indignation, sportive elegance, pathetic and beautiful simplicity, take their turns to controul his pen, according to the nature of the theme. New and striking portraits are introduced of the great actors on the stage. New lights are cast upon the principal occurrences. Every where are marks of profound learning, accurate judgment, and inexhaustible invention. Cicero here exhibits himself in all the forms of master, husband, father, friend, advocate, pro-consul, consul, and senator.

To assume the person of Cicero, as the narrator of his own transactions, was certainly an hazardous undertaking. Frequent errors and lapses, violations of probability, and incongruities in the style and conduct of this imaginary history with the genuine productions of Cicero, might be reasonably expected, but these are not found. The more conversant we are with the authentic monuments, the more is our admiration at the felicity of this imposture enhanced.

The conspiracy of Cataline[5] is here related with abundance of circumstances not to be found in Sallust. The difference, however, is of that kind which result from a deeper insight into human nature, a more accurate acquaintance with the facts, more correctness of arrangement, and a deeper concern in the progress and issue of the story. What is false, is so admirable in itself, so conformable to Roman modes and sentiments, so self-consistent, that one is almost prompted to accept it as the gift of inspiration.

The whole system of Roman domestic manners, of civil and military government, is contained in this work. The facts are either collected from the best antiquarians, or artfully deduced from what is known, or invented with a boldness more easy to admire than to imitate. Pure fiction is never employed but when truth was unattainable.

The end designed by Walstein, is no less happily accomplished in the second, than in the first performance. The style and spirit of the narrative is similar; the same skill in the exhibition of characters and deduction of events, is apparent; but events and characters are wholly new. Portugal, its timorous populace, its besotted monks, its jealous and effeminate nobles, and its cowardly prince, are vividly depicted. The narrator of this tale is, as in the former instance, the subject of it. After his retreat from court, Pombal consecrates his leisure to the composition of his own memoirs.

Among the most curious portions of this work, are those relating to the constitution of the inquisition, the expulsion of the Jesuits, the earthquake, and the conspiracy of Daveiro.[6]

The Romish religion, and the feudal institutions, are the causes that chiefly influence the modern state of Europe. Each of its kingdoms and provinces exhibits the operations of these causes, accompanied and modified by circumstances peculiar to each. Their genuine influence is thwarted, in different degrees, by learning and commerce. In Portugal, they have been suffered to produce the most extensive and unmingled mischiefs. Portugal, therefore, was properly selected as an example of moral and political degeneracy, and as a theatre in which virtue might be shewn with most advantage, contending with the evils of misgovernment and superstition.

In works of this kind, though the writer is actuated by a single purpose, many momentous and indirect inferences will flow from his story. Perhaps the highest and lowest degrees in the scale of political improvement have been respectively exemplified by the Romans and the Portuguese. The pictures that are here drawn, may be considered as portraits of the human species, in two of the most remarkable forms.

There are two ways in which genius and virtue may labour for the public good: first, by assailing popular errors and vices, argumentatively and through the medium of books; secondly, by employing legal or ministerial authority to this end.

The last was the province which Cicero and Pombal assumed. Their fate may evince the insufficiency of the instrument chosen by them, and teach us, that a change of national opinion is the necessary prerequisite of revolutions.

Engel, the eldest of Walstein's pupils, thought, like his master, that the narration of public events, with a certain licence of invention, was the most efficacious of moral instruments. Abstract systems, and theoretical reasonings, were not without their use, but they claimed more attention than many were willing to bestow. Their influence, therefore, was limited to a narrow sphere. A mode by which truth could be conveyed to a great number, was much to be preferred.

Systems, by being imperfectly attended to, are liable to beget error and depravity. Truth flows from the union and relation of many parts. These parts, fallaciously connected and viewed separately, constitute error. Prejudice, stupidity, and indolence, will seldom afford us a candid audience, are prone to stop short in their researches, to remit, or transfer to other objects their attention, and hence to derive new motives to injustice, and new confirmations in folly from that which, if impartially and accurately examined, would convey nothing but benefit.

Mere reasoning is cold and unattractive. Injury rather than benefit proceeds from convictions that are transient and faint; their tendency is not to reform and enlighten, but merely to produce disquiet and remorse. They are not strong enough to resist temptation and to change the conduct, but merely to pester the offender with dissatisfaction and regret.

The detail of actions is productive of different effects. The affections are engaged, the reason is won by incessant attacks; the benefits which our system has evinced to be possible, are invested with a seeming existence; and the evils which error was proved to generate, exchange the fleeting, misty, and dubious form of inference, for a sensible and present existence.

To exhibit, in an eloquent narration, a model of right conduct, is the highest province of benevolence. Our patterns, however, may be useful in different degrees. Duties are the growth of situations. The general and the statesman have arduous duties to perform; and, to teach them their duty, is of use: but the forms of human society allow few individuals to gain the station of generals and statesmen. The lesson, therefore, is reducible to practice by a small number; and, of these, the temptations to abuse their power are so numerous and powerful, that a very small part, and these, in a very small degree, can be expected to comprehend, admire, and copy the pattern that is set before them.

But though few may be expected to be monarchs and ministers, every man occupies a station in society in which he is necessarily active to evil or to good. There is a sphere of some dimensions, in which the influence of his actions and opinions is felt. The causes that fashion men into instruments of happiness or misery, are numerous, complex, and operate upon a wide surface. Virtuous activity may, in a thousand ways, be thwarted and diverted by foreign and superior influence. It may seem best to purify the fountain, rather than to filter the stream; but the latter is, to a certain degree, within our power, whereas, the former is impracticable. Governments and general education, cannot be rectified, but individuals may be somewhat fortified against their influence. Right intentions may be instilled into them, and some good may be done by each within his social and domestic province.

The relations in which men, unendowed with political authority, stand to each other, are numerous. An extensive source of these relations, is property. No topic can engage the attention of man more momentous than this. Opinions, relative to property, are the immediate source of nearly all the happiness and misery that exist among mankind. If men were guided by justice in the acquisition and disbursement, the brood of private and public evils would be extinguished.

To ascertain the precepts of justice, and exhibit these precepts reduced to practice, was, therefore, the favourite task of Engel. This, however, did not constitute his whole scheme. Every man is encompassed by numerous claims and is the subject of intricate relations. Many of these may be comprised in a copious narrative, without infraction of simplicity or detriment to unity.

Next to property, the most extensive source of our relations is sex. On the circumstances which produce, and the principles which regulate the union between the sexes, happiness greatly depends. The conduct to be pursued by a virtuous man in those situations which arise from sex, it was thought useful to display.

Fictitious history has, hitherto, chiefly related to the topics of love and marriage. A monotony and sentimental softness have hence arisen that have frequently excited contempt and ridicule. The ridicule, in general, is merited; not because these topics are intrinsically worthless or vulgar, but because the historian was deficient in knowledge and skill.

Marriage is incident to all; its influence on our happiness and dignity, is more entire and lasting than any other incident can possess. None, therefore, is more entitled to discussion. To enable men to evade the evils and secure the benefits of this state, is to consult, in an eminent degree, their happiness.

A man, whose activity is neither aided by political authority nor by the *press,* may yet exercise considerable influence on the condition of his neighbours, by the exercise of intellectual powers. His courage may be useful to the timid or the feeble, and his knowledge to the ignorant, as well as his property to those who want. His benevolence and justice may not only protect his kindred and his wife, but rescue the victims of prejudice and passion from the yoke of those domestic tyrants, and shield the powerless from the oppression of power, the poor from the injustice of the rich, and the simple from the stratagems of cunning.

Almost all men are busy in acquiring subsistence or wealth by a fixed application of their time and attention. Manual or mental skill is obtained and exerted for this end. This application, within certain limits, is our duty. We are bound to chuse that species of industry which combines most profit to ourselves with the least injury to others; to select that instrument which, by most speedily supplying our necessities, leaves us at most leisure to act from the impulse of benevolence.

A profession, successfully pursued, confers power not merely by conferring property and leisure. The skill which is gained, and which, partly or for a time, may be exerted to procure subsistence, may, when this end is accomplished, continue to be exerted for the common good. The pursuits of law and medicine, enhance our power over the liberty, property, and health of mankind. They not only qualify us for imparting benefit, by supplying us with property and leisure, but by enabling us to obviate, by intellectual exertions, many of the evils that infest the world.

Engel endeavoured to apply these principles to the choice of a profession, and to point out the mode in which professional skill, after it has supplied us with the means of subsistence, may be best exerted in the cause of general happiness.

Human affairs are infinitely complicated. The condition of no two beings is alike. No model can be conceived, to which our situation enables us exactly to conform. No situation can be imagined perfectly similar to that of an actual being. This exact similitude is not required to render an imaginary portrait useful to those who survey it. The usefulness, undoubtedly, consists in suggesting a mode of reasoning and acting somewhat similar to that which is ascribed to a feigned person; and, for this end, some similitude is requisite between the real and imaginary situation; but that similitude is not hard to produce. Among the incidents which invention will set before us, those are to be culled out which afford most scope to wisdom and virtue, which are most analogous to facts, which most forcibly suggest to the reader the parallel between his state and that described, and most strongly excite his desire to act as the feigned personages act. These incidents must be so arranged as to inspire, at once, curiosity and belief, to fasten the attention, and thrill the heart. This scheme was executed in the life of "Olivo Ronsica."[7]

Engel's principles inevitably led him to select, as the scene and period of his narrative, that in which those who should read it, should exist. Every day removed the reader farther from the period, but its immediate readers would perpetually recognize the objects, and persons, and events, with which they were familiar.

Olivo is a rustic youth, whom domestic equality, personal independence, agricultural occupations, and studious habits, had endowed with a strong mind, pure taste, and unaffected integrity. Domestic revolutions oblige him to leave his father's house in search of subsistence.

He is destitute of property, of friends, and of knowledge of the world. These are to be acquired by his own exertions, and virtue and sagacity are to guide him in the choice and the use of suitable means.

Ignorance subjects us to temptation, and poverty shackles our beneficence. Olivo's conduct shews us how temptation may be baffled, in spite of ignorance, and benefits be conferred in spite of poverty.

He bends his way to Weimar. He is involved, by the artifices of others, and, in consequence of his ignorance of mankind, in many perils and perplexities. He forms a connection with a man of a great and mixed, but, on the whole, a vicious character. Semlits is introduced to furnish a contrast to the simplicity and rectitude of Olivo, to exemplify the misery of sensuality and fraud, and the influence which, in the present system of society, vice possesses over the reputation and external fortune of the good.

Men hold external goods, the pleasures of the senses, of health, liberty, reputation, competence, friendship, and life, partly by virtue of their own wisdom and activity. This, however, is not the only source of their possession. It is likewise dependant on physical accidents, which human foresight cannot anticipate, or human power prevent. It is also influenced by the conduct and opinions of others.

There is no external good, of which the errors and wickedness of others may not deprive us. So far as happiness depends upon the retention of these goods, it is held at the option of another. The perfection of our character is evinced by the transient or slight influence which privations and evils have upon our happiness, on the skilfulness of those exertions which we make to avoid or repair disasters, on the diligence and success with which we improve those instruments of pleasure to ourselves and to others which fortune has left in our possession.

Richardson has exhibited in Clarissa,[8] a being of uncommon virtue, bereaved of many external benefits by the vices of others. Her parents and lover conspire to destroy her fortune, liberty, reputation, and personal sanctity.

More talents and address cannot be easily conceived, than those which are displayed by her to preserve and to regain these goods. Her efforts are vain. The cunning and malignity with which she had to contend, triumphed in the contest.

Those evils and privations she was unable to endure. The loss of fame took away all activity and happiness, and she died a victim to errors, scarcely less opprobrious and pernicious, than those of her tyrants and oppressors. She misapprehended the value of parental approbation and a fair fame. She depreciated the means of usefulness and pleasure of which fortune was unable to deprive her.

Olivo is a different personage. His talents are exerted to reform the vices of others, to defeat their malice when exerted to his injury, to endure, without diminution of his usefulness or happiness, the injuries which he cannot shun.

Semlits is led, by successive accidents, to unfold his story to Ronsica, after which, they separate. Semlits is supposed to destroy himself, and Ronsica returns into the country.

A pestilential disease, prevalent throughout the north of Europe, at that time (1630), appears in the city. To ascertain the fate of one connected, by the ties of kindred and love, with the family in which Olivo resides, and whose life is endangered by residence in the city, he repairs thither, encounters the utmost perils, is seized with the reigning malady, meets, in extraordinary circumstances, with Semlits, and is finally received into the house of a physician, by whose skill he is restored to health, and to whom he relates his previous adventures.

He resolves to become a physician, but is prompted by benevolence to return, for a time, to the farm which he had lately left. The series of ensuing events, are long, intricate, and congruous, and exhibit the hero of the tale in circumstances that task his fortitude, his courage, and his disinterestedness.

Engel has certainly succeeded in producing a tale, in which are powerful displays of fortitude and magnanimity; a work whose influence must be endlessly varied by varieties of character and situation of the reader, but, from which, it is not possible for any one to rise without some degree of moral benefit, and much of that pleasure which always attends the emotions of curiosity and sympathy.

Death of Cicero, a Fragment

TIRO[1] TO ATTICUS.[2]

The task of relating the last events in the life of my beloved master, has fallen upon me. His last words reminded me of the obligation, which I had long since assumed, of conveying to his Atticus a faithful account of his death. Having performed this task, life will cease to be any longer of value.

Having parted with his brother,[3] he went on board a vessel which lay at anchor in the road. The master was a Cyprian, ignorant of the Roman language; a stupid and illiterate sailor, whose provincial jargon was luckily understood and spoken by *Chlorus,* who was by birth a Cnidian. He served us as interpreter.

He was a stranger to the affairs of Italy, and his knowledge was so extremely limited, that he had never heard even the name of my master. This ignorance we were careful not to remove; and finding him unengaged, and merely waiting till some one should offer him a cargo, I tendered him a large sum if he would set sail immediately. This incident determined our course. No great deviation from his usual route was necessary to carry us to Tarsus; and there my master would not only be under the protection of Cassius,[4] but in the midst of his Cilician clients.[5] His ancient subjects would not fail to receive, with joy and gratitude, a patron from whom they had received so many benefits, and in case of any adverse fortune, their mountains would afford him concealment and security.

The vessel was small and crazy. It afforded wretched accommodation, but it behoved us to submit to every inconvenience, and to console ourselves with the hope that the voyage would be short. We had scarcely got on board, however, and made our bargain with the master when the wind, which had lately been propitious, changed to the south-east, and with this wind, the master declared it impossible to move from our present station.

This was an untoward event. Our safety depended upon the expedition with which we should fly from the shores of Italy. Our footsteps would be diligently traced, and another hour might bring the blood-hounds within view.

One expedient was obvious. The search might be eluded, or, at least prolonged, by leaving this spot. It was possible to move by the help of oars along the coast. Further south, the country near the sea was still more desolate and woody than here, and we might be concealed in some obscure and unfrequented bay, till the wind should once more become favourable.

Additional rewards and promises induced the captain to adopt this scheme. The wind and the turbulence of the waves increased. My master had always an antipathy to voyages by sea, owing, probably, to the deadly sickness, with which the tossing of the billows never failed to afflict him. This sickness speedily came on, and added to the pent-up air, filthiness and inconvenience of the ship, plunged him into new impatience and dejection. He frequently declared his resolution to go on shore, and offer to his enemies a life which was a burden to him, and relinquished his design not till I had employed the most pathetic and vehement remonstrances.

We had not gone two leagues before night came on. This for a time suspended our toils. We came to anchor near the shore, and being somewhat sheltered from the wind, by the direction of the shore, the sea became more calm, and my master's sickness disappeared. Still he was unwilling to pass the night on board the vessel, and ordered us to land.

This proceeding was imminently dangerous. I endeavoured to convince him of this danger. The town of Circœum[6] was two or three miles distant, but the huts of which it consisted would afford him accommodation little better than that which the ship afforded. He would unavoidably be recognized by the inhabitants, and if they had not yet heard of the proscription,[7] his appearance among them would lead them to suspect the truth, and what reliance could be placed upon their fidelity? This town might contain some tenant or retainer of Cæsar,[8] or it might at this moment be visited by the messengers of Anthony, at least, his appearance there would shortly be known, and would afford to his pursuers a new clue, by which they may be aided in their search. The same hazards would accompany his entrance into any of the neighbouring farmhouses.

These reasonings made him give up his resolution of going to Circœum, but he retained his determination to land. If he should pass the night in the open air, though the ground was covered with snow, it was better than to breathe the poisonous atmosphere of the ship, and remain cooped up with the Cyprian and his crew.

Since he would not give up this design, I endeavoured to find reasons for approving it. One danger against which it was needful to provide, was the suspicion of the sailors. The grief and dejection of my master, our impatience to be gone from Italy, and the secret and abrupt manner of our embarkation, could not but excite their notice and make them busy at conjecture. They would be still more at a loss to conceive why, when a town was so near, we should prefer to spend the night on board their vessel, and the shelter of a tree or a rock, with the fire which might easily be kindled, were, in truth, not less safe or commodious than continuance in the ship. Preparations, were, therefore, made to land.

My caution led me to go on shore before him, that any danger which impended might be seasonably descried. Wandering over the strand, a small hut was discovered which appeared to have been formerly inhabited by fishermen. This was a season when the net was idle, and this hut was therefore deserted. The walls and roof were broken, but a good fire might render it tenable for a few hours. Here my master consented to repose himself.

The ground within the hut, as well as without, was covered with snow. This was removed and a kind of bed of withered sticks and dried leaves was provided for him. On this he lay down, and the servants seated themselves around him. He did not endeavour to sleep, but supporting his head upon his elbow, and fixing his eyes, in a thoughtful mood, upon the fire, he delivered himself up to meditation. A pause of general and mournful silence ensued.

Every one's eyes were fixed upon those venerable features. To behold one, so illustrious, one that had so lately governed the destinies of mankind, seated on the pinnacle of human greatness, and encompassed with all the goods of fortune, thus reduced to the condition of a fugitive and out-law, stretched upon the bare earth, in this wretched hovel, affected all of us alike. Every bosom seemed to swell with the same sentiment, and required the relief of tears. Chlorus set us the example of this weakness, and not one of us but sobbed aloud.

His attention was recalled by this sound. He lifted his head, and looked upon us by turns with an air of inexpressible benignity. My friends, said he, at length, be not discomposed. My life has been sufficiently long, since I have lived to reap the rewards of virtue. Those evils must indeed be great, which would not be compensated by these proofs of your affection. I need extort from you no other testimony of the equity and kindness of my treatment of you, than the fidelity and tenderness with which you have adhered to me in my distress. This is a consolation of which it is not in the power of the tyrants to bereave me. Let their executioners come: I am willing to die.

These words only heightened the emotions which they were intended to suppress. I desired for my own sake, to change or to terminate this scene, and to reflect that my duty forbade me to sit here in inactivity, when surrounded by so many dangers. None of us had eaten a morsel since we left Astura. Our master was too much absorbed in reflections connected with his fallen fortunes, to think of food. It was our duty to contend with his indifference or aversion, in this respect, as well as to supply our exhausted strength, and prepare for the hardships which we were yet to endure.

I determined, therefore, to go, with two or three companions, to Circœum and purchase necessaries, as well as ascertain what danger was to be dreaded from this quarter. My master was careless of necessity or danger, and the task of consulting and deciding for the welfare of himself and his servants, had entirely devolved upon me. This charge, it behoved me to perform with circumspection and zeal.

We set out, and crossing an angle of the forest, quickly reached the village. The utmost caution was necessary to be used, since many of the servants of Cicero, and particularly myself, were nearly as well known, especially in this district, as our lord. Chlorus was least liable to be detected, in consequence of having spent the greater part of his life at the Cuman Villa.[9] He might be effectually disguised, likewise, by mimicking the accents of a Cyprian sailor, and pretending that he came from the vessel. Chlorus went forward, while I and Sura remained at a distance, awaiting his return. He came back in a short time, and with some tokens of alarm. He had crept into a tavern, and after purchasing some bread and dried fruits, had joined a knot of persons who were earnestly engaged in conversation in the portico. One appeared to be a stranger, who had just arrived, and was telling his news to the rest. The coalition of the tyrants was the theme of his discourse. Pœdius, the consul,[10] was said to be included in the sentence of proscription, and a tumult was affirmed to have been raised, on this account, in the city. The populace had aided the magistrate in arresting the emisaries from the armies, and the senate had created Pœdius dictator.

After listening some time, Chlorus ventured to slide into the company, and inquired, in his broken Latin, of what proscription they were talking. The traveller repeated his news with great vivacity, and mentioned, among a thousand incredible circumstances, that the army of Brutus had revolted, and that diligent search was making for the Ciceros. He had just passed near Astura, and was told that a troop had been there, hunting for the fugitives, and finding them to have lately fled, they had dispersed themselves over the country; and he was sure they could not escape. Hearing this, Chlorus withdrew, and hastened to communicate his tidings to me.

The revolt of the Macedonian army was sufficiently probable. This was mournful news, but it shewed with new force the propriety of taking refuge in Asia, rather than in Greece. The last tale was no less probable, and convinced us that no time was to be lost in leaving this fatal shore.

To leave it, however, was not in our power. The present state of the wind imprisoned us in this spot. To change it for another would merely multiply our perils. Here we must remain till it should please Jove to give us a prosperous gale, or till our enemies should trace us to our covert. It only remained for us to hasten back to the hut, and defend our master at the expense of our own lives.

We returned. No interruption or intrusion had been experienced during our absence. On entering the hovel, I found my master in profound sleep. His features were tranquil and placid, and his anxieties were, for a while, entirely forgotten. The bread and fruits we had brought were shared among our companions, and we continued to watch during the night.

Anxious attention was paid to the state of the air, and fruitless wishes and repinings were whispered by one to another. The morning light returned. The enemy was still distant, but the sky was as untoward as ever.

At length, my master awoke of his own accord. After noticing the day-light, and recollecting his situation, he turned to me, and said: Well, my dear Tiro, what is now to be done? I will tell thee what; we will go on board; the Cyprian shall ply his oars and carry us to Formia,[11] and there will I wait for my release.

He noticed the down-cast eyes and mournful looks, which these words occasioned. No one seemed inclined to move to such a purpose. He looked around him, and continued in the same tone; What else, my friends, would you purpose to be done? How unworthy of the saviour of Rome and of Italy is it to be thus clinging to a wretched life, and skulking from ungrateful foes, among rocks and woods? No: I have done my part: All that remains is to die with firmness and with dignity.

Hitherto, I have been the fool of passion and inconstancy. My purposes have wavered from day to day, but it is time to shake off this irresolution and trample on this cowardice. I am now resolved, and will be gone to Formia this moment.

With these words he rose from the ground, and put on an air of sternness and command, which left me no power to expostulate. We obeyed him in silence, and once more put ourselves on board the vessel. The crew were still asleep, but being roused by our arrival, were prevailed upon to row along the shore towards Formia.

My master seemed to have retrieved his wonted tranquillity, in consequence of having formed his ultimate resolution. He was still, for the most part, wrapt in meditation. He forebore to converse with me, but sat upon the deck, with his eyes fixed upon the water, which was now less turbulent than on the former day, and did not occasion sickness.

My own thoughts were occupied in devising some means of escape.

We were now approaching Sicily, and it was possible that some conveyance could be gained to that island. This however must be found after our arrival at Formia, for beyond this the Cyprian refused to go, under pretence, which indeed, was probably true, of being unacquainted with the coast. Neither was I totally without hope that the wind would suddenly change, and permit us to leave the coast. On this event, I did not fear to obtain Cicero's concurrence, with a scheme so conducive to his safety. To despair of himself or the republic while the seas were open, and while Cassius was in arms, and furnished with the wealth of all the Asiatic provinces, was unworthy of his understanding and his virtue.

His purpose to go to any one of his villas was pregnant with danger. These places would be searched, by his enemies. As long as he remained in Italy, it was expedient to conceal himself in unsuspected corners. Could not such be found, where he might remain unmolested for years.

I now reflected that Formia being situated within a mile of the sea, might be the best asylum to which he could betake himself. A ship might be provided, ready to profit by the first wind, to sail away to Sicily, while, in the mean time, my master might be effectually secreted in some part of his dominion. The subterranean vaults, constructed to preserve wine and other provisions, on this estate, might afford him concealment till the opportunity of escape should offer.

While brooding over these images, we came in sight of Formia. It was now time to mention to him this scheme. He received it with disapprobation—I am too old, said he, to undergo once more the hardships and hazards of a camp. I have witnessed long enough the ingratitude and perfidy of mankind. I am tired of the spectacle, and am determined to close my eyes upon it forever.

It shall never be said, that Marcus Cicero[12] fled from the presence of tyrants, that he saved the miserable remnant of his old age, by making himself an exile from his country. I tell thee, Tiro, I am too old to become the sport of fortune, and the follower of armies. Cassius and Brutus are young, they are innured to war; it is their element. They fight for liberty and glory, which their age will permit them to enjoy for many years to come; but as to me, I have reached the verge of the grave already, and should I elude my enemies, and reach Rhodes or Tarsus in safety, I should only have reserved myself for a speedy and ignoble death. No: Here shall be the end of my wanderings.

I will go to my house. I will pass my time without anxiety or fear. When the executioners of Antony arrive, they will find their victim prepared. My resolution, continued he, with some impatience, is taken. It is to no purpose to harass me with arguments and remonstrances, for I shall never swerve from it.

I was not totally discouraged by these declarations. I confided in my power to vanquish this resolution, as soon as the means of escape should be provided. Till then it was indeed useless to contend with his despair. His imagination saw nothing but cowardice and degradation, in hiding himself in vaults and pits. That he who was so long at the head of the Roman state, should seek his safety in shifts and stratagems like these, was ignominious and detestable. Death was not so terrible that it should be shunned, life was not so dear that it should be preserved at this price.

He proceeded to his house with an air of fearlessness and confidence. It was far from certain, that it was not occupied already by assassins, expecting and waiting his approach; of this, however, he testified no apprehension. As soon as he entered the porch, his arrival was rumoured through the building, and his servants hurried from all quarters to welcome him. Their looks betrayed anxiety as well as joy. It was easy to perceive that they were not unapprised of the dangers which encompassed their master, and that his appearance among them had been unexpected. He greeted and smiled upon each, and then retired to his chamber, whither he would not allow any one to follow him.

It was now time to adopt those measures on which my thoughts had been engaged. As soon as I parted from my master, I took Glauco the steward aside. I told him what had lately happened, and what I now designed to do, and desired his assistance to procure a vessel which might carry us without delay to Sicily.

I found that there was need of the utmost expedition, for Glauco informed me that, not many hours before, a troop of twenty horsemen, had come hither. They rode furiously into the court, and without inquiry or permission, rushed into the house. They entered every apartment, and not finding their victim, indulged their resentment in imprecations on the upstart of Arpinum,[13] and in striking their swords against the furniture and pictures. Two busts, of Brutus and Ahala,[14] which stood in the library, they overturned upon the pavement.

The servants, affrighted at the stern and sullen visages of these intruders, fled from their presence. After lingering for some time in the house, they mounted their horses and disappeared.

These tidings shewed me the magnitude and nearness of the danger. Not a moment should be wasted in deliberation or uncertainty. It was possible that the assassins might not speedily return, and the interval was to be employed in procuring the means of flight. The sea was to be crossed, and Cajeta[15] was a league distant. At Cajeta only was it possible to find a vessel, suited to our purpose.

I now called some of the most faithful servants together, and charged them to guard the safety of their master, till Glauco and I should return, which should be in less than an hour. We were going, I told them, to Cajeta, in hopes of finding some immediate conveyance from this shore, and would return with the utmost expedition.

We set out, selecting the fleetest horses to carry us. Three barks were seen in the bay, Glauco imagined that he saw on one the stern and beak which is peculiar to Sicily. To this we immediately transported ourselves. Happily his penetration had not been deceived, and the Sicilian readily consented to take us on board, and proceed immediately to Sicily.

By exerting themselves with energy, they might bring the vessel in a short time to the shore nearest to my master's house. This was better than to bring him to Cajeta, where it would be impossible for him to escape observation, and to which he could come only by a public road, thronged and obstructed with passengers.

I left Glauco on board the vessel, to hasten the motions of the sailors and to direct them to the proper place. Meanwhile, I mounted my horse and rode back to Formia. The vessel would be ready to receive us by the time that we should reach the shore.

The domestics, whom I had posted in the atrium, were still assembled and received me with joy, but one event had taken place in my absence which filled me with foreboding and anxiety. A slave who wrought in the fields, who formerly belonged to the Cornelian family, and whose temper was remarkably perverse and malignant, had withdrawn himself immediately after my master's arrival. Glauco had frequently complained of the turbulent and worthless character of this slave, and had exhorted Cicero to part with him. In the multiplicity of more momentous concerns this affair had been overlooked by my master, and he still continued in the family.

It was now suggested to me that he had gone in order to recall the soldiers, and to avenge himself in this manner, for the punishments which his refractory and rebellious conduct had frequently incurred. This new danger was an additional incitement to my diligence. I went to my master's chamber and found him asleep. This was no time to be scrupulous or tardy. I awakened him.

On recovering his recollection, and finding me beside him, with every mark of trepidation and dismay, and silent, from my uncertainty in what manner to address him, he suspected that I brought fatal tidings. He looked at me without emotion, and said:

How is it with thee, my Tiro? With me, all is well. I have slept soundly, and am prepared to meet the worst. Thou wouldst tell me that they are coming. I rejoice to hear it: the sooner they arrive and execute the will of Anthony and his Octavius, the better.

Saying this, he half rose from the couch, and stretching his feet towards the stove, he continued: Thanks to Jove, that, at a time like this, nothing but my feet are cold. I have done with hope and with fear, and Cæsar's ministers shall find that my heart's blood has lost none of its warmth. He may deface and mangle this frame, but my spirit shall be found invincible.

I could no longer forbear, but while the tears flowed down my cheeks, I pulled him by the arm towards the door, and exclaimed: We have found a vessel that will carry us to Sicily. She lies at this moment near the shore ready to receive us. Hasten, I beseech you, beyond the reach of the tyrants. Why would you glut the vengeance of Anthony, and not rather live to raise up the republic?

He shook his head, and resisting my efforts: It is too late, said he: I never can die in a fitter season and place than the present, and hence I will not move.

O! Heaven! Does Cicero love his enemies better than his friends? Is he willing to sacrifice his country to parricides and traitors? Shall he seek death because, while he lives, liberty is not extinguished; because the triumph of the wicked can only be completed by his death?

Has Antony merited so well at your hands, that you are willing to die, that his ambition may be fully gratified? Is this the issue of your warfare? After contending with his treason so long, do you now fall of your own accord at his feet, put the poniard in his hand and call upon him to strike? Thus will mankind regard your conduct when the means of escape are offered you, when the arms and treasures of Sicily and Greece and Asia are ready to be put into your hand, you reject the gift, you abandon the cause of your country, of liberty, of your friends; you invite infamous assassins to your bosom; you die at the moment when your life is of most value to mankind, and nothing but your death is wanting to ensure the destruction of Rome.

O! let it not be said that in his last hours, Marcus Cicero was a recreant and coward. That so illustrious a life was closed with infamy, that his eulogies on liberty, his efforts for the salvation of Rome, the claims of gratitude and friendship were forgotten or despised. That mankind called on their deliverer, that armies and provinces were offered to be employed by him in the rescue of his country, and the ruin of tyrants, in vain.

The road is open and direct, there is nothing to create momentary hindrance or delay. In a few hours, he may laugh at the impotent resentment of Antony; and arm himself to punish the ingratitude and perfidy of Cæsar—But no, he will thrust himself within their grasp; he will patiently wait till their assassins have leisure to execute their sentence; he will beg them to except his homage, and since his death is indispensable to their success, he will stretch out his neck to receive it.

Perceiving that my master's resolution began to faulter, I redoubled my remonstrances, I called up the images of his brother, his son and his nephew, of Cassius and Brutus and Pompeius.[16] I painted the effect which the tidings of his death would produce in them; their transports of grief awakened not so much by the injury redounding to the common cause, as by the infatuation and folly to which his death must be ascribed. With their humiliation and terror, I contrasted the exultation of his enemies, to whose malice he was thus making himself a voluntary victim. What indignities would not be heaped upon his life-less remains! How would Fulvia[17] and Anthony feast their eyes upon his head, which, torn from the trunk, will be carried to their toilets, and how will the folly of inviting their revenge and crouching to the stroke of their assassins be made the endless theme of ridicule and mockery?—

At this moment, the servants entered the chamber with a litter. I had given previous directions to this effect. I had resolved if persua-sion should prove inefficacious, to carry him away by force. One of the bearers was Chlorus, whose looks betokened the deepest consterna-tion, and by his eyes and gestures besought me to use dispatch. I made a sign to the attendants, who approached their master with diffidence and reverence and prepared to remove him from his couch to the litter.

I renewed my supplications and remonstrances, to which he lis-tened in silence, and though his looks testified reluctance and perplex-ity, he made no resistance. He was placed in the litter. I led the way into the garden. Chlorus had now an opportunity to whisper me that the soldiers had scented their prey anew and were hastening to the house. This intelligence induced me to strike into an obscure path which led through a wood and to quicken the pace of my companions.

The litter was surrounded by sixteen domestics well armed. They were all faithful to their trust. Most of them were grey with age, but vigorous and resolute. All of them had been, during many years, per-sonal attendants on their lord, and were eager to shed their blood in his defence; I was not without hope that should we be overtaken and at-tacked, such resistance might be made, as, at least, to secure the retreat of my master to the shore.

We had now accomplished half the journey, and were inspired with new confidence in our good fortune. Turning an angle, however, a band of men appeared in sight. They discovered us in a moment, and shouting aloud, made towards us with the utmost expedition. There was now room but for one choice. Fly, said I, to those that bore the lit-ter, fly with your burden to the shore and leave us to contend with these miscreants.

The enemy had been discovered by my master as soon as by us. He now raised himself up, and exclaimed in a tone of irresistable authority; No: I charge you stir not a step. Set down the litter and await their coming. Put up your swords, continued he, turning to the rest, who had, in imitation of my example unsheathed their weapons: Put up your swords. By the duty which you owe me, I command you to forbear.

With whatever sternness these commands were delivered, they would not have made me hesitate or faulter. I was prepared to conduct myself, not agreeable to his directions, but to the exigencies of the time; I was willing to preserve his life even at the hazard of offending him beyond forgiveness; but my companions were endowed with less firmness.

Go on, said I, to the bearers, heed not the words of a desperate man. It is your duty to save him, though you forfeit your lives by your disobedience—They once more stooped to raise up the vehicle, but were again forbidden. What! said he, am I fallen so low as to be trampled on by slaves? Desist, this moment! Appalled and confounded by the energy of his accents, they let fall the litter, and stood with their eyes down-cast and motionless.

The delay which this altercation produced, rendered his escape impossible. The veteran and well-accoutred band that was approaching, left us no hope of victory. All that I had meditated, was to retard their progress so long that my master might reach the ship in safety. For this end we were to lay down our own lives, but as long as he continued in this spot all opposition would be fruitless.

To stay and behold violence committed on that venerable head was not in my power. I went forward to meet the assassins. It was not, however, till I had discerned the person of their leader that I had any hopes of diverting them from their design. He was a tribune in the army of Cæsar, and his name was Popilius Lænas.[18]

This man had been formerly accused of murdering his wife's brother. This brother had considerable property to which Lænas expected to succeed, but on some dissention between them, the brother had selected a new heir and Lænas was said to have gratified his vengeance by his death. His wife and children were among his accusers, and there was too much reason to believe the truth of the accusation.

In this extremity he besought Cicero to be his advocate. Lænas had been active in the Clodian tumults, had sided with Milo and the Senate, and had, consequently, promoted the interests of my master.[19] This service was now his plea, and, joined with unwearied importunities, accomplished his end. Cicero was an enthusiast in gratitude, and was not used to scrutinize suspiciously or weigh accurately, this kind of merit. Benefits received from others were, if possible, repaid an hundred fold. He made himself the advocate of a cause, which, without his assistance, would doubtless have been desperate, and Lænas was acquitted. His vows of gratitude and service were unbounded, and now that I discovered him at the head of Cæsar's executioners was scarcely credible.

After a moment's pause, I advanced towards him, and offered him my hand. He rejected it with scorn and rage, and thrusting me aside, Out of the way, villain, said he, and thank my mercy that you do not share the fate of the traitor you serve.

His followers surrounded me with drawn swords, and looking at the tribune, seemed to wait only for his signal to put me to death. Come on, he cried; Our prize is in view. Cut down every one that opposes, but leave the peaceable alone. They left me and hastened towards the litter.

My eyes followed them instinctively. Shuddering and a cold dew invaded my limbs. With the life of Cicero, methought, was entwined the existence of Rome. The stroke by which one was severed, would be no less fatal to the other. It was indeed true that liberty would he extinguished by his death, and then only would commence the reign of Anthony, and the servitude of mankind.

Would no effort avail to turn aside the stroke? Should I stand a powerless spectator of the deed? Might I not save myself at least the ignominy and horror of witnessing the fall of my master, by attacking his assassins or falling on my own sword?

These impulses of grief, were repressed by the remembrance of the duties, which his death would leave to be performed by me and of the promises by which I was bound.

During these thoughts my eyes were fixed upon the litter. My master, perceiving the approach of the tribune, held forth his head, as if to facilitate the assassin's office. His posture afforded a distinct view of his countenance, which was more thoughtful and serene than I had seen it during our flight from . . .

The eyes of the ruffians sparkled with joy at sight of their victim. They contended which should be foremost in guilt. The domestics, struck with consternation, looked upon each other in silence. The soldiers, full of eagerness to secure the reward which Anthony had promised for the head of his enemy, were too much occupied to speak to each other, or to heed any foreign object.

One blow severed the devoted head! No sooner had it fallen, than the troop set up an horrid shout of exultation. Lænas grasped the hair and threw the head into a large bag, held open by one of his companions for that purpose.

Come, lads, he cried: Post we, with our prize, with all speed to Rome? Anthony will pay us well for this service—So saying, they hastened away with as much expedition as they came.

All passed in a moment. Nothing but the headless trunk, stretched upon the floor of the litter, which floated in blood, remained. I approached the vehicle without being fully conscious of my movements, and gazed upon the mutilated figure. My thoughts were at a stand, as well as my power of utterance suspended. My heart seemed too small to embrace the magnitude of this calamity. It was not a single man who had fallen, or whose violent catastrophe was the theme of everlasting regret. The light of the world was extinguished, and the hopes of human kind brought to an end.

My mind gradually recovered some degree of activity. I mused upon the events that led to this disaster. It seemed as if the most flagitious folly, had given birth to this insupportable evil. Nothing was easier than to have fled to the shore; to have embarked in the Sicilian vessel, and quickly to have moved ourselves beyond the reach of our enemies. At one time, I loaded myself with the most vehement upbraidings: Why did I not exert myself to hinder him from leaving the Cyprian barque? Had we proceeded to Cajeta, without delay, we might have put ourselves on board the Agrigentine,[20] and set danger at defiance. The Cyprian refused to proceed, but menaces would have been successful where rewards had failed. He and his feeble crew, would have easily been mastered by our superior number.

But was not Cicero himself the author of his evil destiny? Irresolute, desponding or perverse, he thwarted or frustrated the measures conducive to his safety. More sensible to the stings of ingratitude and his personal humiliation, than to the claims of his fellow citizens; prone to despair of liberty, though the richest and most populous portion of the empire was still faithful to its cause; though veteran armies and illustrious officers were still ranged under its banners in Sicily, Greece and Asia, he lingered on this fatal shore, and threw himself before the executioner.

There were a thousand recesses on this desolate coast, and caverns in the Apenine, and unsuspected retreats on his own estate, where he might have been effectually concealed, till Cassius and Pompey had restored the republic, till the pursuit of his enemies had slackened, and time and his faithful servants had supplied the means of his escape. Had he even permitted the generous sacrifice which his attendants were zealous to make, and profited by the interval, which their contest with the ruffians would have afforded, to reach the shore; had he looked, with a stern eye, on the tribune and his followers, and rebuked them with the eloquence whose force had been so long irresistable; had he called up the memory of past benefits, and thundered indignation in the ears of the apostate Lænas, who knows but the blood-hounds would have been eluded or baffled, or disarmed of their sanguinary purpose? They were wretches, incited by the lust of gain, void of enmity to Cicero, or love of his oppressors. The bribe with which Anthony had bought their zeal, might have easily been doubled by Cicero, to purchase their connivance at his flight. The hope of promotion in the legions of the east, might have changed them into guardians of our safety, and companions of our voyage. Thus had the magnanimity of Marcus snatched him from worse perils, and kept him from despairing of his life, and his cause, though labouring under a greater weight of years, encompassed by enemies more numerous and more triumphant: lonely, succourless, in chains and immured in a dungeon!

But why do I calumniate the memory of Cicero? Arraign the wisdom of his conduct, and the virtue of his motives? Had he not lived long enough for felicity and usefulness? Was there cowardice or error in refusing to mingle in the tumults of war? In resigning to younger hands, innured to military offices, the spear and the shield? Is it more becoming the brave to struggle for life; to preserve the remnant which infirmity and old age had left, than serenely to wait for death, and encounter it with majestic composure? Is it dishonourable to mourn over the triumph of ambition, and the woes of our country? To be impatient of life, when divorced from liberty, and fated to contemplate the ruin of those schemes, on which his powers had incessantly been exercised, and whose purpose was the benefit of mankind?

Yes. The close of thy day was worthy its beginning and its progress. Thou diest with no stain upon thy virtue. The termination of thy course was coeval with the ruin of thy country. Thy hand had upheld the fabric of its freedom and its happiness, as long as human force was adequate to that end. It fell, because the seeds of dissolution had arrived at maturity, and the basis and structure were alike dissolved. It fell, and thou wast crushed in its ruins.

APPENDIX

An Account of a Murder Committed by Mr. J[ames] Y[ates], upon His Family, in December, A.D. 1781

To the EDITOR of the NEW-YORK WEEKLY MAGAZINE.

SIR,

The inclosed Account I transmit to you for publication, at the particular request of a friend, who is well acquainted with the circumstances that gave rise to it.—It is drawn up by a female hand, and she here relates respecting Mr. Y—— what she knew of him herself, and what she had heard of him in her father's family, where he had been an occasional visitant; as I have no reason to believe that this transaction has ever appeared in print, you will be pleased to give it a place among your original compositions.

ANNA.

NEW-YORK, *May* 17, 1796.

The unfortunate subject of my present essay, belonged to one of the most respectable families in this state; he resided a few miles from Tomhanick,[1] and though he was not in the most affluent circumstances, he maintained his family (which consisted of a wife and four children,) very comfortably.— From the natural gentleness of his disposition, his industry, sobriety, probity and kindness, his neighbours universally esteemed him, and until the fatal night when he perpetrated the cruel act, none saw cause of blame in him.

In the afternoon preceding that night, as it was Sunday and there was no church near, several of his neighbours with their wives came to his house for the purpose of reading the scripture and singing psalms; he received them cordially, and when they were going to return home in the evening, he pressed his sister and her husband, who came with the others, to stay longer; at his very earnest solicitation they remained until near nine o'clock, during which time his conversation was grave as usual, but interesting and affectionate: to his wife, of whom he was very fond, he made use of more than commonly endearing expressions, and caressed his little ones alternately:—he spoke much of his domestic felicity, and informed his sister, that to render his wife more happy, he intended to take her to New-Hampshire the next day; "I have just been refitting my sleigh," said he, "and we will set off by day-break."—After singing another hymn, Mr. and Mrs. J—f—n departed.

"They had no sooner left us (said he upon his examination) than taking my wife upon my lap, I opened the Bible to read to her—my two boys were in bed—one five years old, the other seven;—my daughter Rebecca, about eleven, was sitting by the fire, and my infant aged about six months, was slumbering at her mother's bosom.——Instantly a new light shone into the room, and upon looking up I beheld two Spirits, one at my right hand and the other at my left;——he at the left bade me destroy all my *idols*, and begin by casting the Bible into the fire;——the other Spirit dissuaded me, but I obeyed the first, and threw the book into the flames. My wife immediately snatched it out, and was going to expostulate, when I threw it in again and held her fast until it was entirely consumed:——then filled with the determination to persevere, I flew out of the house, and seizing an axe which lay by the door, with a few strokes demolished my sleigh, and running to the stable killed one of my horses——the other I struck, but with one spring he got clear of the stable.——My spirits now were high, and I hasted to the house to inform my wife of what I had done. She appeared terrified, and begged me to sit down; but the good angel whom I had obeyed stood by me and bade me go on, 'You have more idols, (said he) look at your wife and children.' I hesitated not a moment, but rushed to the bed where my boys lay, and catching the eldest in my arms, I threw him with such violence against the wall, that he expired without a groan!——his brother was still asleep——I took him by the feet, and dashed his skull in pieces against the fire-place!——Then looking round, and perceiving that my wife and daughters were fled, I left the dead where they lay, and went in pursuit of the living, taking up the axe again.——A slight snow had fallen that evening, and by its light I descried my wife running towards her father's (who lived about half a mile off) encumbered with her babe; I ran after her, calling upon her to return, but she shrieked and fled faster, I therefore doubled my pace, and when I was within thirty yards of her, threw the axe at her, which hit her upon the hip!——the moment that she felt the blow she dropped the child, which I directly caught up, and threw against the log-fence——I did not hear it cry——I only heard the lamentations of my wife, of whom I had now lost sight; but the blood gushed so copiously from her wound that it formed a distinct path along the snow. We were now within sight of her father's house, but from what cause I cannot tell, she took an opposite course, and after running across an open field several times, she again stopped at her own door; I now came up with her——my heart bled to see her distress, and all my *natural feelings* began to revive; I forgot my duty, so powerfully did her moanings and pleadings affect me, 'Come then, my love (said I) we have one child left, let us be thankful for that——what is done is right——we must not repine, come let me embrace you——let me know that 'you do indeed love me.' She encircled me in her trembling arms, and pressed her quivering lips to my cheek.——A voice behind me, said, 'This is also an idol!'——I broke from her instantly, and wrenching a stake from the garden fence, with one stroke levelled her to the earth! and lest she should only be stunned, and might, perhaps, recover again, I repeated my blows, till I could not distinguish one feature of her face!!! I now went to look after my last sublunary treasure, but after calling several times without receiving any answer, I returned to the house again; and in the way back picked up the babe and laid it on my wife's bosom.——I then stood musing a minute—during which interval I thought I heard the suppressed sobbings of some one near the barn, I approached it in silence, and beheld my daughter Rebecca endeavouring to conceal herself among the hay-stacks.—

"At the noise of my feet upon the dry corn stalks—she turned hastily round and seeing me exclaimed, 'O father, my dear father, spare me, let me live—let me live,—I will be a comfort to you and my mother—spare me to take care of my little sister Diana—do—do let me live.'—She was my darling child, and her fearful cries pierced me to the soul——the tears of *natural pity* fell as plentifully down my cheeks, as those of terror did down her's, and methought that to destroy *all* my idols, was a hard task——I again relapsed at the voice of complaining; and taking her by the hand, led her to where her mother lay; then thinking that if I intended to retain her, I must make some other severe sacrifice, I bade her sing and dance.——She complied, terribly situated as she was,——but I was not acting in the line of my duty——I was convinced of my error, and catching up a hatchet that stuck in a log, with one well aimed stroke cleft her forehead in twain——she fell——and no sign of retaining life appeared.

"I then sat down on the threshold, to consider what I had best do——'I shall be called a murderer (said I) I shall be seized—imprisoned—executed, and for what?—for destroying my idols—for obeying the mandate of my father——no, I will put all the dead in the house together, and after setting fire to it, run to my sister's and say the Indians have done it——'I was preparing to drag my wife in, when the idea struck me that I was going to tell a *horrible lie,* 'and how will that accord with my profession? (asked I). No, let me speak the truth, and declare the good motive for my actions, be the consequences what they may.'"

His sister, who was the principal evidence against him, stated——that she had scarce got home, when a message came to Mr. J——n, her husband, informing him that his mother was ill and wished to see him; he accordingly set off immediately, and she not expecting him home again till the next day, went to bed—there being no other person in the house. About four in the morning she heard her brother Y—— call her, she started up and bade him come in. "I will not (returned he) for I have committed the unpardonable sin—I have burnt the Bible." She knew not what to think, but rising hastily opened the door which was only latched, and caught hold of his hand: "let me go, Nelly (said he) my hands are wet with blood—the blood of my Elizabeth and her children."—She saw the blood dripping from his fingers, and her's chilled in the veins, yet with a fortitude unparalleled she begged him to enter, which— as he did, he attempted to seize a case knife, that by the light of a bright pine-knot fire, he perceived lying on the dresser——she prevented him, however, and tearing a trammel from the chimney, bound him with it to the bed post——fastening his hands behind him.—She then quitted the house in order to go to his, which as she approached she heard the voice of loud lamentation, the hope that it was some one of the family who had escaped the effects of her brother's frenzy, subdued the fears natural to such a situation and time, she quickened her steps, and when she came to the place where Mrs. Y—— lay, she perceived that the moans came from Mrs. Y——'s aged father, who expecting that his daughter would set out upon her journey by day-break, had come at that early hour to bid her farewell.

They alarmed their nearest neighbours immediately, who proceeded to Mrs. J——n's, and there found Mr. Y—— in the situation she had left him; they took him from hence to Tomhanick, where he remained near two days— during which time Mr. W—tz—l (a pious old Lutheran, who occasionally acted as preacher) attended upon him, exhorting him to pray and repent; but he received the admonitions with contempt, and several times with ridicule, refusing to confess his error or *join* in prayer—I say *join* in prayer, for he would not kneel when the rest did, but when they arose he would prostrate himself and address his "father," frequently saying "my father, thou knowest that it was in obedience to thy commands, and for thy glory that I have done this deed." Mrs. Bl——r,[2] at whose house he then was, bade some one ask him who his father was?—he made no reply—but pushing away the person who stood between her and himself, darted at her a look of such indignation as thrilled horror to her heart——his speech was connected, and he told his tale without variation; he expressed much sorrow for the loss of his dear family, but consoled himself with the idea of having performed his duty—he was taken to ALBANY and there confined as a lunatic in the goal, from which he escaped twice, once by the assistance of Aqua Fortis,[3] with which he opened the front door.

I went in 1782 with a little girl, by whom Mr. Bl——r had sent him some fruit; he was then confined in dungeon, and had several chains on——he appeared to be much affected at her remembrance of him, and put up a pious ejaculation for her and her family——since then I have received no accounts respecting him.

The cause for his wonderfully cruel proceedings is beyond the conception of human beings——the deed so unpremeditated, so unprovoked, that we do not hesitate to pronounce it the effect of insanity——yet upon the other hand, when we reflect on the equinimity of his temper, and the comfortable situation in which he was, and no visible circumstance operating to render him frantic, we are apt to conclude, that he was under a strong delusion of Satan. But what avail our conjectures, perhaps it is best that some things are concealed from us, and the only use we can now make of our knowledge of this affair, is to be humble under a scene of human frailty to renew our petition, "Lead us not into temptation."

May, 27, 1796.

NOTES

Like the endnotes that T. S. Eliot added to his poem "The Wasteland," the erudition of Charles Brockden Brown should probably be taken aesthetically—that is, with a grain of salt. Brown aspired to be mystifyingly encyclopedic, and a full clarification of his obscurities risks the kind of deflation likely with a full explanation of the physics in a science-fiction movie. These notes are intended, therefore, to be supplementary—a guide for the curious. Brown's fiction may be enjoyed without them.

For even more complete deciphering, the reader may consult Alexander Cowie's "Historical Essay" in the bicentennial edition of *Wieland; or, the Transformation and Memoirs of Carwin the Biloquist* (Kent State University Press, 1977); chapter 3 of Christopher Looby's *Voicing America: Language, Literary Form, and the Origins of the United States* (University of Chicago Press, 1996); and chapter 3 of Alan Axelrod's *Charles Brockden Brown: An American Tale* (University of Texas Press, 1983). Harry R. Warfel's *Charles Brockden Brown: American Gothic Novelist* (University of Florida Press, 1949) remains the best biography of Brown yet published. Studies that help to place Brown in the context of early American culture include Jay Fliegelman's Introduction to *Wieland and Memoirs of Carwin the Biloquist* (Penguin, 1991); chapter 5 of Robert A. Ferguson's *Law and Letters in American Culture* (Harvard University Press, 1984); Peter Kafer's "Charles Brockden Brown and Revolutionary

Philadelphia: An Imagination in Context," *Pennsylvania Magazine of History and Biography* CXVI (October 1992): 467–98; and chapters 2 and 3 of my book *American Sympathy: Men, Friendship, and Literature in the New Nation* (Yale University Press, 2001). Proper names easily found in a standard dictionary, atlas, or desk encyclopedia are not explained here.

WIELAND; OR THE TRANSFORMATION: AN AMERICAN TALE

On April 12, 1798, William Dunlap recorded in his diary that his friend Brown read aloud to him from a new novel "he calls . . . Wieland or the Transformation." The novel was published on September 14, 1798, in New York by Hocquet Caritat.

1. *an authentic case, remarkably similar to that of Wieland.* Brown is referring to the case of James Yates of Tomhannock, New York, which was reported in the *New-York Weekly Magazine* in July 1796. It is reprinted in the appendix of this edition.

2. *The modern poet of the same name.* Christoph Martin Wieland (1733–1813) was a German poet, playwright, novelist, and magazine editor. Brown probably read his four-canto poem about Abraham, the Old Testament patriarch who was commanded by God to sacrifice his son, in a prose translation published in America as *The Trial of Abraham* (John Trumbull, 1777). Wieland's most popular work was his epic fantasia *Oberon*, the basis for the libretto to Karl Maria von Weber's opera of the same name. In 1799, while stationed in Prussia as a diplomat, John Quincy Adams translated it into English.

3. *the Albigenses, or French Protestants.* It is an anachronism for Brown to describe the Albigensians as Protestants. The dualistic heresy surfaced in southern France, near the city of Albi, in the twelfth century. Its adherents called themselves Cathars, after the Greek word for "perfect." They believed that the world was evil, but that a ritual called the *consolamentum* could absolve them from sin. The Roman Catholic Church brutally repressed the Cathars by means of the Albigensian Crusade and the Inquisition. "Kill them all, the Lord will know his own," a papal legate is reported to have ordered his crusaders. By the mid-fourteenth century the Cathars were no more.

4. *"Seek and ye shall find."* Matthew 7:7 and Luke 11:9.

5. *the sect of Camissards.* The Camisards were a group of Protestant peasants in southern France who between 1686 and 1709 resisted Louis XIV's attempts to convert them to Roman Catholicism. When they were imprisoned and tortured, and their churches demolished, they fought back with guerrilla warfare, encouraged, if not inflamed, by their belief that the end of the world was at hand. They were subject to ecstatic trances, in which

they heard voices and spoke in tongues. (Note that although both the Albigensians and the Camisards were located in southern France, they were separated by nearly four centuries.)

6. *that precept which enjoins us, when we worship, to retire into solitude.* Cf. Matthew 6:6.

7. *the disciples of Zinzendorf.* Count Nikolaus Ludwig Graf von Zinzendorf (1700–60) devoted himself to the Moravian Church, also known as the Renewed Church of the Brethren, a Protestant denomination known for its plain, heartfelt style of worship and its missionary zeal.

8. footnote. *A case . . . published in one of the Journals of Florence.* In April 1792, the Philadelphia-based *American Museum, or Universal Magazine* summarized an article about spontaneous combustion that had appeared in a Florence journal. While reciting his breviary, an Italian priest named G. Maria Bertholi had purportedly burst into flame. Bertholi claimed that "he had felt a stroke, as if somebody had given him a blow over the right arm, with a large club, and that at the same time, he had seen a spark of fire attach itself to his shirt." Four days later, he was rotting to death. "His body exhaled an insupportable smell," his doctor reported. "I saw the worms which issued from it crawling on the bed, and the nails of his fingers drop of themselves." Brown probably cribbed the references to Merille, Muraire, Maffei, and Fontana from the *American Museum* account.

9. *the oration for Cluentius.* In 66 B.C., Cicero defended A. Cluentius Habitus from the charge that he had poisoned Statius Albius Oppianicus. The story line of the case was as complex as it was sordid. Eight years prior, Cluentius had successfully prosecuted Oppianicus for a grisly string of murders, mostly of his own relatives, which he had allegedly committed in order to inherit his victims' estates. In a particularly lurid twist, Oppianicus's co-conspirator and second wife (he poisoned his first) was Cluentius's own mother. After Oppianicus was convicted, rumors spread that Cluentius had bribed the jurors. In the new case, brought by Oppianicus's son, Cicero defended Cluentius by arguing that Oppianicus senior had indeed been guilty of the crimes he was convicted of and had died of natural causes. According to Quintilian, Cicero later boasted of having "thrown dust in the eyes of the jury in the case of Cluentius." But in *Lectures on Rhetoric and Belles Lettres,* a guide to public speaking that Brown undoubtedly consulted in his law studies, Hugh Blair devoted a chapter to the oration for Cluentius, which he praised as "one of the most chaste, correct and forcible of all Cicero's judicial orations."

10. "polliciatur" . . . "polliceretur." These are the third-person-singular present subjunctive and the third-person-singular imperfect subjunctive of the verb *polliceor,* meaning "to make an offer" or "to promise."

11. *the Della Crusca dictionary.* a seventeenth-century Italian dictionary.

12. *the Dæmon of Socrates.* In Plato's *Apology*, Socrates credits his philosophic conduct to "a divine or spiritual [*daimonion*] sign": "This began when I was a child. It is a voice, and whenever it speaks it turns me away from something I am about to do, but it never encourages me to do anything."

13. *a clown.* a rustic.

14. *the siege of Nice under Godfrey of Bouillon.* In 1097, on the First Crusade, Godfrey of Bouillon helped lay siege to Nicaea, today known as Iznik, Turkey.

15. *Murviedro.* Today known as Sagunto, it was called Saguntum by the Romans and Murviedro by the Moors. It is home to the well-preserved ruins of a Roman theater.

16. *the work of the deacon Marti.* The poet, linguist, and numismatist Manuel Martí y Zaragoza (1663–1737), who was appointed deacon of Alicante in 1696, wrote *Descripción del Teatro de Sagunto.*

17. *Zisca, the Bohemian hero.* In Bohemia and Moravia, in the early fifteenth century, the purblind warrior Jan Zizka led followers of the Czech religious reformer Jan Hus in a successful campaign against the military reimposition of Roman Catholicism.

18. *demean myself.* behave.

19. *"They are well," he replied.* Cf. *Macbeth*, IV.iii.176 ff.

20. *I was commissioned to kill thee, but not to torment thee.* Cf. *Othello*, V.ii.87–88.

21. *he told them that his brother had just delivered to him a summons.* Cf. *Hamlet*, I.iv.69–74.

22. footnote. *Mania Mutabilis. See Darwin's Zoonomia, vol. ii. Class III. 1. 2. where similar cases are stated.* In the second volume of *Zoonomia; or, the Laws of Organic Life* (1794–96), Erasmus Darwin, grandfather of the man who discovered natural selection, sorted human diseases according to their qualities. In *mania mutabilis,* or mutable madness, "the patients are liable to mistake ideas of sensation for those from irritation, that is, imaginations for realities." As a treatment, Darwin recommended "endeavouring to investigate the maniacal idea, or hallucination," as well as the then-conventional medical treatments of bloodletting, induced vomiting, laxatives, and "opium in large doses."

23. footnote. *See the work of the Abbe de la Chappelle.* In 1772, Joannes Baptista de La Chapelle published *Le Ventriloque, ou L'Engastrimythe.* Brown probably read about it in the American edition of the 1797 *Encyclopedia Britannica,* which had an entry on ventriloquism. La Chapelle told the story of a grocer who practiced a prankish piece of amateur ventriloquism in a monastery: he threw the voice of a recently deceased monk complaining to his brothers that he was stuck in purgatory because they were not praying for him hard enough. For the history of ventriloquism in early America, see Leigh Eric Schmidt's *Hearing Things: Religion, Illusion, and the American Enlightenment* (Harvard University Press, 2000).

24. footnote. *Dr. Burney (Musical Travels)*. The music historian Charles Burney (1726–1814) was father of the novelist Fanny Burney.
25. footnote. *—Peeps through . . . and cries Hold! Hold!—*. Cf. *Macbeth*, I.v.52–53.
26. *the* man of sorrows! Cf. Isaiah 53:3. The epithet is traditionally associated with mystical images of a resurrected Christ displaying his wounds and crown of thorns.
27. *the Marquis of Granby.* During the Seven Years' War, John Manners (1721–70) served in Germany as commander in chief of the British forces.

Memoirs of Carwin the Biloquist

On September 4, 1798, Elihu Hubbard Smith recorded in his diary that he had read a draft of Brown's "Carwin." Brown never finished the novel, however. He published the fragment in installments in his *Literary Magazine and American Register* between 1803 and 1805.

1. *Mohock.* Mohawk.
2. *Milton's Comus.* John Milton, *A Mask Presented at Ludlow Castle . . .* (1637).
3. thunder heard remote. Cf. Milton, *Paradise Lost,* 2.477.
4. *"Five fathom deep thy father lies."* Cf. *The Tempest,* I.ii.399.
5. *In the Cowslip's bell I lie.* Cf. *The Tempest,* V.i.89 ff.
6. *generosity had been expunged from his catalogue as having no meaning or a vicious one.* Like many of Brown's villains, Ludloe is influenced by William Godwin (1756–1836), who pursued this line of reasoning in his *Enquiry Concerning Political Justice* (1793), book II, chapter 2: "My benefactor ought to be esteemed, not because he bestowed a benefit upon me, but because he bestowed it upon a human being."
7. *He laboured to shun all hurtful and vitious things, and therefore carefully abstained from making or confiding* in promises. In book III, chapter 3 of *Political Justice,* Godwin wrote that "promises are, absolutely considered, an evil, and stand in opposition to the genuine and wholesome exercise of an intellectual nature."
8. *those artificial ties which held human beings together under the same roof.* In the appendix to book VIII, chapter 8 of *Political Justice,* Godwin wrote that "cohabitation . . . is hostile to that fortitude which should accustom a man . . . to judge for himself."
9. *My friend was the eulogist of sincerity.* Sincerity was the most important instrument of social reform in Godwin's philosophy. In book IV, chapter 4 of *Political Enquiry,* he wrote, "If every man today would tell all the truth he knew, it is impossible to predict how short would be the reign of usurpation and folly."
10. *the convent of the Escurial.* a sixteenth-century monastery and palace near Madrid.
11. *He taught me to ascribe the evils that infest society to the errors of opinion. . . . he usu-*

ally proceeded to delineate some scheme of Utopian felicity, where the empire of reason should supplant that of force. Godwin believed that it was out of ignorance and weakness that people obeyed authority figures rather than their own consciences. He looked forward to "the true euthanasia of government" (*Political Enquiry,* book III, chapter 6).

12. footnote. *Paraguay.* In seventeenth-century Paraguay, which includes modern-day Paraguay and Argentina, the Jesuits established settlements known as "reductions," where they employed Native Americans and taught them Spanish customs.

13. *A number of persons are leagued together for an end of some moment.* Ludloe may be hinting that he belongs to the Order of the Illuminati, a secret society founded at a Bavarian university in 1776 that aspired to reform the world according to Enlightenment principles. Though they were widely suspected of espionage, conspiracy, and terrorist violence, the Illuminati probably had little power. In 1800, Thomas Jefferson summarized the ideas of the founder of the Illuminati thus: "He thinks he may in time be rendered so perfect that he will be able to govern himself in every circumstance so as to injure none, to do all the good he can, to leave government no occasion to exercise their powers over him, & of course to render political government useless. This you know is Godwin's doctrine."

14. *Your slave is a woman; and the bond, . . .* marriage. Godwin called marriage "a system of fraud" and "the worst of monopolies." Cf. Brown's dialogue on women's rights, *Alcuin.*

15. *pendragon.* ancient British chieftain.

16. *Salisbury plain.* the site of Stonehenge.

17. *A translation of Aristotle's republic, the political romances of sir Thomas Moore, Harrington, and Hume.* In his essay "Idea of a Perfect Commonwealth" (1754), David Hume mentions Plato's *Republic* and Thomas More's *Utopia* (1516) and briefly discusses James Harrington's *The Commonwealth of Oceana* (1656) before proposing a new system of government for Great Britain and Ireland.

18. footnote. *the voyages of Bougainville and Cook.* Louis Antoine de Bougainville explored the islands of the Pacific Ocean between 1767 and 1769; James Cook, between 1768 and 1779.

THESSALONICA: A ROMAN STORY

In May 1799, Brown published this story in *The Monthly Magazine and American Review,* which he edited. The plot is adapted from an episode in chapter 27 of Edward Gibbon's *Decline and Fall of the Roman Empire.*

1. footnote. *At the conclusion of the Gothic war, A.D. 390.* Theodosius I signed a peace treaty with the Goths in 382. The events narrated in this story took place in 390.

2. *Theodosius.* Theodosius I (c.346–395), Roman emperor of the East from 379 until his death, drove two usurpers from the empire of the West, eventually installing one of his sons as emperor there. A convert to Christianity, Theodosius repressed heretics brutally and promoted the doctrine of the Holy Trinity as set forth in the Nicene Creed. After his death, the eastern and western empires were more formally divided.

3. *Botheric.* Botheric was general of the Roman troops stationed at Thessalonica. As Gibbon explains, he was, "as it should seem from his name, a Barbarian." To ensure a lasting peace, Theodosius I had enlisted many Goths in his army.

4. *a third set of characters, distinguished by a crimson uniform.* According to Gibbon, only a white and a red chariot raced in the earliest Roman circuses; the colors green and blue were added later. Spectators cheered a color much as they cheer a sports team today. Cf. Gibbon, *Decline and Fall,* chapter 40. Brown may have misremembered the order in which the colors were introduced.

5. *a citizen, by name Macro.* Gibbon ascribes the sedition of Thessalonica to "a more shameful cause": "a beautiful boy, who excited the impure desires of one of the charioteers of the Circus." The attractive boy was a slave belonging to Botheric, who imprisoned the charioteer for his lasciviousness. The people rioted because they "lamented the absence of their favourite, and considered the skill of a charioteer as an object of more importance than his virtue."

6. *an equestrian statue of Constantius.* Constantius II (317–61).

7. Mediolanum. the Latin name for Milan, then capital of the western empire.

8. *the prefect.* For the next few pages, probably as a result of hastily merging two drafts, Brown transposes the prefect Julius Malchus from the first to the third person.

9. *Rufinus.* According to Gibbon, "Theodosius had tarnished the glory of his reign by the elevation of Rufinus: an odious favourite, who, in an age of civil and religious faction, has deserved, from every party, the imputation of every crime."

10. *exquisite remorse.* Faced with excommunication by Saint Ambrose for his actions in Thessalonica, Theodosius I would later humble himself publicly before the archbishop.

11. *Antioch, which three years before had committed a less atrocious offence.* Distressed by heavy taxes, the people of Antioch tore down statues of Theodosius I and his family in 387. In retaliation the emperor degraded Antioch to the status of village; shuttered the baths, circus, and theater; and confiscated the property of the guilty. Before citizens were executed en masse, however, he relented.

12. *Scythia.* The Goths were often referred to (inaccurately) as Scythians.

WALSTEIN'S SCHOOL OF HISTORY.
FROM THE GERMAN OF KRANTS OF GOTHA

Brown published this essay-fiction hybrid in *The Monthly Magazine and American Review* in August and September 1799. Walstein and Krants of Gotha appear to be characters invented by Brown.

1. *Newton and Xavier, Zengis and William Tell.* Sir Isaac Newton (1642–1727), Saint Francis Xavier (1506–52), Genghis Khan (c. 1162–1227), and William Tell.

2. *the Marquis of Pombal.* Sebastião José de Carvalho e Melo, marquês de Pombal (1699–1782), was chief minister to Joseph I of Portugal. A practitioner of enlightened despotism, Pombal was both a forward-thinking administrator and a ruthless politician: he rebuilt Lisbon after a 1755 earthquake, exiled and imprisoned the country's Jesuits, and fostered national industry.

3. *his flight from Astura, at the coalition of Antony and Octavius.* See headnote to "Death of Cicero," page 375.

4. *Atticus.* T. Pomponius Atticus (110 B.C.–32 B.C.), a wealthy Roman knight who abstained from politics, was Cicero's benefactor, great friend, and the recipient of his most intimate letters. He owed the cognomen Atticus to the years he spent in Athens, where he studied philosophy.

5. *The conspiracy of Cataline.* Plutarch described L. Sergius Catilina as "a man of bold, daring, and restless character," guilty of cannibalism, incest, and murder. That may overstate the case somewhat, but Catiline was indeed a dangerous man. In the elections of 63 B.C., he ran for consul against Cicero and lost. When he lost again the following year, he plotted a bloody coup. Cicero exposed the conspiracy to the senate, executed Catiline's collaborators without granting them a trial, and was acclaimed as savior of the republic.

6. *the conspiracy of Daveiro.* After an assassination attempt on King Joseph failed in 1758, Pombal had the duke de Aveiro and other political enemies tortured to death.

7. *the life of "Olivo Ronsica."* The life story of Olivo Ronsica, shifted to eighteenth-century Pennsylvania, is the plot of Brown's novel *Arthur Mervyn*.

8. *Richardson has exhibited in Clarissa.* Samuel Richardson's novel *Clarissa; or the History of a Young Lady* (1747–48).

DEATH OF CICERO, A FRAGMENT

"Death of Cicero, a Fragment" was published in late 1799 as an addition to an informal second edition of the third volume of Brown's novel *Edgar Huntly.* Brown seems to have drawn from Plutarch's life of Cicero, a fragmentary account of Cicero's death by Livy, and Seneca the Elder's sixth and seventh suasoriae, which consider whether Cicero ought to have begged for mercy or otherwise exerted himself to save his own life.

In Federalist America, Brown could assume that his readers already knew Cicero's biography in outline. During Julius Caesar's dictatorship, Cicero retreated to writing and philosophy. When Brutus and Cassius murdered Caesar in 44 B.C., Cicero praised them for restoring the republic and returned to politics. But he unwisely allied himself with Caesar's nephew and heir, Octavian—no friend to his uncle's killers. Octavian did not hesitate to betray Cicero in 43 B.C., when Mark Antony demanded the orator's death before he would agree to an alliance. When the news reached Cicero in December that Mark Antony, Octavian, and M. Aemilius Lepidus had joined in a triumvirate, he went to Astura, a town on Italy's western coast where he owned a villa, and fled by sea.

1. *Tiro.* M. Tullius Tiro, Cicero's slave and secretary, was freed in 53 B.C. and wrote a biography of Cicero after his death. He is said to have invented shorthand.
2. *Atticus.* See note 4, page 374.
3. *his brother.* Q. Tullius Cicero, Cicero's younger brother, was also sentenced to death by the triumvirate, as were Cicero's son and nephew.
4. *Cassius.* In 43 B.C., Cassius was raising troops in Asia Minor and preparing with Brutus to fight Mark Antony and Octavian.
5. *his Cilician clients.* In 51 and 50 B.C., Cicero had served as proconsul of Cilicia, which he had governed mildly and well. The capital of the province was Tarsus, later known as Antioch.
6. *Circæum.* today known as Monte Circeo.
7. *the proscription.* Mark Antony, Octavian, and Lepidus condemned their enemies by publishing a list of names, known as a proscription. Once Cicero had been proscribed, his property could be legally confiscated, his protectors risked punishment, and his murderers could look forward to reward.
8. *Cæsar.* That is, Octavian (more formally, C. Octavius). He had been adopted by Julius Caesar in 45 B.C.
9. *the Cuman Villa.* Cicero had a residence in Cuma.
10. *Pædius, the consul.* Q. Pedius became consul with Octavian in August 43 B.C. He was charged with carrying out the proscription. Brown may have invented these rumors about him.
11. *Formia.* Cicero had a residence nearby.
12. *Marcus Cicero.* His full name was Marcus Tullius Cicero.
13. *Arpinum.* Cicero's birthplace, known today as Arpino.
14. *Two busts, of Brutus and Ahala.* L. Junius Brutus expelled the tyrant Tarquinius Superbus from Rome in 510 B.C. and was said to be an ancestor of

the M. Junius Brutus who killed Julius Caesar. C. Servilius Ahala stabbed a would-be tyrant in 439 B.C.

15. *Cajeta.* Today known as Gaeta, it is the port of Formia.

16. *Pompeius.* S. Pompeius Magnus (Pius), the younger son of Pompey the Great, had brought fugitives from the proscription to Sicily, which he was occupying.

17. *Fulvia.* Mark Antony's wife and political ally.

18. *Popilius Lænas.* Plutarch identifies the assassin as "Popillius, a tribune, whom Cicero had formerly defended when prosecuted for the murder of his father." Seneca the Elder, however, maintains that although Cicero may have defended Popillius, the charge against him was not parricide (*Controversiæ,* 7.2.8). In *The History of Rome, from the Foundation of the City of Rome, to the Destruction of the Western Empire,* which Brown may have consulted, Oliver Goldsmith gives the man's name as "Popilius Lænas, a tribune of the army, whose life Cicero had formerly defended and saved."

19. *Lænas had been active in the Clodian tumults, had sided with Milo and the Senate, and had, consequently, promoted the interests of my master.* When Cicero foiled the conspiracy of Catiline in 63 B.C., he executed the conspirators without trial. To avoid prosecution, Cicero fled Rome in 58 B.C., and his enemy P. Clodius Pulcher passed a bill declaring him an exile. Gangs loyal to Clodius destroyed Cicero's property in his absence. The following year, the tribune T. Annius Milo, assisted by gangs as vicious as those of Clodius, engineered Cicero's return.

20. *the Agrigentine.* Agrigento was a town in Sicily. Tiro is referring to the Sicilian boat that he and Glauco had hired earlier.

APPENDIX: AN ACCOUNT OF A MURDER COMMITTED BY MR. J[AMES] Y[ATES], UPON HIS FAMILY, IN DECEMBER, A.D. 1781
This article appeared in the *New-York Weekly Magazine,* 2.55 (July 20, 1796), p. 20 and 2.56 (July 27, 1796), p. 28, where the murderer was identified by his initials only. His full name appears in a letter written by the novelist Ann Eliza Bleecker. Cf. James C. Hendrickson, "A Note on *Wieland,*" *American Literature* 8 (November 1936): 305–6.

1. *Tomhanick.* today known as Tomhannock.

2. *Mrs. Bl——r.* probably Mrs. Bleecker; see headnote.

3. *Aqua Fortis.* nitric acid.

A NOTE ON THE TYPE

The principal text of this Modern Library edition
was set in a digitized version of Janson, a typeface that
dates from about 1690 and was cut by Nicholas Kis,
a Hungarian working in Amsterdam. The original matrices have
survived and are held by the Stempel foundry in Germany.
Hermann Zapf redesigned some of the weights and sizes for
Stempel, basing his revisions on the original design.

Modern Library is online at
www.modernlibrary.com

MODERN LIBRARY ONLINE IS YOUR GUIDE TO CLASSIC LITERATURE ON THE WEB

THE MODERN LIBRARY E-NEWSLETTER

Our free e-mail newsletter is sent to subscribers, and features sample chapters, interviews with and essays by our authors, upcoming books, special promotions, announcements, and news.

To subscribe to the Modern Library e-newsletter, send a blank e-mail to: join-modernlibrary@list.randomhouse.com or visit www.modernlibrary.com

THE MODERN LIBRARY WEBSITE

Check out the Modern Library website at
www.modernlibrary.com for:

- The Modern Library e-newsletter
- A list of our current and upcoming titles and series
- Reading Group Guides and exclusive author spotlights
- Special features with information on the classics and other paperback series
- Excerpts from new releases and other titles
- A list of our e-books and information on where to buy them
- The Modern Library Editorial Board's 100 Best Novels and 100 Best Nonfiction Books of the Twentieth Century written in the English language
- News and announcements

Questions? E-mail us at **modernlibrary@randomhouse.com**.
For questions about examination or desk copies, please visit
the Random House Academic Resources site at
www.randomhouse.com/acmart